Date Due

DEC 4 '68			
FEB 7 '69			
MAR 27 1973			

Overdue

Also by Stephanie Perkins

The Woods Are Always Watching
There's Someone Inside Your House
Isla and the Happily Ever After
Lola and the Boy Next Door
Anna and the French Kiss

Edited by Stephanie Perkins

Summer Days and Summer Nights: Twelve Love Stories
My True Love Gave to Me: Twelve Holiday Stories

Overdue

Stephanie Perkins

SATURDAY BOOKS
NEW YORK

This is a work of fiction. All of the characters, organizations, and events portrayed in this novel are either products of the author's imagination or are used fictitiously.

First published in the United States by Saturday Books, an imprint of St. Martin's Publishing Group

OVERDUE. Copyright © 2025 by Stephanie Perkins. All rights reserved. Printed in China. For information, address St. Martin's Publishing Group, 120 Broadway, New York, NY 10271.

www.saturdaybooks.com

Designed by Michelle McMillian
Case stamp by Manning Krull
Interior and endpaper art: flowers © The natures/Shutterstock; library card © Happie Hippie Chick/Shutterstock

The Library of Congress Cataloging-in-Publication Data is available upon request.

ISBN 978-1-250-31346-1 (hardcover)
ISBN 978-1-250-31348-5 (ebook)

Our books may be purchased in bulk for promotional, educational, or business use. Please contact your local bookseller or the Macmillan Corporate and Premium Sales Department at 1-800-221-7945, extension 5442, or by email at MacmillanSpecialMarkets@macmillan.com.

First Edition: 2025

10 9 8 7 6 5 4 3 2 1

For Jarrod, best friend & true love

January

DATE DUE	BORROWER'S NAME	ROOM NUMBER
JAN 25		

CHAPTER ONE

I had already made one catastrophic decision earlier that week. But I didn't know that it was catastrophic yet, just like I didn't know that—by the end of the day—I would make another. As I opened the double doors and breathed in the cold outside air, my chest swelled with hope. Everything smelled clean and sharp. Delicate and heavy.

"Soon," I said. "It's going to start coming down any minute now."

"That's what you said an hour ago."

I looked back over my shoulder and flashed my coworker a dazzling smile.

"Shut the doors," Macon grumbled. "You're letting out all the heat." But as his eyes returned to his computer, they sparked with telltale amusement.

The doors were old and required a good shove to close. Woodsmoke replaced the scent of the forthcoming snow. A fire crackled inside the stone fireplace in the back room. Flames were forbidden on county property, but the North Ridgetop Branch Library was a registered historical building, so the beloved fireplace had been grandfathered in.

I plopped into my chair behind the circulation desk, pleased as ever to have cracked through Macon's curmudgeonly exterior. I was one of the few people who could do it. Our stalwart desk contained two stations. I had occupied one for the past four years, and he had occupied the other for eleven. Both literally and figuratively, he was my closest work friend.

An oversize book slid across the desk to me. "Lunch?" It was open to a photograph of a rambling cottage garden with a cast-iron table and charmingly mismatched chairs.

"No way," I said. "Not today."

"No?" He sounded surprised.

"Are you kidding? Today is one of the good days."

This was a favorite game of ours: picking out a place where we'd rather be than at work. But today *was* a good day. Snow had been predicted for the high mountains of North Carolina, and our small city of Ridgetop thrummed and jittered with excitement. The library was empty apart from a handful of patrons using the computers. Everybody else was at the grocery store, purchasing milk and bread before the inevitable early closings, and hurrying home. It only snowed a few times a year here, and the reaction was always deliciously overwrought.

"Fair enough," Macon said as I slid the book back to him. He placed it onto the returns shelves and then resumed reading an exhaustive online article about the statistical probability of an imminent global food crisis. Macon enjoyed nonfiction about topics that were terrifying, as well as lengthy classic novels that took weeks to read. I read and liked almost everything.

"I'll meet you in that garden for lunch," I said, referring to the picture, "as soon as the snow melts."

"Supposed to be a big one."

"It'd be nice to have another day off tomorrow."

"To go home early tonight."

We spoke as if we hadn't been engaged in this same speculative conversation for hours, just like we spoke as if everything between us was normal ... because only I was aware that it was not. My stomach flipped and tumbled. For all our talk of lunch, I'd been too anxious to eat during my break.

I wasn't sure how to tell him. The subject had consumed me for days, but now that the time had finally arrived, the task seemed insurmountable.

Because how could I tell the person I wanted to kiss—that I wanted to *more* than kiss—that I was suddenly single, but only for one month? Any which way I framed it, it sounded ludicrous.

This should have been my first hint that it *was* ludicrous.

The doors burst open, and a diminutive elderly man bellowed, "Should auld acquaintance be forgot—"

"Happy New Year, Mr. Garland," I said as he pushed a mystery novel vigorously through the returns slot in my side of the desk. I sat there because it was where most patrons went first, and I was friendlier than Macon. The better greeter. Although I was introverted like many librarians, I wasn't shy. I was a good listener, I was curious about others, and I loved to laugh. *Ingrid Effervescent*, Macon sometimes called me. It was a dig, but I secretly liked it because I suspected that he did, too.

"Ingrid Dahl! Macon Nowakowski!" Mr. Garland beamed at us both. "Did you have a nice holiday?"

I smiled back at him. "I did, thank you." It was the third day of the year, a Tuesday. We were always closed on Sundays and Mondays, but I'd been away for even longer, on vacation since before Christmas. "How was yours? How did that Yule log cake turn out?"

He was already power walking away toward the new releases. "Can't complain, can't complain! Gotta get another book before the storm hits."

Macon had become stone-faced at the intrusion of high energy. Although he had the exhausted spirit of a man approaching retirement, he was only thirty-nine. Ten years older than me. Quiet and grouchy, Macon had a carefully modulated voice and an unnervingly intense stare. His wardrobe was limited, and from autumn through winter he wore the same coat every day, often inside—a large duffel coat with toggles. *The grumpiest Paddington*, I liked to tease him. He was frequently late, prone to rants, and his dark brown hair was always in desperate need of a professional trim. There was purposefully, handsomely messy . . . and then there was Macon.

I found him delightful.

He gestured to his brass nameplate, knocking it over with his coat sleeve. "I'll never forgive the county for forcing us to use these." The public library was funded by the county government, whose rules tended to fluctuate. The mandatory nameplates had shown up on our desk the previous spring, and he was still irritated whenever somebody used his full name.

"It's not so bad." My smile shifted into a grin. "And at least Mr. Garland always pronounces your name correctly. Mason."

"How dare you." But Macon was enjoying his indignation.

My surname was mispronounced everywhere except the library, where most patrons were familiar with Roald Dahl's splendid books even if they were unfamiliar with his untoward bigotry. ("No relation," I was always quick to say, although we both had Norwegian roots. A relation was possible.) It was *Daal*, but the lazier *Doll* was close enough that I didn't mind. But *Nov-a-kov-ski* was too difficult for nearly everybody, especially those who didn't know to replace the Polish *w*'s with *v*'s. And to Macon's everlasting irritation, the butchery didn't stop there. Most people misread his first name, too. "I'm not a canning jar or a fraternal organization," he often groused. Instead, it signified that his family was also Southern, as it was often used in this part of the country as a name for a city or county or street.

Mr. Garland hustled back into the room.

"That was fast," I said.

He dropped a hardcover onto the desk, tossed his stylish scarf over his shoulder, and whipped out his library card. "I'm a man who knows what he wants."

Mr. Garland was in his eighties, and his spiky hair, short stature, and tailored clothing reminded me of a sprite. He only ever checked out new mysteries, and only one at a time because he liked having an excuse to visit regularly. Back when his husband was still alive, Mr. Garland had checked out teetering stacks, and we only ever saw him when they were due. Because of this, I always tried to give him my full attention. Today, however, my mind was elsewhere.

"Tough crowd," he said in a theatrically lowered voice. He was talking to Macon, but his nod was at me. I was already handing the book back to him with the due-date receipt tucked inside. He'd been spinning a tale, and I'd missed the punch line. And the tale.

"Sorry." I winced. "I'm a million miles away. Have been all day."

Mr. Garland pretended to look affronted. "As long as it's you, not me."

I gave him the laugh he wanted. "Stay warm out there, okay?"

In response, he popped his coat collar with a flourish and made his grand exit. "Until next time!"

"Next time," Macon said, standing up to close the doors, which Mr. Garland had left ajar, as always, "I'm going to lock these when I see him coming."

"He just wants a little attention."

Macon shut the doors with more force than necessary.

"He's lonely," I said. A lot of our regulars were lonely. Libraries were safe spaces for people who led solitary lives, including some of the librarians. Including Macon.

"He sings every time he enters the building."

"You love the singing."

He dropped back into his chair and rotated toward me in accusation. "A million miles away."

"What?"

"You just said it, and you are. You're past the moon. Headed toward Mars." I tried to brush him off, but he pressed on. "*And* you're fiddling."

"Fidd—" Realizing what he meant, I dropped my necklace. My fingers had been unconsciously twisting its chain.

"You're going to tangle that, and then I'll have to fix it. Again."

I raised my empty hands. "I let go!" But I was laughing. I had a nervous habit of fiddling with my jewelry. Fortunately, Macon was a patient and skilled untangler. Headphones, charging cords, strings of lights. Balls of yarn for storytime crafts. My hair, caught in a barrette. He could sit with a mess for as long as was necessary to puzzle it out and set it straight again.

"What's going on?" he asked.

"Nothing," I said too quickly. Fear shot through me. I'd been searching for an opening all day, and he'd just handed it to me. Still, I struggled against my own resistance.

He stared at me and waited.

Ask me again, I begged.

But the moment had passed, and he swiveled away with a shrug. It wasn't in his nature to press for more information or overstep boundaries.

The words issued forth in an out-of-body experience. "Cory moved out."

Macon stilled. His chair swiveled back in my direction.

I twisted my necklace around my fingers again. "It happened over Christmas."

"What happened over Christmas?"

The question emerged before its speaker, a woman with a round face and round glasses, who turned the corner behind Macon. We both startled. Alyssa had been in the children's section in the back, replacing a display of winter holiday picture books with one featuring snowmen.

Scrambling for a response that was honest yet withholding, I settled on the beginning of the story. "My sister got engaged."

Macon's brows lifted.

"Engaged!" Alyssa predictably lit up. "To the basketball player?"

"Yep," I said. I glanced at Macon, and his brows settled back down into impassivity. He understood that we were having a different conversation now.

"Thank goodness." Sue appeared from the annex. "Have we officially stopped working? I'm too distracted to get anything done this afternoon."

"Did the email arrive?" Elijah asked, wheeling an empty cart behind the desk. He was the page, which meant he reshelved the books. Sue was the branch manager, and Alyssa was the children's librarian. The five of us comprised the entire staff.

"Not yet," Macon said. The desired email would come from the director at the main library downtown, and it would give us permission to close early.

"We never get the email until it's actually snowing," Sue explained.

"Damn," Elijah said, removing his earbuds to fully join the conversation. He listened to nonfiction science books and sci-fi novels while he worked. He was the youngest employee, only two months shy of his twenty-first birthday. He knew the policy but was still young and optimistic enough to hope it might have suddenly changed. Like the nameplates.

"Ingrid's sister got engaged," Alyssa said.

Sue looked interested. "To the basketball player?"

Everybody was always interested in Jess. My sister's fiancée was a shooting guard in the WNBA and a two-time Olympic gold medalist. She had met my sister, Riley, when they were in a COVID bubble together during a shortened WNBA season that the press dubbed "the Wubble." Riley was one of the nurses who did the daily testing.

"To the basketball player," I confirmed.

"How tall is she again?" Elijah asked. Everybody always asked.

"Regular tall. Five ten."

"Who proposed to whom?" Alyssa asked.

"Jess proposed. They'd splurged on a Disney cruise for the holidays"—this got a laugh; everyone enjoyed the fact that my no-nonsense sister and her pro-athlete girlfriend were adorable Disney nerds—"but apparently, Jess was so nervous that she didn't notice my sister was seasick. She got down on one knee at the exact moment Riley puked over the side of the ship."

The others kept laughing, but Alyssa looked taken aback.

"They thought it was funny, too," I assured her.

"If Tim had proposed to me while I was throwing up, I would *not* have said yes."

"That's unfair," Macon said. "Poor Tim."

I exchanged a glance with Macon, but we both managed to keep our faces straight. We liked Alyssa despite not having much in common with her. She was only a year younger than me, but she was a bit naive. And she could be overly critical, especially of her husband, which was unpleasant. But Tim had these same qualities, *and* he was a bore. Alyssa was mostly fun.

"Would you have asked Dani while she was throwing up?" Alyssa asked Macon about his longtime, but notably ex, girlfriend.

Macon's expression flattened. "There were no circumstances under which I would have proposed."

"Snow or not," I said, eyeing Macon as I steered everyone back to a safe topic, "at least the two of you get to leave soon." I turned my gaze to Sue and Alyssa, who would be off at six o'clock, the usual time. Tuesday was one of our branch's late nights, and if the snow didn't start soon, Macon and I would be there, along with Elijah, until eight.

Sue glanced at the wall clock and sighed. "Not soon enough."

Unlike Macon, who only acted as if he were two years away from retirement, Sue actually was, a fact that she mentioned on a near-daily basis. She was always as ready to go home as the rest of us, but her attitude was relaxed and efficient, and she ran our branch the same way. I admired her and secretly thought of her as a maternal figure—my Ridgetop mom. It was the main reason I didn't want to tell her what was going on with Cory and me. I didn't want her to worry. And I didn't want Alyssa's judgment, and Elijah was too young.

It took ages, but eventually the three of them drifted back to work. The instant we were alone again, Macon pivoted toward me, his brow furrowed with concern. But I shook my head. I didn't dare resume our conversation until Sue and Alyssa actually left the building.

Cory and I had moved to Ridgetop seven years earlier, the day after we graduated from college. Born, raised, and educated in Orlando, we'd driven up for a getaway during our senior year, and that first crisp bite of mountain air had tasted more like home than Florida's sticky humidity ever had. Although both cities were driven by tourism, Ridgetop was an arts haven that attracted dreamers and wanderers. Known for effortlessly—some might say mystically—welcoming its new residents, Ridgetop had a way of making you believe that things would work out, and they had for us.

So it made sense that the fateful call had come while we were back in Orlando, just over a week ago, visiting for the holidays. We were in my parents' kitchen on Christmas morning, glazing a spiral-sliced ham that neither of us would eat—Cory had a limited diet, and I was mostly vegetarian, though my parents never remembered or maybe kept assuming we'd grown out of it—when the landline rang. Riley and Jess were docked in Tortola and asked to be put on speakerphone.

When we heard their news, my mother exclaimed with joy and my father chuckled with satisfaction, and then the rest of our day was spent in a frenzy of marveling and speculating, discussing and planning. It wasn't until that night, after the tins of homemade cookies had been passed around for dessert, that my parents finally realized how quiet Cory and I had become. Tension cloaked the sugar-dusted atmosphere.

My parents didn't ask what was wrong, but they didn't have to. They loved Cory and treated him like family. But they also fervently believed in minding their own business, so the subject of us getting married had crossed their lips only once, after my mother had drunk too many blue margaritas at our graduation party. Cory's family, on the other hand, was loud and boisterous and teased us frequently about the subject. His parents also lived in the suburbs of Orlando, and we always spent half our vacation time with them. But they were laid-back and had never put any actual pressure on us.

Riley's happy news was an unexpected blow. And the more it churned in my mind, the more perturbed I felt. This was my sister. My baby sister. Who had only been dating her girlfriend for two and a half years. And, sure, two and a half years was plenty of time to know if you wanted to marry somebody. Except.

Except.

Cory and I had been together for eleven.

We had met during our first week of community college. *The first minute of the first day of our first class*, we liked to brag to new acquaintances. He took the seat beside mine in Psych 101, and because college was an ideal opportunity to take risks, he didn't wait to ask me out. I was so startled that I said yes. We had lunch together that same day, then more lunches, then dinners, and it was easy, and it had never been easy for either of us before. We'd both been unpopular kids, genuinely awkward, lonely and bullied.

Cory had been my first and only boyfriend, just like I was his first and only girlfriend. But despite our inexperience, our relationship had always been healthy and enviable. We made each other laugh, rarely fought, had a good sex life. And although neither of us was interested in having children, it was understood that we would get married someday. But for whatever murky and uncomfortable reason, we had never discussed *when*. Even as our friends hit their late twenties and began marrying around us, we'd shrugged off their nosy inquiries. *We'll do it when we buy a house*, we would answer vaguely. But we had never discussed doing that either.

I finally summoned the courage to ask him about it a few days after Christmas. During our long and atypically solemn drive home, the question swelled and throbbed and gurgled inside my throat until it became more uncomfortable *not* to ask.

"Why do you think we've never gotten married?"

To his credit, Cory didn't seem alarmed. He continued to stare straight ahead at the road before us as if he'd been contemplating the same mystery. "I don't know," he said, although it sounded like he might have an idea. "Maybe there's just some part of us that isn't willing to commit until we've experienced something else."

The interstate didn't crack open and swallow me whole. Our life as a couple didn't flash before my eyes. It was as if he'd said what I'd been thinking, even though the thought had never occurred to me before.

"Some*one* else," I said.

Macon was reading a review journal and circling titles to add to our collection, but his pages weren't turning very quickly. His pen kept tapping against the desk. And his occasional glances at me felt as weighty as the impending snowfall.

Time itself was restless. The minutes stretched and crawled. Red, blue, green, and gold light illuminated the bookshelves on the western side of the building as the sun began to set. Ridgetop was famous for its stained glass, but the windows at our library were particularly notable.

Arthur Frey Brisson was the man responsible for bringing the trade to town, an artist so skilled that his only U.S. rival was Louis Comfort Tiffany, although many believed Brisson was more deserving of fame. He was also the devoted husband of Mary Brisson, founder of Ridgetop's first public library in 1879. Situated beside a small but pretty body of water called Thistle Lake, her library—our library—was small, too, but it had a cozy lakefront porch where folks could sit in rocking chairs and read for as long as they liked. And it had the windows.

On the bottom, Arthur had installed clear panes that let in enough sunlight to read, but the top panes were a glorious and hectic design of stained-glass books and spines, and beside the porch door, a large stained-glass Mary cradled a book like it was a child. A halo of golden pages ringed her head. It was a remarkable portrait, a blasphemous scandal, and now a minor tourist attraction.

These colorful shards of light had all faded when Sue and Alyssa said their dispirited goodbyes at the regular time. Neither the snow nor the email had arrived.

Macon closed the journal and tucked his pen behind his ear, where it normally sat. I once asked him, "Isn't that uncomfortable with your glasses?" and he had said, "No." But twenty minutes later, he'd added in a defensive tone, "I have big ears." They were only a little bigger than average, though. I liked them, and I liked the pen, too.

He rolled his chair away from the desk to peer into the stacks. Satisfied, he rolled back. Closer to me than he'd been before. "He's plugged in," he said, referring to Elijah's earbuds.

Earlier, I'd been ready to tell Macon everything. Now I was not ready.

"I'm sorry." His tone was sympathetic, though his face was inscrutable. "Breakups are hard."

"Oh." The misunderstanding helped me find my voice. "We didn't actually break up. We're taking *a* break."

I noticed his underlying eagerness only as it fell away, but it spurred me forward.

"My sister did get engaged, which got us wondering, you know? About why we haven't gotten married. And we realized it's probably because neither of us has ever dated anybody else, so we're taking the month off to go out with other people."

His expression fell even further. "And what happens at the end of the month?"

"He'll move back in, and we'll figure out our future. Marriage and all that."

"Marriage," he said. Completely without enthusiasm.

"Yeah."

"And he already moved out?"

"We moved his stuff into an Airbnb on New Year's Day."

Macon shook his head slowly. "That's a hell of a resolution."

It was. But it also wasn't. We had reached our decision with careful, pragmatic thought. It was the most adult decision that we had ever made. January would be a month of promiscuity without repercussions, but it wasn't about dating or kissing or even sex. Not really. It was about getting the unknown out of our systems so we could finally move forward together.

We had agreed that it would be sensible to refrain from contact until February. That was when we would decide to either separate or get married, although we were certain it would be the latter. For the first time ever, we had even discussed our wedding. It would be in autumn, our favorite time of year, with only our closest family members. Or maybe that was even too much. Neither of us particularly liked weddings, so perhaps we'd just get hitched at the courthouse.

However, despite my generally optimistic disposition, I understood that this plan made my vision seem wholly rose-tinted. I understood how it would sound to other people.

"I'm sorry," Macon said, "but this sounds like a terrible plan."

"I know."

"You do?"

I shrugged and smiled. "Sure."

"And that doesn't worry you?"

"Nope."

He removed the pen, then his glasses, and rubbed the space between his eyes.

"It's okay." My smile grew reassuring. "It only needs to make sense to me, and it does. I know what I'm doing."

Unfortunately, this was the exact moment that I realized I did not know what I was doing. That somehow, despite all the scenarios that had run through my head since saying goodbye to Cory, I had neglected to imagine this crucial transition between telling Macon I wanted to date and telling

Macon I wanted to date *him*. The omission now seemed glaring. It also occurred to me only now—at the worst possible moment—that this might be considered using him.

I supposed I figured . . . it would just happen. That he would be up for it. Because he knew, we both knew, that our friendship had always held the capacity for more. The air hummed thicker between us. It startled us with intermittent and unpredictable sparks. This wasn't the one-way charge of seeing somebody attractive; the charge was striking in both directions. It happened whenever we reached for the same object at the same time, accidentally bumped or brushed against each other, ran into each other outside of work. Any time we appeared in a place the other didn't expect us to be, our world shimmered.

There was one late shift about a year ago when the building was empty, and we were slaphappy, and for whatever reason, I wondered aloud if I could still do a cartwheel. Macon said, "Go on," and when I performed one successfully in front of our desk, he cheered. Seized by a mania to keep impressing him—I don't know why I believed cartwheels would impress him—I launched myself toward the stacks and attempted to perform several in a row. I made it to one and a half before crashing into the audiobook display.

"Oh my God," I heard him say, and an instant later he was above me.

In shock, I blinked up at him from the floor. Then I released a whoop of crazed laughter.

His fear fell away, and he gripped me with both hands. But as he helped me to my feet, I landed too close to him, way too close, close enough for his chest to heave against mine. The energy between us pulsed—and then surged. Instead of laughing and taking a quick step backward, we drank each other in. His pupils dilated. The moment lasted only seconds before our hands and bodies flew apart, but those seconds lasted an eternity.

As notable as incidents like this were, however, they hadn't mattered at the time. This energy wasn't anything we would ever speak about or act upon. Until a year and a half ago, he'd been with his girlfriend, Danielle, and I'd always been with Cory, and neither of us was the cheating type. And we were both the type who could have just a friend.

And yet. Even still.

When Cory and I had made our unusual arrangement, my first thought hadn't been picking up some stranger in a bar. My first thought had been Macon Nowakowski.

Without another word, he put his glasses back on, and then the pen, and then wearily pushed away to his side of the desk.

The library felt colder. I'd spent all day yesterday preparing for today—shaving, painting my nails, selecting the right outfit, packing a lunch that wouldn't offensively impact my breath. I'd even placed a toothbrush and travel-size toothpaste into my bag for freshening up afterward, though I hadn't needed it since I'd been too nervous to eat my smashed chickpea sandwich. And then I'd brushed my teeth anyway. My simple plan suddenly seemed a lot more complicated.

As my cheerful poppy nails picked at my favorite vintage trousers, the ones that made my legs, my best feature, look especially long, my pocket lit up. I tugged out my phone, knowing exactly who had sent the text.

How did it go??

Kat was a librarian, too, in a coastal town in Western Australia, in a time zone currently thirteen hours ahead of mine. She had probably just woken up. Even though we'd never met in person, she was one of my closest friends and the only other person who knew about the Cory situation. And she was the only person, period, who knew of my intentions toward Macon.

I have no idea, I replied.

He glanced at me. Unlike the rest of the world, Macon wasn't addicted to his phone, mainly because he didn't trust it. Black electrical tape covered the cameras on his device, and normally when he caught me texting, he made a droll comment. Tonight he said nothing.

I stuffed my phone back into my pocket, paranoid that somehow he'd be able to read the screen.

Ninety minutes remained until closing. Mr. Brember, a permanent fixture of our computer section, was the only patron left in the building. Outside, it was fully dark.

There was still no sign of snow.

Had I been wrong about Macon? He seemed upset, maybe even disappointed in me. Or maybe he was confused because I hadn't explained the situation clearly enough. I'd definitely been too flippant. How could he know I was interested in dating him if I hadn't articulated it—or even been flirtatious? As my panic rose, my breathing grew shallow. My palms sweated. I'd never made a move on anybody before. I had only ever been on *one* first date, and I was eighteen at the time. Had Cory already slept with somebody else? While we were both skilled at talking to strangers, he was more extroverted than me and enjoyed going out. I hadn't gone anywhere yet because I'd been waiting for tonight. Waiting for Macon.

Two clocks were ticking: twenty-eight days until February, eighty-five minutes until closing. And I had no idea what to do.

A stiffness to Macon's presence indicated that he was still observing me. My throat thickened. I lowered my head, trying to hold myself together.

His chair rotated back toward me.

I forced my chin up. Forced myself to meet his gaze.

His eyes were serious and kind. "Are you okay?"

I nodded my head for yes. Shook it for no. My skin flushed like a teenager without social skills or self-control.

"That seems about right," he said. And then he smiled.

It wasn't that Macon never smiled, but he never gave a false smile, which meant that they always reached deeper inside of me. They penetrated at an atomic level, while everybody else's only brushed my skin. This one was meant to reassure me, and miraculously, it did. I wiped away a tear that had managed to leak out and laughed at myself.

"So, how did you choose who got to stay and who had to move out?" He was trying to distract me to keep me from falling apart.

"Of our apartment? That decision was easy. I have more clothes and makeup and stuff. You know, everything required . . ."

". . . for going on a date."

"Yeah." I swallowed to steady myself. "So I got to stay. We're each paying for our own place this month."

"Oh. Shit." His concern shifted. "Is that a lot?"

It didn't bother me that he was asking about money. All of us librarians talked openly about our lack of finances. The government didn't pay us well—fully weaponizing the knowledge that anybody willing to work with books would be willing to do it for a meager salary—so we were all thrifty by necessity.

"It's not bad. I mean, it's not great. But I have enough."

"Still haven't gotten the email?"

A gruff voice interrupted us. Like Mr. Garland, Mr. Brember was in his eighties, but he was far less sprightly. He came in every day to work on his funeral plans, which wasn't as morbid as it sounded. He was in good health; he just wanted to make sure that when he did die, he received the appropriate tribute. The last time I'd glimpsed it, his document was more than a hundred pages long and contained detailed instructions regarding wreaths, choral arrangements, a marching band, fireworks, refreshments, and Clydesdale horses.

"Not yet," I said.

He grunted. "It's getting dangerous. Wind's picking up."

With a start, I realized it was true. The stained-glass windows were rattling. Mr. Brember didn't drive, so I was thankful he only lived around the corner. "Be careful out there."

"You should close," he said, scolding us as he skedaddled away. (Long ago, Macon and I had decided that *skedaddled* was the most accurate verb to describe the way he moved, and I could never unthink it.) "Never wait for somebody else to tell you what to do."

The doors shut behind him with a loud, wind-sucked pop.

"Somebody like you?" Macon said dryly.

But Mr. Brember had a point. Macon would never, not in a hundred thousand lifetimes, tell me that he was interested in taking advantage of my month of freedom. We had been friends and coworkers for too long. He was respectful. Professional. It would be up to me to make the first move.

"Did we get the email?" Elijah called out from across the library.

I cupped a hand around my mouth. "Not! Yet!"

"Fuck it." Macon pushed away from the desk and stood. "We're empty." And then he strode away to prepare for closing anyway.

The familiar clanks and thunks told me he was putting out the fire in the back room, so I searched for shelves to straighten and discarded items to file away. The historic building was shaped like a rectangle with a single wall down its center, which divided the space into the form of an "O." I traveled clockwise through new releases, fiction, and young adult. The wooden shelves were smooth from hands and age, and potted plants were nestled into every available nook. Macon was the plant guy, and his charges were, without exception, full and healthy, even the ones that were supposedly difficult to care for. Patrons were always asking him for advice.

Everything looked crowded but neat and tidy. With so few patrons that day, the shelves were still in order, or perhaps Elijah had already done the work. Most likely both. As I passed the porch door, I discreetly bowed my head at the portrait of Mary Brisson beside it. The stained glass had transformed her into a patron saint for those with a calling to put good books into people's hands, and normally I felt a kinship with her, although she was not currently on my mind. The bow was habitual, maybe even superstitious.

I proceeded through the back of the building, which was divided into three sections: the children's section, with its braided rug and squashy chair; the periodicals section, with its scratched tables and stone fireplace; and the computer section, with its modern tables and glowing screens.

Macon glanced up from his position on the hearth. I startled and stared back too feverishly. His expression grew unsettled, and I hurried away with smoke in my nostrils.

Elijah was shelving in nonfiction. He was a lanky Black kid with a slightly lazy eye, full of exuberant charm. We nodded, and he did a double take at something behind me, but I was already halfway through the media section—audiobooks, music, movies—when he shouted, "It's snowing!"

Sure enough, the first tiny flakes of the year were finally tumbling down. Hope reignited inside me. "It looks like magic, don't you think?" I said, turning to Elijah.

"It looks cold," Macon said as he swished past.

My nerves jolted.

"And a *little* magical," he conceded from the front room. His mouse clicked, and I assumed he was refreshing his email.

"Anything?" Elijah asked as we joined him. He pushed his empty cart into the space where it was stored and then hopped up and sat on it. We were all done working, whether it was official or not.

"No," Macon said. "But it'll come." He typed up a sign that read CLOSED FOR SNOW and hit print.

"Check it again," Elijah said.

The printer kicked on with its loud routine, and I went to fetch the sheet of paper.

"Nothing," Macon said. But then, "Oh, shit. We got it."

My heartbeat stumbled.

"*All Colburn County libraries will close immediately,*" he read aloud, "government bullshit, government bullshit . . . *and will open two hours late tomorrow.*"

"Yes!" Elijah vaulted back to his feet. "Y'all don't need me, do you?"

"Get out of here," Macon said.

Elijah saluted, snatched up his belongings, and then tripped as he exited.

It was almost time to make my move. My heart was pounding now, and my head went woozy. "I'll get the doors."

"I'll get the porch door and computers," Macon said.

With trembling hands, I turned the lock and taped up the sign. Elijah's car pulled out of the lot, leaving only Macon's and mine behind. Macon drove a Volvo sedan, old and practical, and he took immaculate care of it. I drove a sunshiny Beetle, old but impractical. It was constantly breaking down, but he always made sure that my engine started before he left. He always made sure I was safe.

You are *safe*, I reminded myself. *It's only Macon. You can do this.*

The hardwood floor creaked as he moved from computer to computer, turning them off. I closed the register, and the small change for fines, photocopies, and printouts slipped across the desk as I counted it. I had to recount twice. I took the cash into the annex, the only part of the building that wasn't original, and when I returned from locking it in Sue's office, Macon was already holding my coat and my tote bag along with both of our lunch sacks.

"Did you eat any of this?" he asked, frowning at the weight of mine.

I made a noncommittal noise and accepted my coat. The tremble in my hands turned into a shake as I tried to button it. He flicked a switch, and the library darkened. A single emergency bulb glowed and buzzed, highlighting the already-charged atmosphere.

Macon held open one of the doors. The watery mineral scent of snow, fresh and fragile, rushed into my lungs. I took my bags and then ducked and passed underneath his arm. I'd never done that before, and he laughed. "What was that?" he asked.

But when he locked the doors and turned around, he saw that I was not laughing. I was standing directly behind him, unmoving.

His dark eyes widened.

Snowflakes caught in the light of the streetlamps and twinkled like stars, infinite wishes whirling and eddying around us. The flakes had gotten thicker. They clung to our coats and our hair. This was it. *This* was the moment.

I leaned forward—

Closed my eyes—

Parted my lips—

"No." Macon stumbled back and clunked against the doors. "Ingrid. No."

My hands flew to my mouth in mortification. "Oh my God. I'm . . ."

So sorry. So wrong. So ready to hurl myself into the lake and drown.

"No, *I'm* . . ." But he couldn't finish the sentence either. He bolted to his car. His windshield wipers burst into action at the same time as his lights, flinging snow back into the sky, and he was already reversing, already turning, already driving away.

CHAPTER TWO

I didn't turn on the lights. I dropped my keys onto the table beside the front door where they belonged but only out of habit. I sank to my apartment floor in a puddle. Prickly carpeting smooshed into my face. I had sobbed and screamed the entire drive home—*why the fuck did you do that, how could you be so fucking stupid*—and now my body went into shock. I couldn't remember the last time I had felt this humiliated or ashamed. How could I have misjudged Macon's friendship in such a monumental way? It was such a rookie mistake, so pubescent.

The horror in his eyes.

My chest squeezed, and my arms went numb. I thought I'd triggered a heart attack until I realized the numbness was only because I was lying on top of them. I wiggled them out and let them tingle painfully. I relished the physicality of this pain because it aligned with what was happening to me mentally.

The floor vibrated beneath my cheek. A young couple who attended the local college lived below me, and one of them was walking from their bedroom toward their kitchen. The guy called out something that sounded like a question. His girlfriend gave a muffled response.

I fumbled for the phone in my bag, which had fallen onto the carpet beside me.

It was bad, I texted Kat. *So bad. Going-to-have-to-get-another-job bad.*

I stared at the screen, waiting for her usual quick response. It didn't come, which meant she was probably commuting. We'd found each other nearly a decade earlier in the book circles of social media, and we often chatted during our overlapping waking hours. Despite the actual ocean between us, whenever I said or did something stupid, Kat was my first line of defense. But Cory was my second. He was the one who hugged me, who told me everything would be okay—and then reminded me of all the times that he'd done something similarly idiotic. It felt bizarre that he wasn't here. That I couldn't tell him about my day.

All of my muscles tensed as the incident replayed in my mind. Macon had *run away* from me. I cried again: for Kat, for Cory, for a time machine.

My screen lit up, and my heart leapt. Kat!

Did your car start? Are you home?

Macon.

Despite everything, he was still making sure that I was safe. My skin crawled with renewed shame. I wanted to ignore him, but he'd only drive back to the library and then retrace the route to my apartment, worried that I was stranded someplace with a dead phone. He had saved me from the side of the road before. I typed and deleted, typed and deleted, until I finally settled on this: *I'm home. I'm sorry. I don't know what I was thinking. All I can say is that it's been a strange week. If it's okay with you, let's pretend that never happened.*

It took a full minute—I watched the clock—before the three dots appeared. Unlike me, Macon thought about his reply before typing it.

No worries.

That was it.

God. What a disaster.

I hadn't been exaggerating when I'd told Kat that I'd have to get another job. Returning to work and sitting beside him for forty hours a week was unthinkable. The level of not thinking that had gone into all of this was extraordinary. It wasn't as if I hadn't considered the possibility that he might turn me down, but . . . I honestly believed he wouldn't. How could

I have been so cocky, so overconfident to assume that my feelings were mutual? On what planet had I been living for all these years? I didn't know if I could give Sue a single day's notice, let alone a full two weeks. How would I explain my sudden departure to her? Where would I find another job? Would the library at the college hire me or would they require a more advanced degree?

My screen lit up again.

WHAT HAPPENED?

I scrambled to my feet, lurched onto my couch, and burritoed myself in a blanket. *Can you talk?* I asked, and my phone immediately rang with an incoming FaceTime call.

"It was bad," I said through a fresh burst of tears.

"I can barely see you. Where are you? Are you all right?" Kat was standing outside her library. Her hair was in its usual practical ponytail, and her light brown skin was tanned and generously freckled. She glowed in the morning summer sun of the Southern hemisphere.

My own glow was pale and haunted, illuminated only by my screen. "Oh God. It was bad."

"So you keep saying. What happened?" As I told her, she gasped in all the right places. "Are you sure he wasn't just startled?" she asked, although her expression betrayed that even she didn't believe this was a possibility. "Maybe he needs more time to think about it. About you."

"He said the word *no* twice. He couldn't have been clearer."

"No, you're right. No means no and all that."

A thought, appalling and repugnant, seeped through me. "I'm one of those monsters—one of those hideous monsters who sexually harasses their coworkers."

"You are not."

"I am. Oh my God, I am."

"Did you accept his no?"

"Of course, but—"

"Would you ever try anything like this again?"

"Of course not, but—"

"End of discussion."

Seconds passed. I was finding it hard to look at her. "I fucked up," I finally said.

"Yep."

"It's going to be so awkward at work."

"Yep."

I moaned. "What am I supposed to do?"

"About Macon?"

"Macon, my job, everything. All of it."

"Cory?"

"What about Cory?" I asked.

Kat appeared to be searching for the right way to phrase her next question. "Are you sure this is something you still want to do? This arrangement with Cory?"

"Yeah, I just"—my voice lowered into a confession—"thought it would be easier than this."

Her guffaw was sharp and unexpected, and she instantly looked repentant. "Sorry. But you know that's absurd, right? Why do you think the dating industry is worth billions of dollars?"

"I know, but—"

"If you really want to do this, you'll have to pull your shit together and get out there."

"Says the married woman," I said petulantly. Kat was a little older than me. When we met, she was already married, and they had a child now. I hadn't witnessed her dating years.

"Well, you better believe Cory isn't sitting alone in his Airbnb right now, sobbing to a mate on the phone."

Reality dipped. I saw Cory in a crowded room with thumping bass, leaning in close to chat up an alluring woman. The temptress smiled back at him and licked her teeth.

Lightheadedness and nausea rolled through me.

"You need to leave your apartment"—Kat was getting bossy now—"and meet a man you don't work with."

"Okay. Okay." I nodded even though my head was still swimming. "How do I do that?"

"You know, go to a pub or bar or whatever."

"Alone?"

Her eyes widened in alarm. "No. You have to bring somebody, a friend to keep you company and help you watch out for scumbags."

"Right." I shook my head. "It's been a long time since I've done this."

"You've never done this."

"Right. I've never done this."

"Here's what you're gonna do: Wash your face, eat dinner, go to bed. And while you sleep, I'm going to come up with a brilliant plan."

Panic bubbled back to the surface. "No, I need to go out tonight. Now."

"You need to go to bed now."

"I'm serious, I can't stay here. I can't sit with this. I have to get out."

"Out to where?"

"To a bar! Like you said."

"With whom?"

It was a good question, and it stopped my spiral. Sue and Alyssa were out of the question, and most of the other people I hung out with were actually Cory's friends from work. "What if I went alone," I said, "just for tonight—"

"Abso-fucking-lutely not. You're a disaster."

"Thanks," I said, managing to feel even worse.

"Listen to me. I'm saying that it would be dangerous for you to go out alone tonight. You're in a bad headspace, and I don't want you doing something you'll regret."

This got through to me, and I relented. Deflated.

A flash of light, a reflection, shone behind Kat. My library overlooked a glorified pond while hers overlooked an entire ocean. "What about Brittany?" she asked.

I hesitated. "I don't know. Cory and I are both friends with her."

"But aren't you *closer* friends with her?"

"I guess. Maybe."

I was. When our former downstairs neighbors, Brittany and Reza Najafi, had moved into a house across town the previous autumn, I was the one who'd made the extra effort to stay in touch. Cory had only visited their new place once for their housewarming party, but I'd been over a few additional times to help them paint and decorate. I'd also helped Brittany scour some garage and estate sales for furniture to fill up all that new empty space.

"So," Kat said, "claim her before Cory can."

The notion chilled me. We hadn't broken up, yet lines were being drawn. Kat wasn't wrong, though. "I wish *you* could come with me," I said.

Her face fell, and I knew she wished it, too.

"Stupid Australia," I said glumly.

"Stupid America."

"You have to get to work."

"I do. Text me if you need me, all right?"

We hung up, and I called Brittany, no text beforehand, no chance to change my mind. She answered on the third ring, sounding worried. "What's going on? Are you okay?"

It depressed me that most people assumed a call meant something bad had happened. Unfortunately, it was often true. "Yeah." I sniffed. "I mean, no. But yeah."

"Are you crying? Did your car break down again?"

Cory and Macon weren't the only people who had saved me from the side of the road. Reza had jumped my car once in a Taco Bell parking lot.

"Is she okay? Where is she?" a voice asked in the background.

"I'm at home," I said.

"She's home," Brittany said to her husband.

The whole complicated and humiliating story spilled out of me. Although I was speaking to Brittany, I was aware of Reza's presence, too. They were shocked to hear about the situation with Cory and equally shocked that I had made a move on my own coworker.

"You have to help me," I begged. "Go out with me."

"To a bar?" Brittany asked.

"Yes! I don't know what I'm doing."

"And you think I do?"

The question was valid. One of the reasons we had all become friends was because we were the same age and in committed relationships when none of our other young friends were. We were all twenty-two at the time, fresh out of college. Brittany's parents were devout evangelical Christians from Alabama, and Reza's parents were devout Shia Muslims from Pakistan, and the only way they could live together without upsetting everybody was by getting married. So they did. Like Kat, they were already married when we met, but like Cory and me, they didn't have children.

"Please." My voice cracked, the dam readying to burst again. "I can't do this alone."

Resignation descended on the other line. "Fine. Once. I'll be your wingman *once*. Wingwoman. Oh God. The wingwoman isn't also trying to sleep with strangers, is she?"

Gratitude overwhelmed me. "I have no idea. But obviously mine isn't."

"So on Friday, we'll find a bar or wherever single people go these days—"

"Friday?" My gratitude plummeted. "That's three days away."

"O-kaaay. We'll go tomorrow—"

"That's a whole twenty-four hours from now!"

"I'm sorry," Brittany said. Not sorry. "You're asking me to go *tonight?*"

"Please." I was on the verge of hysteria. From the heated silence, I could tell that Brittany and Reza were frantically communicating in some way.

"I can't," she said after a minute. "You can't. For one thing, it's snowing."

"People in Minnesota drive in the snow every day, and they're fine."

"Everything will be closed."

"No way. There are always people who need alcohol. Something will be open."

More silence on the other end of the line. More assumed communication.

Reza picked up. "Hey, Ingrid." He still had a light accent from his childhood in Karachi. "We understand your emergency, so here's our offer. Brit isn't comfortable driving in this weather, so I'll come get you—"

"I don't mind driving. It's barely snowing." It was snowing more than barely, but who cared?

"Ah, but you see, I *do* mind you driving to a bar in your crappy Volkswagen when there's ice on the road. My Subaru has four-wheel drive. So I'll drive you and Brit wherever you need to go, I'll stay invisible and sober, and then, whenever you're ready, I'll drive you home."

"Isn't the point for me to go home with somebody else? Or for somebody to come home with me?" I wasn't sure.

"She's right," Brittany said in the background.

"This is a nightmare," Reza said.

Brittany texted when they arrived, and I dashed outside. Reza drove a truck—a package car, they called them—for UPS, so he placed a high value on speed and punctuality. Fear gripped me. As I'd cleaned myself up, I realized Kat was right. I should have gone to bed and cried myself to sleep. This was insanity. All of this could wait until tomorrow. But I had already begged, and Brittany and Reza were going out of their way to help. There was no backing out now.

A gust of snowflakes whirled in behind me as I slid into their back seat. Reza stared me down in the rearview mirror. "For the record, I still think this is a bad idea. I'm only here to make sure you don't go home with Ted Bundy."

"Understood," I said.

"I mean, all of this is bad. This temporary breakup is a terrible idea. The worst idea I've ever heard."

Brittany turned to face me. "Don't listen to him. We're just ... a little weirded out. We support you—you know we support you *and* Cory—but ..."

"I know," I said so she wouldn't have to finish the thought.

Reza shook his head but began to drive. "Where are we going?"

I was embarrassed not to have an answer.

"Also for the record," he said, "I agree that every place will be closed because of the snow. I'm getting that out of the way now so I won't have to gloat later when I'm right."

"Oh, you'll gloat if you're right," Brittany said.

"I will absolutely gloat," he said.

Thankfully, Brittany had come prepared and was ready with the save. "I thought maybe that cider house by the river? The one with that giant Friar Tuck mural. I've never been there, but there are always tons of cars out front. I bet they'll be open."

"They will not be open," Reza said. But he glanced at me for the okay.

"That'll be fine." I nodded vigorously. "That sounds perfect. Thank you."

The large number of apple orchards nearby had given rise to Ridgetop's unusual alcohol of choice, hard cider, and the town had several rival cideries. Locals and tourists flocked to these establishments year-round, but I generally only went when we were meeting up with Cory's friends. I preferred going out for dinner, not drinks. Or even better, not going out at all.

I fidgeted with the large buttons on my coat. I had changed out of my work clothes—I would have to burn them—*the horror in his eyes as he stumbled backward—No. Ingrid. No.*—and into a cute thrifted dress and my nicest coat. I was paranoid that wherever we were going would be filled with carefree youths in trendy denim, but I also believed it was better to be overdressed than under.

Brittany turned to give me an encouraging smile. "You look great."

"You do, too," I said. She always did.

Brittany wasn't merely beautiful; she was dramatically gorgeous. She was curvaceous and fat with tremendous breasts and a heart-shaped face. Her dark eyes and dark hair were always exquisitely made up, and because she was a seamstress, her clothing always hugged her in all the right places. Tonight her dress was violet with a pattern of flying cranes. The fabric looked like silk, and the neckline plunged, but she had paired it with a casual jacket that effortlessly toned the whole thing down. Her appearance was living and breathing art.

I was her physical opposite. When I was young and scrawny, my mother had assured me I would grow into my body in adulthood, and I mostly had.

My hips had filled out, a little, and my breasts had rounded, a little. But I did have long legs for my average height, and my hair was naturally blond, a color that other women paid a lot of money for. The mole on my left cheek that I'd lobbied so hard to have removed as a teenager now added character, and my eyes were large and wide, which lent an unusual openness to my face. As a child, strangers had found it spooky and off-putting. As an adult, it made them want to tell me their secrets.

I had settled into a quiet type of pretty. *Like a Scandinavian deer*, Cory had said not long after we'd first met. I still treasured the compliment. I had felt gawky and gangly, eyes bulging and limbs knocking, and he'd been the first person to frame it as something beautiful and mysterious. He had changed the way I thought about myself.

"Just to be clear," I said, scooting forward to talk to Reza, "Cory and I are still together. Earlier you called it a 'temporary breakup,' but we haven't broken up. We're taking *a* break. There's a huge difference."

"'We were on a break!'" Brittany said in a very particular voice.

I flinched, and Brittany cackled.

"Is that *Friends*?" Reza asked. "You know I've never seen a single episode, but even I'm aware that after Ross slept with somebody else, Rachel never forgave him."

"Which is why Ingrid and Cory are both sleeping with other people," Brittany said.

"And we planned this," I said, grateful for the unexpected backup. "Ross and Rachel didn't plan anything."

"Ross and Rachel also hadn't been together for over a decade," Reza said.

"How do you know if you've never seen a single episode?" Brittany asked.

"Had they?" he asked, indignant.

"No."

Brittany and Reza dissolved into the easy laughter of best friends. With a pang, I realized they sounded like Cory and me. Or Macon and me.

I needed to stop thinking about Cory and Macon.

The snow was still coming down steadily, and the streets were deserted, so it was a surprise when we finally caught sight of the cider house. Its parking lot was packed, and its windows blazed with life. The jovial friar painted on the side of the building was laughing and toasting our arrival with a sloshing tankard. Brittany crowed to Reza, "It's open!"

But his eyes had already snagged on something else. "Uh, I don't want to alarm anyone, but—"

The next four words reached me in a ringing haze.

"—isn't that Cory's car?"

It was Cory's car. I could tell even with the curated mass of vinyl on his rear windshield—stickers of obscure DIY bands and comic books and demands to buy local—covered by snow. It'd been parked for a while. My vision dimmed, and I grew faint.

Reza slowed as he drove past it. "Now what?"

"Are you okay?" Brittany asked me.

"I need instructions!" he said.

"Go! Isn't there another place just up the river? There must be a dozen of them around here."

Their voices faded as I searched for the familiar figure though the crowded windows, which were framed in blinking Christmas lights. I couldn't make out anything inside, but the lights flashed a redundant warning. Cory was in there, and I was out here, and our town was way too small.

The next several cider houses we tried were all closed, but Reza didn't gloat. Seeing Cory's car had shifted something inside him. He was serious now, more determined to help. Or perhaps his motivation stemmed from sympathy and resignation.

We drove around for half an hour before landing at Blue Glass Brewery. Even from the outside, the location wasn't promising. Few cars were parked out front, and there were no friendly painted ambassadors to greet us. But the lights were on, and the door was unlocked. Desperation propelled me forward.

The microbrewery had all the bland hallmarks of modern design: polished concrete, reclaimed wood, chalkboard menu, Edison bulbs. The potent bleach smell underscoring the aroma of fermentation was the only thing that separated it from any other taproom in the country, not to mention any coffee shop or boutique hotel. Brittany and I selected a table in the warmest-looking corner. Remembering his role, Reza took a seat alone on a barstool overlooking the street.

"I'll get us something to drink," Brittany said.

Beer excited me even less than cider, but there was no way I could handle doing this sober. I supposed that was the whole point of meeting people in bars. Unfortunately, this one was quiet. There were eight other people here, seven of them men. The most attractive, who wasn't even my type, was wearing a wedding band. The second most attractive was the bartender. I wasn't positive, but it seemed like bad etiquette to hit on the person who was being paid to serve me. Another man was on a date. One was old enough to be my father, one was sloppily drunk and monologuing to the table beside him, and the two at that table looked like they might have stormed the Capitol building. My mood grew even bleaker.

I gave the bartender another look. He had a ring on, too.

Brittany returned with two glasses. "We suck at this. You should have been the one to go up there, not me. The bartender . . . he's not bad."

I gestured to my ring finger.

"Oh. Shit. I forgot to look for that."

"I feel awful. Reza's over there alone, drinking water."

"He's fine. He's playing a game on his phone."

"It was nice of him to drive us."

"He's the best," she said simply as she scoped out the rest of the room. Her face slackened with disappointment.

"Yep," I said miserably.

"So . . . we wait? For other people to arrive? Is that how this goes?"

"I don't know. Maybe?" I sipped my beer. It was all wrong, too citrusy and sunny for a night and a place like this. "I guess we should have looked around before ordering."

"That's okay. This is how people learn, right? We're learning."

"I don't even know what I'm supposed to do if I see someone I *am* interested in. Like, am I supposed to just . . . approach him? And what are we supposed to talk about?"

"I don't know. Whatever you'd normally talk about, I guess."

"Books? Somehow, I don't think talking about books would be considered sexy."

"For the right person, it would be."

My heart sank. "Please don't."

"Don't what?"

"Don't say his name."

"Who?"

"Macon."

It seemed impossible that she wasn't referring to him, but she looked genuinely confused. "Oh," she said. "Right."

I supposed she didn't know much about him, though. Maybe she'd heard me mention him as a work friend, but she hadn't heard of him as an object of interest until tonight.

"Maybe"—Brittany sounded hesitant—"you should go flirt with those men?"

She was talking about the insurrection guys. "Oh my God. No."

"For practice!"

I glared daggers at her.

She shrugged helplessly. "It's just that I'm still not sure what we're doing here."

"Well, I'm not sure either, okay?" I hadn't meant to snap at her, and I shrank back and into myself. "I'm sorry."

"Hey. *Hey*," she said, waiting until I looked at her. Her expression was serious, and for a moment, it grounded me. Then it reminded me of Macon again, and my heart cracked back open and bled. "We'll figure this out," she said. "Let's give it some time."

We drank slowly. The taproom was lackluster and quiet, and even the music was so low that I could barely hear it. I felt awful for dragging my friends into this listless hellhole. I checked my phone and found a message from Kat: *How many men have you kissed so far?*

None, but a guy my dad's age keeps leering at Brittany.

"Look at us, hanging out at a bar and checking our phones," Brittany said, and I wondered if she'd been texting Reza. I didn't tell her about the lech sitting behind her, because I didn't want to make her night even worse. "This place sucks." She shoved her drink away. "Blue Glass Brewery. And yet our glasses are clear."

I pointed at an industrial pendant light. "They couldn't even make the fixtures blue."

"I'm so sick of these places that look like they were designed by one of Zuckerberg's shitty algorithms."

I pushed my drink across the table and clinked it against hers in a low-key cheers.

The brewery had a drafty chill. I stood to shrug my coat back on, giving up on looking cute, and noticed Reza still sitting by himself. I headed over to his barstool. He glanced up from a colorful jeweled puzzle game, and I jerked my head toward our table. He slipped his phone into his pocket, grabbed his sparkling water with lime, and joined us.

"We were just talking about how awful this place is," I said, which made Brittany sort of laugh, so I sort of laughed, too. "God. What did I expect would happen?"

"That you would meet some strapping bar hunk who would whisk you back to his place and fuck your brains out?" Reza said.

My laughter grew louder as humility mixed in with my humiliation. But then my emotions turned again, and I started crying and gasping, and nothing was funny at all.

Reza placed a solid hand on my back. "Breathe. Breathe."

I couldn't. I couldn't.

"You don't have to do any of this tonight," Brittany said, hastening to my side and whispering the permission I needed. "We can leave right now."

The moon's reflection on the fallen snow illuminated the town with an eerie brightness as they drove me home. It looked like the midnight version of high noon. In the raucous cider house, phantom women circled Cory. Maybe he'd already taken one of them back to his place. Or maybe he was inside one of their apartments, naked and warm and tangled into a new position, something I wasn't flexible enough to achieve.

I saw Macon stumbling backward against the doors. *No. Ingrid. No.*

The snow was coming down harder. My cold fingers grasped each other. I held my own hand because no one was there to hold it for me.

CHAPTER THREE

It snowed eight inches that night, which hadn't happened since the year Cory and I moved to town and went sledding on pizza boxes in the woods behind our apartment. Powder collected on bare branches. It outlined the deciduous trees in white shadows and toppled from the evergreens in small avalanches. Rooftops transformed into blank canvases. The roads and sidewalks and grass all vanished, but by dawn the wind had calmed, and the smoothed earth was crisscrossed with squirrel and rabbit and bird tracks. Everything sparkled with the promise of a fresh start.

But it didn't feel like one. I had slept terribly, in fits and starts. An endless loop of the attempted kiss tormented me while I was awake but also whenever I dreamed. I was only able to recognize the difference because time slowed down in my dreams, forcing me to relive each millisecond while still withholding any ability to change the outcome. The loop reset whenever I reached Macon's horrified expression as he drew away from me.

No. Ingrid. No.

My jaw ached from grinding my teeth against my night guard. Despite the cold—Cory and I kept the thermostat low to save money—my chest was soaked with sweat. I got up to pee, blotted off the sweat with a tissue, then returned to bed and my phone.

Surely Sue would text soon. It had snowed enough to keep the library closed, but I needed her confirmation. I needed a day off to figure out how to quit. What explanation, what lie, could I give to her? Perhaps I could request a meeting before work to avoid seeing Macon.

Relief arrived around 8:30 A.M. when she confirmed in our group text that the library would remain closed for the day. The snowstorm had already moved on, so we'd be back at work tomorrow, but at least this gave me a buffer, a whole day to formulate a plan.

Alyssa replied first with three party emojis.

Elijah was next: *snow day!!*

I waited anxiously for Macon's response, hoping it might reveal something—anything—about his mood. It finally arrived ten minutes later: *Great news. See you all tomorrow.*

How typical of him to remain professional. My frustration and disappointment were unreasonable, but I couldn't help it. Afraid of giving away something about my own emotional state, I responded with a thumbs-up emoji and then hurled my phone across the bed.

It lit up immediately. Heart thumping, I scrambled over to fetch it.

How are you doing?

Not Macon.

I disappeared back underneath my blankets and hit the call button. Kat's face appeared. She was in bed, too, bathed in the light of her reading lamp. Night darkened the room behind her. I was familiar enough with her family's schedule to know that her three-year-old son, Howie, was probably already asleep and that her husband, Lachlan, was probably watching television.

"Congratulations!" she said. "You made it to morning."

I moaned, which made me realize my night guard was still in. I set it on my bedside table and filled her in. When I finished my bellyaching, her body shifted from a listening position to a speaking position. "Here's what I've come up with," she said. "My plan for you."

I stared back at her with dead, swollen eyes.

"You aren't going to quit. Not yet. Not until you know what the situation is. Macon is an adult, and he's your mate, so it might not be as bad as you think it is."

"Oh, it's bad—"

"Yeah, it *is* bad. And yeah, sitting beside him at work will be awful. But we don't know how awful or for how long, and I don't want you making another rash decision before we have all the information."

"Another," I said a little coolly.

She toughened, but it was with love. "You and Cory decided to experiment with other people. You tried to kiss your coworker. This isn't the best time for you to lose your income and health insurance and try to find new employment."

"I can't go back. I *can't.*"

"You can, and you will, and you'll pretend like everything is fine and normal. Because it is normal! Being humiliated is a regular part of the dating process. You can't be reduced to a puddle every time some guy rejects you."

"Macon isn't some guy. He was one of my closest friends—"

"If it's unbearable," she said, cutting me off, "I'll support you quitting. I'll support you launching from your desk in the middle of a shift and rocketing out the door. But I won't support you quitting before we even know what you're dealing with."

"It'll be unbearable. It might actually kill me."

"It won't. But if it does, I promise to fly to America and remove anything scandalous from your apartment before your parents show up."

"I don't own anything scandalous."

"Give it one day," she said. And she kept repeating it until she won.

Once Kat had made the stressful decision for me, my body rapidly shut down. Several hours later, I awoke, gasping back to life. Anxiety tightened around my heart as two names pounded back and forth inside my head: *Cory, Macon, Cory, Macon, Cory, Macon.*

People were shouting outside.

I jolted upright before realizing it was the downstairs couple throwing snowballs at each other in the parking lot. The physicality of my distress was staggering. I pressed a hand against the pain in my chest and stumbled to the bathroom. I understood I was having an extended panic attack, but I couldn't shake the sense that my life was actually in danger. I'd lost my dignity and—no matter what Kat said—possibly my job, too.

I brooded on the toilet until my legs fell asleep. What the hell was I supposed to do today? In times of crisis, I found it useful to stick to the basics.

Eat, I decided. Breakfast. Lunch. Whatever.

My feet were still prickling as I stood before the fridge. The situation was dire. Cory and I hadn't gone grocery shopping since before the holidays, and he'd taken the entire contents of the freezer with him when he'd moved out. He was particular about his diet and still ate like a child. His food pyramid consisted almost exclusively of pizza, nuggets, and fries. Produce was rare, but sometimes I could pressure him into eating a few apple slices or baby carrots dipped in ranch. It wasn't that he was difficult, though. He never turned his issues into a problem for anybody else, or at least he tried not to. Mainly I worried for his health.

I made peanut butter toast because I didn't have the energy for anything more substantial. The meal was basic enough that Cory might have even eaten it, except the peanut butter was the natural kind, and his needed to be creamy. I also used the butt of the bread because all the regular slices were gone. He wouldn't have liked that either.

My mind conjured another unwelcome image: Cory and some stranger in bed, lazy nude limbs draped over each other, gazing out her window together at the snow. Unconsciously, I found myself pulling up his social media. We had agreed not to post about any of this online because we didn't want our families asking questions. He was sticking to the plan—of course he was—so there wasn't anything for me to see. I desperately wanted to text him: *Isn't it weird that we aren't talking? That I don't even know where you are right now?*

I couldn't text Kat either, because she was asleep, and the only other person I texted with regularly was my sister, who couldn't know about any of this. And then there was Macon, who obviously I would never text with again. We had never texted much anyway due to his inherent Luddism. What was he doing right now? What must he think of me?

No. Ingrid. No.

The loop was punishing.

Sorry about last night, I texted Brittany. *Thanks for taking such good care of me. You two are the best, and I promise I'll never put you through anything like that ever again.* I did want to apologize, but I also longed for a comforting response. *No problem! Happy to do it! Everything will be okay, and you're doing great!*

Brittany didn't text back.

The last few bites of toast were so thick and dry that I gagged. I shoved the remains down the disposal and slumped against the sink. Each day that passed was another opportunity lost. What would I have done if a man at the brewery *had* wanted to go home with me? The question filled me with fear and dread, which suggested I might be stuck with dating apps. I feared and dreaded those, too, but at least the safety of a screen would make it easier to start a conversation. Yet I didn't pick up my phone and create a profile. I stared at the greasy smears around my drain.

No. Ingrid. No.

My eyes squeezed closed. Several minutes passed before I was able to release my grip on the sink. I rinsed away the peanut butter, but it still looked dirty. I got out the cleanser and scrubbed, and then I noticed that the counters needed help. Then it was the appliances, the floor, the small window that overlooked the parking lot. It wasn't long before everything in the room was clean. Our whole kitchen—our whole apartment—was small, not just the window.

This was the second place we'd lived together. We had lived with our respective parents during the first three years of college—two at the community college and one at the University of Central Florida—to save money to help pay for our education. Thriftiness was necessary and long ingrained. Our families did okay but never had much to spare. My parents were high school teachers, which meant college wasn't optional, but they also couldn't pay for all of it. By the time Cory and I were seniors, we were eager to move out and start our life together.

We found a one-bedroom near campus, tiny and dark with only two windows on the same wall. The apartment was part of a massive complex full of rowdy neighbors. Mold speckled our ceilings, insects scuttled through our cabinets, and we had to haul our laundry to a dismal facility overrun with mosquitos and lizards and, on one occasion, an enormous snake that management assured us (too many times for it to be an actual assurance) was *not* a Burmese python. We had jobs, of course, but we still took a significant financial hit by leaving home a year early. We were also happy.

That wasn't to say we didn't take notes. When we moved, the upgrade from tiny to small was thrilling. Our new one-bedroom had three hundred additional square feet, windows in every room, and a closet that contained a stacked washer and dryer. No mold, few insects, no pythons. The entire complex was only six two-unit buildings, and each unit had a balcony overlooking some woods. Most glorious of all, it was still within our price range.

It wasn't easy, money never was, but the previous year we'd finally managed to pay off the last of our student loans. Now we paid that same amount into our separate savings accounts because neither of us had been able to shake those financial fears. We weren't broke, but we *felt* broke. Or maybe it was just that money still felt so precious. Spending it was stressful, so we lived like we had none to spare. Squirreling away every spare dollar had been hardwired into us. Mostly I felt angry about college—that it hadn't been worth the expense, worth the burden, and we'd invested so much in order to obtain jobs that barely paid a living wage—but we were still lucky. Our student loans had been relatively small; I had majored in English, Cory in hospitality. If we'd been interested in fields requiring more than four years of study, we would have been paying back those loans for decades. But there we were, debt-free at last.

And we were still there.

When we'd moved in, Brittany and Reza had lived in the unit below us. Now it was occupied by a young couple, clones of our former selves. Most of our neighbors were either in college or had recently graduated, which contributed to the nagging, unshakable feeling that our friends had moved into the next phase of adulthood while we were still stuck in the past.

What would our apartment look like through the eyes of a potential suitor? What might it reveal about us? Cory and I were clean, relatively tidy, and took care of what we had. That was important. But our landlord wouldn't allow us to paint or hang art, so our walls were beige and bare. And our furniture was largely made of particleboard, items from IKEA and Target that we'd pieced together ourselves, flimsy and sagging under the weight of time.

At least the hypothetical suitor would also notice our extensive collections of books (mostly mine) and vinyl (mostly Cory's). We were interesting! We were cultured! Yet our apartment didn't reflect the way I saw myself. I was more vibrant than this. I was more structurally sound. Guests felt comfortable around me, able to cozy up and pour out their hearts. However, if it weren't for the books and music, this space could belong to anybody.

I threw myself into cleaning the rest of our apartment, sweeping, dusting, spiraling. *No. Ingrid. No.* I scrubbed and scoured. The potential suitor narrowed his eyes and judged, so I staged Cory's vinyl to make me look cooler. I hid the framed photos of us in the bottom of our closet.

The temperature rose. The snow began to melt. I sweated and did the laundry. As I stripped off the bedsheets, I wondered: If the situation were reversed—if Cory were here and I were in an Airbnb—would I ever want to sleep on them again?

No. It was the only easy answer that day.

I laundered the sheets anyway and remade our bed with my least favorite set, in case I had to trash them later. Maybe I shouldn't bring anyone into our bedroom at all.

My gaze snagged on my night guard, which was still on the nightstand. It had been embarrassing enough when I'd had to start using it after I began grinding my teeth during the pandemic. I couldn't fathom wearing it in front of anybody except for Cory or Kat. I checked my phone to see if Kat was awake yet and discovered a text from Brittany.

Any interest in being set up with one of Reza's coworkers?

The chaos froze. My hands shook as I responded: *Maybe. Who is he?*

Thankfully, Brittany was still near her phone. I felt nervous as she typed. I hadn't even considered being set up, but it sounded significantly more appealing than my other options.

Nice guy. Funny. Recently divorced. Thought that might be useful since he's probably not looking for commitment either. He got custody of their kid, so that's a good sign, right?

It was a good sign.

What's his name? I asked so I could search for him.

Brittany sent me a link. Adam Coughlin's social media mainly contained photos of his daughter and their spunky shepherd mix, but there were a few photos of him, too. Unfortunately, he wasn't dressed for work in any of them. It was a well-established fact that UPS had somehow accomplished the impossible by making brown uniforms with shorts attractive, although perhaps this was only because their employees were in such good shape from lifting all those heavy boxes. Like Reza, Adam did appear to have strong arms and muscular legs. Cory wasn't muscular—muscular wasn't even my type—but there *was* something alluring about a UPS man. And Adam looked cute enough and friendly.

Yes, I said. *Thank you!*

K. I'll get Reza to ask.

I set down my phone, jittery and excited, before it struck me that Reza would be sending Adam links to *my* social media. Snatching my phone back up, I reminded myself what he would see: books. An endless scroll of what I'd read and enjoyed. My skin grew hot as I remembered being the geeky kid at school, nose buried in the pages of the novels that were my closest friends. But if books turned Adam off, I wouldn't want to date him. "If you go home with somebody, and they don't have books, don't fuck 'em," right? (The John Waters quote was popular online, but I knew it first from reading the essay in *Role Models*.) Except I wasn't looking for a normal date. So did it matter? I wasn't sure, but I suspected it did.

I inspected the few photos of myself that I had posted. They were good—like everyone else, I only ever posted the good ones—although most of them were selfies with Cory. Still, my spirits lifted with tentative hope, and I kept my phone in hand for the remainder of the day, waiting for an update from Brittany, staring at Adam's photos and my own.

By the next morning, the snow had melted into slush. I arrived at work on time, but Macon was late, which wasn't unusual. I was always on time, and Macon was often late, always with a grumbled excuse. Alyssa was sitting at my station, manning the circulation desk. Thursday was our branch's other late night, so she and Sue had already been there for two hours because they always opened. Macon and I always closed. Of course our next shift had to be a late shift.

"How was your day off?" Alyssa asked when I returned from putting my tote bag and lunch in her office. The annex was small, so her desk shared a space with our break room.

"Fine," I said. But my voice sounded tremulous. It seemed best to keep her talking so that I wouldn't have to. "How was yours? What did you do?"

Alyssa had read—that's what we all usually did—some new novel by some debut author about . . . something. I was pulsating with dread. Sweating in my sweater. I'd been as careful about selecting today's outfit as I had been before my previous shift. Because what *did* a person wear to work after throwing themselves at a colleague? Corduroy pants and a bulky sweater, I'd decided. Clothing that concealed and comforted.

"Blah blah blah Macon blah," she said.

I startled, catching only the part that interested me. "Sorry. What was that?"

She jerked her head toward the front windows. He was getting out of his car. The phone rang, so I grabbed it, praying for a long call.

"Ingrid, dear? Is that you?"

The voice was raspy and familiar. Not a long call. I barely restrained my exasperation and dove in with false cheer. "Good morning, Ms. Fairchild!"

"Is the fire lit today?"

Doreen Fairchild was one of a handful of elderly regulars who fought for the chairs beside the fireplace during the winter months. It was a satisfying place to read the periodicals and do the *New York Times* Sunday crossword, our most photocopied item. The rule was that we lit the fire whenever the temperature dipped below fifty, but no matter how many times we gave out this information to that particular subset of patrons, the inquiries still came. On the rare occasions that we got too busy to light it, the firebugs became downright belligerent.

A soothing crackle issued from the back room. "It sure is."

"Are there any chairs available?" she asked.

Normally I loathed this follow-up question because it required leaving my seat, but Macon had almost reached the doors. "Hold on," I said. "I'll go check." I hurried away, aware of the gust of cold air behind me, aware of Alyssa and Macon greeting each other. The low rumble of his voice made my cheeks flush. I pressed my hands against them to cool them down.

If it's unbearable, you can quit. Kat's promise returned to me like a guiding mantra. *If it's unbearable, you can quit. If it's unbearable, you can quit.*

I glanced back, and our eyes met across the full length of the stacks. My gaze dropped straight to the floor. I slowed my steps in an attempt to calm my palpitating heart, but as soon as I picked up the receiver again, I realized I'd returned to the desk without checking the chairs.

"You're in luck!" I said, too enthusiastically. "One of them is empty." If they were all occupied when she arrived, I could pretend it had just happened.

"Thank you, dear," she said. "I'll be right down."

I hung up, not daring to look at Macon. "Sorry I'm late," he said to Alyssa. "Edmond showed up again this morning."

Edmond showed up every morning. He was Macon's almost-cat who belonged to a neighbor but preferred Macon's house. The cat's real name was Phish, with a *ph* the neighbor was careful to specify, but Macon called him Edmond Dantès after the wrongfully convicted protagonist of *The Count of Monte Cristo*, who makes a patient but determined escape from prison. Edmond had arrived last autumn, entering Macon's house through a previously unknown gap in the foundation. Macon had discovered the cat grooming himself on the couch. He'd patched the hole, but then the cat hopped in through a tear in a window screen. Macon patched that, too. Then the cat slipped in through the back door while Macon was fetching a tool from his shed, then through the front door while his arms were filled with groceries. To make his point, Edmond began planting himself on the welcome mat every morning until Macon finally gave up. Now Edmond spent all day at Macon's, napping and snacking, and was sent home only at night. Apparently, he always protested vehemently, and Macon always argued back that the cat didn't belong to him. Someday Macon would have to accept that he did.

I once asked why he'd named the cat after an escapee and not, say, a burglar. (A cat burglar! It was right there.) Macon said if I knew this particular neighbor, I would also think of Edmond's house as an unjust punishment worthy of a triumphant escape.

"Of course he showed up again," Alyssa said. "You feed him."

"If I didn't, he'd starve himself," Macon said, incensed.

"You buy him the expensive food."

"Because the cheap stuff is garbage. It'd be like feeding him a Happy Meal and then grinding up the plastic toy to go with it." Macon was anti–fast food, so none of us were surprised when his opinions on diet extended to cats. I suspected that he spent more money on Edmond than he did on himself.

"Oh, sorry!" Alyssa popped up. She'd noticed me standing around awkwardly and assumed it was because she was still sitting in my chair. "I'll get out of here."

The previous summer, she'd jokingly referred to Macon and me as "work husband and work wife," and instead of acknowledging our indisputable closeness as colleagues, we'd grown flustered with overlapping denials that sounded more like confessions. For months afterward, we'd been instinctively less chummy when she was around, as if we had something to hide.

But we'd never had anything to hide. Not until now.

If only I could have begged her to stay.

I took my vacated seat, still unable to look at him. Our silence was loaded. The situation *was* unbearable, and I *would* have to quit. Today. This morning. Right now. I would tell Sue how sorry I was, but that I couldn't stay, and I couldn't explain why, though I was grateful for everything she'd done for me and—

Macon cleared his throat. Then again, as if it hadn't worked the first time. "What, uh, how was . . . yesterday?"

The shame burned, more painful and intense than ever.

"What did you do?" Any trace of prickliness had vanished. He sounded nervous and polite. Gentle, even.

I couldn't ignore him. I owed him that much. My gaze flickered over to him for an instant only, but I'd never forget what I saw: a man pushing through his extreme discomfort out of genuine concern. I felt foolish and mumbled something unintelligible back.

"I made that kale salad, the one I told you about? With the lemon and ricotta salata. It was good." He paused here because usually I would comment. "Went through some seed catalogs, narrowed down my picks for the year. Uh, went to bed early. Read."

Silence returned, swift and all-consuming.

"Not very exciting, I guess," he said.

It was an exceedingly un-Macon-like effort to put me at ease. It was what I wanted—he was doing exactly what I had asked for, pretending like I hadn't done what I had done—but I was too ashamed to accept his kindness. I had forever tainted our friendship with my misdeed.

"I . . ." I had to get this one thing out, at least. "I'm so sorr—"

He weakly lifted an embarrassed hand and waved, cutting me off. *Don't worry about it. Let's not talk about it.* And that's how we left things for a long time.

My self-consciousness had infected him, and we worked in excruciating silence. But I didn't talk to Sue either. The wave had been enough to hold me back. Instead, I monitored my phone for updates from Brittany and mentally scanned through all the Adams I had ever known, trying to find universal personality traits among them. I typed his name into the library's system. He had an account, but his card had expired. The system didn't allow us to view a patron's checkout history unless they had overdue fees related to a specific item. The policy was good for privacy but bad for my curiosity. Adam had no overdue fees.

If I didn't hear from Brittany by that evening, I'd send her a text.

I texted Brittany on my lunch break. She didn't respond, but twenty-three messages pinged back and forth between Riley and our mom in our group text re: potential weekends for the wedding.

By the afternoon, the only snow that remained was in the shadows. Kat had asked for a photo, but I'd forgotten. We often traded pictures of the ocean for mountains, kangaroos for black bears. I darted outside and snapped a sad photo of a glistening white patch in our mulch. When I returned, Alyssa was hanging out behind the desk again.

"Photo for Kat," I explained, still avoiding eye contact with Macon. I talked about her often enough that they both understood.

"Hey, you know those teens who live next door to me?" Alyssa asked, and we did. She complained about them regularly, but for some reason her complaints felt pettier than Macon's. Or perhaps the things that bothered her just weren't the same things that bothered us. "They had this garland in their window that said LET IT SNOW, but yesterday they switched around the letters, and now it says WET SNOT. Can you believe that?"

Macon and I let out the same surprised snort, which was immediately uncomfortable because we were unable to share anything right now, even a joke or an opinion.

"I said something to their mom," Alyssa said, "but she just laughed. She didn't even make them change it back."

"Why should they have to change it back?" I snapped. "It's funny."

Alyssa looked surprised. Even Macon seemed taken aback by my sudden crossness because normally I was the peacemaker. "Weird vibe over here today," Alyssa said, eyeing us suspiciously and grabbing a stack of damaged graphic novels to repair.

Sue's head popped out of the annex doorway. "Ingrid, would you mind coming in here for a minute?"

Relieved for an excuse to escape yet still feeling like I was being sent to the principal's office for something she surely wasn't even aware that I'd done, I followed her back into her compact office. Stacks of jumbled books, papers and review publications, and framed photos of her husband and twin sons cluttered every available surface. Afternoon light streamed in through the stained glass, casting rainbow shadows across all of it. Obviously the annex's windows weren't original to the building, but a craftsman in the seventies had done a remarkable job of matching their style.

Sue sat behind her desk and gestured for me to take the extra chair. "I was just on the phone with Constance, and she asked me to remind you that this is the final year you can apply for library school and still receive the full financial reimbursement. The deadline is this spring if you want to start classes this summer."

Well. Shit.

Constance, the library director, had been encouraging me to apply ever since I'd been hired. A few decades ago, a local wealthy book lover had bequeathed his estate to the public library, and part of the endowment had been earmarked for continuing education. If I returned to college full-time through a distance learning program, I could receive my MLIS, master of library and information science, in two years. The money would run out in two and a half.

I wasn't keen to return to school, and I'd been putting it off. Every time I thought about it, it felt like trying to swallow a pickled egg. A master's wasn't required for the lesser-paying jobs in our system, but obtaining the degree was the only way to advance into a higher position. I wasn't sure I actually wanted any of those positions, but if I didn't get the education now, I might regret it later, *and* I would have to pay for it myself. What kind of person turned down a free education? It felt like I had no choice.

"The deadline is at the end of April, right?"

Sue nodded. "I know you're not looking forward to it, but I agree with

Constance that you should do it. You're a great candidate. You could have a good future here."

"Thank you." And I meant it, even as my heart sank.

"Have you given any further thought to what you'd like to do next? Run a branch? Work in reference? Administration?"

"I'm not sure."

The admission sounded feeble to my ears, but Sue gave me a thoughtful look. "You know, when I retire in two years—"

Ding! Even in my despair, I tallied the mention of her favorite subject.

"—Alyssa will most likely take over this branch. But there are two other managers close to retirement, and I can see you running a branch someday. You have the right leadership skills."

Sue was one of the few Black librarians of her generation in Colburn County. She'd had to work twice as hard to rise to her position, and she'd been the esteemed head of this branch for nearly four decades. Her staff and patrons loved her. I loved her. A compliment from Sue carried a lot of weight.

I smiled so that she could see my appreciation, not my uncertainty. I had given a lot of thought to running a library—the idea of being in charge of a collection was admittedly seductive—but some mental block I didn't understand prevented me from getting excited about it. Maybe it was the inherent bureaucracy, though the rise of book banners didn't help. They weren't our regular patrons, but postpandemic, we'd been coming into contact with them on a regular basis. Their fury and ignorance were draining, so much so that our usual method of dealing with infuriating people—flipping them off underneath the desk while gritting our teeth in the approximation of a soothing smile—wasn't enough. A number of our fellow librarians had quit in the last year. They couldn't handle the abuse any longer, nor should they have had to.

I hadn't set out to be a librarian. My first job in Ridgetop had been as a gift shop cashier at the Tamsett Park Inn, a sprawling historical hotel where Cory still managed the front desk. I hadn't enjoyed working exclusively with tourists—it had reminded me too much of Orlando—but thankfully, it hadn't taken me long to find a new job at the Tick-Tock Bookshop.

The Tick-Tock was named after the magnificent grandfather clock that gave the store its heartbeat. I loved working there and had stayed until it closed. Len's emphysema had forced him into retirement, and no buyers had been willing to take on his struggling business. I had wanted to stay in the industry, but the only options in town were a handful of ragtag used bookstores with employees who never vacated their positions and the Christian bookstore by the mall. I'd been facing a bleak reunion with the inn when the library job had appeared. Now I'd been here nearly twice as long as I'd worked at the bookstore. What I really wanted was my old job, but sometimes the best you could do was reach for the thing closest to your dream. This was the closest.

Still, when I returned to the desk, I couldn't hide my misery.

"Whoa," Alyssa said. She had yet to leave to repair the damaged books. I'd interrupted a conversation between her and Macon about his mother, who lived in town and had severe agoraphobia. He spent a great deal of time taking care of her. "What was that all about?"

Macon was watching me, too. His posture had grown tense and disquieted. Perhaps he was wondering if—or hoping that—I had just quit. I told them about my conversation with Sue.

"Jeez, don't sound so excited," Alyssa said.

"Just because I'm applying," I said, "doesn't mean I have to be excited."

"You're really applying?" Macon was surprised. He knew I'd been dreading it.

I shrugged in a way that said, *I guess I have to.*

"I liked it," Alyssa said. She'd taken advantage of the reimbursement program immediately upon being hired.

"I didn't." Macon's surliness had returned. Library school hadn't been continuing education for him; he'd done it the first time around. But despite being as qualified as Sue and Alyssa, he'd never shown any interest in upward mobility.

"Yeah, but you hate everything," Alyssa said.

"I do," Macon agreed.

Although it didn't seem to bother him, it bothered me when other people accused him of being a curmudgeon. I often teased him about it, too, but Sue and Alyssa didn't have quite the same faith in him that I did. They didn't seem to understand that a large portion of his crankiness was a wink, his sense of humor, and that his actions consistently revealed the truth: he was kind and thoughtful and generous, and people who actually hated everything were not.

It also bothered me that he'd been doing this job—this same job as me— for eleven years. I understood not wanting the responsibility of running a branch or managing a staff, but Macon belonged at the reference desk at the main library. The pay was better, and he'd be great at it. Selfishly, I'd never encouraged him to apply. Selfishly, I'd liked having him beside me.

If only I hadn't been so selfish. Maybe then he still wouldn't have been here, and I wouldn't have made a move, and we wouldn't have been at odds.

Normally I preferred the late shift. The library was quieter, and apart from the stressed schoolchildren and parents amassing sources for last-minute reports, the patrons tended to be friendlier and more relaxed. But nobody was writing reports during the first week of January, and all the convivial patrons must have been doing something else that night.

It was too quiet and too empty.

The corduroy pants had been a bad idea. The swish of wale against wale was a constant signal of my presence. I tried to stay still, but the silence was so uncomfortable that it verged on the profound. Even without eye contact, I felt Macon observing me just as I was him, yet I still had no idea what he was thinking or how long we'd be able to keep this up.

It isn't UNBEARABLE, I texted Kat. *But it is unsustainable.*

My phone was in hand because I was still waiting to hear back from Brittany. The most reasonable conclusion was that Adam wasn't interested in what he'd seen, which, fine, whatever. (Not whatever.) Mainly I was mad at myself for not using the snow day to sign up for a dating app. It was stupid to have put all my eggs in the Adam basket.

The monthlong clock was ticking: five days lost, twenty-six days left.

Macon stood so suddenly that I looked up. Mumbling something about plants, he vanished into the annex to grab the watering can. Thursday was his plant-watering night. At least this would give us a few minutes of relief.

Kat lit up my phone. *Are you going to quit??*

All the libraries had been closed during the early months of the pandemic. The county had sent Sue to an outreach center for the unhoused, Alyssa to the food bank, and our previous page lost his job altogether because he'd only been part-time. Macon and I were both sent to the 911 call center. Initially, we—along with a handful of other librarians and some people from election services—had been intimidated, but then we realized during training that we'd only be fielding low-priority calls, things like rabid raccoons and violations of the stay-at-home order. After that, we felt useful. This was something we could do to help. But two weeks into it, the dispatchers got hit with a large-scale situation, and I was forwarded an actual emergency. It was a domestic dispute. A woman was being followed by her ex-husband in a truck, and I had to stay on the line and build the call for the responding officer so they'd know what to expect when they arrived. I had to keep the woman calm and ask questions about their location and whether it was possible he was armed. The woman made it through, and I did, too, but I was still shaken up in the parking lot after work. Macon had waited with me until I was steady enough to drive home.

"I'm glad we were both assigned here," I said. The sidewalk was cold underneath my ass. We were perched on the curb, socially distanced at six feet apart. "I felt safer knowing you were there. Like, if I had messed up, I knew you could have stepped in and handled it."

"You wouldn't have messed up. You didn't. Honestly, I think that's why we were both sent here. We're levelheaded."

"You are," I said.

"You don't give yourself enough credit."

"Still. I'm glad you're here. I would have really missed you."

It was the plain truth, and I hadn't meant anything weird by it. But his ears reddened, and his words caught in his throat. "I would have missed you, too."

My whole body grew hot in response.

Macon's metal watering can clanked against the rim of a potted plant, jolting me back to the present. My body was burning again.

No, I texted Kat. *Not yet.*

She was right that quitting my job while my life was in upheaval wouldn't be smart. But it also didn't feel safe. I needed the safety of this job and these coworkers, and Macon was the safest of all. I promised myself that I would honor our past and do right by him: I would search for a new job in February so he could feel safe at his job, too. I wouldn't let this terrible silence hang in the air between us for so long that he'd be forced to quit first.

But I did need time. I did need this month.

My phone lit up again.

Adam wants to know if you're free tomorrow night, Brittany said.

CHAPTER FOUR

We met at a popular rooftop bar that served glitzy, overpriced cocktails. I'd heard of it but had never been there before due to my abiding distaste for places where people who cared about popularity and appearances and money gathered, a predictable remnant of my unhappy school years. Drinks had been my idea, the location Adam's. Even with my extremely limited dating knowledge, I understood that if drinks went well, they could lead to a meal, which then could lead to a bedroom. But if they went poorly, I'd be able to make a fast escape.

The ability to escape quickly seemed crucial.

Although I was a punctual person, I wasn't necessarily an early person, but I arrived a full twenty minutes before we'd planned to meet. I assumed Reza wasn't unique and that being on time mattered to all UPS employees, so I hadn't wanted to risk even a second of tardiness. It turned out the rooftop was closed for the winter and the bar area was limited to a heated top floor, but there was still a crowd and a view. I went ahead and purchased my own drink. This seemed like a good strategy; the rooftop had made me think about roofies, which made me think about how unfair it was that women *had* to think about roofies. (I doubted Cory was thinking about roofies.) My nerves were frayed as I waited alone in a too-tall chair at a too-tall table. It seemed as if bar tables existed only to make adults feel infantilized, and I didn't need any help there. This date was already playing on all my childhood vulnerabilities.

Cory and I had both been late bloomers. While the average age for menstruation to begin keeps dropping due to God knows what hormones in our food and damage to our environment, my own period didn't show up until I was sixteen. And by the time my breasts and hips finally followed, I was already too entrenched in the art of invisibility—head down, shoulders rolled forward, seat in the back of the classroom—for it to make a difference with the boys. I already believed I was undesirable.

Cory had looked even younger at sixteen and was often mistaken for twelve. When he'd first told me, I couldn't believe it had been that bad. But later, once we fully trusted each other, he'd shown me the photos. He hadn't been exaggerating. His body had been devastatingly childlike, more like a middle schooler than somebody who could drive. And whereas I had turned my shame inward and become sad and reflective, he'd turned his outward and become angry and disruptive. We both still carried resentment over these hurts, but mine was mostly under control while Cory's actively simmered. However, as my feet dangled above the floor, I felt young and invisible all over again. Was dating making him feel the same way? Suddenly it seemed impossible that I was meeting somebody who *wasn't* Cory. That anybody apart from Cory would even want to meet me.

Adam arrived a few minutes early, looking like his photos—and unlike Cory. He was taller and more muscular than my boyfriend. Olive skinned, not fair skinned. His eyes were brown and unobscured, not blue and framed with glasses. The whole package was so unfamiliar that I had to fight the urge to duck and army-crawl away.

When he scanned the room, he seemed surprised to find me already there. He approached with a nervous smile. "Ingrid?"

I stood and gave him a light hug. "It's nice to meet you."

"Same." He removed his coat and draped it over the chair across from mine. "I'm impressed. Most of the women I meet for drinks show up late."

Several thoughts dominoed through me: *I was right! Thank goodness I* arrived early. *He sounds a little judgmental. How often is he meeting women for drinks?*

He winced. "That came out weird. I only meant to say I appreciate that you're already here."

I blushed as if the blunder had been my own.

"I'd offer you a drink, but . . . can I bring you something else?"

I declined, and he promised to return.

Don't be invisible. I sat on my hands to stop them from shaking. *Head up. Shoulders back.* I wanted to spy on him while he ordered, but he deserved a chance to pull himself together in private, too, so I forced my gaze to the skyline instead. Most of downtown Ridgetop still had its original art deco architecture. I'd learned from Macon that a lot of towns in this part of the country had once had similarly elegant and ornate buildings, but most of them had been destroyed in the seventies and replaced with the blocky, uninspired boxes of the time. Ridgetop had been too broke to modernize. "A bad thing that turned into a blessing," he'd said.

It had been another awful day at work with us barely able to acknowledge each other. Another book banner had even graced us with her hateful presence, though she might have regretted it because Macon nearly tore off her head. Normally he handled the complainants well. He had the patience and belligerence to outlast them. Exhaust them. He could outmaneuver almost anybody in any argument without ever raising his voice, but this afternoon he had *roared*, and the woman had threatened to have him fired.

"You will not win that argument, and you won't win this one either," he'd fumed, snatching the offending young adult book out of her hands.

The snatching *was* enough to get him into a bit of trouble with the director, but he was right that he wouldn't be fired. If we'd still been friends, I would have cheered at his outburst and done another double cartwheel into the audiobooks. But if we'd still been friends, I doubt he would have lost his temper. I was very aware that I was the reason for his unhappy mood, and that made me feel even worse.

"Sorry. I forgot it's not rooftop season." Adam reappeared, looking embarrassed again as he followed my gaze and guessed at the reason for my uneasy expression.

"I don't mind!" It came out with an unnatural zeal, so I called myself on it. "I swear that wasn't sarcasm. I'm just nervous. It's been a while since I've been on a date."

I wondered if I should have admitted that, or even called this a date, but he smiled with understanding. "Yeah, Reza mentioned something about that. And I can relate. My first few dates after my divorce, I was a mess. Not that you're a mess," he added quickly. "I just mean that I understand. This stuff is difficult."

"Does it ever get any easier?"

"A little. But sometimes it gets harder, too."

It wasn't the answer I wanted, but it sounded truthful, and a measure of my anxiety receded.

"You're going to do great," he said. "I promise."

I gave him a rueful smile. "How do you know?"

He shrugged, but it was a warm shrug. "Just a feeling. It doesn't hurt that you're an attractive woman," he added. "Men will always be glad to see you."

I made a face.

"Oh my God." His eyes widened as he laughed in disbelief at himself. "I told you, this stuff is hard. I didn't mean for that to sound creepy, but I think I just creeped you out."

I laughed, too, if only to lessen the tension. But what he couldn't have known was that it was the first time any man apart from Cory had so pointedly complimented my appearance. I wasn't sure what to do with this, yet our conversation did grow easier. He wasn't much of a reader, but Brittany was right that he was nice. And he had a decent sense of humor, even though he wasn't as naturally funny as Cory or as slyly funny as Macon. He'd played soccer as a kid and had recently joined a casual adult league, which tracked. He looked like the type of handsome guy who wouldn't have noticed me in high school but who would have at least apologized if he'd accidentally bumped into me in the hallway.

Adam will remarry, I thought. Perhaps to someone who also had children.

He mentioned his daughter, Lily, several times, and I was glad that he wasn't one of those men who pretended his children didn't exist. I was also glad that I would never have to meet her.

I'm not sure what I told him. Not because of the second drink, which he'd purchased and I'd kept my eye on, but because the whole experience was so surreal that my mind kept wandering. I didn't think he would reject me if I tried to kiss him. The vibe between us seemed to be okay. But how would I know when to do it? And how did people—people who had just met!—transition from kissing to sex? I hoped he'd take the lead. I also hoped he'd have protection on him. I was on the pill, but still. There were diseases. Oh God. What if I got a disease during one of these non-Cory encounters? (What if Cory got a disease?) How was I supposed to ask a stranger if he had an STD?

"Ingrid?" Adam had clearly asked me a question, but I hadn't heard it.

"I haven't eaten dinner," I blurted. "Wanna grab a bite somewhere?"

He gave a startled laugh in a way that made me wonder if he'd just said something similar. "Wait," I said. "Did you just ask me that?"

"Uh, no. I asked if you enjoy being a librarian."

My cheeks lit like bonfires. "Sorry, I was just—"

"Hungry?" It was a polite tease.

"Yeah," I said weakly.

He smiled, and his crow's feet crinkled in a way that I liked. "Let's go."

As we headed down the stairs toward the street, I remembered that Kat and Brittany had both asked me to check in because they were paranoid about serial killers. (Cory didn't have to be paranoid about serial killers.) "You're the one who set this up!" I had said to Brittany.

"Yeah," she had replied, "but some psychopaths are *secret* psychopaths."

I texted them each a thumbs-up emoji and hid my phone back in my pocket.

"So, do you?" he asked.

"Do I . . . ?"

"Enjoy working at the library."

"Oh, um—"

Swooping in, he kissed me. It was unexpected and shocking. We had been descending from the fourth floor to the third, and then we weren't. Flummoxed, I immediately laughed. He pulled back in alarm.

"No," I said. Then, with another unwanted flash of memory, I corrected myself. "I mean, yes. It's okay."

It was happening much faster than I'd anticipated, but perhaps this was how these things went. Our mouths met again, tentatively at first, and then energetically. *My second kiss!* I thought with a thrill. Well, not my second *kiss*. But Adam would now and forever be the second man I had ever kissed in a romantic way. It felt like a victory.

He tasted different than Cory. Not unappealing, but odd. I continued to catalog the differences as if I were an outside observer: My head was tipped farther back. The hand on my waist was bigger. The neck that my arms were wrapped around was thicker.

"We could skip the restaurant," he said against my lips.

My spine stiffened from bottom to top.

He pulled away again. "I only meant if it would be easier for you."

I swayed as I took a step back.

"I'm sorry." There was a beat, and then his expression turned apprehensive. "I promise I didn't mean anything by that. I just thought with your situation, maybe . . ."

I hugged my coat around my body. "My situation?"

"This deal with your ex. Or I guess he's still your boyfriend?" As he observed my reaction, he shrank even further. "You didn't know. You didn't know that I knew."

"No," I said tightly.

"I'm sorry. Oh God. This is awkward."

My thoughts were tumultuous, confusing, and contradictory. Casual sex with a kind and attractive man was what I wanted, but not with someone who already knew I was an easy lay. But I was using him, too, so wasn't it better to be on equal footing? Wasn't this all a good thing?

"You call the shots," he said. "We could go to your place. Or mine. Or we could still go to a restaurant first—"

"No." I winced at how fast I said it, because I hadn't meant to say it at all.

"No to the restaurant, or . . ."

The night tilted at a wrong angle. He wasn't being vulgar or doing anything I wasn't doing, too, but it was wrong. I didn't understand why, I just knew that it was.

"To all of it," I said.

"You can't tell a man that she wants no-strings-attached sex," Brittany said to Reza.

"But she *does*," he said, panicked.

My mortified friends apologized over the phone as I cried and scalded my tongue on a London fog. As ashamed and disappointed as Adam had looked, it couldn't touch the shame and disappointment that I felt. As soon as I was out of his sight, I'd fled to my car, only to become paranoid about the two drinks. A few blocks away, there was a teeny walk-up tea kiosk inside a modified red British telephone booth, so I'd gone there to sober up. Normally I loved the quirky kiosk. Tonight it seemed lonely and pathetic and confused about its place in the world.

"Please stop apologizing." I sniffled, shivering and huddling with my disposable cup behind a stunted oak tree. The temperature was freezing, but people were still milling around downtown. I didn't want to be seen. "It's my fault. I don't know what's wrong with me."

"There's nothing wrong with you," Brittany said. "You just weren't ready."

I wiped my runny nose on my glove because I'd forgotten to get a napkin. "I thought I was ready. I wanted to be ready."

"He wasn't the right guy," Brittany said.

"The whole point was that it didn't need to be the right guy," I said. Adam was the second person I'd ever kissed, but this no longer felt like a victory. It was special when there had been just one. Now it seemed unfathomable that there had been only two.

"Well," Reza said, "maybe it doesn't need to be *the* right guy, but it still needs to be *a* right guy."

"I wish we knew somebody else we could set you up with, but everyone at my studio is a woman," Brittany said. "And the rest of our friends are either married or literally on the other side of the planet."

I ground the toe of my shoe into a knobby tree root. "That's okay. I would never ask you to do this again. And I'm sorry I put you in such a weird position at work, Reza."

"Don't worry about it," he said, although a catch in his voice made it clear that he'd forgotten about the awkward conversation that awaited him the next time he saw Adam.

It was humiliating to have entangled my friends in all this. And I didn't mean to tell Sue and Alyssa, and definitely not Elijah, about any of it either. But the problem with being temporarily out of my mind was that I was saying and doing all sorts of things against my best interests.

Because our branch was open Tuesday through Saturday, I had to work the morning after my disastrous Friday-night date. I arrived late, even later than Macon, and everybody was already chatting and doing the morning prep. Saturdays were our gossipiest days, so I went straight to scanning the overnight drop so I wouldn't have to join in. I was able to play it cool for about five minutes before Alyssa called me out. Perhaps my unusual quietness gave me away, or perhaps it was my disheveled state. It had been another night with little sleep and lots of sobbing.

I don't remember what she asked—probably something as mundane as *Are you okay? You look a little fucked up*, except Alyssa didn't swear. Whatever it was, my mouth unlocked. Everything spilled out in a torrent, except for the part about Macon. But he was standing right there with everyone else, listening, and I just vomited it all out in front of him again.

Alyssa looked shocked. Sue looked skeptical. Elijah's youthful brow was pinched with bafflement. At least we weren't open yet, so there weren't any patrons.

"But it's okay." I frantically scanned another stack of returns, trying to convey via my body language that everything was fine. "We know what we're doing."

"Let me get this straight." Sue crossed her arms. "You and Cory are going to live as singles for a month. And then you're getting *married*."

"Yes," I said.

She exchanged a concerned glance with Macon. He shook his head once at her, slightly. I often looked to the two of them for advice, but I couldn't handle their opinions or judgments right now—especially not Macon's, even though he was still being discreet about the part I had left out. Sue watched my herky-jerky movements, and her tone grew merciful. "I'm only wondering if a month is enough time for an experiment of this magnitude."

"It's enough," I said, perky and bright. "It'll be fine. I'm fine, don't worry."

"See," she said, "it's statements like that that worry me."

"That guy last night . . ." Alyssa lowered her voice as if there were still a single person here who did not know my most personal business. "You were going to sleep with him? This is about sex?"

I balked. Had I actually told them that? "No. I mean, yeah. But that's only part of it."

Macon had been putting the money in our register. At this, he stilled.

My ears rang. My stomach dropped. Macon had only known that I wanted to kiss him. *Date* was the word I'd used: Cory and I were going to *date* other people. Now I had all but confessed that I would have slept with him, too. I crumpled—nearly fainted—into my chair. If he'd thought about my actions, and surely he had, he'd already surmised sex had been on the table. But maybe he hadn't. Either way, my confirmation struck us both anew.

Alyssa didn't seem to notice. "Does this mean you and Cory are polyamorous?"

"What?" I blinked up at her. "No."

"That's the literal definition of polyamory," Elijah said. Literal meanings were important to him.

"It's temporary," I said. I wasn't sure why the word sounded so jarring. I was in favor of polyamory for consenting adults, but it wasn't something I had ever desired for myself. And it didn't seem connected to my own situation. "Temporary," I repeated.

Sue placed a hand on my shoulder and stared down Alyssa and Elijah until they retreated. She asked me quietly, "Do you need to go home?"

"I just need a minute," I said. Breathed.

"Are you sure? It's been a slow week. Macon can handle the desk."

He still hadn't moved. Nobody else seemed to have noticed.

I tried to give Sue a reassuring smile, but the smile wavered. Her grip tightened on my shoulder to give me strength.

By midday, Sue and Alyssa were hanging around the desk again. I had become the main subject of interest, so interesting that neither of them noticed the misery radiating from Macon. I was too inside my own head to resist their attention, so when they pressured me into creating a dating profile right then and there, I didn't protest for long.

"'Are your parents ugly?'" I asked.

Sue put on her reading glasses to scrutinize my phone. "Good lord. It really says that."

The app I was signing up for required me to answer at least fifty algorithmic questions, although it recommended that I answer a few hundred or even a few thousand. Supposedly, the more I answered, the better matches it would find for me. I'd answered a few dozen so far. After the predictable lifestyle queries about sex and recreational drug use—some of which I'd read aloud to Sue and Alyssa, but all of which I'd answered privately—the questions had grown stranger. I was reading everything aloud now, to great amusement.

"Go on," Alyssa said. "Answer it."

"No." I clicked. "My parents are not ugly." The next question revealed itself. "'Do you believe in dinosaurs?'"

Sue huffed. "Only in this country do they need to ask that."

Alyssa shook her head in agreeable disbelief. She was religious, but not that kind of religious.

"'Would you and your ideal match feel comfortable farting around each other?'" I asked.

Sue burst into laughter.

"Yes," I said.

Alyssa raised a judgmental eyebrow. "That was quick."

"Are you suggesting that you and Tim don't?" Sue asked.

"No!" Alyssa laughed. "We're polite. We hold it in and take it out of the room."

"Oh, Russell and I are decades past that. There's joy in letting it rip."

They dissolved into even deeper laughter, which I interrupted. "'Do you own any dice with more than six sides?' I don't, but I should check yes, right? A D&D guy would be fine."

"Check yes, then," Alyssa said.

Sue agreed. "You have to read between the lines."

"'Do you think women have an obligation to shave their legs?'" I asked.

"Jesus," Macon finally said, though he still refused to swivel in our direction.

I clicked no, obviously. "'Do spelling and grammar mistakes irritate you?'"

"Yes," Alyssa said.

"Some people just aren't wired for it," Sue said. "Unless they're willfully ignoring spell-check, I wouldn't hold it against someone."

"Do these questions irritate you?" Macon asked in a tone that eviscerated.

I put away my phone, chagrined. But that weekend, I lived on it. I answered more questions, tweaked my profile and liked others, waited for contact. Received contact. It didn't take long for me to line up multiple dates. I hadn't realized I would be messaging several different people at the same time, feeling them out and testing who was worthy of further pursuit. I'd been naive to have found Adam's "most of the women I meet for drinks" line to be off-putting. That's just what dating was: quick interactions with tons of people until something stuck. Sometimes the textual flirtations were dizzying, sometimes disgusting. But I was gaining the experience that Cory and I had wanted. Finally, I was doing something right.

I swiped past the shirtless pics and the guys posing with dead fish. (I had no idea I would see so many deceased trout.) I set the age parameters from twenty-five to forty-five but then quickly bumped that first number up to twenty-seven. In terms of message quality alone, those two years made a difference. And then I was off to the races.

My first date was with Brandon, a thirty-three-year-old welder with scarred hands and a big goofy laugh. Like Adam, he had a library card, but it had expired. We met at a cider house near the river—not the one with the friar and Cory's car—and although we discovered we had nothing in common, we liked each other enough to make out in the parking lot afterward. The skin of his fingers was rough, but his kisses were sloppy and gentle, and I drove home feeling bubbly and elated and wishing nothing but the best for him.

The next night, still buzzing with optimism, I went out with Lawrence, a twenty-eight-year-old sous-chef with a handsomely crooked face. No library card. We met for dinner at a Korean barbecue joint, where he spent most of the meal complaining about his job at a restaurant that served Southern gourmet. I heard about his interests, his education, his friends. He only cared about the details of my life as they related to his. He didn't try to kiss me, which was surprising because he seemed so into himself that I figured he'd assume I was, too. But then, as we parted ways, he said this: "Just so you know"—he tapped his teeth—"bulgogi. Right there."

I did not wish the best for Lawrence, and I did not make the mistake of accepting a sit-down meal invitation again.

Two days later, I met Geoff (thirty-two, wildlife rehabilitator, active library card but nothing checked out) for coffee on my lunch break and then Mike (thirty-eight, surveyor, possible library card because two people had his same name) for drinks after work. Geoff removed a purple sweet potato from the bulging pocket of his cargo pants and gave it to me as a gift, claiming the purple ones would make me live longer. Macon often gifted me produce from his garden, so I'd never realized that there was an off-putting way to do it. And then Mike waxed on and on about weed strains, which caught me off guard because he was wearing khakis. This was fine, but also not for me. Neither getting high nor khaki pants had ever been my thing.

I did not make out with Geoff or Mike.

My next date was with a different Brandon—twenty-nine, paramedic, no library card—and I was pleased that we did make out. Again, the only thing we had in common was enough physical chemistry to press our bodies against each other inside my car, but he was more intense than the first Brandon in a way that transformed me back into a horny, groping teenager. He asked if I wanted to go out again. I said yes and then waited nearly a week for him to text. Finally, I texted him. He never responded, and I realized I'd been ghosted for the first time.

I wasn't even that upset. Another adult merit badge earned.

But I *was* annoyed about the lost time and dove back into the dating pool with frenzied desperation. I met up with Kenji (cute and nerdy and extremely my type but could not have been less interested in me), Jay (slow-moving and depressed except when he spoke about radio antennas), Cameron (showed me pictures of his 3,400-square-foot house and kept repeating that it was 3,400 square feet), and Sunil (asked if I'd be willing to keep my toenails painted year-round). I did give in and kiss Sunil goodbye after several uncomfortable seconds of pressure and guilt, which left me feeling icky and angry and mad at myself instead of him.

Kenji had an active library card but nothing checked out.

Jay had an expired card and $4.25 in fines for a book about, I am not making this up, radio antennas.

Cameron and Sunil did not have cards, and I was not surprised.

Back on the app, I exchanged messages with a nice guy named Chad who talked about what a bummer it was to be named Chad, and then I felt bad when I decided not to meet up with him either. (He wanted to take me out to karaoke. Cory also liked karaoke, and I dreaded those nights when we went out with his coworkers, and I had to pretend to enjoy them all singing songs that felt three times as long as the original versions.)

I considered messaging the first Brandon again. Sweet Brandon with the goofy laugh! Had I judged him too quickly? February was approaching rapidly. I still hadn't slept with anybody and was positive that Cory had. I'd never thought of myself as competitive, but now I felt its sting. Nor had I thought of myself as prudish, but now I wondered if I was.

The truth was, I just hadn't wanted to sleep with any of them.

During my giddier shifts at work, the swollen-lipped days after a night of heady fumbling and bumbling and making out, I attempted to be friendly with Macon again. I tried engaging him in conversations but received monosyllabic answers. I leapt to assist the woman whose clothing always reeked of gag-inducing mildew, and I volunteered to kick out the guy who'd been permanently banned the previous summer for public masturbation to a tome on horse anatomy. Once I even slid a travel photography book toward Macon's side of the desk, open to a spread with a sweeping ocean cliffside on one page and a bluebell-carpeted forest on the other. Did he want to meet me at either for lunch? The phone rang, and he grabbed it. He never answered the phone if he could help it, and as he testily guided the patron through placing an online hold for the new Kazuo Ishiguro, he closed the photography book and filed it away on a cart.

On my own phone, a prolonged and heated argument was raging between my mother and Riley. My holiday-loving sister wanted a Christmas wedding, and our practical mom was doing everything in her power to convince her that civilization itself might collapse if that happened.

I ignored them and refreshed, refreshed, refreshed the dating app.

Sue and Alyssa asked how I felt about the forthcoming end of the experiment. I didn't know how to respond. I had only just gotten started, and I was still an inexperienced beginner. It wasn't as if I had expected to become an expert—or even advanced—in one month, but shouldn't I have at least graduated to intermediate? I felt disappointed and frustrated. Overwhelmed and underwhelmed. What might have happened if I'd had more time? And what had Cory been able to accomplish in the same number of weeks? I hadn't considered the possibility before that we might no longer be equals when we reunited. Our experiences with other people were still supposed to represent a shared experience. We were supposed to have similar months. And although I didn't know how his month was going, it was difficult to imagine him second-guessing any opportunities. He was, by nature, a go-getter. Up for anything.

I had missed the *friend* half of my boyfriend. I'd missed him during the downtimes, the hanging out times, the cooking dinner and cleaning up times. I had also missed his warm presence in bed, despite not missing the sex, because I was so consumed by the notion of having it with somebody else. If only I'd had more time, I could have gotten out of my head and made it happen. Then the two of us would still be on the same page.

On the last day of January, I jolted awake in a panic reminiscent of my first week alone. Our plan was to meet in a restaurant the following evening after work. That was where we would discuss our future, and then he would either come home with me or never come home again. But of course Cory was coming home. My panic was because I wasn't ready. Our *apartment* wasn't ready. Because he hadn't been there—because I'd barely been there—discarded clothes were heaped in piles all over the floor, makeup was caked on the bathroom sink and countertop, and dirty dishes and frozen food wrappers littered the entire kitchen. I cleaned for two hours before work and then kept cleaning afterward until three in the morning.

Will he have a ring? I wondered, scrubbing furiously at the face powder that had become one with my toothpaste scum. Were we about to get engaged? I scrubbed so hard that the handle snapped off our cleaning brush. He would wait until we'd had a chance to discuss it, I assured myself, running my finger over the jagged plastic edge.

We had both always been so practical and rational.

February

DATE DUE	BORROWER'S NAME	ROOM NUMBER
JAN 25		
FEB 19		

CHAPTER FIVE

I arrived ten minutes late to the restaurant. I'd always taken pride in my punctuality, but my life had gotten so erratic that now I ran late for everything. Tonight the delay had been my outfit. I had removed my work clothes to exchange them for something nicer, but then it had felt strange to dress up for Cory yet equally strange to wear something I'd worn on a date with somebody else. I'd ended up riffling through our closet for too long, willing something new to appear, before finally accepting defeat and putting my work clothes back on.

It was unusual for Cory to be late, too, but his car wasn't in the lot. A glance around the restaurant confirmed that he wasn't inside. I sensed the observant stare of the host, an older brawny man with a lumberjack beard who gave off the vibe of owning the place, even though the diner was called Lottie's and the name on his shirt was KEVIN. He was often stationed here at the front. "I'm looking for my . . ." *Boyfriend* still wasn't sitting right on my tongue, so I let the sentence hang in the air, unfinished. "I don't think he's here yet."

"Booth for two?" Kevin asked.

"Yeah. Yes," I said, doubling down on my hesitant confirmation.

He guided me past *Grease, Moonlight, After Hours, Waitress, Swingers,* and *When Harry Met Sally* to the *Back to the Future* booth. Cory and I never called this place Lottie's, or even Kevin's. It was the "diner-themed diner," and it was one of our favorite places in Ridgetop. Rainbow flags welcomed the guests out front, the seats were sparkly pink vinyl, and the employees wore matching pink shirts in a fifties-style cut with their names embroidered on the fronts. Embroidered! Nobody did that anymore. But the real standouts were the tabletops, lovingly themed and collaged. Tonight I stared at Marty McFly in the original diner as well as the eighties-themed diner from *Part II*. Apparently, the saloon in *Part III* didn't count.

As anxious as I felt, it was comforting to be somewhere familiar after a month of new bars and cideries. This was the everlasting charm of a diner: familiarity. Cory appreciated the predictability of their menus, but I also liked that a person always knew what to expect when stepping inside one. For the first time ever, I didn't know what to expect.

Cory.

I started at the sight of him. My heart squeezed with pain and joy. He noticed me, too, and grinned. Our hands lifted in a wave. Mine trembled. As he crossed the checkered floor, I stood for a hug but suddenly became nervous to touch him.

Our embrace was loose. Out of practice, out of sync.

"Sorry I'm late," he said as we sat down on opposite sides of the booth. "There was this thing with a canceled reservation, and then Mitchell caught me on the way out, and you know how he is—"

"I do know," I said with a laugh. The doorman at the Tamsett Park Inn, Cory's workplace, was a good guy but also very chatty and very boring. He had a lot of theories about the Knights Templar. "I actually just got here, too."

His grin widened. "Who are we anymore?"

The question was valid. Under the nostalgic glow of the diner's pink globe lights, he still looked like Cory. He had the same gingery hair with its upward, Tintin-like swoop, the same closely spaced freckles that in certain lights made him look tan instead of Irish-pale, and the same friendly smile that always put everyone else at ease. A college friend once told Cory and me that we had matching smiles. We were also the same height and had been born with the same poor vision, although I'd gotten Lasik during my first year on the county's health insurance while he still wore chunky black glasses. His overall appearance was cute and cartoonish. But something about him was different tonight, some infinitesimal thing.

"You look..."

"I know." He was staring back at me, similarly mystified. "You look the same but dreamlike. Like my eyes can't fully process you."

"That was the longest we've been apart in eleven years."

"I've wanted to call you so many times."

I leaned forward. "Me too. Anytime something happened, it was weird not being able to tell you about it."

"*So* weird." His fingers drummed against the tabletop.

It was his energy, I realized. He'd always had a lot, but tonight he was fidgety and jittery. Perhaps even a bit manic. He pushed his menu aside to reveal young George McFly ordering "a milk, chocolate." "What a good get!" Cory said. "Although still not as good as—"

"*Diner*," we said in unison.

Long ago, we had decided that the *Diner*-themed table in the diner-themed diner was the apex table. Unfortunately, we'd never been seated there. We could have asked for it, I'm sure, but we joked that we were waiting for it to happen naturally. We shared a fondness for silly theming, a holdover from growing up in Orlando. Neither of us wanted to live in the theme park capital of the world anymore—we both sort of hated it, and we definitely hated all the recent legislation in Florida—yet a good theme still recalled some of the happier memories from our childhoods.

Cory's smile was soft and a little sad. "Yeah."

"So...uh. Hi."

"Hi," he said.

We laughed again. It was awkward but nice. It really did feel like a date.

"How are you, Iggy? You look good."

I hadn't heard that name in a month. Cory and Riley were the only people who called me Iggy, and I was still ignoring her texts. As the older sister, I'd been christened with the family name. Ingrid Dahl had been our paternal grandmother. Farmor and Farfar—"father's mother" and "father's father"—were immigrants from Norway, and my father was their only child. And although my name was more common now, when I was a kid it had *felt* like an immigrant grandmother's name. I'd been jealous of Riley, two years younger, who'd received the American name. But Riley had given me "Iggy." As a baby, she hadn't been able to pronounce my name, and the nickname stuck. Everybody had called me Iggy for years until I finally embraced my real name in college.

It was Riley, of course, who'd been the one to call me Iggy in front of Cory not long after we'd started dating. "Iggy Doll would be the coolest rock-and-roll alter ego," he'd said. Although he wasn't a musician, he was passionate about music, especially unconventional artists who played in styles I didn't quite understand. And so the nickname stuck again. But I didn't mind. Now it was something only my most beloved could call me.

"You look good, too," I said.

"How was . . . your month?"

"Uh. I don't know." I tried to smile to cover my discomfort, but I couldn't maintain it. "I'm not sure how you want to talk about this. How was yours?"

"Um, fine. Strange. Good. I've had a good time."

Good.

"But I don't want to make it weird or whatever," he said. "I mean, we're not going to talk numbers, are we?"

By the way he said *numbers*, I knew he didn't just mean his number and my number. It was a pluralization, a confirmation. Cory had slept with multiple women. I felt ill.

"Yeah," he said, correctly interpreting my expression, "I don't think I want that sort of information from you either."

We jumped as two red plastic tumblers of water thunked onto the table. Our server was a lithe man with a dancer's body and a shaved head. The name HANK was embroidered on his shirt. "Hey there. I'll be taking care of you folks tonight. Can I get you something else to drink?"

"Water's fine," I said, already grabbing it to cool myself down.

"A Coke, thanks," Cory said. "Actually, I think we're ready." He glanced at me, and I nodded. We always ordered the same thing here: he got the chicken tenders and fries, and I got the grilled cheese and tomato soup. Hank tapped his smooth head to say he didn't need to write it down and then strolled gracefully away to place our order.

"We'll keep it general," Cory said. "Did you ... have a good month, too?"

We were stuck on that adjective. I didn't know how to respond and flushed with embarrassment.

"Uh-oh." He rubbed his hands in anticipation of a juicy story.

It would have been easy to lie. I could have slipped my own pluralization into the conversation and let him draw the wrong conclusion, but honesty was required. "I haven't."

He didn't get it yet. "You haven't ..."

I widened my eyes.

"Oh," he said. And then, "*Oh*."

"I've met people, I've gone on dates. But ... no."

Cory sank back against the sparkly booth. He looked disturbed. I hadn't known what reaction to expect, but it wasn't this. "I—I'm gonna need a moment to process this. I mean ... what *does* this mean? Is this something you even wanted to do? Did I pressure you into this?" His breathing quickened. "Oh my God, Iggy—"

"No." I reached for his hand. It took a moment for him to realize what I was doing and give it to me. I squeezed him hard. "I wanted this, too. It doesn't mean anything except that"—I shrugged helplessly—"I'm really, really bad at this."

The alarm faded, but he still seemed hurt and confused. "I don't understand."

"I'm out of practice. That's all."

"But I am, too. Neither of us was ever *in* practice." His hand wriggled free of mine as his panic spilled back over the table. "I'm an odd-looking dude, and you're an attractive woman. This should have been so much easier for you."

I lowered my voice to help calm him down. "There were men I could have slept with, but ... I don't know. None of them seemed right."

"Well, yeah, but we weren't looking for soul mates. We were just messing around." He shifted forward again as a new thought occurred to him. His voice became hard-edged. "Were you afraid they might hurt you? Were they creeps?"

"No, nothing like that." When he continued to stare me down, I released an unhinged laugh. "I don't know! I don't know why it hasn't happened for me yet."

Cory sat back a bit. "Yet."

I bit my bottom lip, as if that could prevent the word from having slipped out.

"Are you—" He stopped himself. "No. Tell me what you mean by that."

Blood rushed to my head. I wasn't okay with ending our experiment, not when I was still in the middle of it. Not when he had numbers and I had none.

"I'm not ready," I said. "I need more time."

Cory deflated. At first I assumed he was devastated. But when he bent over with laughter, I realized he was relieved. "Thank God." He removed his glasses to rub his eyes. "That month, like, flew by. I'm not ready either."

"You're not?"

"No!"

He burst into another laugh that sounded more hysterical. I began laughing, too, though mine was clouded with shock. I wasn't the only one who wasn't ready. There wasn't a ring. Up until that moment, I hadn't allowed myself to feel the full disappointment of my failure. Of having January be it, forever. But I was getting a second chance. My shock and despondency were swept away by an exultant relief that matched his.

"What were we thinking?" he said.

I gasped. "A month! As if we could do all this in a month."

"I was terrified to say it because I didn't know how you'd feel, but . . . one month!"

We continued to mock our stupidity until Hank interrupted with the food. We dug in, elated, refueled with foolish confidence. Cory smashed his fries into his ketchup, and I slopped my grilled cheese into my soup. Red stains splattered onto our work clothes as we extended our plan by another month and discussed our time apart.

"So who have you told?" I asked.

"Well, you know . . ." He named most of his coworkers. "I didn't want them to think I was cheating on you or that we had broken up."

"Yeah. Same."

"Really?"

"Yeah. Why do you look so surprised?"

He ripped into a chicken tender and then took a moment to chew and swallow. "I thought my coworkers might see me at one of our bars, but I have a hard time imagining Sue or Alyssa going out drinking. I guess I assumed you wouldn't tell them."

The Tamsett Park Inn contained multiple restaurants and bars. Somehow, it had never occurred to me that he might try to hook up with a guest. Surely that was against the inn's policy, but maybe not? Or maybe everybody just looked the other way. It would have been convenient for him to go straight up to their rooms. I also couldn't help but notice that he hadn't mentioned Macon. For whatever reason, Cory had always disliked him.

"Yeah, but Sue and Alyssa see me every day. They would have known something was up. And what if one of them did see me or caught me using a dating app? I didn't want them to think I was cheating on you either."

"I guess that makes sense."

"Is that okay?" I felt affronted.

Cory shook his head to explain that wasn't what he'd meant. "Of course it is. It's just weird to think about your coworkers knowing our business."

"How is it any weirder than yours?"

"You know. Your coworkers are all so . . . adult."

That was true enough. Most of Cory's coworkers—the ones he hung out with, at least—were under thirty and single. And sure, Alyssa was also younger than us. But she was married, dependable, and responsible. Unlike his coworkers, she'd never called in sick with a hangover.

"What does Macon think about it?" he asked.

I squirmed, and the vinyl cushion beneath me squeaked. "What do you mean?"

"Ah, forget it."

My face grew warm again. "No. What do you mean?"

"Nothing." He crumpled up his napkin and dropped it in surrender. "The guy's a little judgy, that's all."

That didn't feel like *all*, and it wasn't a fair assessment of Macon, but we left it there. I certainly didn't want to explore the topic any further.

"So," Cory said after several seconds of awkward silence. "You're using a dating app."

The tension broke. He'd ventured onto the same app, so I told him about the men with dead fish, and he told me about the women with duck face, and we shuddered and laughed at the idea of running into each other there. Beneath our plates, Marty McFly sat beside George McFly and gaped at how young and innocent—and weak and clueless—his father had been at his age.

One more month would be enough time, right? We actually believed this.

CHAPTER SIX

February was the shortest month. Cory and I had both forgotten that. This particular February contained twenty-eight days, and although that was only three fewer than in January, I still felt the shortage like a too-tight belt. The weather was growing unseasonably warm. The compact yellow buds of the daffodils and forsythia were a breath away from bursting into an early, global warming–fueled bloom. There was no time to waste.

The morning after the diner, Alyssa and Elijah were surprised to learn that Cory hadn't come home. Judging by the glance they exchanged, Sue and Macon weren't. No doubt they had been discussing me in private. If either of them were acting similarly out of character, I'd be gossiping behind their backs, too.

Sue asked about rent. Last month, while paying double, Cory and I hadn't needed to touch our savings accounts, but we'd been unable to contribute anything to them either. This felt almost as bad. Thankfully, our expenses would be back to normal this month. Before meeting at the diner, he'd already vacated the Airbnb and packed his car, but—anticipating where our conversation might lead us—he had also already asked his closest work friend if he could crash in her spare room. While I was grateful that he'd had the foresight to ask Robin, I was equally grateful that he hadn't actually moved in with her until we'd discussed it.

As for Robin, I liked her. And she dated women exclusively, so there was nothing to worry about there. The way Cory had gotten agitated about Macon made me wonder if he'd hooked up with one of his co-workers. It suddenly seemed possible, if not probable. This shouldn't have bothered me, but it did. I didn't want Cory sleeping with people we knew. Even as I thought this, I understood that it was hypocritical. Perhaps I even sensed that it meant something about my feelings toward Macon, although I was unwilling to explore the notion any deeper. He remained as closed off as a cinder-block wall, enough to make me reconsider quitting. Because it *would* have to be me who walked, not him. But it still wasn't the right time. I had only one short month left, and I needed every minute.

That evening I temporarily brightened out of my gloom when a familiar patron walked through the double doors. "Hey," I said, "it's been a few weeks since we've seen you."

Gareth Murphy was one of our movie patrons and a regular on Thursday nights. He worked in construction, and even though his clothing and skin were always speckled with paint and drywall mud, he wasn't a gruff and burly stereotype. He was good-natured and average-sized, and his taste in film was broad and comprehensive.

He smiled back at me. "Yeah, I was doing a job out in Fairfax, so I took the opportunity to dip into their collection."

"Did they have anything good?"

He laughed as he handed me his returns. "No. They had the same collection you guys had last." Our Blu-rays rotated between branches every six months to keep the selections fresh.

"Oh no."

"At least it gave me the opportunity to watch the rest of the *Up* series."

"Oh my God," I said. "I'm always so worried about how Neil is doing."

"Yes!"

We talked excitedly for a few minutes in the way that people do whenever they discover they've seen the same gripping documentary, and then he headed off toward our spinning racks.

"Ask him out," Elijah said in a low voice as soon as Gareth was out of earshot. He was behind the desk, filling his cart with cookbooks, one of the worst subjects to shelve. They all began with the same Dewey Decimal number, which made the numbers after the decimals so long that they wrapped around the spines and onto the front covers. To shelve a single heavy cookbook, tons of others had to be pulled out just to check those last few digits.

A wave of heat rushed through me. "What?"

"Ask him out," Elijah said again. "Dude is into you."

I became so flustered that I didn't know how to respond. "I'm not asking out a patron," I finally said.

"Why not? Is it against the rules?"

"No."

"He seems cool. He always chats you up. What's the problem?"

I turned toward Macon for a second opinion, forgetting for a moment that he was Macon. He scowled and shook his head. This could have meant either *don't ask me* or *don't do it.*

Elijah shrugged as he pushed his cart away. "Doesn't hurt to ask."

I strongly disagreed. Gareth would be standing before me in person, not on my phone. I'd never asked anybody out in person before, and it could hurt a lot. Besides, I wasn't about to ask him out with Macon sitting right there. I'd never even considered dating Gareth before, and I wasn't sure what I thought about him—or what he might think about me. I did like him. And I was aware that he usually came to my station, not Macon's. But I had also always assumed it was because I was the friendly one. Gareth had been coming in for years. If he'd wanted to ask me out, he'd had plenty of time. Unless I'd mentioned Cory at some point?

I was still stumbling through these new thoughts when he returned to the desk. Macon's posture straightened, an invitation for Gareth to check out at his station.

Gareth set down his stack in front of me. As always, he had selected five movies, the maximum we allowed patrons to check out at one time. "So many Criterion titles, I hardly knew where to begin."

Macon's chair squeaked as he slumped back against it. Dark energy radiated off of him.

Gareth held up a box. "Have you done Tarkovsky yet?"

"No," I said. "I've always been intimidated."

"Me too. But I'm doing it. I'm diving in."

"I'll expect an update—are the long takes meditative or punishing?"

After promising a full report, he continued to chat lightheartedly about his other selections. Gareth appeared to be close to my age, and he was attractive in an approachable way. He had sleepy blue eyes and a short scruffy beard, light brown flecked with golden red. As I realized his coloring was similar to Cory's, the knowledge unexpectedly slammed into me: *Yes*. I could sleep with this man.

I glanced at his left hand, which was freckled with gray paint and ringless. Perhaps he took it off to work, though. It seemed like something that people in construction might do for safety reasons. And his friendliness might be only that. I'd been in the opposite position often enough, patrons mistaking my professional affability for something more. I would notice them checking for a ring and then brace myself, knowing the absence of one would make them ask me out or slip me their number.

Gareth said something I didn't catch, and I stumbled my way back into the conversation. He gave me a funny look. Had he clocked me checking for a ring? My cheeks warmed as I handed him the receipt.

The instant he was gone, Elijah's head popped around the corner. "Did you do it?"

I glowered at him.

He clucked his tongue, disappointed in me, and suddenly I was disappointed in me, too. The thought of asking out Gareth was terrifying, but this experiment was about gaining new experiences. Asking somebody out, no matter the outcome, counted as a new experience. And sure, I didn't know Gareth well, but at least he wasn't a stranger. He wouldn't show up to our date and be an unpleasant surprise. If he even agreed to a date, that is.

A low-frequency anxiety hummed in the pit of my stomach. He'd be back when the movies were due. That gave me a week to figure out how to ask him.

In the meantime, I lost my second virginity to a man in high-top Converse All Stars. I hadn't been expecting it. We'd swiped right, we'd chatted, and we'd arranged the perfunctory meeting after work. I wasn't excited. He didn't have a library card, and I'd been on another uninspiring date over the weekend—a guy whose dream was to open a gym called Live Laugh Swole. My full attention was on the Gareth issue. I was tired. I wanted to go home and fret and stress and figure out a plan for the following day when Gareth would return.

One more, Kat had texted. She was doing her long-distance best to help me get laid.

You said that last time.

Just one more before Gareth. For practice.

One more, I agreed.

Before leaving work, I didn't make any effort with my appearance beyond blotting the oil from my nose and reapplying my lipstick. Sue and Alyssa didn't even see enough of a change in my appearance to crack a knowing joke, and Macon didn't get weird. But from the moment Justin and I spotted each other across the crowded cider house, this date was different: Justin was hot. And he seemed to think that I was, too.

A grin broke out across his face.

A smile spread across mine.

Justin seemed both older and younger than me. Technically he was two years older than Macon, and he had the prematurely silver hair to prove it, but it was cut in a youthful style, and his clothing was as playful as his sneakers. He was energetic and funny, and he laughed a lot—a silver fox, although there was nothing distinguished about him. He was a kit who still ran and chased and pounced.

Our conversation was easy. He was born in a rural county and still had a rural accent. He asked good questions and told good stories. His age gave him the maturity and respectfulness toward women that I craved, but his disposition was waggish and fun. We joked and laughed, and his eyes sparkled behind his horn-rimmed glasses. I've always been a sucker for men with glasses.

We downed our drinks and ordered a second round. He'd been married before. He had a kid. I lied and said I'd recently gotten out of a long-term relationship. I told the truth and said I didn't want to talk about it. He managed a local outfitters and was on the volunteer crew that rescued missing and stranded hikers. He was passionate about climbing and downhill mountain biking. He wasn't a reader. I would never be able to keep up with or marry a guy like him.

He was perfect.

Everything was so much easier with a man who was genuinely into me and not just looking toward a goal, even though a goal, mutual and unspoken, was clearly on the table. We ordered another round. We excused ourselves to go to the bathroom at the same time, which cracked us up again, and then we made out in the poorly lit hallway outside the restrooms. He was tall with long, strong limbs. His five-o'clock shadow rubbed against my cheeks and chin. I felt ravenous, and for the first time since this whole thing had begun, I didn't overthink it.

We went to his place, which was my choice. I texted his address to Kat and Brittany as well as a photo that he happily posed for. I was self-conscious when he removed my clothes, but I gasped when he touched me. When he entered me. When I came.

I awoke around dawn to another new experience: somebody else's home. As the first light of day slipped in through the windows, Justin's bedroom began to reveal itself. A chair over there piled with clothing, a sconce with a swing arm beside my head, a dramatic black-and-white photograph of a cliff above a sturdy dresser that didn't look like he'd had to assemble it himself. It was reassuring that the room aligned with how I'd seen him the night before—as an adult responsible enough to own a house and keep his laundry clean but whose priorities did not involve putting the laundered clothes away. I felt safe and happy. I sneaked out of bed to use his bathroom, which was unremarkable except for the fact that it was bigger than my own, and then gathered my things to leave. He woke up as I was putting on my shoes.

"That was fun," he said in a voice thick with slumber.

"It was," I agreed. "Keep sleeping. I'll see myself out. I've gotta get ready for work."

"Have a nice day," he said, and sounded like he meant it.

We didn't discuss seeing each other again because we'd both gotten the experience we'd wanted. As I crept toward his front door, I lingered to inspect each room that I passed: a bedroom with a BB-8 bedspread and shelves of completed Lego sets that must belong to his son, a living room with a banana tree and more black-and-white mountain photography, a kitchen with heavy oak cabinets that were more dated that the rest of the house, an entryway with a rack for climbing gear and a console table with a pile of mail. Few things interested me more than the books a person owned, but I saw none apart from some chapter books in his son's room and a few guidebooks in his living room. A whole life, briefly visited and departed.

"Not only did I have sex," I bragged to Kat over FaceTime in Justin's driveway, "but I had a one-night stand."

I floated through work that day. My pelvic floor felt pleasantly warm, like a good secret. I was chatty and even a little flirty with the patrons, and the atmosphere inside the library lifted to meet my mood. Macon was the only one who seemed suspicious. That evening, as Gareth and I had our usual animated discussion about his rentals—Tarkovsky verdict: meditative *and* punishing—Macon vibrated beside me like a storm cloud ready to burst.

"You decided not to ask him out?" he asked the second Gareth left.

I was taken aback. This was the first time he'd addressed my situation directly.

"I'm not asking anybody out," I said, cool and poised. As if that hadn't been my plan all week.

Macon *hmph*ed but became a fraction less disagreeable. It was a confusing reaction from somebody who didn't want to kiss me, and I wasn't sure how to interpret it. At least what I'd said was true. I didn't need to ask anybody out, because I finally felt fulfilled.

The hunger returned that night, more insatiable than ever. I dug out my vibrator and then ordered a new one. I scrolled through the app and rejected everybody. I regretted not asking out Gareth. I would ask the next time I saw him.

Justin messaged me through the app on Saturday. I gave him my actual number, we texted, and then my one-night stand became a two-night stand.

I packed my first overnight bag, which was just my regular tote with a few additional items tucked inside. It didn't include a number of the practical items I normally required, like pajamas or my night guard, but surely everybody's overnight bags were a lie. Maybe that was how people even knew when a relationship had advanced from a fling into something more: the night guards and orthopedic pillows and CPAP machines came out. But Justin and I were not there, nor would we ever be there. That wasn't the point of Justin.

I felt shy about disrobing in front of him again, but although this self-consciousness had yet to abate, the stimulating, shuddering, overwhelming sensations of something familiar yet completely brand-new hadn't either. I was a spring bud exploding into exquisite blossom. These experiences were important to me personally, but they didn't feel important to me specifically. I understood that these early blooms wouldn't—couldn't—last the entire season. Did the flowers outside sense the killing frost, too? By design, they were temporary pleasures. Ecstatic in one moment, withered the next.

Sue brought us all hot chocolate with pink marshmallows for Valentine's Day. She and Russell were going salsa dancing that night. Alyssa said Tim had made reservations at the fancy steak restaurant inside the Tamsett Park Inn, and several of her storytime kids dropped by to give her cards and drawings. And while Macon seemed like the type who would rail against ugly baby Cupids and the environmental impact of out-of-season roses, he didn't join in when I griped. He was content to let other people enjoy it. Macon was above Valentine's Day.

Cory and I were in agreement that the holiday was stupid—yet another by-product of being undatable teenagers—but we always made cards for each other and baked a heart-shaped pizza for dinner. Did he have plans that night, or would he also be eating a frozen pizza for one? He'd probably go out with his coworkers. Alyssa and Tim might even see them at a bar at the inn. I didn't like the idea of them seeing Cory flirting with other women. It made me angry with Cory and angry with Phoebe (the coworker I suspected he was most likely to sleep with) and angry with Kayla (the coworker I suspected he was second most likely to sleep with) and angry with Tim for making the reservation in the first place. Of course fucking Tim wanted a fucking steak. Meanwhile I'd be stuck at home, forced to listen to the downstairs neighbors, well, fucking.

I didn't expect to hear from Justin, but a text arrived in the late afternoon: *This holiday sucks. Wanna come over?*

I did.

A couple of days later was another Gareth night. Upon his arrival, I grew hot and stumbled over my greeting. I could feel Macon's side-eye. Was I still going to ask out Gareth? I tried to decide while he made his selections, but my mind was a buzzing void of unintelligibility, and soon he was back at my station. No, I wasn't ready. Or maybe I didn't need to ask him out anymore, now that I was sleeping with Justin. I wasn't sure how I felt, so the risk didn't seem worth it.

When he left, the tension left the building, too. Macon settled back into an article he'd been reading about the United States shooting down four objects in eight days: a spy balloon from China and three UFOs. The events were strange, but even stranger was seeing the word *UFO* in the headlines. Even though it was only meant in its most literal sense—three of the objects had yet to be identified—a lot of people were suddenly interested in the aerial phenomena. All of our books on the subject had been quietly checked out.

And I do mean quietly. They had arrived at our circulation desk sandwiched between other books on less stigmatized topics, barcodes arranged for quick scanning so that we wouldn't notice or judge or ask questions. We always noticed, but we never judged or asked questions. We were professionals, after all.

Experts were reporting that these new UFOs were most likely errant sky junk, possibly civilian, possibly military—balloons or drones or some other type of science or surveillance crafts. Non-human intelligence was low on the list of suspects.

"What do you think they are?" I asked.

"Hm?" Macon glanced over and saw that I was staring at his computer. I missed our conversations and sensed that he did, too. Work was dull without them.

"Probably something boring," he said. "Not like they'd tell us the truth, anyway." Although he wasn't a conspiracy theorist, he was deeply mistrustful of the government. I didn't trust it either—what American did these days?—but he had mistrusted it for longer. Also, I didn't dwell on my mistrust the way he did.

I wasn't sure what prompted my next question. It wasn't something I'd asked anybody, apart from Cory, since childhood. The topic was too culturally shameful, especially for those who prided themselves on being well educated. Perhaps I just wanted to keep him talking. "Do you believe in them? UFOs?"

"Sure," he said.

I was startled by his answer, but also by how casually he said it. Over the years, I'd read a few of our books and watched a number of documentaries. I'd gone from not believing in the phenomenon at all to believing that *something*, who knew what, was there. It was an open loop inside my mind that I returned to and picked at but never grew nearer to closing.

"In the sense that there are things up there that we, the public, and maybe even the government and military, can't explain, yes. That's straightforward enough," he said.

I nodded, a little disappointed.

"And most of the answers are surely mundane. But it seems like some of them aren't. And the implications and possibilities are all... pretty extraordinary."

I felt so close to him in that moment, over this silly thing that wasn't actually a silly thing. Macon was smarter than me. He'd had a full decade longer to read and research and think and observe the world. What he said carried weight with me. I had assumed he would dismiss the subject out of hand, but his curiosity and open-mindedness made me feel better about my own. I had expected to be ridiculed. Instead, I felt comforted.

"I think so, too," I said.

And his eyes lit up, just a bit, just enough for me to notice.

It was the first time I wondered if maybe he didn't feel as confident about his opinions as he appeared. Maybe he worried about what I thought of him, too. The energy between us realigned, and for the rest of that shift we couldn't stop talking, wondering, puzzling, and marveling at all the possibilities that existed in the universe.

It didn't take long for our tenuous friendship to disintegrate again. We'd had a good Friday and an even better Saturday morning, and that afternoon I was in the back room helping a polite man who'd just been released from a long prison sentence sign up for an email account. So much of my job was tech support, guiding people through filling out tedious forms online. Mr. Brember was shooting the man dirty looks, and I was shooting them back. *Be kind*, I mouthed. Mr. Brember's face soured even further, but he returned to his funeral plans. Thankfully, the man didn't notice the exchange. He was too absorbed in the overwhelming work of reintegration.

A question cut through the building's din. "Is Ingrid working today?" The voice was loud and assured with a strong rural North Carolinian accent.

My heart jolted. I spun around in my seat to find Justin at the circulation desk.

Macon affirmed in his low, respectable library voice that I was. Although I couldn't hear much, I detected a touch of surprise and wariness in his tone, perhaps because Justin wasn't a regular. Macon must have mentioned the computers, though, because Justin looked in my direction. Our eyes caught, and he grinned. I gave him a small wave. He gave me a huge one back and gestured that he'd wait up front until I was done.

"How do they expect anybody to memorize a password this complicated?" the man beside me mumbled.

It took ten minutes to guide him through the rest of the process, and the whole time I was flushed and distracted by overheard snippets: Justin inquiring about the stained glass, and Macon giving unusually abridged answers. Justin joking about the dangers of having a lit fire around all these books, and Macon not bothering to pretend we didn't hear this same joke several times a week. Why was Justin here? Our relationship so far had been purely carnal. His presence was embarrassing—I wished he'd stop trying to engage Macon in conversation—but also flattering. It was another warm winter day, and he was wearing a light jacket over a T-shirt. His posture was as assured as his voice, and it was clear, even with the jacket on, that he had a nice body. A climber's body. I felt a stir that was indecent for work.

Still, as I approached the desk, my plan was to slip behind it to avoid the awkwardness of making physical contact with him in front of Macon. This plan was thwarted when Justin reached me first, swooped me into his arms, and pecked my cheek. Though the greeting felt natural, I quickly pulled away and placed the barrier between us. "What are you doing here?" I asked. I didn't look at Macon, but I was conscious that we were being observed.

Justin's hips leaned seductively against my station. "I was picking up a new sump pump at the hardware store over there, and I thought, I wonder if Ingrid is working today?"

I spread out my arms. "I am."

"And then I wondered if you'd want to go out tonight. Maybe to an actual restaurant this time. Or a movie. Or, I don't know, this might be really out there, but: dinner *and* a movie."

"Oh, um." I couldn't help but beam. "Yes."

"Good," he said.

"Good," I said.

"Okay, then. I'll text you the details." His eyes twinkled as he gave the desk a little tap of triumph.

The second he was out the door, Sue and Alyssa appeared from the annex.

"Who was *that?*" Alyssa asked.

Sue raised an eyebrow. "'Maybe to an actual restaurant this time'?"

"We've met up a few times for drinks," I said. We'd had drinks once. The other times, I'd driven straight to his house. I was as surprised as they were by this turn of events; Justin showing up and publicly asking me out went against everything movies and television (and even most novels) had taught me about relationships built on sex. But we had been hanging out a bit more, before and after. I had no idea if any of this was normal or unusual.

Alyssa hooted. "Look at your face."

I blushed harder. I wasn't even sure how much I liked him, only that I did and that it had been exciting to see him again. "His name is Justin."

"How old is he?" Sue asked. The silver hair.

"Forty-one."

"It suits him," Alyssa said.

Macon's jaw was clenched as he grabbed an armful of new fiction and stalked away to shelve it. I'd been trying my best to keep all of this away from him, but it had been difficult with the others teasing me and requesting stories about the dates that had gone awry. They couldn't get enough of those. But this was even worse. Our workspace had been invaded by the man I was sleeping with. My coworkers were too polite to ask, but none of them needed to ask. *Macon* didn't need to ask. Justin and I had the body language of two people who had fucked.

What did Macon think about me sleeping with somebody older than he was? Sometimes I wondered if this was why he had rejected me, if the decade between us made me seem young and immature. But I had always been attracted to guys who were older than me, Macon obviously included. However, I did realize that this was an odd thing to admit, considering my longtime relationship with a man who was exactly my same age.

Justin told me to pick the movie, and we met at the indie theater downtown. There was a new one about Emily Brontë, but I knew better than to do that to him, so I went with my second choice, a film that had made the Oscars shortlist for Best International Feature. The poster made it look dangerous and edgy, but I should have read the reviews, because it turned out to be somber and introspective. Long pensive shots of the protagonist forced us to sit with her sadness and self-destruction. I was into it, but the entire two-hour running time was tinged with the discomfort of being aware that Justin wasn't. He fidgeted in his seat, not having the patience for such a slow pace. The long takes brought to mind Tarkovsky and Gareth, and how I could have relaxed beside Gareth. Even if he didn't like the movie, he would have been interested in it. A dangerous step further: I wouldn't have taken Gareth to the Brontë film either, since he wasn't a reader. But Macon was. I could have taken Macon to either film.

"I could wipe you from my life with a snap of my fingers," the protagonist said to her boyfriend in a devastating scene.

Justin wasn't my boyfriend, but I heard the snap all the same.

When the movie finally ended in an ambiguous manner, Justin whispered, "That's it?"

Although he'd promised "an actual restaurant this time," he drove me to the cider house where we'd first met up. "You like this place, right?" he said. But I could tell it was more for his comfort than mine. We shared an appetizer sampler platter, and it wasn't like our first date at all. We had reached our conversational limit. He was telling me about a trail he wanted to hike, and I felt him sussing me out, trying to see if it was something I'd be game for doing. Hiking was okay, but this particular trail sounded long and strenuous, the outdoor equivalent of the film we'd just watched. We'd had enough sexual chemistry for both of us to be curious about dating chemistry, but it wasn't there. And what would I have done if it *had* been there? Date him for the ten remaining days and then ditch him when Cory returned? I'd seen him too many times now. Any more, and the situation might get messy.

I was about to ask him to drive me back to my car when a group of Cory's coworkers entered the cidery. My blood chilled. I blinked and checked again. Cory wasn't with them, thank goodness, but before I could angle myself away from them, they spotted me, and their chatter stopped. Then it started up again, whispered and fervent. My gaze drifted casually back to Justin, as if it wasn't a big deal that they'd seen me. As if I hadn't started to sweat.

Justin glanced over his shoulder to see what I'd been staring at, but Cory's friends had turned and were heading toward the bar. "Everything okay?" he asked.

Something came over me. My energy dialed up, and I became flirtatious again, laughed harder at his jokes. He seemed confused but not displeased. I wasn't proud of my behavior, but I also couldn't bear to let word get back to Cory that I was unhappy.

As we left, I linked my arm through Justin's and pulled him close against my body. My eyes shone until I was back inside his car and the doors closed.

The mood dropped.

"Do you want to come back to my place?" he asked uneasily. It had become a question again, not an assumption.

I couldn't look at him because I couldn't look at myself. "I'm kind of tired."

He took that in, and then nodded. As he dropped me off, he seemed disappointed but not hurt. "Call me if you change your mind."

"Thanks," I said, and I meant it. But I knew it would never happen.

The situation with Justin left me antsy and unfulfilled and ruminating about dating. Not dating like it had been with the app, but dating like it had been with Cory. Conversation and laughter and connection. I decided to ask out Gareth on the final Thursday of the month. The worst he could do was say no, and he was a nice guy, so at least he would say it politely. And sure, if he turned me down, I'd have to hide in the annex every Thursday night for the rest of my librarian life, but the miserable situation with Macon would probably force me to quit soon anyway.

My plan had been to ask him out to the movies—a safe, obvious bet—but then Amelia Louisa Hatmaker, one of our favorite regulars, a funny and slightly batty middle-aged woman, regifted us a generous present. "I'd say I'm too busy, which I am," she said, "but *really* I'm too chicken." None of us had wanted it either, but we promised to find a good home for it. Hours later, nobody had bitten, and the novelty and freeness of the gift had wormed its way into my psyche. By the time Gareth arrived, I was so nervous that I fleetingly lost touch with reality and could barely verbalize when he checked out his five discs, which was how I found myself bursting outside and chasing him into the parking lot before I missed my chance forever.

"Hey!" I blurted.

He startled and turned around.

I hurried up to him, rushing the question, too. "I was just wondering if you wanted to go on a"—oh my God, these were the most ludicrous words ever to come out of my mouth—"hot-air balloon ride with me this Sunday."

His expression circled from confusion, to surprise, to the pleasure of being asked out—he was going to say yes!—and then back to confusion. "A what now?"

I understood why he thought he'd heard incorrectly. "It's ridiculous, I know. It's a gift from another patron. We all laughed it off, but then I couldn't stop thinking about it, and I wondered if . . . maybe . . . you wanted to go."

Nope. He was *not* going to say yes.

"Uh, yea—yeah." It came out in an adorable stammer. "Sure." His voice grew confident and jokey again. "I mean, I love ballooning."

"You do?"

"No. I haven't thought about hot-air balloons since I was a kid. I mean it. Not once." He laughed and scratched his scruffy beard. "But yeah, I think I'd like to ride in one . . . with you."

The pause before *with you* made me flutter. We exchanged numbers, he gave me a dizzy smile of disbelief, and my heart soared as I sailed back inside through the double doors.

"Did you just ask him out?" Macon demanded.

I hesitated. Then I said it like a challenge. "I did."

I thought you said you weren't going to ask out any patrons. He didn't say it out loud, but it hung between us all the same. I moved behind my station and avoided his gaze. A minute later, he removed the pen from behind his ear and pointed it at me. "What about that other guy?"

"I'm not seeing them both, if that's what you're asking."

He tapped the pen rapidly against the desk, about to say something more, but then shoved the pen back into place. "Sorry. It's none of my business."

It wasn't. But I also couldn't help but feel like I'd dragged him into it. "It's okay," I muttered, retrieving the gift voucher from the desk drawer and slipping it into my pocket.

"*Ballooning?*" Macon said. "You're actually going ballooning with him. With Gareth Murphy."

"No," I seethed. "I'm going with Mr. Brember."

Our rhythm was so off that it took him a few seconds to realize I wasn't serious. His confusion clicked into understanding.

"Yes, with Gareth Murphy," I said.

His expression darkened with fury. "Yeah, I know."

"Then why did you ask?"

"Forget I said anything."

"That won't be hard since you never talk to me anymore," I snapped.

He winced, and immediately I felt like a tremendous piece of shit.

"I'm sorry." My voice dropped into a quiet plea. "I understand why you don't, and I know you want me to quit, but I can't. Not yet."

He looked flabbergasted. "I don't want you to quit."

"Oh."

His expression collapsed and then screwed into wretchedness. I sensed him wanting to explain himself and then, after a struggle, closing back up. The smell of smoke from the fireplace seemed to intensify, but it was only because the spark between us, tentative but volatile, had been extinguished.

CHAPTER SEVEN

"This is the strangest date I've ever been on," Gareth said. "Also the earliest."

We had arrived in separate cars at a derelict JCPenney parking lot at 6:30 A.M. and had been shuttled in a transit van to the launch site fifteen minutes away. This turned out to be farmland that was currently empty of grazing cattle. The pilot used a helium party balloon, of all things, to test the wind speed and cleared us for flight at sunrise. Components were laid out, connected, and checked, and then a large fan began inflating the balloon. Gareth and I stood nearby, watching the enormous swath of patchwork rainbow fabric ripple and billow and fill.

My laugh was somewhat desperate. "Yeah, sorry about that. I didn't realize." I hadn't realized a lot of things until I'd forwarded him the instructions from the business. We had also been instructed to wear warm layers, comfortable shoes, and hats. Hats were mentioned twice.

Gareth smiled. "All part of the adventure, right?"

I was grateful that it sounded like he meant it.

We shivered and sipped our coffee. He had brought two thermoses from home, a thoughtful gesture that boded well for our date, despite the temperature being forty-one degrees. It was warm for a February morning but cold for an outdoor activity. As requested, we were both wearing beanies. His was plain and burgundy, and mine had a fluffy pom-pom on top. When he saw it, he booped it and said I looked cute. This was the first time I'd seen him in clothes that weren't soiled from construction work. He looked good, too, and I told him so. His expression shied with pleasure, which increased my attraction. We had already chatted a bit about ourselves, but mostly we'd been making polite conversation with the three balloon company employees who were here with us. Somehow, I had forgotten the obvious: We wouldn't be on this date alone.

"You know," he said, "I've always wanted to ask you out."

This filled me with more warmth than the coffee, more than from exchanging compliments. "You have?"

"Yeah, but it felt inappropriate. Like asking for a server's number in a restaurant."

"It felt inappropriate for me to ask you out, too," I confessed.

"Also, for some reason I was under the impression that you lived with a guy?"

"Ah," I said.

"You did."

"Yes."

"And it's way too early—in the date and in the morning—to talk about that."

I laughed. "Definitely."

The balloon envelope had filled with air, so the pilot lit the burner and blew fire up into it from the propane tanks. The heat brought the structure upright. Up close, a hot-air balloon was a gigantic and impressive thing. Suddenly I wasn't sure I wanted to climb inside it. Gareth also looked a touch queasy. "You're not afraid of heights, are you?" I asked.

"I'm not, but now I'm wondering if I am."

"Thank goodness, because me too."

"Why are we doing this again?" he asked.

"Because it's free?"

"And remind me why it's free?"

"Time to fly, kids," Tom shouted. We'd already learned that he'd been piloting balloons since before we were born, so neither of us minded the diminutive. We left our thermoses in the chase van and hustled forward so we wouldn't disappoint him. It surprised us both when the youngest member of the crew, whom I'd assumed would stay with the van driver, sprinted past us and hurdled neatly into the basket. Tom caught our reaction and grinned. "Connor is a student pilot. He'll be assisting me. That's why y'all got such a good deal today."

"I didn't get the deal," I said. "It was a gift."

Tom guffawed. "Guess you've got a cheap friend."

I didn't bother to explain that Amelia Louisa Hatmaker was the one with the cheap friend, but I also couldn't wait to relay Tom's line back to her. I knew she'd find it funny.

"Don't worry," Connor said. He had a mustache, but just barely. A starter mustache. "I've only crashed once, and only two passengers died."

Gareth and I laughed gamely at the hacky joke.

The gondola was taller than I'd expected, the top above waist height, and it had no door, for safety reasons. The whole thing looked as quaint and insubstantial as a wicker basket in a grandmother's living room.

"No graceful way of doing it," Tom said, enjoying our discomfort. "Just hop on in—and hurry up."

Gareth and I threw our legs over at the same time. I didn't want to seem scared, and presumably he felt the same way. He *oofed* as he landed, and Tom clapped him on the back. I got stuck midway, so Connor reached out to assist me. Staggering over the side, I crashed into him, and then he crashed into Gareth and Tom. Immediately it was apparent why: the gondola, which would have felt snug with three, was even more crowded with the extra pilot. There would be no changing positions or moving around.

"Smile for the camera," the van driver shouted.

"Oh my God," Gareth and I chorused as we were spun around and crammed against each other in a Tom-and-Connor sandwich.

"We'll make sure you get a copy of that," Tom said.

"Now's a good time for selfies," Connor said, "especially if your camera or phone doesn't have a strap. Two thousand feet's a long way down."

Our eyebrows simultaneously rose to touch our hats, both at the mention of the height and at the idea of taking yet another photograph together. "It'll probably be weirder if we don't," I whispered, and Gareth agreed, so I pulled out my phone and snapped a picture of us laughing in confusion and mild fear. Tom finished lecturing to Connor behind us and stretched his arm above me to untether us, and then it was happening.

Liftoff was gentle—so gentle. I realized I'd been expecting something as extreme and lurching and windy as a biplane with an open cockpit, but leaving the earth felt smooth and effortless. Upward we drifted in a dreamlike floatation.

"I keep imagining myself falling out of the basket," Gareth said.

"Just when I was feeling good about all this," I said.

"You'll probably be fine, though, since you're shorter than me. More difficult for you to topple out."

I pointed upward. "Hey, did you see how thin and flimsy that balloon fabric is?"

"Look how close it is to the fire," Tom said, gleefully joining in.

"Now it's your job to help us watch out for power lines, houses, trees," Connor said. We laughed again, but he added, "Not a joke. Four sets of eyes are better than two. Let us know if you spot any obstacles that you think we haven't noticed." He had switched to serious pilot-in-training mode, and his fingers smoothed his faint mustache with authority.

I gave Tom a nervous glance, and he grinned at me again. There was another explosive burst of fire above our heads. Gareth and I startled and ducked, which launched Tom into a spiel about how it all worked: The hot air was less dense than the surrounding cold air, and that was why the balloon rose. Navigation was all about climbing and descending to catch winds going different speeds and directions. And eventually we would land . . . wherever we landed. Every flight was different and unrepeatable, Tom explained, and that was why he would never tire of it.

This was the same reason why some people weren't right for monogamy.

Their energy was restored by the new and unknown, so that's what they would always crave. That wasn't me, though. I was only a visitor to this world, cutting across it like the balloon through the sunrise. As titillating as it was to feel Gareth's arm bump against mine, to be so close that I could smell the sharp cleanliness of menthol in his shampoo, I desired a lifelong relationship with a single person. And when this was all over, that person would still be Cory.

What might my future look like with Gareth instead? It was impossible to imagine, but I supposed this was because I didn't know him. More unsettling was that it was also difficult to imagine the specifics of my future with Cory. When would we buy a house? What would it look like? Where would we travel? How would we spend the rest of our lives?

The balloon was gliding over the mountains now, which were still cloaked in misty morning fog. The trees were mostly bare, but the view was majestic, and the basket felt safe and peaceful. The sky glowed in purples, pinks, oranges, yellows. Our shadow trailed below.

Connor monitored the altitude and wind speed and other things I didn't understand while Tom observed. Since we were traveling with the wind, we couldn't hear it, and the only time we felt a breeze was when the altitude changed. The flight would have been almost silent if not for Tom's communications with the chase van and the occasional blasts of fire, which revealed the true purpose of the hats: to protect our scalps from the heat of the burners.

Gareth shifted to look at something and knocked into me. "Sorry. Are you okay?"

I was fine and told him so. We had been making accidental physical contact and apologizing since the flight began.

"How long have you two been together?" Tom sounded genuinely curious as opposed to professionally polite, and I understood at once that he'd been observing our body language.

"Uh—" Gareth began. He glanced at me, and we both squirmed.

"Well, we've known each other for a few years," I said.

"But this is actually . . . our first date," he finished.

We knew it was coming, and it did. Tom and Connor erupted with incredulous laughter. "In my forty-three years of flying, I've witnessed a lot of proposals and honeymoons," Tom said, shaking his head, "but only a handful of first dates. I knew you two were special."

"That's a lot of cash to drop for a first date," Connor said to Gareth.

"It was free, remember?" Tom chortled harder.

"And I asked *him* out," I said, because I sensed Tom was the sort of man still clinging to outdated notions who would find this hilarious. He did.

Mercifully, Gareth also decided that it was easier to join in than to fight it. We played along as Tom and Connor ribbed us about the romantic sunrise, wondered if that pair of red-tailed hawks was bonded for life, grazed an evergreen and encouraged us to grab some needles for a souvenir, dipped the gondola near a waterfall and told us to make a very special first-date wish. And because Gareth and I had committed ourselves to having a good time, we did.

Cory was also easygoing, but if he wasn't having fun, he wasn't able to fake it. If the dating jokes struck a nerve, anger and misery would have been radiating off him. Macon was equally unable to fake a good time. Justin would have enjoyed the flight—hell, it was easy to imagine him as a pilot—but I was glad that none of these men who haunted my thoughts were here. For once, I was glad to be with the person I was with.

After about an hour, Tom pointed out a plowed field to Connor and the chase van. "Perhaps you've been imagining that we would float down gently for an easy landing," Tom said to us. "But the wind has picked up, so I'm gonna need you to follow my instructions carefully."

The enjoyment slid from Gareth's and my expressions.

"No need to be scared," Tom said, delighted by our fear. "We're gonna lean against the basket, turn sideways like this, and then bend our knees a little to soften the impact."

"Uh, how hard do you expect this impact to be?" Gareth asked.

"Just keep holding on to those rope handles for support."

"Connor? You got this?" I joked while fiercely wishing that Tom were the one piloting. I grasped the thick, prickly rope with both hands and all of my strength.

"We're fine," Gareth said, looking straight at me with wide eyes.

I stared straight back. "Totally fine."

His blue irises were piercing, and I held his gaze with a racing heart.

"Land ho!" Connor cried, and the gondola jolted us as it hit the earth. The basket skipped daintily across the field a few times before toppling pathetically onto its side in a complete stop. We all laughed again in a release of emotion as if we'd just been on a theme-park thrill ride.

Gareth and I clambered out and squelched across the muddy ground. "Land, sweet land," he said. Mud streaked our pants from the knees down, and our sneakers were caked. The van driver greeted us with a cheer and waved two bottles: champagne and orange juice.

"Oh dear God," I said. "There's more."

"I'm not opposed to a drink right now," Gareth said.

Tom bombastically recited something called the "Balloonist's Prayer" and then led a toast to celebrate our successful first date—ha ha, he meant flight.

We clinked our mimosas together and downed them.

Now that the adventure was over, the cold weather felt biting as we helped the team deflate the balloon, roll it up, and load it and everything else onto the utility trailer hitched to the van. They didn't ask for our help, but it seemed impolite to do nothing. Job done, we trundled out of the field and back to the JCPenney parking lot. I tipped Connor, and Gareth tipped Tom. Then they all stood around watching us, so Gareth and I clumsily hugged goodbye to their catcalls, got in our separate cars, and drove home.

Better or worse than Justin? Kat texted that evening, as soon as she woke up.

We didn't do anything, I replied.

WHAT? But!! Romantic balloon ride!

Exactly. Too much pressure. We had to keep joking so it wouldn't get weird.

She FaceTimed me. "That's bullshit. Not even a kiss?"

"We would have had to do it in front of an audience. The pilots wouldn't leave."

She laughed. She was still in bed, and the room behind her was bright and sunny. "So that's it?"

"I have no idea. I guess so? I told you, the whole thing was weird."

"Well, it's been a weird two months. But at least you're going out on a high." She grinned. Held the grin.

"Oh. That was a balloon joke."

"Yes, it was."

"Did you see the pictures I sent?"

"You both look terrified. But he's cuter than the pictures I could find of him online. Have you kissed anybody with a beard yet?"

"No, but First Brandon was a day or two unshaven and had more facial hair than Cory can grow."

She sighed. "I guess that'll have to do."

I was surprised to receive a text from Gareth the following night. I supposed I shouldn't have been. After all, I'd asked him out—signaling my interest and availability—and then we'd had a fun time despite everything. Of course he would follow up. He didn't know that my boyfriend was moving back in with me in two days. He didn't even know that I had a boyfriend.

I should have taken you out to breakfast, he said. *Let's do breakfast.*

I called Kat again. "He wants to have breakfast. What do I do?"

"What do you mean?"

"I mean, is it ethical for me to have breakfast with him tomorrow so I can try to make out with him? You know, check that beard box?"

"Do people make out after breakfast?"

"*I* will make out after breakfast."

She hesitated. "I'm not sure you're looking for a real answer."

"So . . . that's a no." I knew she was right, but I still felt irritated.

"Maybe it is, and maybe it isn't. But if you want to do anything with him, the *ethical* move would be to tell him what's going on first."

I moaned. "What's my other choice?"

"Don't meet him for breakfast."

"And my other, other choice?"

"Don't tell him, have breakfast, pop a mint and feel each other up, never contact him again, and then feel guilty about how you treated him for the rest of your life."

"I mean, most of that sounds good."

"Listen, I think you want me to tell you to do it, and I'm not going to stop you or judge you. But I'm also not going to encourage it. He sounds like a nice guy."

Gareth was a nice guy.

How's tomorrow? I texted him, ignoring Kat's advice and my gut.

He responded quickly. *I have to be on site early. Doubt you want to meet me at 6! Wed?*

Wednesday, the day after tomorrow, was March. I wouldn't be seeing Cory until that evening, but it definitely felt unethical to break my word to him. *I don't have to go into work until late, and you met me at 6:30 for the balloon. We'll call it even.*

Is a restaurant okay or should I book a rafting trip?

It made me laugh out loud. *I'll settle for a restaurant.*

Lottie's? They're open that early.

My heart twisted. Lottie's belonged to Cory and me. *What about that British phone booth downtown? They have pastries in the morning.*

It's a date, he said. And then, *See you in . . . a few hours?!*

A few hours later, he was waiting for me beside the phone booth with an expression between a smile and a grimace. "They don't have food here, or even coffee. Just tea."

"Oh no!" I greeted him with a hug. He was wearing his construction clothes, but he smelled like a new day, fresh and clean. I was bundled up in a cheerful and colorful coat that I knew he'd never seen before. "I could have sworn they did."

"I did wonder how they could fit any pastries into that tiny kiosk."

I groaned. "I'm sorry. Do you need coffee?"

He confirmed that he did but bought me a chai latte before we set off to locate it. "Maybe we should have tried to squeeze in there with the barista," he said. "You know, do a reenactment of the balloon ride."

"Are they called baristas if they don't serve coffee?"

"You're the librarian." He gave my arm a playful nudge. "You tell me."

I was surprised by how light and happy I felt to be there with him. We already had banter and inside jokes. This was what I had been missing with Justin. We located an open coffee shop, and when he walked me back to my car an hour later, my chest was vibrating like it was filled with hummingbirds. I could tell he was thinking about kissing me but was nervous to do it.

I reached for his jacket lapels. The durable cotton was thick in my hands, and he smiled and sort of laughed as I pulled him into me. His coffee breath was comforting, and my whole body mushed and went giddy with the pleasure of kissing him. His strong arms wrapped around me warmly. I wanted to take him somewhere private and do private things to him, but instead we made out on the sidewalk until he realized he was about to be late for work. His lips were as red and raw as my skin was from his scratchy beard.

He said goodbye in a daze, and as he disappeared from view, my body released a quake. This unexpected physical reaction escalated quickly. Violently. I hurried into my car and shuddered, splitting apart at the seams. I wept and howled. I opened the door again and threw up my latte onto the street. Mortified, I sped away from the scene. Then I engaged in another two hours of uncontrollable, primal anguish at home.

If only I had asked Gareth out sooner. A loop existed inside me now that I would never be able to close. Cory was coming home tomorrow. I wanted him to come home—I *wanted to want* him to come home—but I didn't. I wasn't ready. These thoughts felt disloyal, even though I'd followed our rules. I just needed more time, that was all. *Not yet*, my body screamed as I took a second shower to calm myself down. As I drove to work. As I greeted patrons and scanned their books. As Macon gave me a wide berth, then guardedly asked if I was okay.

No, jackass, I am not okay! I shrieked.

"I'm fine," I actually said.

That night I tried to clean the apartment for Cory's return, but the emotional hurricane had exhausted me. What if he needed more time, too? The possibility made me feel a little better and then much worse. I had no appetite, so I skipped dinner and went straight to bed, but then I couldn't fall asleep. I turned on my lamp to read, wincing at the obnoxious *ding ding ding* the pull chain made as it settled back down. We'd both always hated our lamps. The books piled high on my nightstand shamed me as I debated which one to try again. I kept starting them, and each one seemed fine, but I always lost interest after that first reading. Another book would distract me. Then another after that. But I also didn't want to give up on any of them, because what if I missed out on something exceptional? So the stack kept growing, and I still hadn't finished a single one. I doubted I'd made it past page thirty in any book this year.

On top of the stack, my phone flashed with a text from Gareth: *We're bad at breakfast. Let's skip it and go straight to lunch.*

I picked up the phone instead of a book. But I was a coward, so I did not text him back.

March

DATE DUE	BORROWER'S NAME	ROOM NUMBER
JAN 25		
FEB 19		
MAR 30		

CHAPTER EIGHT

Groundhog Day. Not the holiday, but the booth. I felt the weight of the movie as if Kevin had sat me here as a bad joke. Cory and I were both late again, and I sensed we were about to have the same conversation as before, too. He had requested another meet-up at the diner, and I wasn't entirely sure why, although the location seemed right to me, too. Perhaps it felt like neutral territory. Perhaps the apartment already felt more like mine. Did it unsettle him to imagine who might have been there in his absence? I wondered if I should tell him that nobody had, that it felt wrong to bring somebody home who wasn't him.

When he finally arrived, he looked wilder than at our previous meeting. The mania had been turned up a notch. The comparison to the character Phil Connors felt accurate, except that Cory and I had chosen this time loop and Phil had not. We hugged before sitting down and discovered that the looseness and distance between our bodies had also increased.

Our friendship was still there, though. Cory was grinning at me, and it spread into his voice. "*You* had a date. My coworkers saw you."

I blushed and dropped my gaze. "Yeah. I figured they'd tell you."

"So? Did you?" If it had been a text, a dozen question marks and exclamation points would have followed the words.

I nodded, and he cackled with glee. Halted and sat there in silence. Shook his head and knitted his brow. Fell motionless again. "You know," he said. "I don't know how to react to that."

I laughed once, low. "Imagine how I feel."

"This is weird, isn't it?"

"That's the word I keep using." Underneath the table, I gripped my thighs for support. For the first time, I realized that I hadn't worried about him bringing a ring tonight. And looking at him now, I was positive my instincts were correct.

"Iggy, I have to say it. I'm still not ready."

I had expected a powerful rush of relief, and it came. Yet an irrational part of me was also hurt and upset. I didn't want him to come home, but I wanted him to want to come home. I wasn't sure if I wanted to marry him, but I wanted him to want to marry me.

"Say something, Ig. Talk to me."

My fingers clawed deeper into my legs. "I need another month, too."

He'd been leaning toward me, but at this, he collapsed back into the booth. "Oh my God. You scared me. For a second, I thought we weren't on the same page anymore."

It was a strange thing for him to say. Sure, we were still on the same page, but our page was currently in two separate books. We were acting out two separate stories.

"You do still want this, though? Us?" I asked.

He sat up again, nervous and ready to reassure me. "Of course. February was just such a short month, you know?" His expression shifted into fear. "Do *you* still want this?"

"Of course," I said, because I thought I did. I reached for his hands—I needed to touch him—but just then two red plastic tumblers of water thunked onto the table between us. We jumped. It was Hank, the same lithe server we'd had a month earlier.

"Hey there," he said. "I'll be taking care of you folks tonight. Can I get you something else to drink?"

"A Coke, thanks. Actually, I think we're ready," Cory said, glancing at me to confirm. "I'll have the chicken tenders and fries, and she'll have the grilled cheese and tomato soup."

Hank tapped his shaved head and then strolled gracefully away to place our order.

Cory said something I didn't catch.

"Huh?" I was still watching Hank. "*Groundhog Day* vibes are strong tonight."

"What? Oh yeah. The table."

That wasn't quite what I had meant, though. We were out of sync and confused, but what mattered most was clear: Our groundhog had seen its shadow. We both needed more time.

I texted Gareth from the diner's parking lot. *Lunch tomorrow?*

Our schedules weren't compatible, so we arranged a date for the weekend instead. But I'd forgotten the following day was a Thursday, his library day, and was excited when he pointed out that we'd see each other anyway. I wore a dress to work and put some effort into my hair.

"Aw, look at you," Alyssa said when I walked in. She was sitting behind my station doing the morning desk shift. "Cory must be coming home."

I started at the name.

"Sue and Macon said it wouldn't happen," she continued. "Elijah was less sure. But I knew Cory would be back."

Heat flashed through me. "You've all been placing bets?"

"Not betting. Speculating."

I thumped my tote bag down on the desk. "Well, you're wrong."

"Who's wrong?" Sue asked, appearing from the annex. It wasn't a general question. She had been eavesdropping on our conversation.

I'd been dreading having to tell them but couldn't avoid it. "Cory and I extended our experiment."

"Ha!" Sue said to Alyssa, who looked disappointed in me. I wasn't sure if it was for moral reasons or because she'd lost.

Macon slouched into the building. "We were right," Sue said to him. "No Cory."

I expected him to brush her off—he was always grouchiest upon arrival, so it was too early for gossip—but instead he stopped. Stared at me. I glared back. "Are you okay?" he asked, and then the others remembered their manners because they asked, too.

Before I could respond, Elijah swaggered in for his shift. He hooted when he saw me. "It's that guy!"

"What guy?" Sue and Alyssa asked.

"Thursday-night dude. I forgot you asked him out. You're all dressed up for him, right?"

I hadn't been aware that Elijah had overheard my fight with Macon about asking out Gareth. Alyssa leaned forward eagerly. "What Thursday-night dude?" she asked. She and Sue didn't know about Gareth because he always came in after they were already gone.

Macon stalked into the annex to put his lunch in the fridge. When he returned, the other three were still crowded around me, hounding me. "Leave us alone," he barked.

Elijah and Alyssa scattered. Sue lifted her hands in surrender and moseyed away, but then she glanced back over her shoulder. One eyebrow was raised.

Us. Macon hadn't said *leave me alone* or *leave her alone*. He'd grouped us together again. It was a small thing, but I clung to it.

"Thanks," I said.

He flumped into his chair in an exhausted response.

How had he known that Cory and I would need another month? And what did he think about it? I hated that his opinions still mattered so much to me, but thankfully, I had a distraction. As the clock drew nearer to the Gareth hour, my adrenaline surged. I wasn't sure why I felt less embarrassed about Macon seeing me with Gareth than seeing me with Justin. Maybe because he already knew about Gareth, or maybe our fight had made me stubborn. Or maybe I was just so frustrated that some unkind part of me wanted to rub it in his face.

He never gave me the opportunity. The instant Gareth appeared, Macon disappeared to water the plants. It didn't matter, though. I was thrilled to see Gareth again. We didn't hug, and he didn't peck me on the cheek like Justin had done. His initial approach was bashful, but then we flirted exhaustively, and by the time he finally left—after spending much longer at the desk than usual and being throat-cleared out the door by another waiting patron—I felt delirious with wantonness.

Macon slammed the watering can down onto our desk, and I jumped. The jarring clang of metal reverberated through the quiet library.

"Yo," Elijah called out.

I stared at Macon in astonishment until he looked at me. He crumpled with embarrassment. "I have a headache," he muttered, as if that made any sort of sense.

If I hadn't known any better, I would have thought he was jealous. Except, actually, I was still pretty sure that he was. Excitement flickered inside me until anger flared and overtook it. I had tried, and he had said no, and he had no fucking right to be fucking jealous now.

My mood clearly showed, because Macon rose to the challenge. His back stiffened. His expression hardened. We stared each other down like two beasts in the wild.

"I found bacon in my mystery novel," somebody sang.

Our attention jerked to the man entering the library. "My word," Mr. Garland said, eyeing the two of us with delight. "What have I interrupted?"

"Nothing," I said, as Macon said, "Bacon?"

"A strip of cooked bacon," Mr. Garland confirmed, opening the hardcover in his hands. "The person who checked this out last must have been using it as a bookmark."

Macon sighed. "For fuck's sake."

"That's what I said," Mr. Garland said. "I couldn't wait to show it to you."

Macon plucked out the bacon with two fingers, dropped it into the trash can, and inspected the greasy pages with disgust.

"Do you need me to order a copy from another branch for you?" I asked.

Mr. Garland waved a hand airily. "No, I just turned the page and kept reading. It's a good one."

Although the tension had been defused, Macon and I remained sullen and aggressive toward each other until late the following morning. The post-storytime rush was nearly over when the phone rang. I answered, and it was an older woman with an unsteady voice. "May I please speak to Macon Nowakowski?"

"Of course. He's helping someone, but it'll only be a moment."

"Thank you," she said.

As I waited for Macon to finish checking out a stack of picture books for a mother and her son, an affable preschooler who loved whales and sharks and especially whale sharks, I had a delayed reaction. The voice pinged in my memory bank along with the realization that the caller had correctly pronounced Macon's last name. I clutched the phone against my chest.

He sensed the change in my energy and glanced over.

"I think it's your mom," I said.

His face fell. I stepped in to finish the transaction so he could take the call. In all the years I'd worked there, his mother had never phoned. I only recognized her voice because we'd met a number of times when I'd first started and she'd come into the branch. She still lived in town, but her agoraphobia had grown to the point where it was keeping her from leaving the house. Like her son, she was an avid reader, so now he brought the books straight to her. He also ran her other errands, cooked many of her meals, and did her yard work. Caring for her was essentially his second job.

"What happened?" he asked her. And then, "Is she okay?"

But his mother wasn't the sole person he had to worry about, and it was obvious that today's bad news had something to do with his aunt. Macon was an only child, his father had never been in the picture, and the only other family member he was close with was his mother's sister, who had helped raise him before she'd gotten married and moved away. Her husband had passed away a few years ago, and shortly afterward, she'd injured her back trying to clean out the gutters. Her doctor had prescribed opioids for the pain. It went as terribly as these things could go. She'd overdosed more than once and had been in and out of multiple rehab facilities.

"Is she still there?" he asked.

Christina Castillo, the mom of the preschooler, was also listening to the call. We exchanged a worried glance. She gave me a tight nod—*I hope everything will be okay*—and then put on an overly animated expression to lead Miguel and his shark books out of the building.

"I'll figure it out," Macon said. "No, that's okay. I'll call Will. Yeah, I'm leaving right now. I'll be careful." He hung up.

"I've got this," I said. "Go."

"Bonnie was arrested again. She's being transferred to another rehab facility, or she's already been transferred—I'm not sure—but her neighbor called my mom, and apparently Bonnie's place is a disaster. I've got to drive to Durham to sort it all out." Bonnie's stepson, Will, usually handled these situations, but he was living in Myanmar for the year while his wife did a stint with Doctors Without Borders. Macon had been expecting to have to step in at some point and help. He grabbed the back of his chair for his duffel coat, but it was already on. He'd been wearing it all day. He was making plans, half in his head and half out loud. "I'll have to call my neighbors so they can feed Edmond— Shit. They're on vacation."

I stepped forward. "I can feed him. Mornings, right?"

"And evenings."

"Oh. I thought his owner fed him at night?"

"Edmond doesn't live with him anymore. He lives with me. He's my cat."

My head drew back. "Really? When did that happen?"

"Uh, end of January. Shawn moved to the coast and didn't want to take him."

"Oh my God," I said. Because I couldn't imagine leaving a pet behind. Because Macon hadn't told me, and I'd been sitting beside him this whole time. It stung.

He disappeared into the annex to talk to Sue and returned a minute later, fishing for his keys in his pocket. "Mornings and evenings," I said. "I can do that."

"Are you sure?"

"Of course. I can feed him, play with him. Get your mail. Whatever you need, for however long you need it."

"I don't want to inconvenience you. I know you've been busy—"

"Jesus, Macon. It's not an inconvenience." I didn't mean for it to come out so short.

He stared me down again before relenting. "I'll put a spare key underneath the smallest planter by the door, and I'll leave instructions inside."

I drove straight to Macon's house from work. His neighborhood was older and darker than most in Ridgetop. Fewer streetlights. Street*lamps*. He was lucky to live in an area that still had the city's original decorative posts. They gave off less light than the taller posts along the main roads but added a whimsical charm to the twisty, woodsy neighborhood. Macon had once told me that he preferred the lamps because they produced less light pollution, which was better for the birds and animals. I'd never considered the effects of light pollution before, but now I often did—all those miserable chickadees and chipmunks trying to sleep.

I'd been to Macon's house once before, a long time ago, during my first year as a librarian. He had invited us all over for a dinner party: Sue and Russell, Alyssa and Tim, Cory and me. Our former coworker Richard and his wife, Lucy, had also been in attendance. Rail-thin and white-bearded, Richard resembled a skinny Santa Claus and was generally as mild-mannered, apart from his zealous diatribes on climate change. He and Macon still met up a few times a year to rage. Richard was in his mid-seventies when I was hired, already retired from the National Park Service. The paging job was supposed to be temporary—a supplemental income to help with Lucy's medical bills—but he'd ended up working at the library for six years.

Next month would mark my fifth year. The library job was supposed to be temporary for me, too, until it wasn't. I wasn't sure when it had turned into my career. It was a good career, and I felt fortunate, so I wasn't sure why I didn't love it as much as I should. I didn't know how to reconcile having a desirable job that I could do well yet still not be satisfied with. It stank of privilege. But even though I was bored and restless, I still panicked whenever Sue mentioned library school, which could get me a job away from the desk. It made no sense. She'd been nudging me again, and I knew I had to apply, but it wasn't the right time. I couldn't picture myself back in school any better than I could picture my life with Cory being anything other than what it already was. Why did my future always look so static?

I would apply to library school when Cory returned, I promised myself. When things were steady again and we were moving forward.

I slowed my car so I could read the house numbers, and sure enough, number twenty-four was exactly where I had remembered it. Strange how I could recall its location after all these years. Even in the dark, Macon's house had been easy to find.

I parked in the driveway and checked the mailbox. Nothing was inside, so I went and found the key where Macon had promised it would be. His front door had a unique round window. I remembered this, too. It was dark now, but that night it had beamed like a sun.

His whole house had been warm and inviting that night. Candlelight in every room, soft bohemian wall hangings, plants and rugs and pillows, crystals and rocks arranged on the windowsills, and enough chairs that everybody had a comfortable place to sit. The dinner had been thoughtfully prepared, a full menu with courses, and Sue and Richard had each brought a bottle of wine. I'd felt bad that I hadn't thought to bring a gift, but thankfully Alyssa hadn't either. We'd been young and hadn't known the rules of adults, and we'd exchanged giggles of relief away from the others. The food had been outstanding, the conversation lively, and my usual party jitters had relaxed with the easy companionship, everyone flushed with wine and laughter.

It wasn't until now, as I crossed back over the threshold, that I realized how much I treasured those memories. Whenever Macon mentioned his house, I pictured it trapped in amber, warm and candlelit. But when my patting hand located the light switch—it was a little button, another charming detail—there were no candles, no pillows, no sparkling quartz or prisms. There was hardly even any furniture. His house was tidy and clean, but it was also sparse and empty.

I was looking at the absence of a person. The absence of *Danielle*. Because of course his ex-girlfriend had been at the dinner party, too.

A forgotten but familiar squirm wriggled through me. Macon and Dani had been partners for a long time. I had liked her well enough, but I had also not liked her. I had known her, but I had also hardly known her at all and had grasped on to every breadcrumb of information that Macon had ever dropped. She was one of those good people who'd made me feel bad for not being as good as her. She taught at the Appalachian School of Herbal Medicine, and she ate healthfully, like Macon. Meditated and did yoga. Never wore makeup, but she had perfect skin, so big deal. If I had perfect skin, I wouldn't wear it either. But she was also a pessimist like Macon, only with far less levity. And she'd never seemed to like me much—I suspected I was too smiley, too unserious for her. But that night, in my memories, she had also been happy and filled with laughter.

"Edmond? Edmond Dantès?" I called out into the darkness that lay deeper inside the house. "We've never met before, but I'm your dad's friend." Although it felt silly, it seemed important to explain myself to the cat. Even if *friend* might not be the correct word. It was like talking to a young child and leaving out the difficult bits.

The house responded with silence.

I'd never had a cat, but growing up, my family had lived with a basenji. Trixie'd had a beautiful red coat with white markings, adorable pointy ears, a sproingy curled tail, and a calculating mind that knew exactly how long to wait for Riley and me to leave the room before destroying our favorite toys. Her bark had sounded like a yodel, she had stolen food directly off our plates, and she had refused to walk on grass. I had loved our mischievous and rotten dog, but Trixie had been devoted to my mom and hadn't given a fig about the rest of us.

Cory had been raised with a number of Labradors. "They're big, they're playful, and they wear down my boys," his mother had once told me. Cory was the youngest of three brothers, and when they were together, they all had fighting-wrestling energy. Cory and I did want to get a dog eventually. We planned to adopt a mutt from the shelter, but we were waiting until we had a fenced yard.

I felt a surge of triumph at this glimpse into our future: a dog. We would have a dog. Yet despite my love of dogs, this vision didn't fill me with excitement or longing.

"Edmond? Ed? Eddie?" I set down the key and my tote bag and then inhaled, deep and slow. The air smelled like Macon. My heart panged with loss.

A black-and-white tuxedo cat slinked into view.

"Hi there. Am I allowed to pet you?"

Edmond seemed interested but uncertain.

"Want to show me the kitchen? It's back here, right?" I pressed the buttons to turn on more lights as I moved through the house. My footsteps echoed through the quiet rooms.

Edmond followed behind me at a cautious distance.

The feeding and care instructions were on the kitchen counter, exactly where I expected to find them. The handwriting gave me a second pang. It felt good to be close enough to somebody to be able to recognize their handwriting. Seeing it was almost like seeing the person themself. The disheveled yet precise scrawl in front of me distinctly, unmistakably belonged to Macon. I touched the piece of paper and felt the indentations left by his pen.

Edmond stirred behind me, reminding me of my purpose. I fed him a mackerel and lamb mix, rinsed out the can, and plopped it into the recycling bin. The instructions informed me that changing his water bowl and cleaning the litter box were morning activities.

Beside the sink was a dish that contained two bars of soap. The note didn't specify which was for my hands, so I guessed. Then I snapped a picture of Edmond eating and drafted an accompanying text. *All is well! Hope you made it to Durham safely and hope your aunt is okay.* After a moment of deliberation, I added a red heart emoji and hit send. I often added hearts to my texts, so I knew he'd understand that it was out of concerned friend-love as opposed to anything romantic. A text from me would be more suspect if it didn't have a heart.

Edmond was still eating. His plate gently scraped against the tile floor, and the disgusting scent of wet meat wafted through the room.

"Mm, yum. Does that taste good?" I asked, bending down to pet him.

His ears flattened against his head, and he backed away from my outstretched hand. He wasn't ready for any physical interactions with a stranger. I understood and respected that.

"Loud and clear, bud. See you in the morning."

But halfway to the front door, I paused.

The ghostly loneliness of the house swept through me. It had been built in the thirties, and the structure itself looked as if it had resisted modernization. The floors, trim, and fixtures seemed to be original, and the overall appearance was of a lot of bare wood. The walls and surfaces were mostly empty. In the dining room sat a breakfast table, two chairs, and nothing else. The living room was unusually long, stretching across nearly the whole front of the house, and Macon had created a sitting area with a tired couch, a coffee table, and an end table with a lamp. Across from this setup was a dusty television. The rest of this large space was desolate apart from a scratching post and several fur-covered blankets and beds scattered around, proving my suspicions correct: Macon did spend more money on Edmond than on himself.

The darkness in the back of the house beckoned to me. I turned on the hallway light, and four doors appeared, three open and one partially closed.

In my memory, these rooms were small and the first one was a study, so I was pleased to discover that it still contained Macon's desk and crowded bookshelves. Naturally, I took a few minutes to inspect the spines. His collection was separated into fiction and nonfiction, and everything was arranged alphabetically. Tons of classics and Everyman's Library editions, some still stickered with prices from the used bookstore. Tomes about the environment and history and science and economics. Several worn and beloved novels from his childhood. Gardening books, some of which I recognized from our Friends of the Library sales. A cat care book that looked like it had been purchased new. My chest ached with recognition. If I had been shown a list of these titles, I would have known exactly who they belonged to. Everything here was right.

The room beside it used to belong to Dani. The walls had been crowded with furniture and other items, but the center of the floor had contained only a circular rug, a lavender zafu, and a low table with a bell. The room had stunk of incense. Now it smelled like a litter box. Honestly, the incense might have been worse. Cardboard boxes cluttered the floor, a perch was positioned in front of the window, and the litter box and all its accouterments were tucked into one of the corners.

Edmond darted past me, startling me, and leapt onto his perch.

"Does Macon call this 'Edmond's room'? I bet he does."

Although he could have gazed out the window, his body was facing me. His vigilant eyes were green and intense.

I moved along. The next room was the bathroom—the old house had only one—and I took the opportunity to use it. It was even smaller than the one in my apartment, but it was also significantly more appealing. Like the rest of the house, the fixtures looked original, and the tile was in good condition. With a fresh coat of paint and some decorative touches, it could be darling. I washed my hands with another bar of soap that smelled like Macon. I sniffed my fingers, and sorrow draped over me like a shroud. Unexpectedly, tears threatened to well up.

Edmond was waiting for me back in the hallway.

"Oh. Hey there." I reached out my fingers for him to sniff.

He didn't budge. He was intrigued, but I required further observation.

The final room had the partially closed door. It was the only one I hadn't seen on my previous visit. I glanced back at the cat as if he might tell on me, then gingerly pushed the door open. I couldn't bear to turn on the light. Instead, I stood on the threshold of Macon's bedroom and looked at what the hallway light was strong enough to reveal. It wasn't much. A large dresser and a mirror, a bed that was made, two side tables and two lamps.

Sadness returned and enveloped me. Aside from the two chairs in the dining room, these tables and lamps were the only evidence I'd seen of a second person—or the hope of a second person. I didn't know if Macon wanted to date again. It was one of those subjects that we never broached. His future self lived inside my mind in both versions: in another long-term relationship and peacefully alone for the rest of his life.

I pulled the door back to where it had been.

He hadn't mentioned the porch light in his instructions, but I turned it on anyway. It was too upsetting to leave Edmond and the house in the dark. I locked the door and lifted the planter to return the key. But . . . it was mine to keep until he returned. I lowered the planter and tucked the key into my pocket. It glowed warmly inside.

CHAPTER NINE

That night as I was trying to fall asleep, it occurred to me that something else had been missing: I hadn't seen a single houseplant. Had they been there before? I wasn't positive, but they were present in my memory. And Macon took such tender care of the library's plants and devoted so many hours to his garden. It was impossible for me to imagine him not surrounded by greenery. Had Dani taken them when she'd moved out, or had he gotten rid of them when Edmond had moved in? Many common houseplants were toxic to cats and dogs.

I turned over in bed, thinking about the garden. I'd been saving food scraps for Macon's compost pile for years—I'd literally been helping fertilize his garden—yet I'd never seen it. I'd always bagged the scraps and brought them to the library for him to take home. Ridgetop didn't have curbside composting, so residents had to either drive their scraps to a commercial facility or create piles in their own backyards. For most people, both of these options required too much effort. Macon was not most people. He was doing me a favor by taking my scraps, but I was also doing one for him. His garden was notoriously huge, every inch cultivated around his entire house, so he needed the compost. But how was it possible that I had never seen it myself?

It had been too dark earlier, but it had also been dark on my previous visit. And while it was true that we were only work friends, I spent more waking hours with him than with anybody else. The garden mattered to Macon, and he mattered to me. I should have asked him to show it to me. Maybe if I'd attempted to hang out with him away from work, our friendship would have been more solid, and then I wouldn't have tried to kiss him. Everything came back to that failed kiss. My heart had a physical ache, a scooped-out hollowness, in the shape of Macon. I should be trying harder to be his friend again. I shouldn't be provoking him into fights. Especially because if I did go to library school—if I didn't quit my job—he *would* remain in my life, at least until I got another position elsewhere. And that would take a few years. My only option was to try to make it work with him. The decision was practical, but I also missed my friend so badly.

All night long, I lay awake thinking about Macon.

I did not think about Cory or Gareth.

CHAPTER TEN

I arrived at Macon's house early the next morning, a full hour before work. His neighborhood was one of the most desirable in Ridgetop, and I was able to appreciate it even more in the daylight. The trees were large and established, and the houses were a fetching assortment of Arts and Crafts bungalows, rambling Victorians, and adorable cottages. Fifteen years ago, the residents of this neighborhood had been old, and everything had been falling apart. But as they'd passed, younger residents had moved in, and the cycle of life—and home restoration—had begun again. It was a neighborhood that had been affordable somewhat recently but was now wildly out of most buyers' price ranges.

Macon lived in a smaller house with a full stone exterior, and in the morning light, it looked so much like a fairy-tale cottage that it stole my breath. I loved it so much on sight that it made me furious. Covetous. The force of these emotions surprised me. I hadn't known it was possible to fall in love with a house, but how dare this belong to him and not to me? How dare some people get to own houses at all while I was still stuck in a crummy apartment?

Macon wouldn't have been able to afford the house either had it not first belonged to his aunt. After marrying in her mid-forties and moving to

Durham, Bonnie had rented it out. Many years later—around the time Macon was considering leaving his college town of Chapel Hill—the renters had vacated the premises, and Macon had taken it as a sign that he should return to Ridgetop, his place of birth. He had stayed in the house rent-free for six months before Bonnie sold it to him with a hefty family discount. Six months after that, Dani had moved in.

What an idiot! How could Dani have ever left this house?

I slammed my car door shut and stomped toward the front door. And that was when I saw the fucking garden.

Not much was growing yet apart from some kale and onions and early lettuce. But the sizable vegetable beds were surrounded by picket fencing to keep out the animals, and they were covered with some kind of protective crop, and I could picture exactly how it would all look in the summer—like a storybook garden, the kind that fucking Peter Rabbit would try to steal from. I spotted the compost pile, which somehow looked neat and tasteful, and then absorbed the rest of the landscaping, which was wild and robust and artistic. Artistic! There was no other word for it. Two pear trees were halfway toward their enchanted white bloom, and the buds of a cherry tree hinted that pink clouds wouldn't be far behind. Grape hyacinth clustered in pockets, and leaves from bigger bulbs suggested imminent tulips.

I knew Macon's garden was substantial—I *knew* this—yet I'd still been picturing something pleasant but modest. Perhaps because I'd witnessed him trading meager cuttings with patrons and heard about him rescuing other people's dying plants, and these exchanges had all seemed small and thrifty. But even out of season, his garden was abundant. Every nook and corner of his property was in use. I'd never had a green thumb, but now I longed for one. I longed for the whole house!

jesus fucking christ macon, I texted while shoving the key into the door, too angry for capitalization and forgetting my vow to be his friend again. The key scratched against the lock, and my whole body shuddered. "Oh my God. I'm so sorry," I whispered to the lock. The beautiful lock! In the daylight, I could see the hardware was original, too.

Macon's scent blasted me again upon entering the house, as if it were reminding me who it belonged to. As if I could forget. I called out to Edmond before realizing he was staring at me from the back of the couch. "Oh. Hello."

My phone lit up in my hand.

What?? Macon texted. Double question marks. I didn't know he was capable of such a crime. I reread my message and realized it might have caused him some alarm.

Your house is beautiful, and I'm jealous.

Oh. Thank you?

I headed to the kitchen. Edmond leapt off the couch and tagged behind at a safe distance. My phone lit up again.

But you've seen my house before, Macon said.

Not in daylight! You didn't tell me you were a storybook witch.

I waited nearly a minute for him to respond. Edmond made a low meow-grumble. "Oh my God. I'm so sorry." It was the same apology that I'd given the lock. I opened a can of duck pâté. My screen lit up again, and I hurried to exchange the new plate of food for the old one. I put the dirty dish in the sink and checked my texts.

I assumed my witchy demeanor had already given that away.

I smiled and sent him another picture of Edmond eating.

Macon's original farmhouse sink stood in front of a window, and as I scrubbed last night's plate, my eyes settled on the back porch for the first time. It was made out of the same stone as the rest of the exterior, and a wrought iron table and two chairs were perfectly centered on it. It looked like a photo from our game—a place where we'd rather be than work. Farther out in the yard rested a stone toolshed that looked like a miniature version of the main house, as well as a quirky greenhouse constructed out of salvaged windows.

Fuck you, I fumed inside my head.

My phone lit up. Macon had sent me a photo of mostly bare shelves containing a pitiful number of cans—I could make out asparagus spears, fruit cocktail, and Vienna sausages—an open sleeve of Ritz crackers, a box of Minute Rice, and a mousetrap. Thankfully, I couldn't tell if the trap had an occupant. The picture was blurry because Macon hadn't cleaned off the lens after removing the electrical tape that usually covered his camera.

My anger deflated. *Edmond's breakfast looks better*, I texted. *Is that Bonnie's pantry? Have you seen her yet?*

This response took a while, too, and I grew anxious as I waited.

Yeah. I'll see her later today, he finally said.

It was a conversation ender. Disappointed, I headed into Edmond's room, selected an empty tortilla chip bag from Macon's eclectic stash of litter bags, and then scooped my first box. Easy and uneventful. I set the bag by the front door so I could throw it away in his outside trash can when I left, washed my hands, and then checked my phone again.

No new texts. Forty-five minutes left before work.

Edmond appeared, so I waved a stick toy with a fleece ribbon at him. He removed his eyes from me to watch it, tempted, but didn't engage.

I sighed. "Well, would it bother you if I read for a while? I don't want to go in early."

He didn't respond, so I dug the latest novel that I'd been trying and failing to read out of my bag and then dropped onto the couch. As they always did lately, my eyes struggled to stay on the page. The couch was old and saggy with upholstery in a geometric pattern of textured neutrals that surely had been designed for the sole purpose of hiding stains. It was unquestionably the most appalling item in the house. My guess was that it had been free.

I texted Kat a photo of the upholstery, but she didn't respond.

I was about to give up and leave when Edmond sprang onto the cushion beside me and then up onto the back of the couch. He sat behind my head and stared out the window. Even though most of the garden was still dormant, it was easy to imagine how spectacular the view would be in the summertime. I didn't want to seem rude, so I picked the book back up. Edmond's ears swiveled back to listen to the sound, but his eyes remained fixed outside.

Trust. A small victory.

After a few more minutes, I finally got lost in the pages.

On my way back to Macon's house that evening, I picked up a refried bean burrito. I'd decided to eat at his place so that I could keep Edmond company, but truthfully, I wanted the company, too. My apartment was lonely, and my date with Gareth wasn't until the following day.

After doing some research at work, I'd learned that reading aloud was a good method for getting a shy cat used to your presence. I wasn't sure that Edmond qualified as shy—he wasn't hiding from me—but I still hadn't gotten to pet him or play with him, and I was determined to get him to like me before Macon returned.

We ate together, Edmond on the floor and me at the table, and then I headed back to the hideous couch with my book. After a few minutes, he took his place behind me. I hadn't heard from Macon since that morning, so I sent him a photo of Edmond at the window. *He's waiting for you to come home!* I texted. I had no idea if it was true, but I hoped it would cheer him up.

I cracked the book back open and began reading to Edmond. I didn't bother to explain where we were in the story; I figured he could catch up. It was the book that Mr. Garland had recently returned. I was intrigued by the idea of a novel so enthralling that even somebody else's uneaten bacon couldn't ruin it. It was a locked-room mystery set at a luxurious and remote inn in the French Alps between world wars. A seemingly immovable boulder had just crushed an unlikable maître d' to death, and a brilliant young governess—clearly inspired by Poirot, despite her age and lack of mustache or official detective status—was suspicious that it hadn't been an accident. She was currently scrutinizing a guest who might have been a German spy, but it was too early for this to be anything but a red herring.

I felt like my mother, reading aloud to Riley and me when we were young. Her reading voice was soothing and wise and humorous, and she was great at making all the characters sound different. Although I had never desired children of my own, nor did I have any interest in being a children's librarian—too many songs and activities—I did enjoy filling in at storytime whenever Alyssa was on vacation, and I enjoyed reading aloud to Edmond now. It felt gratifying to share a book with somebody else.

Sometime later, my phone lit up. I reached for it, expecting my memories to have summoned my mother and sister. They were still blowing up my phone. Riley had won the fight about the wedding date, and the event was set for the weekend before Christmas. The venue had been booked after further quarreling, and the current argument was about floral arrangements—red poinsettias or red roses. My mother believed poinsettias were too obvious, which had prompted my sister to retort, TELL THAT TO THE ROSES. It was odd that our mother was even arguing with her. My headstrong sister would have her way here, too.

Even more odd was that our mother was inserting herself into Riley's decision-making at all. Our parents loved us—they had always been caring and encouraging—but they also weren't very involved in our adult lives. Both of them were teachers, professionally but also naturally born, and they had taught us how to do everything as children. But then Riley and I had been *expected* to do everything. "You're smart, figure it out," they always said once we grew old enough. So we did. We stopped asking for help, and our parents never offered it. It would have felt like we were disappointing them to ask. Or disappointing ourselves.

I'll be home in time to feed him on Monday night. Is that okay or should I call a neighbor to help?

I was so glad it was Macon that I didn't think before I texted back. I held up the book and posed for a selfie between it and Edmond. *I told you, I've got this! We're bonding.*

You're still at my house?

Ooh, was that weird? Probably, but it was too late now. I had to roll with it. *I thought he might be lonely.*

It took a minute for Macon to respond. Finally he said, *That's sweet. Thank you.*

I don't know what compelled me to keep going. Perhaps because he'd used the word *sweet*, which tingled inside me like faraway music. *I ate dinner here, too.*

Something from my fridge?

What? No. I'm not stealing your food.

There's some leftover manicotti about to go bad. You should eat it. It's mushroom, not beef. Macon knew that I sometimes ate poultry and fish but never any other kind of meat. He rarely ate meat either and was an excellent cook. His leftovers would be significantly better than what I'd been consuming lately. I had assumed my meals would improve in Cory's absence, but without our regular routine, my habits had nose-dived into cheap takeout and frozen dinners.

I might actually take you up on that, I said.

Good.

As stilted as his texts were, Bonnie's place must have felt as lonely as my apartment, because these last two conversations were the longest we'd ever had over the phone.

Did you see Bonnie today?

I did, for about an hour. It was rough.

I'm so sorry.

I spent the afternoon paying overdue bills and cleaning. I found needles. I had no idea. I threw it all away.

Oh, Macon. Fuck. How awful.

Yeah. I didn't expect to find those in my seventy-four-year-old aunt's house, but there you go. America.

He told me that he was going to keep cleaning and then he would fill Bonnie's pantry with better canned goods. He wasn't sure when she was coming home, but at least she would come home to a safe space. *Not that it will last,* he added.

It was all so heartbreaking. I wished I could help him, and he insisted that I was. He meant Edmond, but there was subtext, too. Being able to talk to me was also helping him, and I wondered if we'd accidentally stumbled onto a solution to our problem. Perhaps it would be easier to revive our friendship through our screens. Perhaps it was already happening.

CHAPTER ELEVEN

I met Gareth for lunch the next day at Tommy Chickens, a Nashville hot chicken restaurant that was popular both because of its cuisine and how much fun it was to say the name out loud.

"Hot-air balloon, British telephone booth—Tommy Chickens felt suitably absurd," Gareth said.

Tommy Chickens was the perfect amount of absurd. It was tricky to maintain a sauce-free face, but I did my best and so did he, and we laughed whenever it escaped the bounds of our mouth and required a napkin. Afterward, we strolled along the river to keep the conversation flowing. I wanted to hold his hand but felt too shy to reach for it, yet I didn't feel shy at all when we came upon an unpopulated area and made out again.

Strange how holding hands now seemed like the more intimate act.

We spent the whole afternoon together, and I lost track of the time. "Shit. I need to go feed my coworker's cat. He's out of town."

"The guy who sits beside you?"

I laughed. "Oh, right. Yeah. Macon. Of course you already know who he is."

"He's kind of a serious guy, isn't he? He never really smiles."

I squirmed, realizing I didn't want to talk about Macon with Gareth. "He *is* serious, but he's fun when you get to know him."

"I work with some guys like that." Gareth snatched the end of my coat sleeve and swung it a bit. Almost my hand. "I could go with you, if you'd like. To feed the cat."

My shoulders tensed. Macon wouldn't appreciate me bringing Gareth into his house, but it wasn't something I desired either. I didn't want to discourage Gareth, though, so I switched to flirtation. "Ah, but then that would bring us to dinner. And this was lunch."

His eyes twinkled. "I'll have to think of something good for dinner, then."

A playful escalation was happening, and it seemed like we both understood that dinner would equal sex. The subject was still on my mind when I entered Macon's house alone and his scent bombarded me. I forced myself to push away the illicit thoughts.

Edmond must have heard my car arrive because he was waiting for me. I extended my hand to pet him, but he still wasn't ready, which was frustrating because I'd thought we'd made decent progress that morning. He had sniffed my hand but had backed away when I'd tried to touch him. I was hoping he might be up for it now.

"Fine, be withholding," I muttered. "Like father, like son."

Eager to get to my own dinner, I fed him briskly. I hadn't forgotten about the leftovers waiting for me. As I opened the fridge, my eyes snagged on a huge mason jar sitting on top of it. I let out a startled cry. Edmond bolted, leaving his plate rattling in a circle on the floor. The offending jar was filled with slimy brine and . . . a dead sea creature?

I sent Macon a photo. *What is this thing??*

Edmond skulked back into the kitchen, so I plucked up my courage, too. I heated the manicotti and tried not to look at the submerged stack of mucus-y pancakes. I swore it was watching me. It didn't seem to have eyes, but whatever it was, it was alive. Or had been alive.

Macon's response was so quick that I wondered if he'd been expecting me. *Kombucha.*

WHAT?

The big one on the bottom is the mother, and it eats tea and sugar and grows babies. The fermented liquid they're expelling is kombucha.

But what IS it??

A bacteria culture.

For several seconds, I was speechless. *This is so upsetting.*

You've drunk my kombucha before.

I know, but I didn't KNOW.

There was a pause, and then he said, *You can have one, if you'd like. One of the babies.*

I sent him eight million crying emojis. He would never respond with an LOL, but I knew it was happening all the same.

The microwave dinged, and I snapped a photo of the manicotti. *Thank you for this but nothing else,* I said.

Are you reading the bacon book?

Whiplash. I wondered if there was a hidden camera in the house but then remembered my selfie with Edmond. Had Macon scrolled back through our texts to look at it again?

It IS the bacon book, but it's not THE bacon book. It's East's copy. It's good!

Dinner was better than anything I'd eaten in weeks, and we chatted throughout it, breaking another record. I washed the dishes and then carried my phone to the couch. If Edmond had been a human, he would have been annoyed at how often I stopped reading the novel out loud to respond to my texts. Instead, it was as if he sensed Macon's presence on the other end because he hopped off the back of the couch and sat beside me. At last, he accepted my hand. His little tuxedo was so soft.

I spent longer than intended at Macon's house that evening and longer than intended the following morning. Edmond allowed me to pet him straight away. We did our usual routine of feeding and reading—our cozy book club of two—and I exchanged more texts with Macon. I had just reached the penultimate chapter when he told me he was getting on the road. My time there had come to an end. The last thing I needed was to get so comfortable that I fell asleep on his couch, only to wake up when he opened his front door. I used his bathroom one last time, sniffed his soap, told his cat goodbye, and left his spare key underneath the planter.

Let's do dinner, Gareth texted a short time later. *Fri?*

I was empty and antsy and didn't feel like finishing the book anymore. *What about tonight?*

As always, he was game. It was Monday, so he was working and would need to grab a shower first, but we met downtown that night at a restaurant with bland American cuisine and mediocre ambiance that neither of us had been to before.

"You ruined my plans," he said with a laugh.

"Oh no. What'd I do?"

"This isn't our date."

"It's not?"

"Nope. This is our pre-date. Our real date is next door." He grinned at my confusion. "The pinball machine museum! They don't serve food, but I was going to make a picnic for us on Friday and sneak it in. I didn't have time tonight."

I brightened with relieved laughter. "I wasn't going to say anything because I didn't want to hurt your feelings, but this place *does* feel like a misstep."

He clutched his heart. "I would have never knowingly done this to you."

I'd been to the museum a few times with Cory. Every machine was in working condition, and for one flat fee, you could play any of them for as long as you liked. It was all ages during the day, but after hours it became adults only, and they served boozy slushies. The building was packed for a weekday and rang with chimes, knocks, clacks, thunks, and bells. The volume was loud and overstimulating, and I wasn't any good at pinball, but I did enjoy trying. It was an appropriately silly location for us. He paid the fees, and I bought the slushies. I thought I was being smart by ordering watermelon—at least my mouth wouldn't be stained blue—but then he ordered piña colada, and I realized I could have had a completely neutral color.

We wandered around, triggering the flippers and watching the balls fly around and objects spin and light up. He liked the same row of antique machines that I did. They were also less crowded. The atmosphere amplified the nervousness and excitement bouncing around inside me. We flirted harder than ever, finding excuses to touch, standing so close that I could see a few stubborn splatters of gray primer on his left cheek and ringed in his nail beds. It was as if we were both waiting for the other to be brave and say, "That's enough. Let's get out of here."

A woman with influencer makeup and influencer wavy hair tripped behind us, spilling her pinky-red drink onto the carpet and the back of Gareth's jeans.

"Whoa," he said. "You okay?"

She kept stumbling toward her bachelorette party and didn't apologize.

When he looked back at me, we both cracked up. I was glad that he wasn't angry. "Your poor pants," I said. "Are *you* okay?"

"I think she had the same flavor as you. They're watermelon pants now."

"It's madness to allow drinks near all these machines."

"I assume the cost of repairs is built into the price? I noticed they weren't cheap. Thanks again," he added.

Examining the backs of his legs, I realized this was an opportunity. "If you want to save those, they need to go straight into the wash. We should go back to your place."

His eyebrows rose, and it was on.

I followed his car to a newish apartment complex near the library. Of course he lived near my branch, and I felt dense that I was surprised by this. I'd only driven past the building before, but its generic exterior reminded me of the one where Cory's friend Robin lived. I'd been dragged to several parties there. As challenging as the last few months had been, no part of me missed having to socialize in large groups of mostly strangers. Cory and I were both good with new people, but he enjoyed it more than I did and genuinely loved meeting them. Their stories gave him energy. They drained mine, and after a long day at work, I preferred returning to the familiar to recharge. Our shared days off required negotiating and compromising and taking turns with how the free time was spent.

"It's not much," Gareth said as he opened a door on the second floor.

The interior looked so much like my own apartment that it knocked me sideways. It was beige and unadorned and filled with the same build-it-yourself furniture from a decade ago.

"Okay, so it's worse than I thought," he said, taking in my expression.

I explained that I was only startled by the similarities. He relaxed, seeming comforted by this. I couldn't explain why I did not feel the same comfort.

"Something else to drink?" he asked. "Cider, soda, water?"

Another serving of alcohol seemed useful. He grabbed a cold cider for me, then excused himself to change pants. If we'd been more confident, that would have been the moment for us to lose our clothes altogether, but neither of us was Justin.

I glanced around and discovered a shelf of books beneath his extensive movie collection. Most of them appeared to be assigned novels and textbooks from his school days, but there was also some film history and criticism. I flipped through a newer biography about Buster Keaton.

"Oh no," he said, reappearing behind me. The washing machine sloshed in another room. "I've been dreading this. Please don't judge me by my books."

I forced my mouth into a smile. "I would never."

This was a lie, but his books were also fine. I wasn't sure why I felt uneasy. Maybe because he'd imagined me in his apartment before, inspecting and scrutinizing his life, but I had never imagined him in mine. This did make me feel bad—I had more information about our lack of a future than he did—but something else was rumbling inside me, too.

We settled onto his couch, ostensibly to watch something. It reminded me of my earliest dates with Cory, when we still needed an excuse to sit beside each other and fool around. I started, realizing Gareth's couch was the *exact* same model as mine, only with navy upholstery instead of red.

"What?" he asked, alarmed.

"This is my couch. We have the same couch."

He laughed in relief, and I pretended to laugh, and after a few seconds it eased into the real thing. I was nervous, that was all. Condensation slipped down the bottle in my hand. He was asking what I wanted to watch when the tiny splatters of primer on his cheek caught in the television's flickering light. They looked like a constellation of stars. I set down my drink and touched them gently. His eyes closed, and unlike those earliest dates with Cory, the situation escalated immediately into sex. But we fumbled more than Cory and I did now, which made sense because this was new, yet we also fumbled more than I had with Justin. Perhaps this was because Gareth and I never left the couch. Our bodies were too aroused to take it elsewhere. The correct buttons were hit and experiences were had. Yet afterward, I felt deflated.

The way he gazed at me warned that he did not feel the same way.

A siren went off inside me. I did not spend the night with him. He offered, but I used work as an excuse. I was so rattled that I forgot I'd be seeing Macon in the morning and didn't get nervous until I was sitting behind the desk the next day and saw his car pull into the lot. Were we friends again? Or would things still be weird in person?

My heart was thumping as he entered through the double doors. Our eyes met, and he halted. His expression looked hesitant and exhausted . . . but it also held a glimmer of hope.

I broke into a warm smile that seemed to surprise him.

He smiled back reflexively. But then self-consciousness engulfed him, and he hurried off to the annex, presumably to catch up with Sue. I awaited his return anxiously and regreeted him enthusiastically. His skittish response reminded me of Edmond. I was coming on too strong. I backed off to let him get used to my physical presence again.

That week, we resided in a liminal space between politeness and friendship. We conversed about subjects other than work, but we didn't tease each other as we used to. We were overly respectful of boundaries. We stayed on our own sides of the desk. But we were taking steps in the right direction and finally seemed to be on our way to course correcting.

The hiccup occurred on Thursday night when Gareth arrived. Macon disappeared with his watering can again and didn't reappear until Gareth had left, but there was no way he hadn't overheard us discussing our upcoming plans. Once more, Macon's mood soured, but he didn't lash out at me, nor did I try to provoke him. Instead, we retreated into frustrated silence. He was jealous—it was so obvious—yet I still couldn't decipher the implications.

No. Ingrid. No.

That weekend, against my better judgment, I did spend the night at Gareth's. I thought that being in his company would quell my loneliness, but as I lay beside him in a bed strikingly similar to my own—as he slept soundly and I kept checking the clock on my phone—the truth shook loose and broke inside me. I liked him, the dates were fun, and the sex had improved. But I wanted to run screaming from his apartment. Something was deeply, fundamentally wrong.

"Maybe it's his coloring," I said to Kat as soon as I could escape to FaceTime her. "His hair and eyes are so similar to Cory's."

"He doesn't look anything like Cory," she said.

He did, though, a bit. His sense of humor was similar to Cory's, too, not to mention the shared appreciation for a themed location. But why was it so distressing that we had the same pathetic furniture? It wasn't like Macon—it felt shameful to still be comparing other men to the man who had rejected me—had amazing furniture. Arguably, his couch was even worse.

"But Macon's couch is inside a house," Kat pointed out. "And he cooks adult meals and tends an established garden. His decor might be shit, but he's firmly in another phase of life. It sounds like Gareth is making you anxious because he's in the same phase as you and Cory."

"Shouldn't that be a good thing? To be in the same phase of life?"

"Maybe. Unless you don't want to be there anymore."

It hit me like a sledgehammer. One sentence shattered me into pieces that could never fit back together the way they used to be.

"You need to break up with him," Kat said, not realizing what she had done. "It's already gone on too long."

I could barely say it. "Cory?"

"*Gareth*." Her expression changed. "Oh my God. It finally happened. You finally just realized that you need to break up with Cory."

It wasn't true, though. As startling as it was to learn that she had been expecting it this whole time, I hadn't reached that conclusion yet. I still didn't understand that breaking up had always been the inevitable and only possible way this could end. I reeled and sputtered.

Kat realized her mistake and backtracked to refocus my attention on Gareth. "One step at a time," she said. "Let's do this first. Then we can figure out Cory."

"What am I supposed to say to him?"

"To Cory?" she said.

"*Gareth*," I said.

She advised me to tell the truth, but how could I do that to him? From Gareth's perspective, we were heading in the direction of becoming an actual couple. He wasn't living inside my world of pretend. I'd asked him out, we'd gone on a series of adorable dates, and then we'd slept together multiple times. I'd given him no reason to suspect that I was already taken.

I'm sorry, I texted him that evening, after ignoring his texts all day. *I can't see you anymore because I'm getting back together with my boyfriend.* I didn't know if I was lying, but it was close to the truth. Cory and I would at least be seeing each other again. I was simply withholding a few crucial details that would only make the situation worse.

Normally Gareth responded immediately, but this reply took several minutes. The three dots appeared and disappeared. *I don't understand. Is this a joke?*

I'm sorry, I said again. *It's not. You're a great guy, and I had so much fun with you. I wish you all the best.*

WOW. Seriously?? Fuck you too.

An arrow shot through my chest. His hurt and pain leapt off the screen as if they were written in pulsing neon. Heat flushed my skin. He was a nice person. I was a nice person. I hadn't meant to do this to him. I didn't treat people this way. Kat's words from late February rushed back to me: *and then feel guilty about how you treated him for the rest of your life.*

My world tipped over sideways. I supposed it had tipped over on Christmas, but I hadn't noticed how tightly I'd been holding on to the edge until I finally lost my grip and fell.

The next few days spun in a nauseous whirl. Kat tried to press me about Cory, but my thoughts were unraveling so quickly, so catastrophically, that I didn't dare speak any of them out loud. I began to ignore her calls.

I had never been able to see my future with Cory in any kind of detail. There wasn't anything, apart from a vague sense of *more*, that I was looking forward to. The realization was devastating. Cory himself had been the only part of it that I could see, but now it seemed this was because he'd been blocking the view of every other possible future, and I had been doing the same for him. Maybe. Probably. I couldn't be sure yet, but I was certain there would be no threat of a ring in April. Perhaps there never had been.

My mood and behavior at work became so erratic and abnormal that Macon's attitude toward me shifted again, and he grew protective. He tried to provide space for me. He answered the phone, jumped to help patrons approaching the desk, volunteered to assist people with the computers. He didn't know what was going on with me because I didn't tell him. But on Thursday, he dared to ask, "Is your boyfriend coming in tonight?"

He didn't mean Cory. My reply was sharp but guarded. "I doubt it."

He did not ask any follow-up questions.

The days continued to slip by, out of control. An outraged book banner showed up during another late shift. Macon was straightening the periodicals in the back when the woman marched straight to my station, screeching about a list of books in our collection she hadn't read—they never read the books, which was part of the problem—and then accused me of being a pedophile. I wasn't strong enough to take it. My backbone had broken. And although I had a personal rule to never let the hatemongers see me cry, it was too late. She spat another abuse behind me as I ran full throttle toward the annex, and then Macon was roaring at her to exit the premises.

I burst into the restroom—and into racking sobs. My body collapsed against the wall beside the sink, searching for support, and slid down until my limbs crumpled onto the floor. I heaved and gasped. Wailed. Gasped again, in shock, and covered my mouth. Snot and tears bubbled into my hands. I was breathing so rapidly that I *couldn't* breathe.

A knock on the door. "Ingrid?"

I cried and choked, gripping onto myself so tightly that my nails dug into my flesh.

"Ingrid?" Macon said again. He tried the handle and let out a noise of surprise when it wasn't locked. "Ingrid, I'm coming in."

The door opened cautiously, just wide enough for his head to poke in. When he saw me, he hastened inside and began grabbing paper towels. He was the one who'd placed the REMEMBER . . . THESE COME FROM TREES stickers on our dispenser, but now he kneeled beside me and handed me an entire fistful like a bouquet.

I was aware that I was sprawled on the floor of a public restroom and felt all the accompanying revulsion and self-loathing, yet I was helpless to do anything about it. I wiped my face with the paper towels, continuing to sob, still unable to breathe.

"Do what I do." His voice was firm. "We're going to make our exhalations longer than our inhalations." He demonstrated loudly, shortening his inhalations to mirror mine but then exhaling for a few seconds longer. "Look at me. *Look at me.*"

He forced my eyes to meet his. With each breath, our inhalations lengthened. Our exhalations lengthened even further. We inhaled. We exhaled. Inhaled. Exhaled.

"There," he said a minute later.

I was breathing again.

"That woman was abhorrent," he said. "A goblin. I will murder her."

I laugh-choked. But although my tears had quieted, they still spilled. He pried the crumpled paper towels from my hands, threw them away, and handed me a fresh one.

My voice wobbled. "It's not just her."

"I know," he said.

I couldn't speak anymore, and he didn't ask me to.

"Hello?" a man called out at the circulation desk.

"Shit." Macon started to leave but just as quickly stopped. He took off his thick duffel coat and draped it over me like a blanket. The tile floor was cold, and I was shivering. He left, but two seconds later the door swung back open. His head was shaking as if he were the fool. "I just remembered there's a handkerchief in the pocket. If you need it."

He left again.

My muscles felt weak, my bones heavy. I hugged the coat with my whole body the same way I hugged Cory's pillow in bed. It was the closest I could get to the comforting presence of another person, and some nights, it was the only way I was able to fall asleep. Did I imagine Cory in its place? I did, sometimes. But other times it was somebody else, somebody nameless because my loyalty to Cory still lingered. The coat was warm and weighty and smelled like Macon. Smelled like his house. I breathed in the concentrated scent.

A few minutes later, he returned with an oversize hardcover about the Faroe Islands. He squatted beside me again and opened it to a photograph of a stone cottage with a sod roof that overlooked a windswept sea.

"Let's close early and go here," he said. "We'll light a fire. Put the kettle on."

"We'll wear our oldest and most comfortable sweaters."

He smiled. "I'll bake bread."

"I'll sleep."

We held each other's gaze until it became too much. He broke away first and placed the book into my lap. "I'll handle everything out there. Stay here as long as you need to."

He meant both the floor and the cottage.

CHAPTER TWELVE

And then, one blustery morning, Cory texted me. *We need to talk. Can you meet me after work?*

The unexpected contact shocked me. A few days had passed since the restroom incident, but eight days still remained in the month. The fact that he couldn't wait one more week thrust me into a spiral. My head separated from my body.

It was happening. I knew it was going to happen, and I was preparing for it to happen, but I was not ready for it to actually happen.

Thankfully, Sue believed in mental health days. "I'm only surprised this is the first one you've taken," she said, though not unkindly. It was more than mental, though. I spent the day physically immobilized in bed.

This time, however, I managed to arrive early to the diner.

This time, however, Cory was already there.

My heart leapt—and then plummeted back down. He was sitting at the *Diner*-themed table. The universe was gifting us the providence of closure. A strange calm washed over me.

He held up his hands. "I swear I didn't request it."

I smiled even though my soul was splitting. "I know."

He stood and hugged me, and we held on to each other for a long time. It didn't matter that we both wanted and needed what was coming. The *Pulp Fiction* table would have been more appropriate because I felt as if I were about to be annihilated.

We sat down, quiet and already close to tears.

"Thanks for meeting me on short notice," he said.

"Did you work today?" I asked, glancing around for our server. It didn't feel right to break up before ordering our food. I didn't want to be interrupted.

"Uh—no." He said the word *no* with a certain hesitation and weight. There was more to the story, but I wasn't sure what. "Did you?" he asked. And then he shook his head. "Of course you did."

"I didn't, actually. I just . . . couldn't."

"Yeah," he said. "I get that."

A woman who looked to be in her early twenties appeared with our waters. She had dyed-black hair and black short shorts, and her pale legs were covered in colorful tattoos. The name on her shirt read JO. "Can I get you all something else to drink?" she asked.

"A Coke, thanks." Cory seemed anxious for us to be left alone again. "And I'll have the chicken tenders and fries, and she'll have the grilled cheese and tomato soup."

"Actually"—after the day in bed, my body craved breakfast—"I'd like two eggs, sunny-side up, whole-grain toast with strawberry jam, and hash browns."

Jo scratched her pad. "You got it."

Cory's eyebrows rose a little behind his glasses.

"Shit," I said, remembering who I was with. "No eggs."

"It's okay," Cory said, even though eggs grossed him out more than anything. I never ordered them when he was around.

Jo waited for me to make the decision myself.

"You sure?" I asked Cory, and he said of course. "All right. The eggs, too."

When we were alone again, he teased me, "Something new, huh?" He was only talking about my order, but as he heard the words out loud, his smile faded. Our silence was awful. Forks and plates scraped and clinked around us, diners chattered and guffawed, and the jukebox played the movie version of "La Bamba." Cory's expression squinched in agony. "I don't even know how to tell you this, so I'm just going to say it—"

"You want to break up," I said, as he said, "I met someone."

There was a moment of quaking stillness. And then the dam broke.

"Oh," I said. "*Oh*."

His eyes brimmed with tears. "I didn't mean for this to happen. I'm so sorry."

A flood of emotions was rushing through me. Drowning me. "Who? How?" My hands waved as if for a life preserver. "No, don't tell me. I don't think I want that yet." What I meant was, *I don't think I want that information yet*. But I didn't want this either. I didn't want Cory to already have somebody else.

"I'm so sorry," he said again.

Any eloquence I had was gone. "This sucks."

"It does."

"I was going to break up with you next week, and it *still* sucks."

"You were?" He was bent over with misery and guilt, but at this he perked up.

"We aren't right for each other."

"No."

"Do you love her?"

He blew his nose on a napkin. "I don't know. We aren't actually dating. It's complicated. I asked her out, and she laughed at me and said I needed to get my shit together. But . . . I have this feeling. I'm wild about her. I haven't felt this way in a long time." He watched my face fall. "Oh, Ig—"

"No." I stopped him. "I get it. I haven't . . . felt that way either."

Jo reappeared with our plates. "One chicken tenders, one breakfast." She clocked the condiments area on our table. "Shoot. No ketchup." As she ducked into the booth behind Cory to grab a bottle, my eyes caught on her legs. Most of her tattoos were flowers, but the hippo-like body of Moomintroll jumped out at me from among the blooms. And then I spotted Wilbur the pig, Pippi Longstocking, and Winnie-the-Pooh. I'd been holding my feelings in, but at the sight of these childhood friends, my lip wobbled. Triumphantly, Jo set a bottle of Heinz between us, but then she saw our expressions. I pried my gaze up from her legs, because the last thing I wanted was to make her any more uncomfortable. She scooted away with an apologetic mumble.

When Cory realized I was crying, he cried again, too. He moved to my side of the booth. We clung to each other in the pink light through three songs on the jukebox.

"Who is that?" he finally whispered, pointing to the collaged picture beside my plate of a handsome young man with swooping hair pouring sugar into his mouth.

"Mickey Rourke," I said.

"*What?*"

I wiped my cheeks.

"That is not Mickey Rourke," he said.

"Haven't you seen *Diner?*"

"Yeah, but not the one where Mickey Rourke is hot."

We laughed, and he squeezed me again before moving back to his side. "So," I said, poking a yolk and letting it run. He squirmed a little, which gave me a stab of pleasure. "She thinks you need to get your shit together."

He cleared his throat. "Oh my God. I'm a mess."

"Tell me more so I'll feel better."

"Well, I got fired."

"What?" I almost choked on the egg. Cory had always been responsible and reliable. A valuable employee.

"I don't want to get into it," he said, which made me wonder again about the hotel's policy regarding sleeping with the guests.

"What are you gonna do?"

"A guy I know who runs a B&B is going on vacation and needs an inn-sitter."

I didn't know inn-sitters were a thing, but it made sense. Otherwise their owners would never get out of town. We discussed the job until the conversation trailed off.

Diner was about being an adult but not being grown-up yet. It was about old friends finally being forced into adulthood, even though they're mostly doing a bad job of it. They're terrified of who they might become, who they might marry, and where their lives might be headed. It had taken less than three months for Cory and me to destroy something that we had believed was indestructible. We had spent our entire adult lives together. Now he was moving on, and I was alone.

"So . . . there's nobody?" Cory asked.

Another server, arms laden with platters of food, passed our table. A pen was tucked behind his ear.

"No." I set down my fork, unable to stomach the rest of my meal. "There's nobody."

CHAPTER THIRTEEN

I looked for her on social media. The search was easy. Who had Cory recently followed? I expected to find a gaggle of new women, but it turned out he'd only followed one.

Her name was Holland.

She was a musician.

She had dimples.

Cory had been liking her photos since the beginning of January. That stung. I scrolled further back and found a post of her celebrating her thirty-third birthday. It made sense to me that he'd fallen in love with somebody older than us. We'd both been searching for the same elusive thing that we couldn't find in each other: a future. There was a future in that sort of maturity and stability, in that wisdom and guidance. We each wanted somebody who we could grow into the next stage of our lives with. Although we had entered adulthood together, at some point we'd begun to hold each other back. We had both been stuck in our youth for so long.

CHAPTER FOURTEEN

Of course her name was cooler than mine. Of course he'd fallen for a musician. Of course her dimples were so deep they were visible even when she wasn't smiling.

Of course I wanted him to be happy.

Of course I wanted her to break his heart.

Of course I didn't *actually* want that.

Of course I just wanted to be the one who was happy first.

CHAPTER FIFTEEN

I called in sick again the following day, and Cory came by to pick up the rest of his belongings. He planned to store everything in Robin's spare bedroom while he was inn-sitting, which would give him time to figure out where to go next.

"It feels weird to be back." He scratched his head, taking it all in. "Kind of like visiting my parents' house."

I bristled.

"I mean it's like visiting home when it's not actually your home anymore. But some piece of you, a ghost, is still wandering the rooms."

I thought about that and softened. "I've felt your ghost."

"I guess it would have been hard not to with my stuff still here. Are you planning to stay?" He knew that money would be tight. I probably wouldn't have to dip into my savings, but I would no longer be able to contribute to it. My paychecks would be fully stretched.

"I'll stay until the lease runs out this summer. Or who knows, maybe I'll renew. I'm not in any state to find a new place to live."

He laughed, but he was choking up. "Right there with you."

Which he was. But it was also sort of the point that he wasn't.

We grieved as we loaded his car with his clothes, his record player and vinyl, his novels and comic books, some of the kitchenware. Our shared items weren't difficult to divide because neither of us was attached to any of it. He didn't take a single piece of furniture. Everything was particleboard, cheap and disposable. We had never put down roots anywhere or in anything or in each other, yet we cried and clung to one another in the parking lot.

"I wish it had been you," I said into his shoulder.

"I wish it had been you, too," he said into mine.

That night, when the stupid pull chain on my bedside lamp dinged loudly against its metal base, I recalled the lonely matching lamps and side tables in Macon's bedroom. I had tried to convince Cory to take his, but he hadn't wanted them. I didn't blame him for that, nor did I blame him for anything else. I shivered as the temperature plunged below freezing, and when I awoke, many of the flowers on the trees—the most fragile and tender spring buds—were dead.

I thought I'd used up all my tears before we'd broken up, but it turned out those had only been the tears that were immediately accessible. I was tapped into the reserves now, and my spout was all the way open. The waterworks never stopped. I cried so much that first week that I became dehydrated. I began crying while chugging glasses of water, crying in the shower, crying outside in the rain. Water went in, water went out, water was everywhere.

I apologized to Kat for ignoring her calls. "There's nothing to forgive," she said. "I understood what was happening." But I still had to tell my coworkers. I dreaded having to admit that Cory and I had not survived our experiment, just as I dreaded the look that might pass between Sue and Macon, who had known it all along. Kat, Sue, Macon—they had all seen our future. Why had it been obvious to them but not to us?

By the time I arrived on Tuesday morning, my coworkers had already divined my truth again, and there was not a trace of smugness to be found. Sue and Alyssa each held me in a long embrace. Macon did not hug me, but he was worried and kind, and he covered for me whenever I needed to go outside to cry. That day was also Elijah's twenty-first birthday. Sue had brought in a drenched rum cake that I couldn't stomach, and that night we received a message in our group text in which Elijah proclaimed himself to be *LEGALLY DRINK!!* instead of *DRUNK!!*, which Macon would razz him about forever. Apart from that, I retained few memories from that first week without Cory.

One more does jump out, though. My fridge was bare, so I forced myself to stop by the grocery store one evening after work. I was trying to be responsible. I was trying to feed myself.

I was not hungry.

My sister called and found me lost in the produce section. The options were overwhelming, and I couldn't remember what I needed or wanted or even liked. So far, I'd placed an onion and an out-of-season carton of blueberries into my basket.

"Hey," I said. Carrots? Maybe carrots?

"So you *are* alive," Riley said.

"Sorry. I've been busy."

"Busy."

"Yeah." I picked up a bag of carrots. Set it down. Did they have the unbagged kind?

"So are you busy *now*?"

"No. What do you want?"

Her silence was so sharp and bladed that it cut through to me. *Oh my God*, I realized. *I answered the phone. I'm going to have to tell my sister.* Obviously, I would have to tell my family eventually, but I wanted to wait until I wasn't so broken. I didn't want to answer their questions about what had gone wrong. *I didn't even know what had gone wrong: nothing, but everything?*

I clutched my phone harder but affected a brighter tone. "Sorry, I was distracted! You okay? Have you and Mom settled on the floral arrangements yet?"

"The floral arrangements."

"Isn't that why you're calling? For backup?" I was grasping. "Mom wanted something, and you wanted . . . that other thing?"

"We settled on the arrangements weeks ago, and I'm calling because I've barely heard from you all year." When I didn't respond, she pressed. "What's going on? Because it feels like you're avoiding me, and I just texted Cory, and he said I should try calling you again, but then he wouldn't tell me why. Which is extremely unlike Cory."

"I guess I feel like I don't have much to offer. You and Mom seem to have this covered."

"That's not what I'm talking about. Are you okay? Where have you been?"

"Here! I'm here, I'm working. I've been busy."

Riley grew terse again, an angry nurse tired of dealing with other people's bullshit. "Yeah. You mentioned that."

"Fuck," I said, my voice wavering. A woman with a toddler strapped into her shopping cart glared at me, so I turned around to face a dusty mound of baking potatoes. "I can't do this right now," I whispered.

"Do *what?*"

And then I began to cry again, and Riley's frustration transformed into alarm. I'd never cried on the phone with her before. "Iggy. Ig! You have to tell me what's going on."

"Cory moved out," I choked.

"Oh my God." My sister was stunned. "When?"

"Just after Christmas. After your engagement."

"*What?* Why didn't you say something? Why didn't you tell me?"

I set down my basket and stumbled outside in a sobbing haze. It didn't occur to me to get into my car. Instead, I crouched beside the big metal box where bagged ice was stored and used it as a protective shield. I told her about the experiment, the failed dates, the successful dates, the breakup. I told her about everything except for Macon. Those redactions were still too humiliating, too private. There was something *more* there that I wasn't ready to touch.

Riley took a shuddering breath, internalizing my story and holding it safe for me, little sister morphing into big. "I wish you had told me. I understand why you didn't, but I could have at least taken you off the wedding texts with Mom."

"Oh God. I have to tell them. Mom and Dad."

"You do," she said. "But you don't have to do it today."

"I don't think I want to tell them that Cory and I have been dating other people. I don't think they'll get it."

"Do *you* get it?"

"I thought I did?"

Her laughter was crestfallen. "I've missed you. And I wish I'd known. I wouldn't have texted you so many pictures of white dresses."

"No, I'm sorry I haven't been there for you. For the record, I'm always on your side. Who cares what Mom wants? She already had a wedding."

"Thank you," Riley said, as if to say, *That's what I've been saying this whole goddamn time.*

"She's probably just being overbearing because it's something she's helping pay for."

"Yeah, well, I would have preferred if she and Dad had put their chunk of the wedding money toward my nursing school instead. *That* would have been more helpful."

"Seriously," I said. "Although she's also probably being like this because she figured I would've gotten married years ago, so she's had all of these plans piling up and going nowhere."

"In that case, I'll tell her she can save them for you."

"Oh God. I'm never getting married."

My sister quieted. "You know, I can't tell if you mean that you don't think anybody will ever want to marry you or that *you* never want to get married. It's okay if you don't want to," she added quickly. "But if you do . . . you can still have that. Cory is only one guy."

I didn't know what I meant. When I was younger, I had wanted to get married, but then not wanting to marry Cory had confused the situation. Not to mention the fact that if he had asked me, I think I would have said yes. It would have seemed like the correct thing to do. What was I supposed to do with that knowledge about myself? It made me so ashamed.

"Excuse me," a new voice said.

I started and blinked up from behind the ice box. It was the woman who'd glared at me for cursing in front of her toddler. Her expression was sympathetic as she held out a plastic grocery bag. "I don't mean to intrude," she said, "but I saw that you were still out here."

She gestured for me to accept the bag, and I did. Inside was my onion, the carton of blueberries, and a box of tissues.

Kat, Brittany and Reza, my coworkers, my sister, this stranger.

I was never as alone as I thought I was. I often had trouble seeing it, but in this moment—with my sister in my ear and this stranger in front of me—it shone like the waxing gibbous moon rising over the darkest edge of the parking lot. I was lucky, and I knew it. I was grateful to be surrounded by so many steady hands.

April

DATE DUE	BORROWER'S NAME	ROOM NUMBER
JAN 25		
FEB 19		
MAR 30		
APR 17		

CHAPTER SIXTEEN

I had always disliked April Fools' Day. Like most librarians, I prided myself on knowledge—knowing at least something about almost everything—so it felt unbearable to be caught unawares, proven gullible, or deceived. For instance, I knew the holiday had been around for centuries but that historians still weren't sure where it originated. I also knew that I was a fool. I had been caught unawares, proven gullible, and deceived myself. It felt as if Cory and I had spent the last eleven years playing an elaborate and cruel prank on ourselves.

Telling my parents about the breakup had been harder than telling Riley. I hated having to admit to them that I had failed at something very big and very basic, something that should have been obvious to me because it had been obvious to so many others. But my parents didn't treat me the way I was treating myself. They were sad for me and surprised. They were understanding and kind. And they told me, as they often had, that I could handle it. I would figure out how to get through it.

It was one of those evenings when my loneliness was so raw it was incapacitating. When I wished I had the sort of parents who would go the extra mile, drive the literal miles up from Florida to comfort me in person. They had only visited me twice, though, once when Cory and I had first moved here, and then again a couple of years later. It was the first Sunday of the month, and I had been home alone all day. Weekends were hard. At least work provided a distraction. It was still early, but I was already in bed when there was a muffled *thunk* outside my front door.

My eyes shot open. I listened.

Nothing.

Realizing it was probably a delivery I'd forgotten about—perhaps even the care package of Australian chocolates that Kat told me she'd sent, although it was too quick to actually be that—I settled back down. But then my phone illuminated in the blackness of my bedroom: Macon. We hadn't texted since I'd watched Edmond, so I reached for my phone with curiosity. He was the only person apart from Kat and Riley that I would have picked it up for. A blurry photo showed a stack of containers on my welcome mat.

Try to eat something, the message said.

I lurched out of bed. I was expecting to find him already down in the parking lot, but when I threw open my front door, he'd only just reached the stairs.

He turned around in surprise.

"How do you know where I live?" I wasn't sure why this was my first question because I didn't mind that he knew where I lived.

"I dropped you off once when your car broke down."

"Oh. Right." I was still confused, though. "But how did you know which apartment was mine?"

"Library card," he said, as if it was obvious. I supposed it should have been. He winced. "Sorry. I tried to do this quietly. I haven't seen you eat anything all week, so I thought you might need . . . something."

I hadn't even told him about my unsuccessful trip to the grocery store, so I was surprised that he'd noticed. I looked down at the containers. There were five, neatly stacked by size. Every week, he doubled most of his cooking and delivered the extra meals to his mother, who lived in his same neighborhood. This week, he must have tripled it. I lifted the Pyrex off my welcome mat, a half circle of a yellow sun with cheerful rays.

"I like your mat," he said.

I snorted.

"I do," he insisted.

We stared at each other for a moment.

"See you on Tuesday morning," he said, and turned abruptly to leave.

I thanked him as I tried to get back inside, but it was tricky holding all the heavy glass containers. He noticed and hurried over to hold open the door. I caught his curious glance into the darkness behind me. "You can come in," I said, already heading toward the kitchen.

Macon hesitated.

And then he followed me inside. The door shut softly behind him. I set the Pyrex on my counter and flicked on the switch. As he stepped into the light, he inhaled in a way that meant he was smelling something in the air. "Oh God. Does it stink?" I sniffed myself. "I didn't shower today. Or clean all week. Or for the last month."

"No." He looked embarrassed, as if I'd caught him doing something secret. "I was only noticing that it smells like you."

"Oh," I said. Because I wasn't sure what else to say. Also, I hoped I didn't smell like a dirty apartment. Suddenly I became aware that I had been lisping. That I was still wearing my night guard. "Shit," I said, taking it out. *Thit*. I rinsed it off in the sink and set it in the dish rack to dry. "I'm sorry. That's so gross."

"It's not gross," he said.

Under the harsh overhead light of my kitchen, I felt exposed in my sadness and night guard and pajamas. The pajama bottoms were old and thin with stripes of pale pink and white. I was braless underneath my white camisole. Thankfully, I had also worn a thick cardigan to bed. I wrapped it over my chest, blushing, wondering if he'd noticed and what he'd seen.

He took an unusually large step toward my counter. "Uh, so it's just a few things that I thought would be easy to eat and would keep well in your fridge." His gaze was averted, determinedly giving me some privacy as he unstacked the containers. "Kale salad with spiced walnuts, sesame noodles with edamame, avocado and tempeh bacon sandwiches—"

"Sandwiches?"

"—salsa verde bean enchiladas, and roasted pumpkin soup. Maybe eat the sandwiches first. They'll taste better now."

"A few things," I said.

His embarrassment seemed to intensify, so I backed off and started loading everything into my fridge. "Thank you. It all sounds great." I picked up the soup container and examined the pretty pale orange color. "You said this is pumpkin?"

"From my jack-o'-lantern last Halloween. I had some puree left in my freezer."

"You carved a jack-o'-lantern?"

"My neighborhood gets a lot of trick-or-treaters."

I turned to look at him directly again. "Are you one of those people who hands out boxes of raisins?"

His eyes held mine. "Granola."

It made me smile.

"I give them candy," he said.

My smile deepened. "I know you do."

We stared at each other for a beat too long. A pulse of energy ricocheted between us. It was the same charged thrill I had felt during all those years before I'd tried to kiss him. My smile faded. I turned away from him, hurt and confused.

"Ingrid," he said.

I had never heard him say my name like that. With sorrow.

I was crying again. That damned faucet, wide open.

"Oh God," he said with surprise. He glanced around and saw that my living room was littered with crumpled tissues. He grabbed a handful. They weren't clean, but he picked up the snotty dried tissues anyway and brought them to me.

"Sorry," he said. "I don't see the box."

"What's wrong with me?" I asked. But what I meant was: *Why can't I stop crying? Why didn't it work out with Cory? Why didn't I see it coming? Why didn't you want to kiss me?* I wanted his arms to wrap around me. I wanted to be comforted and tightly held. I would have accepted even a loose hug. I didn't know what he thought of me, but I did know he cared for me. That much was obvious. Yet he didn't touch me.

"Nothing's wrong with you," he said, reaching for the empty spot behind his ear where his pen normally sat. His hand ran through his hair instead. "It just takes time."

"I'm so tired of crying."

"You'll stop eventually."

I managed to laugh. "Like, soon?"

"Eventually."

"Fuck," I said, and blew my nose.

"Your apartment looks different from how I imagined it." He was trying to get me to think about something else. His arms crossed, as if he were giving himself the hug that I wanted, before he drifted away to examine my belongings. There wasn't much to look at, but he stared at my bookshelves for a long time.

"How did you imagine it?" I finally managed to ask.

"Like your welcome mat. Colorful. Warm. Friendly."

"Ha, no. It's very beige. Our landlord won't allow us to decorate the walls."

He peeked into my bedroom, but the light was off. Mirroring my own behavior at his house, he didn't turn it on.

"Decent view, though," I said. I'd stopped leaking, so I led him onto the back patio that overlooked the woods.

"That is nice," he agreed.

"Maybe I'll eat your sandwiches out here."

He laughed.

"You're one to talk," I said, circling the conversation back around. "Making fun of my apartment when you've got that whole empty house."

"I wasn't making fun of it. It was an observation."

"Ah, okay. Sure."

We leaned against the railing and stared into the sky. It was a clear, cold night, and the moon was a breath away from fullness. The pines tasted fresh and sharp in my lungs.

"So. Did Cory take all the good stuff, too?" he asked.

"We didn't have any good stuff. But yes, I noticed Danielle took all of yours."

He laughed again, but it was darker and more tired.

"Seriously, what's that about?"

"It was her stuff." He shrugged. "I've been meaning to replace it, but . . . I don't know. There's always so much work to do in the garden."

"What about winter? Couldn't you liven it up during the offseason?"

"When it's cold outside, I'd rather read."

I understood this instinct—understood it completely—yet I still didn't accept it as an excuse. "It could be so cute, though. Your house has great bones. And it wouldn't take much, not really. A few curtains and rugs, some new furniture, definitely some paint—"

Macon was already grumbling.

"Seriously, that bland kitchen is not worthy of your vegetables and herbs."

"Oh God. Now I'm bland."

"Your *kitchen* is bland. Your house shouldn't look so much like my apartment."

I thought I could score another laugh, but his expression grew somber again. "I took care of the outside," he said, "and Dani handled the inside. It was unspoken, but that was the deal. When she moved out, we had just gotten vaccinated, and I still wasn't comfortable going into stores." He sighed, and it puffed in a visible cloud. "Now it just seems like a lot of effort."

"You *took care* of the outside. She *handled* the inside."

"I don't know why you're emphasizing it like that."

"I'm just saying . . . maybe it's time to take care of the inside."

"Look who's talking."

"Hey." I nudged him. "My relationship ended a week ago. You've had two years."

"You're right," he said, touching the place on his arm where I'd bumped him. And then he shoved away from the railing. "I should go."

"What?"

He was already headed back to my front door. I trailed after him. "I'm serious," he said, avoiding my eyes again. "Eat something, okay?"

Macon abandoned me to a familiar turmoil, although this time I wasn't sure what I had done to make him leave so suddenly. But I did decide to eat the soup because he'd gone to all that trouble. As I reached for the refrigerator door, I froze. A dozen faded images of myself with Cory were smiling back at me. I'd remembered to hide our framed photos from potential suitors, yet I'd looked right past these. They were such a part of the landscape that they'd become invisible. Cory and I had forgotten about the photos still hidden in the closet, just like we'd forgotten to divide these. Or perhaps he'd left them all behind on purpose, forcing me to make the decision about whether to keep them or throw them away.

I never had brought another man into our apartment. I wasn't sure why, other than that I hadn't wanted them there. Yet I'd invited Macon inside without any thought.

My tears fell again for what Cory and I had lost by breaking up. For what we had lost by staying together for so long. I wondered if breaking up had been a mistake.

I knew that it wasn't, and that felt even worse.

CHAPTER SEVENTEEN

And then my tears dried up, and I was empty.

CHAPTER EIGHTEEN

The shell version of me appeared. My consciousness climbed out into the universe, searching for a new vessel, and my body was left behind, hard and empty. The shell went to my job and stood in my place. It spoke, answered questions, and made decisions. I had felt everything all at once for months. Now I felt nothing.

Mostly I don't remember what happened while I was a shell.

But my shell did make two big declarations without me.

The first: My coworkers were chatting and doing things around my shell at the circulation desk. Alyssa asked if I was still using the dating app. My shell answered that I didn't plan on dating anybody for a long time because I needed to figure myself out first. (Actually, my shell said, "I need to date myself first." Which was a good sentiment, I guess, but kill me.)

Macon was standing right there when those words came out of my mouth.

* * *

The second: My fifth anniversary as a librarian arrived. Sue gave me a congratulations card and pointed out that it was also, coincidentally, the last day that I could apply to library school.

My shell thanked her for the card but announced that it had decided not to go.

CHAPTER NINETEEN

Something needed to change, and I began to believe it was my hair. "I think I'm gonna get bangs," I said, holding my hair over my forehead to show Kat.

"Under no circumstances," she said.

"Why not?"

"I refuse to allow you become a cliché. If you still want a fringe in three months, fine. But you are in no condition to be making major decisions about your hair right now."

I dropped my hair, dejected. "But I think it might be cute."

"Hold on." By the way she was staring at her screen, I could tell she was pulling up an app. "I'm writing it down: July. If you still want a fringe in July, you'll have my full support. I'll even pay for it myself. Consider it an early birthday present."

"Oh God. I'm turning thirty this October."

"I know."

"This isn't how I imagined my life would be at thirty."

"None of us thought this would be our lives at thirty. Our parents never told us that the economy would be shit and that we'd have no jobs or money or houses." Kat and Lachlan were saving up for a place outside of town with some land for Howie to run around on, but they wouldn't be able to afford it for several more years.

"My parents got married right out of college," I said.

"And mine got divorced when I went to uni."

"I think I do want bangs, though."

"Absolutely not," she said.

That evening, I hauled my boring sad hair and boring sad self over to Brittany and Reza's house for an invitation I had been unable to refuse. Brittany could be forceful when she wanted something, and she wanted to lay her eyes on me and make sure I was doing okay after the breakup. Also, I still felt like I owed them for what I'd put them through in January.

"Ramadan Mubarak," I said, lifting a wooden salad bowl in greeting. I had looked up the phrase on my way over, as I did every year.

"Hey, look at you." Brittany smiled as she ushered me inside. It smelled like spicy fried food and chaat masala. "Ramadan Mubarak."

"Is she here?" Reza called from the kitchen.

"It smells incredible," I called back. This was a lie. I still had no appetite, so it was going to take some serious effort to politely eat a little of everything. "Ramadan Mubarak."

Reza's head popped out. "Hey, look at you," he said in the way longtime couples speak the same language with the same intonations.

Even though I was an unlovable shell, I pretended to be glad to be there. I hugged Brittany with my available arm and placed my quinoa salad on their table. It had been set with a tablecloth and a pair of unlit tapers. Two bowls rested between the candles, one empty and one filled with dates. Reza grew up in a practicing family, and although he didn't practice now, he still observed some of the traditions. "A faint wash," he'd explained the first time Cory and I had been invited over for dinner. "The rituals are comforting."

"Do you fast?" I'd asked.

"I eat light," he'd said. "I drink water."

It was mid-Ramadan, and every year, they hosted a whole schedule of dinners. His family always visited for one week, and then they used the other weeks as an occasion to check in with friends. This was the first year that my dinner with them was alone. Were they hosting only me, or had Cory been invited separately? There wasn't a polite way to ask.

As far as I knew, he hadn't been here since their housewarming party the previous autumn. We'd taken the tour, admired the additional rooms and second bathroom that our apartment unit didn't have, strolled through the modest backyard, and listened to their giddy chatter about future projects—tile floors, landscaping, new countertops. Everything had been bare then. The photographs and art had yet to be hung, and the rooms were mostly devoid of furniture. But even though the house hadn't felt like a home yet, it had shimmered with potential.

The memory reminded me of Macon's house now, although his had the advantage of age and beauty. Brittany and Reza's house had been built in the aughts. But despite its plainness, I had left their party feeling envious. That night, I'd dreamed their house was mine, and it was moving day. My apartment was crowded with marvelous furniture and objets d'art that I'd been collecting for years, everything stacked and teetering, crammed into the small space, but as I moved each item into the new house, I was amazed to discover that everything fit precisely.

When I woke up, I'd felt compelled to help my friends settle in. Cory hadn't understood it, but I'd gone back weekend after weekend. I'd helped Brittany and Reza paint the rooms and fill the empty spaces. It didn't look like my dream home, but it did look like theirs. It gave me pleasure, like recommending the right book to the right reader.

My shell *oohed* and *aahed* performatively as Brittany narrated a new tour, showing me what they had updated in the months since I'd been there.

"Show her the room!" Reza called out across the house, and I was surprised when she blushed. But then I knew. During the first tour, they'd told us that a particular room near the back of the house would be their shared office and maybe perhaps eventually—nervous titters—a nursery. The last time I'd seen it, it had still been untouched.

Now the room had soft green walls and a charming wooden crib. "We'll put a rocker over there, I think." She spoke a little too quickly, and my heart lurched, signaling that it was not so dead after all. "And maybe the changing table there? I'd like to find those used, if we can. Reza can refinish them, but I wanted the crib to be new."

"*Brit.*"

She sheepishly placed a hand on her stomach, and I threw my arms around her.

"Did you tell her?" Reza appeared behind us, down the hall. "You told her," he said, answering his own question.

I detached from her and launched myself at him. "Congratulations."

He wrapped me in a hug. A real hug. It was the embrace I had desired but not received from Macon, and it filled me with a powerful longing. Not for one of my friends, necessarily, but for someone of my own, someone with a Reza-shaped body.

"Are you excited?" I pulled away despite not wanting to. "You must be so excited."

"I'm terrified." He laughed. "But happy."

"It happened quickly," Brittany said. "I had my IUD removed after we moved in. It took my sister three years to get pregnant, so I guess I was expecting something similar."

"How far along are you?" She didn't look very pregnant, but every body carries pregnancy differently.

"I'm due in mid-July."

"Do you know if it's a girl or boy yet?" I didn't know enough about pregnancy to know how far along you had to be to get that sort of information. Kat had been on the other side of the world when she'd been pregnant with Howie, and only a few of my other friends had reached that stage of their lives, and they were all still living in Florida. I hadn't been there to witness any of their pregnancies firsthand. I also hadn't been thoughtful enough to ask many questions.

"A girl," Brittany said, and then Reza—wanting his wife to say it first but wanting to say the words, too—quickly echoed, "A girl."

I met someone, Cory had said. But later that night at the *Diner*-themed table in the diner-themed diner, he had also confessed that he wanted to have children. It wasn't this new woman who had changed his mind. He said he'd been thinking about it for a while, but he'd been afraid to tell me because he knew my own mind had not changed. It was more proof that our futures weren't aligned, so it didn't hurt in the moment—it only surprised me. But it hurt now. Seeing this happiness, this shared future, before me was excruciating.

My shell cracked and threatened to leak, but thankfully I was still dry.

I smiled and squeezed my friends again and repeated my felicitations enthusiastically.

How much longer until I could go home?

"It's time, it's time," Brittany said when we were interrupted by an alarm on her phone. Exact sunset meant iftar, so we hurried back to the dining table. We ate our dates to break our nonexistent fasts, deposited the pits into the empty bowl, and then Reza returned to the kitchen, refusing my offer of help. At that moment, I would rather have been inhaling all of those formidable food smells than be left alone with a pregnant woman. But I did my job and asked questions and kept Brittany chatting readily about her new daughter, even though surely she'd already had the same conversation with countless friends during the past few weeks.

"Late July," I realized, doing the math. "We drank in early January."

I said it before realizing this was inconsiderate and unhelpful, but she didn't seem bothered. "Yeah, I became suspicious later that night when that single beer made me violently ill. Luckily, I only had that beer plus a glass of wine around Christmas." She shrugged. "My period was irregular anyway, and . . . I don't know why I didn't know. But I didn't."

Reza entered with the first few plates, and I told them they were going to be great parents, which was true. They kept the conversation flowing as Brittany and I helped bring the rest of what he'd cooked to the table: vegetable pakoras, eggplant kebabs, fried cauliflower, red lentil dal, and several other dishes that I didn't recognize. It was way too much—both in terms of what I could stomach and how much effort Reza had put into it—but he insisted that it wasn't a big deal and that some of it was leftovers from previous nights.

"I'm sorry," Brittany said. My melancholy had descended over the table.

"We've been going on and on, and we haven't even asked how you've been doing."

"Oh, I'm fine," I said in a tone that was so un-fine that I had to laugh at myself.

Brittany and Reza set down their forks pityingly, but not without compassion.

"We had dinner with Cory a few nights ago, and he was in rough shape, too," Reza said.

"Don't read anything into the order of invitations," Brittany said. "It was only because that was when he was available, and this was when you were available."

I shook my head. "No, it's okay. I'm glad you saw him." I was also glad to hear that he wasn't thriving. Though I was alone, I wasn't alone in my suffering.

"Do you think you can still be friends since the split was amicable?" Reza asked.

"I don't know," I said. "I hope so, someday. Not yet."

"No," Brittany agreed, but then she seemed unsure of how to continue. "Nice to finally be able to eat more than plain breakfast cereal and saltines." She picked her fork back up and speared a cauliflower floret. "And just in time. Can you imagine if we'd served you Cheerios?"

She was trying to give me an easy out of the conversation about Cory, and perhaps also about the baby. She knew I didn't want children. Perhaps she also knew now that Cory did.

"Cory would have been fine with Cheerios," I said.

Thankfully, they laughed. "Yeah, we had pizza that night," Brittany said.

"Well, I'm happy to be a greedy receptacle for your wonderful cooking, Reza. And I'm glad you can eat again," I said to Brittany. I felt compassion for her but also relief that I would never be in her situation—followed by additional relief that I *could* love this particular joy for her without longing for it myself. It was further proof that Cory and I had never been each other's future. For the first time, the thought comforted me.

My hunger emerged from its cave. I dipped a pakora into the cilantro chutney, and my first bite was full of contrasts: the golden pakoras were crispy and tender, the zingy chutney spicy and cooling. I moaned with appreciation, and Brittany and Reza laughed again as I fully dug in to the spread. It tasted like a revelation. I didn't have to nibble and pretend.

Their house looked beautiful that night. The table itself was new and large enough to fit their growing family, and the beeswax tapers gave everything a warm glow, honeying the air. I had never considered beeswax candles before, but now I yearned for tapers of my own. I wanted this feeling of home, this same love and hope and abundance.

Unfortunately, now that I knew I wanted it—now that it was so clear to me—it felt further away than ever.

CHAPTER TWENTY

Mika asked if I wanted to meet up for coffee. She was one of my coworkers from the bookstore days. I liked her a lot, and we had these coffee dates to catch up about twice a year. I'd turned down an invitation from her the previous month, and although I still wasn't in the mood to socialize, the visit with Brittany and Reza had been mostly enjoyable. It felt more exhausting to have to think up another excuse. Better to go and get it over with.

We met at a new place that she was excited to try. It was off the main roads and tucked into a neighborhood not far from Macon's. The building was small and old, but it had a fresh coat of indigo-blue paint, a lemon-yellow door with matching window frames, and a clawfoot tub planter filled with pink and orange cosmos and herbs.

I spotted Mika right away. She'd chosen a table by the front window.

It was raining, and as I ducked inside, the café enveloped me in its warmth and calming energy. Scents of coffee and baked goods and potted plants mingled with a general vibe of cleanliness and friendliness. Some slumbering part of me stirred.

Mika had a huge smile on her face as she stood to greet me. "Is it okay if I hug you?"

I was still desperate to be hugged, but I appreciated when people were thoughtful enough to ask for permission first. It wasn't something I'd considered before the pandemic. I had given hugs to everybody back then, even to people who, frankly, probably hadn't wanted them. I felt bad about that now, how much personal space I had invaded. Now I was careful with my hugs. It made sense that Mika was, too. Her soul was gentle and attuned to the needs of others. She moved through the world with a delicacy and light touch that I had always admired. It felt good to hug her.

"I got here early, so I already ordered," she said. "I hope that's okay."

"Of course. What is that? It smells delicious."

"The wildflower latte." Her eyes widened and her smile grew. "Crushed flowers, buds, and a homemade floral syrup. Everything here is plant-based."

I smiled back, my first easy smile in a while. Mika's was so infectious that it was hard not to mimic it. I set my umbrella beside the table and went to the counter to place my order. The baristas were as friendly and approachable as their surroundings. I ordered a wildflower latte with coconut milk and then bought a vegan cinnamon roll, too.

Had Macon been here yet? He'd never mentioned it, but it seemed like his kind of place. He didn't eat out often, though, so maybe he hadn't heard of it. I'd have to tell him.

I was already feeling more alive as I took the chair across from Mika. "How have you been? How's Bex?"

"Ooh, that looks good," she said, admiring my cinnamon roll. And then, "They're doing well. They're about to receive their fifth-degree black belt." Bex was Mika's spouse who co-owned a taekwondo studio.

"Fifth! How many degrees are there?"

"Nine. Actually ten, but that last one is only given out posthumously."

"Seriously?"

"Dead serious," she said—and then laughed at her own joke.

We were already in. I loved all my friends, but I especially appreciated the ones who required no training wheels, no remedial courses to slide back into the rhythm of conversation.

"There's a title change with the fifth degree, too. They'll go from

Instructor to Master Instructor. I told Bex that under no circumstances will I be calling them Master."

"Master Bex," I said, delighted.

She laughed again. "Under. No. Circumstances."

"Well, please pass along my congratulations to Master Bex. I'm thrilled for them."

"And Cory? How's he doing?"

The café dimmed. I slipped out of my protective shell and into the driving rain.

"Whoa," Mika said. "Where'd you go?"

It wasn't surprising that she'd noticed the change, but it was surprising that she'd phrased it like that. I repeated the long, humiliating story I had been telling all month. I wasn't that far into it when Mika reached across the table and grasped my hand. Many people had given me commiserations and reassurances, but nobody had held me like that. It was pure Mika.

The rain softened against the window.

"I am so sorry," she said when I was done talking.

"It's okay," I said, like always. Except I meant it a little more this time. And then I said something new. "I think we were so stuck in our relationship that creating this overly complicated plan was the only way we could get out of it. Like, it *had* to be done in steps. I don't think we ever could have just faced each other and said, 'This isn't working for me.'"

These words rang with truth inside me, and I felt a burden lift. I was relieved to finally understand what we had done. That there had been a reason for everything. I didn't have to feel so much shame and confusion anymore. Our plan had served a purpose all along.

"That makes sense," Mika said. "It's still strange."

"It is. But we also made it through lockdown together, you know? And so many other couples didn't. I guess we figured, 'Hey, we're set. We're good here.'" My cinnamon roll was still untouched, so I released her hand to fork off the end piece that stuck out from the bun. "I mean, Macon and his girlfriend broke up, like, the second the vaccine came out."

"Who's Macon?"

"Oh." My cheeks reddened. "My coworker."

Her eyebrows rose.

"It's nothing like that."

She continued to gently stare me down.

I couldn't lie to Mika. "Maybe I *was* interested, but he's not."

Her brows lowered, and she sat with that for a moment. Sipped her latte. "Are you still interested?"

"I'm not looking for anybody right now. And when I do want somebody, I want them to want me back."

"That's a healthy answer."

"Hey." I sort of laughed. "Progress."

She laughed, too. "So, apart from this single coworker—who for some unimaginable reason is not interested in you—how's work?" Her expression fell as she watched mine fall. "Oh no. That bad?"

Mika was one of the few people to whom I'd admitted that I didn't love my job. The library was such a perfect fit for me that I felt ashamed for not liking it as much as I should. In that regard, it wasn't that dissimilar to the situation with Cory. Things between us had been good but not right, which had left an unsettling disconnect. It didn't make sense for me not to love my job. I was working with books, my coworkers were great, the building was beautiful. What was wrong with me that I couldn't feel satisfied with what I had?

But Mika understood because she was also stuck with an enviable job that she was skilled at but didn't love. She'd been working for the last few years as a buyer for a popular gift shop downtown. I told her about turning down library school, and she listened sympathetically. "So that's it, then?" she said. "You'll never be able to move into a higher position?"

"No, I could still pay for school myself. But the thought of going back makes me ill. It's so much time and money, and I don't care about the more technical aspects of the field that they'd teach me. I doubt it would feel worth it. And it'd be hard swallowing those fees now knowing that I could have taken the classes for free. I should have just done it, but . . . it was like there was this force inside me physically stopping me from doing it."

"I disagree. I think you were right to listen to that force. It was there for a reason. It was protecting you from making a mistake."

"Maybe," I said miserably.

"No, I really believe that." She said it with such conviction that it was comforting.

I asked about her job and allowed her to unburden herself of her usual complaints—her frustration about having to stock products she didn't respect, her displays being underappreciated by the owner, her artistic side feeling stifled. The store was bigger than most gift shops, a busy mainstay downtown that attracted a lot of tourists and had a large staff. Mika had a great position and was paid decently for it. She liked being a buyer, she liked working downtown, and she liked helping customers. All of this made the job just good enough that she couldn't justify leaving it.

"Why does stability feel so much like settling?" I asked.

"Not always. I don't feel this way about Bex."

"Sometimes I wish we could have our old jobs back."

"Or that we'd been able to buy the store. Remember how we wanted to buy it?"

Mika had loved the Tick-Tock Bookshop as much as I had. Born in Japan, her family had moved here when she was a tween, and she'd become a voracious reader as a way to get a better grasp on the language. We'd both started at the bookstore around the same time, and we'd both been devastated when it had closed. We had spent so many shifts fantasizing about what we would do if it were ours, but Mika was only two years older than me, so we'd both been young and broke. Saving it hadn't been an option. Instead, the space had turned into a boutique for hot sauce and hot sauce–related apparel.

"I honestly can't believe that in a town like this, we *still* don't have a good bookstore," I said.

"That used store on Dogwood sells a few new titles, the popular ones. The same ones available at the box stores. But mainly everyone's just buying their books from the Bad Place."

Neither of us ever invoked the name of the online retailer that had a stranglehold on the industry. All these years later, it still tasted like a curse on our tongues.

"We should open a new bookstore," I said, not meaning it.

"Yeah. With a huge banned books display right in the front window on opening day." She smiled because she'd heard my stories about the banners at the library.

We continued to rhapsodize, adding reading nooks and local art and sustainable goods. I could see it all so clearly. By the time our conversation shifted back to the real world, the seed had already begun to germinate inside my mind. By nightfall, it had taken root. I went to bed early and, like always, struggled to fall asleep. But instead of thinking about being alone, instead of thinking about a man, I thought about the store. I thought about what if.

CHAPTER TWENTY-ONE

I called Mika in a fevered state the next morning. "What if we did it? What if we opened a bookstore together?"

She could tell that the question was serious, so she gave me a serious answer. "I'm sorry. I wish I could say yes, but we already co-own the dojang with Bex's business partner. Owning a business is stressful. We barely made it through the pandemic. I don't want to take on another."

I was crushed. In that early morning headspace, still so close to dreaming, I was positive that she'd be excited. That I could convince her to do this with me. But I couldn't argue with her reason. "I guess I got carried away. It was a silly idea, anyway."

"It wasn't silly," she said. "Thank you for asking me."

I wanted to return to bed and savor my dejection, but it was a Monday. Mondays were when my coworkers and I scheduled things like haircuts and dermatologist appointments, and that Monday, I had a particularly unpleasant errand to run that couldn't wait. My car was overheating again. I drove to my mechanic to get a patch on the leaking radiator, and he chastised me instead. What I needed, Harvey said, was a new radiator and new hoses. But a patch was a hundred bucks, and replacing the whole thing would be closer to a thousand. I demanded the patch, and we both felt surly about it. "It'll be a few hours," Harvey said with unveiled contempt.

I was prepared for this, so I grabbed the bag of food scraps for composting that I'd brought from home and trudged the half mile to Macon's house. Because spring had arrived in February, the town already glistened with an aura of early summer. Sure, April was still occasionally showering, but the May flowers were in bloom, hanging baskets of ferns were swinging on porches, and wind chimes were tinkling in the breeze.

I found Macon in his garden, harvesting tender crowns of broccoli. He startled to see me at his gate. I'd never shown up at his house uninvited before.

"Drop-off for the shit pile," I said, borrowing Cory's old phrase because it matched my mood.

But Macon didn't seem to mind my sudden appearance. I thought I might make him nervous, but since he was in his element, he took everything in stride. I explained about my car, and he gestured in the direction of his compost pile and wheelbarrowed over some weeds to add. He was wearing a dirty black T-shirt and crummy work pants, and he smelled like sweat, soil, and sun. The scent was warm and comforting. I felt the urge to lean toward him like a seedling reaching for sunlight, but managed to resist.

Wooden boards surrounded the compost on three sides to keep it neat, and the pile spilled onto the ground in front of the open side. In addition to the expected food scraps, yard waste, and shredded brown paper, I was intrigued to see toilet paper rolls and cotton balls and other household surprises. "Is that dental floss?" I asked as I dumped out my bag.

"Yep."

"Could I bring you *my* dental floss?"

"Probably not. I buy a special kind." He picked up a pitchfork that was resting against one of the walls and leaned his weight against it, taking pleasure in what he was about to say next. "But you could bring me your nail clippings and hair."

"What?"

He laughed. "They're organic."

"Oh my God." It made me laugh, too. "I will. Just you wait."

"Hey, since you're here and you have some time, would you mind giving me some advice?"

"Really?" My curiosity was piqued. I was the one who usually sought advice from him.

"I've been thinking about what we talked about the other week—about my house needing help—and was hoping you might be able to provide some guidance."

He set down his pitchfork, and I stuffed the bag into my pocket and followed him inside through the back door. The kitchen still looked tired and empty, but buttery sunlight warmed the room, and a round loaf of freshly baked bread was resting on the counter. I was tempted to poke it to see if it was warm, too. "I'd like to fix it up," he said, removing his work gloves to wash his hands, "but I don't know where to begin."

I wandered toward the front of the house. All of the wood—floors, baseboards, crown molding, door casings—was scratched and dinged up. But it was also original and unpainted. Mostly it just looked thirsty. The living room was a good size and had lots of windows. Two had been shuttered with cheap mini blinds, and the whole row of them spanning the longest wall were unadorned, but all of them looked out upon the garden.

My throat thickened with envy. "You're so lucky."

He trailed into the room behind me. "Why?"

"Because of this house. I would love to have a house. My entire generation would love to have a house."

Thankfully, he wasn't the type to deny or downplay it. "I am lucky," he said, although he also sounded weary. Perhaps it was the same weariness that shrouded these rooms.

I put my hands on my hips as I looked around the void that was his living room. "God, Macon. It's so *bare*. I still don't get it."

"I have a couch." He pointed in one direction. "I have a coffee table." Pointed in another.

"Have you been waiting all this time for—" I stopped. My question was rude.

"Waiting all this time for what?"

I shook my head.

"Oh, come on," he said. "You can't do that."

He was right, so I spoke more carefully. "Do you think you've been waiting for her to come back?"

My directness seemed to startle him, and I sensed that he had been expecting a different question. I became afraid of his answer. I tried to wave it off—*never mind, too far*—but he interrupted the gesture.

He spoke carefully, too, and firmly. "No."

Relief shamed me anew, that some part of me still wanted him for myself. I knew better than to want him. Mostly I thought I didn't anymore. But there it was, proof that the desire still existed.

He was watching me closely. Thankfully, his cat chose that moment to slink into the room. "Edmond!" I said, and the slink became a trot. I dropped to the floor, and he greeted me with a head bop. I rubbed his cheeks. He purred and pressed his chin into my hands.

"Edmond likes you," Macon said.

"Is that unusual?"

He considered it. "I don't actually know. I know that he likes me, and he didn't care for his previous owner or the vet. But of course he likes you."

"What do you mean?"

"Everyone likes you."

"Thank you," I said. "I think."

"It was meant as a compliment."

I stood back up and brushed my hands together to remove the fur. "Well, you don't often like things that other people like."

"You aren't a *thing*." He sounded offended on my behalf.

It made me laugh. "Sorry, I was teasing you. I'm well aware that you like me. You never would have invited me inside your house otherwise." I said it lightly and with enough offhanded flirtatiousness to convey that I was still talking about our friendship. But the truth was that I was feeling muddled. "Speaking of!" I said too enthusiastically. "Your house."

"My house," he said, blinking. He seemed muddled, too.

I couldn't look at him directly anymore. "So the basic idea, I think—and granted, you're getting your advice from a woman with a shitty apartment—isn't to fill the space with whatever. It's to add more of the things you already love."

"I'm a forty-year-old man who owns nothing."

"Thirty-nine."

"So what's more of nothing?"

"Oh my God, Macon." I turned back toward him in exasperation, but there was a twinkle in his eye. He'd purposefully tried to provoke that reaction. It made me laugh again.

"Tell me what I love," he said.

My heart painfully skipped a beat. But my smile only faltered for a second. "Well, reading, obviously. Cooking. Gardening."

"So I need to buy more books, food, and plants."

"No—"

"And my couch is fine. That's good."

"Your couch is *not* fine."

"And I don't need a china cabinet, or china to put inside the cabinet—"

"Nobody needs china anymore, unless they love it."

"Oh, I love it."

He was trying to bait me again, so I ignored him. "You love to read, so I'd create a beautiful space for your books. You love to cook, so I'd create beautiful spaces to prepare your meals and eat them. You love to garden, so I'd fill the inside of your house with plants, too. That's where I'd start."

"What about the rest of it?"

"Eh. The rest comes later."

He picked up Edmond and held him against his chest and shoulder. "Okay. Pretend I would like nice places to read and cook and eat. *Pretend.*"

"I'm pretending."

"How does one design those spaces?"

"Well, how did you learn how to garden?"

"My aunt taught me."

"Damn. I thought you were going to say *books*. It was such a perfect setup."

At this, Macon finally broke and laughed.

"Hey, how is Bonnie?" I was careful to keep my voice light. She was still in rehab, and he didn't receive many updates. But I always asked anyway, whenever I saw an opportunity.

"Maybe better? Probably the same." He shrugged—an uncomfortable shrug that was doing a lot of work—before steering me back on topic. "So, what would you do if it were your house?"

"I'm not designing this for me. It needs to be for you."

He brushed this off. "I'm asking what you would do if it *were* your house."

"Oh." My gaze softened. Then it wandered, absorbing everything again until it landed on the kitchen. The walls and cabinets were painted the same dull shade of decades-old, beaten-up white, but the natural light still warmed the faded gloss of the cabinets, almost making the little doors glow. "I'd start in the kitchen. I'd paint the walls a buttery yellow to match the sunshine. And I'd scrub the cabinets and give them a fresh coat of paint, too. Curtains on the window above the sink. A pretty utensil crock to keep all my wooden spoons handy."

"That sounds cheerful," he said.

"Too cheerful for you."

"This is your house, remember?"

I smiled. "I'd put a big round table in the dining room. Enough chairs for me to sit somewhere new every night of the week. Though of course I'd always sit in the same spot."

"Of course."

"Colorful woven placemats. Mismatched cloth napkins."

"Why mismatched?"

"So when I inevitably lose one, it's not a big deal. I don't have to replace them all."

"Ah. Practical."

"Sometimes I'm practical."

"Go on," he said.

"I'd lose the mini blinds and put curtains on all these windows, too. Lots of comfortable seating and pillows. Reading lamps and rugs. And I'd display my bookcases in here, right in the front room, because—I don't know if you know this about me—I like to read, too."

"I've heard something about that."

But I was already past the joke and back inside the dream. "No! I'd turn that whole wall into shelving. I'd just . . . completely surround myself with books. And I'd paint the door a friendly color. I'm not sure what yet."

"It sounds perfect."

I made a face.

"I'm serious. That all sounds great. Well, maybe not the friendly door. I wouldn't want anybody to get the wrong idea."

"Oh, stop it."

"I'm being honest." He laughed. "It sounds like an incredibly cozy house that I would like to live in."

The mood shifted, subtly but swiftly. Because Macon did possess the ability to make my dream a reality—for himself—while I was still stuck in a beige one-bedroom.

"At least put up some art," I said, hastening toward the exit. "Bare walls are sad."

His expression faded. "Noted."

I gave him a tight smile as I marched back outside. "See you tomorrow."

But he picked up his gloves and followed me toward the garden gate. Suddenly he swore, and I glanced back over my shoulder. He was holding the broccoli that he'd been harvesting when I'd arrived. It had wilted in the sun.

That night, while I was mourning the loss of a hundred dollars to the mechanic—and eating instant ramen in an effort to rebalance the financial scales—I received a text from Mika.

I've been thinking about your store all day, she said. *You should do it anyway.*

CHAPTER TWENTY-TWO

"I've been thinking about it," Macon said to me a few days later at work. "I'm going to paint my kitchen yellow."

"Really?" I no longer remembered that I'd left his house feeling angry and envious. I only felt a stir of excitement that my vision was about to become a reality.

"Yeah. Ever since you said it, I can picture it clearly."

I straightened. It felt good to be useful. I hadn't felt that in a while.

"But is it okay? I feel like I'm stealing your idea."

I waved away his concern. "That's what I would paint *that* kitchen. I have no idea what my own future kitchen will look like. Steal away."

Several hours later, though, it was still on my mind. How charming it would look with the correct shade of yellow. How repellent it could look with the wrong one. "Are you going to paint your kitchen soon?" I asked.

He nodded, slowly at first but then faster as he considered it further. "I think so."

"May I help?"

He seemed surprised. "You want to help me paint?"

"Yeah." I had surprised myself, too, but this was the most interest I'd felt in anything since I'd stopped dating. Also, I couldn't tell him that I was concerned he'd pick an ugly color. That I was concerned for the integrity of his house.

He'd been looking at me askance, but his gaze sharpened. "You're serious, aren't you?"

"Of course I am."

"Have you ever even painted a room? Since you live in an unpaintable apartment?"

"I helped Brittany with her house. And Cory's friends held a lot of painting parties." The blankness of his response prodded me to elaborate. "That's when you invite your friends over to paint the walls of your new place, and you pay them in pizza and beer, and supposedly it's fun."

"That sounds horrible."

"It *is*. And everyone else would always get drunk, and somehow the painting was always left to me. And I would do it!" A thought occurred to me. "That's probably why I was invited to so many parties."

"You're too responsible."

"I am."

"If it's so bad, then why do you want to help?"

"Because it sounds better than sitting alone in my sad apartment."

He frowned, but a man interrupted us, wanting to replace a lost card. Macon asked to see his ID, and while the guy was digging it out, Macon shook his head. "I don't know. You'd be doing me another favor, and I still owe you for watching Edmond."

"You're not in my debt. I was helping out a friend. You'd do it for me."

"You don't have a cat."

"Come on."

He threw up his hands. "Okay. I'm not going to stop you from painting my kitchen."

"*Helping* paint. This isn't a painting party."

His expression turned vexed as he snatched the driver's license out of the man's hands a little too aggressively.

"When do you want to start?" I asked as soon as we were alone again.

"Sunday?"

"If we start then, we won't be able to finish it over the weekend."

"My kitchen isn't big. It won't take two days to paint."

I explained that he was forgetting about the prep work: patching, sanding, cleaning, taping, priming. More importantly, he hadn't factored in the time it would take to select the color. "But we're painting it yellow," he said, baffled. "A buttery, sunshiny yellow, like you said."

"You're underestimating how many shades of yellow exist in the world." I did a quick search. "Okay, so the hardware store down the road closes at seven. That gives us plenty of time to pick up samples after work."

"You mean *tonight*?"

"Do you have anything else going on?"

"I might," he grumbled.

A few hours later, I was thrusting paint sample cards into his hands. After I helped him eliminate the most obvious nos, he was still left holding dozens of cards. "Tape these to your kitchen walls," I said, removing another that was too pastel. "Move them around and study them in different types of light. Take down the rejects as you spot them and keep narrowing it down until you're left with only a few that you like. I'll come over before work on Saturday and help you pick the right one."

"Why before work?"

"So I can see them in the daylight. That way you'll be ready to buy the paint after work, and then we can start early the next morning. In the meantime, you should spackle any holes and repair any cracks."

He seemed overwhelmed. "How do you know all this?"

I felt gleeful at being more knowledgeable about something than him for once, and I lectured him on small rollers versus the regular size. "The small ones are so lightweight that your arms don't get tired. You'll have to tape, but then you won't have to cut in, so it's worth it."

He agreed to try them only to shut me up. But like any good librarian, he made up for his ignorance with diligent research. By Saturday morning, his walls were prepped and cleaned, he'd created a list of remaining supplies to purchase, and four paint sample cards were taped up.

I read them aloud. "Midsummer Magic, Sun-Kissed, Rise and Shine, Goldilocks."

"Which one do you like?" he asked, handing me a mug of green tea with honey. I enjoyed all varieties of caffeine, but this was a particular favorite. Unsurprisingly, he'd been the one to hook me on it in the first place. I blew across the surface and took a sip. Also unsurprisingly, his tasted better than mine.

"They're all good," I said, admiring the colors.

His shoulders relaxed, and I could tell that my approval pleased him.

"Maybe Goldilocks is a touch too gold. And Sun Kissed is a tad bland?"

He took them off the wall.

"Rise and Shine," I said. "That's the one."

"That's the one I was leaning toward, too."

I removed the card and slapped it onto his chest. "Done."

The unexpected contact startled us both. I'd never just . . . touched his chest before. He made a whole production of slowly untaping the card from his shirt while giving me a hard look.

I shrugged because I honestly didn't know why I'd done it.

He tutted with mock disappointment. "Rise and Shine it is."

Macon was an early riser, despite his grumpiness upon arriving to work every day. ("My mood has everything to do with leaving my house, and nothing to do with the morning itself," he once told me.) I still wasn't sleeping well, so we made plans for me to return early again on Sunday. I'd wanted to go with him to the hardware store to pick up the paint and supplies, but I'd spent our whole Saturday shift trying to think up an excuse to join him and never did.

We both laughed when he greeted me at the door. We were wearing the same shirt, a gray Colburn County logo tee that we'd received as a holiday "gift" from our employer two years earlier. Other notable gifts included brown paper lunch sacks that each contained a pitiful orange and five chestnuts, and logo coffee mugs that we were ordered to stop using a few months later because they turned out to be contaminated with lead.

"Merry Christmas," I said.

"Humbug," he said.

He'd already taped around the cabinets, windows, and trim. Everything was ready and waiting for me, including breakfast. He'd texted an hour earlier: *If you value my sanity, please don't eat another Pop-Tart. I'll make something for us.* He'd seen them on my kitchen counter and had been pestering me about it ever since. "I only bought one box," I said, heading for the little table in his dining room. "Desperate times and all that." Then I gasped. Two plates were piled with matching heaps of home fries and tofu scramble. "This is so nice. Thank you."

He set down another mug of tea in front of me. "You're welcome."

I moaned at the first mouthful of scramble—peppers, spinach, onions, and herbs. "I assume these are all from your garden?"

"Yeah. Are the peppers okay? They were still in my freezer from last year. I'm trying to use everything up before I fill it again this summer."

"Everything's delicious. I can't wait to see what you make for me tomorrow morning."

"I'd be happy to feed you again tomorrow morning."

My fork paused halfway to my mouth. "I wasn't serious."

He shrugged. "I was."

And he did seem content, watching me tuck in. I thought I understood, though. No part of me blamed Cory or was angry with him, but it had always made me sad not to be able to cook for him. Not to be able to share in the preparation and presentation and pleasure of a good meal. I also suspected—so perhaps I did blame him a bit—that this had held me back. Although my diet wasn't usually as unhealthy as it had been lately, I might have made more of an effort in general if we could have shared our meals. The want and need to feed the people we cared about was primal. It was why families gathered for dinner, why coworkers baked each other rum cakes. And tofu scrambles.

Macon fought with me about cleaning up afterward. "You can't *not* let me help," I said.

"It's okay. I'm weird about dishes. I like them done a certain way."

"We're librarians. We all like things done a certain way. Tell me how you do them, and I can help." I started to put a plastic lid into his dishwasher, and he made a strangled noise. I held it up. "This?"

"No plastic in the dishwasher."

I set it back down on the counter. "Got it."

Soon I learned which bar of soap was for hands and which was for hand-washed dishes (I'd guessed wrong before), which dishes needed to be dried immediately (normally just the cast iron, but today everything because we had to remove it from the room), and how to start the dishwasher (with a scoop of unlabeled powder). Then we moved the last few remaining items into the dining room and set out the drop cloths. It was finally time to roll the primer.

I started on one side of a corner, he started on the other, and soon our rollers met up in the middle. The primer was flat and streaky, but covering the battered old white already made the room look brighter. We washed up and had a couple of hours to kill while it dried. As strange as it sounded, we'd never hung out like this before, just the two of us with nothing specific to do. Concerned that it might get awkward, I asked for a full garden tour, and he obliged.

Everything was greener now, although most of the growth was still small and new. He showed me the early vegetables planted in neat rows and the numerous trays of labeled seedlings in his greenhouse. Their tiny leaves were so sweet. There was an herb garden laid out in a stone spiral that his aunt had built, plump beds with the first hints of native perennials, hidden birdhouses and feeders, and a sign declaring his yard to be a certified pollinator habitat. He was so proud of everything, and I liked seeing him happy.

"How much of this was here when you were a kid?" I asked.

"The spiral planter, some of the fruit trees, and that Japanese maple beside the driveway. The renters had let the weeds and grass claim the rest. Bonnie was livid. But a lot of it does look similar to how she used to have it, though more for practical reasons than sentimental." He gestured to the vegetable garden as an example. "That's the only area that gets enough sunlight for those beds."

"Did she surround them in picket fencing, too?"

He laughed. "Chicken wire. Every time I had to fix it, it'd cut the shit out of my hands." Nostalgia crept into his voice. "She taught me how to do all this, you know."

"I do know. She must have loved visiting you here and seeing you in your adult life, puttering around in her garden, rehabilitating it."

His expression fell into somberness, and I realized I'd said the wrong thing, turning her visits into the past tense. Not allowing for the possibility of *her* rehabilitation.

"I'm sorry," I said.

He shook his head as if to say it was okay, even though nothing about Bonnie's situation was okay. "She did love it."

A thought struck me. "Was it a difficult decision to paint the kitchen?"

He understood what I was getting at. "Because it's looked like that my whole life?"

"I'm just suddenly wondering if *that's* why you hadn't touched anything for all these years. If maybe the house—the way it is—holds a lot of happy memories for you."

Macon considered it before replying. "It's true that I was always happier here than I was at my mom's house," he said, referring to the difficulties with her agoraphobia. His aunt was the one who had taken him places, and his childhood had become more isolated after she'd gotten married and moved away. "Bonnie was the fun one, the one who let me break the rules. In fact, I broke my arm falling out of that tree when I was seven." He pointed to one of the cherry trees, and we laughed.

"Your mom must have lost her mind."

"It took half a year before she allowed Bonnie to watch me again, even though the accident was definitely not Bonnie's fault. I was up there reading and lost my balance."

"You broke your arm *reading?*"

Our laughter grew.

"I can't believe you've never told me this story before," I said.

"I absolutely have."

"I would remember," I insisted, because I would.

"Anyway," he said, "when I took ownership of the house, Bonnie encouraged me to make it my own. And then Dani filled it with her stuff, which was fine. Honestly, I just hadn't been motivated until you brought it up again. I guess I'd stopped seeing what shape it was in. I had to see it through your horrified eyes," he added. His tone was pleasurably offended.

It made me smile. "So is Bonnie the older or younger sister?"

"Younger."

"Figures. They're always the fun ones. They're allowed to be. They don't have the same pressures and responsibilities on them."

"*You're* fun."

He was still joking around, but I blanked on a witty response. God, it was mortifying to always be so eager for him to like me. We had circled back to the porch, so we sat in the wrought iron chairs. "Does Edmond ever join you out here?" I asked, needing to draw his attention away from my flustered nonreaction. "Since he used to be an outdoor cat?"

"Sometimes he'll follow me around for a while. Sniff the earth, chase the bugs. But usually he'd rather enjoy the garden through the windows. He's very stubborn. And lazy."

"Well, I'll have to come back this summer when everything's in full bloom."

"You're welcome here anytime."

He didn't say it offhandedly. He said it like he meant it, and—there it was, that charge hovering in the air between us. I burned with renewed hope and confusion.

His brow furrowed as he turned toward his toolshed. "Can I ask you a question?"

My pulse thumped inside my throat.

"Why did you decide not to go to library school?"

It was upsetting that he could still do this to me, make me think he was going to ask about something else even though we were firmly back in friends territory. I didn't want to feel this way around him. I didn't want to ruin things between us again. I needed to stop misinterpreting him just because some lonely part of me wanted something that wasn't there.

"I can't really explain it," I said after collecting myself. "But every time I thought about going, I felt sick to my stomach."

"Was it the school part? Or the library part?"

I hesitated. I felt bad admitting the truth to him because even though he complained about his job, it was what he wanted to do. "Both."

His gaze left the shed and returned to me.

"I don't want you to get the wrong idea. I'm glad that Sue and Constance think highly of me. I'm grateful for the steady work, and I love the branch. And my coworkers," I added.

Macon gave a sad but knowing smile.

"It's like I have the second-best job in the world, and that should be enough. But it's not."

"What *is* the best?"

I winced. "It's going to sound stupid."

"I doubt that."

"I loved working in the bookstore."

He frowned. "Why would that be stupid?"

"Worse hours. Worse pay. But yeah, best job." My posture turned defensive. "And I know it's hypocritical, because we're always talking about saving money and using what we already have and buying things used, but... books are different. For me, at least. And the book business means more to me than any other business, so it's where I want to spend my dollars. So I don't think it actually makes me a hypocrite. It's just investing my money where I believe it matters."

He let that sit for a few seconds before cocking his head. "If you're trying to justify why somebody might want to purchase a book new or work in a bookstore, you know you don't have to convince me, right?"

I looked away from him, laughing, but I *had* worried about what he would think. Macon, with his nontoxic cleaning supplies and organic vegetable garden and environmental economics books. Macon, whose opinion always mattered so much to me.

"Have you ever thought about opening one yourself?" he asked.

I snorted with surprise. "Actually, I have—and recently—but no. I couldn't do that."

"Why not?"

I made a face like he was nuts. "Because I don't know anything about starting a small business."

"And you think all those other shopkeepers do? You think the guy who owns Vape or Dare knew anything about starting a small business? Or that pervert who owns Mastervaper?"

"Yes!" I laughed again. "Because they did it."

"So you can, too."

I shook my head, still smiling.

"I'm serious. If the vape shop guys can do it, anybody can."

"Yeah, but the vape shop guys sell legal drugs. They don't have to have *great* stores, they just have to have *stores*. They're not hurting for customers. Bookstores are hurting."

Macon shrugged.

"They are."

"I know. But . . . maybe that's not enough of a reason not to try."

"Yeah, but I could put *everything I own* into it and lose *everything I own*."

"And if that happened, you could come back to the library and do the second-best job in the world. Or move into the country and learn how to make cider. Or move to a remote Canadian island to study puffins. The world wouldn't end."

I continued listing reasons why it was a bad idea, all the duties of being a store owner that I didn't know how to do or that sounded boring or difficult. All the duties that I *did* know how to do that *were* boring or difficult. But Macon shrugged these off, too. "No job is perfect. The trick is to find one with enough parts that you love to help you get through the shitty parts."

"Speaking of jobs," I said.

The first roll of color was the highlight of any painting job. Our rollers moved upward like synchronized swimmers, and the yellow was so flawless that I gasped.

"I agree," Macon said. As good as a gasp.

The buttery warmth spread, and in less than an hour the first coat was done. Macon had pre-prepared lunch for us, because of course he had, so we returned to the patio and ate barbecue jackfruit sandwiches. The sauce was tangy, and the sandwiches were topped with a coleslaw that contained crisp green apples. Bumblebees hummed, and leaves danced in the breeze. It was as if we'd stepped into our old game: *this* was the place where we'd rather be than work. Our conversation flowed as it had in the before times, as it had that weekend over text, and it never slowed during the second coat, the break, the final coat. The walls glowed in the setting sun.

"You were right," he said. "This color is perfect."

It *was* perfect. I swooned.

He held up one of the small rollers. "You were right about these, too."

I laughed. That was also a satisfying win. And I couldn't believe how quickly we'd finished, a full day early, but he'd done more prep than I'd anticipated. We removed the blue painter's tape, and I did touch-ups with a thin brush while he cleaned and put things away. Edmond wandered in to inspect our work, curious what all the fuss had been about.

It was fully dark before everything was back where it belonged. I scrubbed my skin at the sink and washed off the paint, but a few stubborn flecks of primer remained on my hands and in my nail beds. It made me think of Gareth, which reminded me of how poorly I had treated him, and my melancholy—absent for an entire day—drifted back in and settled down for the night.

"You okay?" Macon noticed I'd gone quiet. His tone changed. "Oh no."

"What?"

"Paint in your hair. It's in the back, near your ponytail."

I patted my head and cursed when I found the offending spot. After removing the ponytail holder, I tried to ease the paint down the strands. It barely budged.

"Shit," I said. "I think it's primer."

Macon had been cradling Edmond but set him down to help. He reached out—and then hesitated. He'd touched my hair a few times over the years to untangle rogue barrettes. Doing it in the stillness of his own house felt different.

He was gentle. Careful and slow, just like when he detangled any other object. He was able to pick out most of the primer with his fingers, but then he had me lean over his sink to wash out the rest. Our bodies were so close that I smelled his sweat. No doubt he could smell mine.

"Oh," I said, my eyes catching on something.

"Sorry. I'm trying to be careful."

"No, you're fine. But you've got some, too." I gestured to the spot behind his ear where a pen normally sat. He'd probably touched it out of habit. It was also in an awkward location, so I squeezed the dripping water from my hair and instructed him to remove his glasses. I reached out—and then hesitated. Just like he had done. In the five years we'd known each other, I had never touched his hair. My fingers made contact, and he stopped breathing.

I didn't understand, but there it was again: that familiar jolt and frisson. Touching his scalp was too intimate. I fought the urge to rake my hands through his unkempt hair, pull his head toward mine, and kiss him.

I suspected that he would allow it this time.

It was only the yellow latex, so the paint came off easily. I let go. He released a shuddering breath, which I ignored by turning on the sink full blast to wash my hands—and to wash away the feeling of danger. Maybe he *was* attracted to me, but he'd also had his reasons for rejecting me. It didn't matter that I didn't know what they were. I had to respect them. I did respect them.

"Well, Mason." Sometimes I called him Mason because it needled him. Tonight I needed that crowbar, the distance of humor. "We did good."

He put his glasses back on, and my heart tightened with lust. Goddammit. I was *so* attracted to men in chunky frames. He stared at the cabinets for several seconds. I thought he was collecting himself, but then he said, "They seem dingy now, don't they?"

"A little." A lot, actually. They'd already looked sad, but the fresh paint on the surrounding walls made them appear even worse.

He sighed. "I guess that's my next project, then."

"Repaint them in white if you want to keep it classic," I said, because it had been on my mind all day. "Or use the same yellow if you want something more interesting—purposeful oversaturation."

"What would you do?"

"It's not my house."

"But what would you do?"

"I'd . . . have to think about it." I switched the point of view back to him, where it belonged. "But you'll have plenty of time for that. First, you'll need to take off the doors, remove all the hardware, and sand everything. I've heard it's a terrible job."

He rubbed his temples. "Oh good."

"My friend Brittany has an electric sander," I said, collecting my tote bag and preparing to leave. "I'm sure you could borrow it."

"That'd be great. Would you mind texting her?"

"Wait. Now?"

"Might as well start tomorrow."

I raised my eyebrows.

He leaned against the sink in an exhausted way that wasn't meant to be suggestive but that I would think about later that night in bed. "You wouldn't happen to have any interest in helping out with a terrible job, would you?"

CHAPTER TWENTY-THREE

Brittany texted me back early the next morning. *You want me to lend my sander to the guy who crushed your heart back in January?*

Yes, I said.

The one who made you feel humiliated and ashamed?

He's INCREDIBLY responsible. He'll return it to you in better shape than he receives it.

It took more than a minute for her to respond. Her disapproving sigh was audible. *Fine.*

She left it on her porch along with a Ziploc filled with sanding pads, and I picked them up on my way to Macon's. Another breakfast was waiting for me on the table when I arrived: oatmeal swirled with blackberry compote and topped with toasted almonds. The cabinets had already been emptied and drawers pulled out, and their contents were separated into tidy piles in the dining room. Edmond was batting around a small whisk that clanked against the baseboards.

"Sorry," I said, catching an overripe whiff of myself. "I should have worn something else." I'd put the Colburn County shirt back on because it was the one I always used for hard labor, but clearly I should have christened a second work shirt.

Macon was wearing the plain black shirt I'd seen him gardening in. "I promise I only smell you a little."

I buried my head in my hands.

"Would you like to borrow something?" He sounded uncomfortable even as he offered it.

"That's okay. I'll just stink." I was still in a mindset where the best option in any situation was to wallow in my own misery. Besides, the thought of wearing his clothing discomfited me, too.

I tried to keep some distance between us as we washed the breakfast dishes, but it didn't take long for me to give up. Caring took too much effort, and he didn't like me that way anyway, so whatever. What was I even doing here?

"Are you okay?" he asked. Apparently, my vibes weren't great, but it looked like he was beating himself up, too. "I shouldn't have asked you to help. I put you on the spot last night."

"Hey, no. I want to help." When he gave me a skeptical look, I said, "I literally have nothing else to do right now. Not a single thing on my calendar until my sister's wedding."

He scrutinized me harder.

"Too honest?"

"No." His gaze dropped as he picked up the drill on the counter. "Do you know how to use one of these?" He didn't mean it in an insulting way. He knew enough about me to know that I'd probably never had a reason to use one. He was correct, and I shook my head.

"I think you might enjoy it this morning," he said.

Soon I understood. Drilling was loud and aggressive. I was a quick student, and it was satisfying to be the one making a racket. After I removed the first few screws, he left me to it and moved outside to figure out the sander. I joined him when I was finished. He was watching a tutorial on YouTube. "I think I've got it," he said uncertainly.

"I'm sure we can figure it out," I said.

He glanced at me, and I almost expected him to point out the boost of confidence that the drill had just given me. But he simply took me in and then returned his attention to the task at hand. And with a little trial and error, we did figure it out.

It turned out, though, that sanding was the terrible part of the terrible job. Finally I said, "Fuck this. They're *your* cabinets," and stormed back inside. I used sandpaper to scuff up the paint on the cabinet frames and listened to a novel about women who become so enraged that they turn into actual dragons.

We worked until lunchtime—he'd prepared vegan banh mi—and then continued all afternoon. We were only two-thirds of the way done when it was time for me to leave.

Macon removed his safety goggles and mask. "At least let me order a pizza to thank you." From the neck down, he was coated in a thick layer of chalky white dust.

"You've been feeding me all weekend," I said, turning off the faucet. I was so tired that I'd nearly nodded off as I bathed my arms in his sink again. And then, "You order pizza?"

"Sometimes I think you believe I'm not human."

I stared at him.

"No chain restaurants, vegetable toppings only, and I compost the box," he said angrily.

At last, I smiled. Although I was tempted, I wasn't sure I would be able to stay awake long enough for the food to arrive. "Maybe next time," I said.

It was the first night all year that I fell asleep easily and slept deeply.

That week at work, Macon kept me updated on his progress. He was still sanding late into the night, but he could only do so much given the upkeep his garden required. He spoke with such restraint that I couldn't tell if he wanted me to come over and help. My evenings were restless, and I began to long for the distraction of physical labor.

On Saturday, he returned Brittany's sander and the extra pads. Every crevice had been wiped clean, and the cord was neatly wrapped. Then he casually-but-not-casually mentioned that he was ready to start painting. Finally, he was fishing for assistance.

"I can help!" I said. Too eagerly, perhaps. By the way he appraised me, it was clear I'd given something else away about myself. I just wasn't sure what.

"Okay," he said, "but you have to pick the paint color."

"You still haven't decided?"

"Not my strong suit. Obviously."

"White it is."

"Great," he said. But then a minute later, "You said yellow was the more interesting choice."

"For me. But I would never stick you with an all-yellow kitchen. What if you hated it? Or wanted to sell your house?"

He looked offended. "I don't want to move."

"Good. You shouldn't. Your house is amazing."

"So . . . white."

"It's classic," I said.

A fifty-something man with a pinched mouth entered the library, and we stopped talking. It was the patron with our favorite name, Ken Fondness. Ken Fondness spoke as little as possible and was one of the Old Boat Guys, a small but staunch group of men who only checked out historical naval fiction by Patrick O'Brian and C. S. Forester. They would plow through one series, then the other, and then start back at the beginning. I once made a pirate joke, and Ken Fondness blew up at me because pirates were *not* a laughing matter and he was sick of Hollywood portraying them as lovable antiheroes. After that, he exclusively went to Macon's side of the desk.

Macon pulled his holds from the shelf—Ken Fondness always had two books on hold—and placed holds on the next two. Ken Fondness was nearing the end of the Horatio Hornblower series and was about to return to the Aubrey-Maturin series, which he preferred. (Old Boat Guys always preferred O'Brian.) Ken Fondness nodded his thanks, Macon nodded back, and Ken Fondness exited the building.

"He's so sad that he couldn't join the Royal Navy," I said with a hand over my heart.

"How many knots do you think he can tie?" Macon asked.

"He absolutely has a poster of sailing knots framed on his wall at home."

"I hope that when he retires, he'll be able to move to the coast."

"I bet he would be a great lighthouse keeper."

"*I* would be a great lighthouse keeper," Macon said.

It was true, and it delighted me to imagine him as a salty, grizzled old fellow polishing the lens to keep the boats safe.

The phone rang, and I answered. It was another regular, a woman I knew only by voice. She'd had another unsettling dream and wanted me to look up what an owl sitting on a saguaro cactus meant in one of our dream dictionaries. By the time we decided that her prickliness toward others might be preventing her from gaining new wisdom, I'd long forgotten what Macon and I had been discussing.

"But white is safe, right?" he said.

"She said the owl was tawny."

"My cabinets. Painting them."

"Oh." I slammed the dictionary closed. "Yeah. But don't you want safe? Although matching the cabinets to the walls is safer than it sounds. It's also a classic look."

Macon yanked the pen out from behind his ear and threw it at me.

I followed him to the hardware store after work and was selecting the correct brushes for the job, debating between the cheaper brand (cheaper!) and the more expensive brand (longer lasting!), when I overheard him tell the clerk at the paint counter, "One gallon of eggshell in Rise and Shine."

I leaned back, met his eyes, and widened mine.

He shrugged.

I let the brushes swing back into their display and hurried over.

"It's what you would pick," he said defensively. "And I asked for your opinion."

Giddiness washed over me. "Rise and Shine in satin," I told the clerk. "Not eggshell." And then I explained to Macon, "A little gloss in the finish will make them easier to clean."

Another shrug, but this one was accompanied by a hint of a smile. "You're in charge."

I hadn't been in charge of anything in a long time. I returned to the brushes and then handed him the sizes we needed in the expensive brand. They were the better value because I knew he would take good care of them.

May

DATE DUE	BORROWER'S NAME	ROOM NUMBER
JAN 25		
FEB 19		
MAR 30		
APR 17		
MAY 10		

CHAPTER TWENTY-FOUR

Painting the cabinets was almost as terrible as sanding them, and I wouldn't recommend the task to anybody unless they were already unhappy. Luckily, I was, so I took to it with gusto.

Macon kept us fed, and we worked as we listened to another audiobook—the new Louise Erdrich, which was great until the pandemic showed up in the story, and then we had to take a breather. Those wounds were still too raw. But the main plot involved a woman who worked in a bookstore, so Macon asked if I'd given any more consideration to the idea of opening my own.

"I haven't considered anything except your cabinets," I said, which wasn't true, but the bookstore fantasy was nearly as agonizing as wondering if anybody would ever love me enough to want to marry me, or if I would ever love somebody else enough to want to marry them.

We worked the whole weekend, and by the end, I had even convinced Macon to lose two cabinet doors and leave some open shelving on either side of the window above the sink. This required painting the insides of those cabinets, too, which we didn't have time for.

"I can come over after work tomorrow," I said.

"Tomorrow is a late shift."

"Wednesday, then. I can finish this, and you can get back to the garden." He tried to protest, but I interrupted. "I've seen the anguish in your eyes whenever you catch a glimpse of those weeds." I was teasing him, but I also felt a critical need, a *neediness*, to return. To keep going. With reluctance, he agreed. He didn't feel good about doing a fun job while I was doing an unfun one. I assured him that I did not consider getting bitten by mosquitos to be more fun.

It was nearly midnight on Wednesday when I finished the final coat. "I can come back tomorrow," I said, "and put the hardware back on."

"Another late shift," he said, distracted because he was reading the paint can.

"Fuck. Friday. I'll do it then."

"This says we need to wait a month for the paint to cure."

It was late, and I was exhausted. It was impossible to imagine any news more devastating. I burst into tears for the first time since becoming a shell, and he laughed. He actually laughed!

"I'm sorry," I said, taking in the mess of kitchen items crowding and scattered across his dining room. Edmond had continued to move things around, and the piles weren't tidy anymore. "I didn't mean to do this to you."

"Do what? Give me free labor? Make my kitchen beautiful?"

I kept crying.

His laughter died as if his heart were breaking, too. "Oh, Ingrid."

"It's been so hard." I didn't understand where this outburst was coming from.

And then Macon did something that he hadn't done since before the pandemic. Something I had been wanting desperately. He hugged me. I was surprised by the tightness of his grip. By the strength of his arms. I melted into him and cried against his shoulder.

"Okay," he said, but he didn't let go. "You're gonna be okay."

"Can I come back?" I blubbered.

I felt him laugh against me. "Yeah."

"On Friday?"

"For as long as it takes."

They were the exact words I needed to hear.

It had turned into May without me realizing it. As the cabinets began the slow process of curing, the bookstore idea continued to linger and harden inside my mind.

I texted Mika. *How did Bex learn how to start a business?*

You're still thinking about it! she said. *That makes me happy.*

Just curious.

Instinctively, Mika knew not to push. *Ridgetop Means Bizness. They're a nonprofit that teaches people how to open small businesses. They're affordable, and they guided Bex and Craig through the whole process.*

I clicked on her link and was disheartened to discover that there were no private appointments. It was an actual school with actual classes. And unlike Bex, I had no Craig, no business partner. I'd have to do it alone.

I put the idea back onto the shelf.

I slept each night at my apartment and went straight home after our late shifts, but every other hour of my days was spent in Macon's company. I worked like a maniac. No doubt it *was* mania. Because I couldn't screw the hardware back on yet, I polished each individual handle and knob and oiled the exposed insides of the cabinets. Then I oiled the window frames, back door frame, crown molding, and baseboards. Then the ceiling looked shabby, so I painted that, but it was the wrong task to do last, so then I had to do more touch-ups.

"I don't think there's anything else you can improve," Macon said, dropping off a clump of scarlet radishes dusted with rich black soil beside the sink. He'd long stopped helping, at my request. He purchased the supplies and assisted with the prep, but then he disappeared into the garden while I worked.

"A rug for the sink area," I said. "And curtains, café style, so you can still see out into the garden. Red and white stripes. Or maybe gingham. I bet Brittany could teach me how to sew them."

His silence was so acute that I knew to pivot.

The backsplash was original and in great condition; any chips only added to its charm. New countertops would have been fantastic, but the cost put them out of the question. A different light fixture also would have been good, but if I went antiquing and found something I loved, I would be tempted to keep it for myself.

He was right. I was done here, but I wasn't done.

"Your bathroom," I said.

His hackles rose. "What's wrong with my bathroom?"

"It's not gross, don't worry. But it's dreadfully boring."

"*Dreadfully*" was all he said, although it wasn't a denial. The bathroom was another drab, all-white space.

"Blue. You have that little window high up that shows off the sky, so it would bring that color down into the rest of the room. Plus, it's a bathroom. Blue is a clean color."

"There's ceiling paint in your hair," he said, stepping back outside and letting the door slam shut behind him.

This was as good as a yes, so my attention shifted and stayed on the bathroom for the next week and a half. It was a faster job, and I was already more experienced. I painted the ceiling first, then the sink cabinet, and then the walls, all the same delicate shade of a robin's egg. Macon was absurdly blessed to have an original tub and hexagon-tile floor, and he clearly knew it, because his grout was clean. Cory and I had been good about cleaning but bad about grout. As renters, the chore had never seemed important. Seeing the history contained in this one small room made it seem important now.

"I suppose I should be grateful that I have no secrets," Macon said, approaching from down the hallway and passing all of his belongings.

"You should consider new towels," I said.

His head popped in.

I was scrubbing his medicine cabinet. "Sorry. This will be good to go as soon as I'm done, but the sink cabinet is another you won't be able to use for a month."

"You don't sound sorry."

I stopped to give him a smile. "I'm not."

We stared at each other for a moment, and then he seemed embarrassed. "I can't get over how beautiful it looks," he said, turning his gaze and admiration toward the room. And I did sense that it was a turn. That he had been admiring me.

It made me nervous. I didn't trust myself. "Thanks."

"I mean it. I don't know how to repay you for all this."

I assured him, as I already had a dozen times, that the distraction was helping me.

"Speaking of distractions," he said, "have you given any more thought to that bookstore idea?"

I was surprised that he was bringing it up again. Unenthusiastically, I told him about the business school. "And you don't want to go to school," he said.

I pointed at him as if to say *bingo*. "I do, however, want to paint your dining room."

He leaned against the doorframe, tired but amused. "Oh yeah?"

"I'd like to bring the yellow into that room to marry those two spaces."

"Marry the spaces."

I hid my pinkening cheeks behind the door of his medicine cabinet. "Yes."

He stayed quiet while I finished cleaning. As a person who could, on some extremely notable occasions, be impulsive, I had always admired that he was comfortable taking his time. I asked him to hand me the items from the hallway that belonged inside the medicine cabinet, and he urged me to sit instead. So I sat on the toilet lid while he carefully put everything away—the toothpaste on this shelf, the razor on that one. He didn't have much. Only what he needed.

"Just how deep into my house is this yellow going to spread?" he asked.

"Your living room will be green."

"My study?"

"Red, maybe. A dark, classic red."

"My bedroom?"

"I haven't seen your bedroom," I said, making it awkward again. I remained highly aware that *he* was aware that I had wanted to sleep with him, that I'd accidentally admitted as much out loud in front of him and our coworkers.

Our coworkers. They knew I was helping him paint, but they didn't know I was spending more time at his house than my own apartment. Macon and I hadn't discussed it—hadn't meant for it to be a secret—but it was. Whatever I was doing over here was strange and private. The only other person who knew the full depth of the situation was Kat.

"There's nobody here who you'd want to fuck, but will you come paint my rental house next?" she'd asked.

"I do not still want to fuck Macon."

"Yeah, okay," she'd said.

"Okay," he said. "Dining room next."

While painting the dining room, I was also able to convince Macon to buy a new table. We spent an entire Sunday driving around to garage sales, estate sales, and thrift stores. It had been a while since I'd ridden in his car. Like all cars, it smelled intensely of its owner. He was a safe driver, and I felt as if I were snugged in a protective cocoon as I breathed in his scent all day.

We found it at the Humane Society's thrift store: a huge round wooden table.

"They never have furniture this good here," I said.

"It was mine." The woman behind the counter's voice was jolly and sweet, and her petite body was shaped like a gumdrop. "I brought it in this morning. My ex-husband loved that table. I did, too, but I hate the lying cocksucker more."

I promised her we'd take good care of it. It was easy to slip into that *we*, easier than explaining who *we* actually were. Macon paid, the woman slapped a SOLD sign on it, and we agreed to pick it up within the next twenty-four hours.

"Do you know anybody with a truck?" I asked when we were back in his car.

"Richard still has that big van," he said. Our old coworker had needed it to help his wife get around town in her wheelchair. Lucy had died during the pandemic, and he'd had to bury her alone. We'd all attended her memorial a year later at the bird-watching park near Thistle Lake. I felt resistant about asking, but when Macon texted him, Richard was happy to let us borrow the van. Librarians were always happy to lend and borrow. We picked up the table the next morning, and Macon surprised me by donating his old table and chairs to the store.

"You could sell those and make a little money," I said.

"Passing along the good luck to somebody else feels more important," he said, probably enjoying the fact that his donation would also help out all those unloved cats who still needed homes.

It was too much for me. Kat was right: I did still want to sleep with him. I had never stopped wanting to sleep with him. And, even worse, my feelings were about so much more than wanting to sleep with him. I *liked him* liked him, I realized, reverting straight back to childhood and all of those unreciprocated crushes. The sensation was torturous.

No. Ingrid. No.

The circular table fit perfectly into the square room. I touched up the yellow walls and tried to tamp down my useless raging infatuation while Macon conditioned the wood and asked me about chairs. He'd already brought the two patio chairs inside to use in the meantime.

"Thrifted," I replied. He was bent in an odd position to reach one of the table legs, and his shirt had ridden up enough to reveal a triangular slice of abdomen. His stomach wasn't muscular or toned or anything particularly special, but it hinted at the exercise he received while gardening, and it was *his* skin, and it was bare. I wanted to bite into him. "Mismatched. All wood. But seats the same height and all painted the same color."

"So, mismatched but matched," he said.

"Exactly."

"Just like your napkins."

It took a moment for me to realize what he was talking about. He'd remembered. It was unfair for him to be this romantic right now. "Yeah."

"What color?" he asked.

I shook my head, reminding myself that I was still an emotional disaster. I could get through this. I was an adult. These feelings would pass.

"I don't know," I finally said. "I haven't thought it all through yet."

He paused to look at me, searching for something. I wasn't sure what. "Fair enough."

My feelings did not pass, but I had so much practice managing them around him that it was easier to keep managing them than I expected. Near the end of the month, the weather took a chilly turn, and he started wearing his duffel coat again (cute) and fretting about his Japanese maple (also cute). The fire at the library had been lit all week, and everyone was bemoaning climate change. Normally I liked the cold, but a cold Memorial Day weekend was unsettling. Still, I felt a nervous excitement as I pitched him my most ambitious project yet.

I wanted to bring the outside inside and turn his strangely long living room into a cozy green reading room. It didn't make sense for his books to be tucked away in his study and his television to be out on display, so my plan was to switch them. The rarely used television would go in his study, and his library would go in the living room. I planned to build my dream shelves all the way across the longest wall. I wasn't sure *how* I would build them but felt confident I could figure it out. Books would also add warmth and art and texture, which his house still lacked. And I'd make their colorful spines stand out by painting the shelves and walls the same deep shade of green.

I knew he'd be willing to add some cat-safe plants to enhance the greenness, but I also needed to persuade him to ditch the mini blinds and buy some curtains and rugs. The room had no softness apart from Edmond's beds and the couch. The couch depressed me, too, but I was spending Macon's money, not mine, and could only encourage him to purchase so many items.

I laid out my plans, expecting him to look weary and overwhelmed. Expecting him to declare that enough was enough. Instead, something rare happened: He perked up.

"So, the room would become sort of a . . . book forest?"

I brightened, albeit hesitantly. "Or a garden, depending on the sort of rugs and curtains you want. Or if that's too much, I could help you find those things later. I know all this paint hasn't been cheap."

But he waved that off. "I can do rugs and curtains."

Because he wasn't much of a consumer, I imagined he had some savings. I was glad he was willing to spend some of it to enrich his daily life. He would be happy in this room, and I wanted my friend to be happy. Complicated feelings aside, I did love being his friend again. And I suspected that I was his *best* friend, which felt even better.

We sat at his new table and put together a task list for the living room. When we were finished, he added one more item.

I sighed. "Ridgetop Means Bizness."

"I loathe the *z*, too."

"Macon."

"I looked into it. Orientation is free. After that, *if you're interested*"—he emphasized this, interrupting my protestations—"it's six weeks of classes, but only one class per week. And it's only four hundred dollars, which may or may not be a lot on your budget, but it's reasonable."

I pushed away from the table, but he wasn't deterred. "You don't even have to sign up for the orientation. You can just show up."

"I'll think about it," I said, exiting the room to end the conversation.

But I underestimated his stubbornness. For the rest of the week, he hounded me.

"Orientation is this Saturday," he said, as I repainted the living room ceiling and he repaired the spidery cracks in the plaster walls.

"You'd have to leave work a few minutes early, but you know Sue won't mind," he said, as I pushed a cart through the double doors to empty the outside book drop.

"They're not going to try to sell you a time-share," he said, as he helped me put painter's tape around his windows. He was unknowingly doing his best to make himself less appealing, and it was almost working.

I climbed off his stepladder and set down my roll of tape in defeat.

"Excellent," he said, and kept taping.

June

DATE DUE	BORROWER'S NAME	ROOM NUMBER
JAN 25		
FEB 19		
MAR 30		
APR 17		
MAY 10		
JUN 03		

CHAPTER TWENTY-FIVE

I was still feeling hostile about being pressured into it when I took my seat at the Ridgetop Means Bizness orientation. The stackable chairs were modern and lime green and matched the rest of the building's decor, which gave off the vibe of a derivative tech start-up, further inflaming my distrust. There were fourteen of us. Everybody was older than me except for one person who looked to be a few years younger. This did provide a smidge of encouragement. Starting a business was a job for adults, and if they were one, I supposed I was, too.

A man named Jamal with a friendly smile and a lime-green Ridgetop Means Bizness polo shirt walked us through what the organization had to offer. He was good. His enthusiasm seemed genuine, and I felt myself being a little swayed. Classes started in two weeks, but I could take them at night while still working at the library. They also had their own loan department and—because they were a nonprofit organization as opposed to a bank— they could lend to people whom traditional banks couldn't. They could afford to take greater risks on their students.

Despite being unsure, I took home their paperwork.

When Macon asked how it had gone, I told him *okay*. My lack of elaboration was a signal for him to leave me alone about it, which he did. Instead,

I asked the stained-glass portrait of Mary Brisson what she thought about me leaving to open a bookstore. Mary met my inquiry with stoic silence, still cradling her book as if it were a holy baby, but I swear a new spark lit behind her eyes. It might have been light reflecting off the lake, though.

At Macon's house, the moment finally arrived: The cabinetry's paint had cured, and it was time to reassemble the kitchen. All other projects were put on hold while we reattached the hardware, slid the drawers into place, and screwed the doors on.

We stepped back to take in the result of our hard work.

The effect was a magical heightening of reality. The room gleamed with light and warmth and sunshine. It looked both inviting and comforting, and it spoke of enchanted kitchens of yore—of braided bread loaves and bundles of herbs drying upside down and piping hot bowls of nourishing soup. It was a space that encouraged love and gathering.

"I'm a little speechless," I said.

We were standing side by side, and his voice thickened. "Thank you."

I fought the urge to lay my head on his shoulder.

A number of frequently used items were already sitting on the shelves, but now we took our time adding the rest and arranging everything so that the most beautiful items—the drinking glasses and a collection of ceramic mugs made by local potters—were positioned in the open shelving. Then we refilled the drawers with everything that had been crowding his dining room. Suddenly both rooms looked better, and the clean spaces also highlighted all the recently conditioned wood. This corner of his house no longer looked weak and empty. It had *life*.

"Is it okay for me to say that it looks even better now than it did when it was filled with Danielle's stuff?"

It was a tease, but he answered matter-of-factly. "It is okay, and it does."

"I think we're restoring your house's spirit."

He let that sit for a moment before asking, "Just the house?"

I'd thrown my whole self into the work as a distraction. The need to do it had felt beyond my control. A compulsion, or maybe I was being compelled by something bigger. Macon was right. My spirit was in the process of being restored, too. And I was changing.

"I've decided to do it," I said. "Open a bookstore."

His brows rose in surprise, and I laughed—also with surprise.

"I decided just now," I clarified.

"Oh my God. But that's great."

Library school had filled me with dread, but whenever I thought about business school, I felt nervous. It was that tingly anxious nervousness that could often be mistaken for a bad feeling but actually meant something was important and shouldn't be ignored.

"I know it'll be hard—" I started.

"You can do hard things," he said.

"And I know it might fail—"

"It's not going to fail."

"It might. But even so, I want to do it."

Unexpectedly, Macon sprang toward his fridge with a rare level of excitement and rummaged around until he found what he was looking for. "It's not champagne, but it is bubbly."

It was a golden-brown liquid in an unlabeled, repurposed bottle. "What is that? Vinegar?"

"Close. Kombucha."

I laugh-groaned. "I didn't recognize it without the amoeba pancakes."

"Yeah, the mother is in my bedroom right now, making more."

"Oh, Macon. The *mother* is in your *bedroom*."

He ignored this and gave me a practical response. "It creeped you out, so I moved it into my closet where you wouldn't have to look at it."

I didn't expect such a touching reason. "Aw. You hid the monster for me."

He tried to scowl as he poured the beverage into two tumblers, but the corners of his mouth twitched. He shoved one of the glasses at me. "Just drink your celebratory fizz."

I held it aloft for him to clink.

"To your bookstore," he said.

"To my bookstore." The words were as terrifying as they were jubilant.

Mika shrieked with joy. "I want to be your assistant manager. Promise me I'm your first hire."

I wished I could hug her through our phones. "Of course you're hired."

On my first day of community college, I'd met Cory. On my first day of business school, I gave Sue my six weeks' notice. On both occasions, the ground slipped out from underneath me, but while the former had given me a giddy floating sensation, the latter felt more like being unmoored. I was preparing to say goodbye to stability, a regular paycheck, and health insurance.

"Yes," Sue said. "But you're saying hello to the opportunity for a bigger life."

After some initial concern and a lot of questions to make sure my decision wasn't as impulsive as it sounded—I had the money I'd been saving ever since I'd paid off my student loans, which wasn't insignificant, plus the business school's loan department had a solid track record of providing assistance—she was proud of me. She said everything my parents had already said over the phone, and although I was grateful for their support, it meant even more to me coming from her. Perhaps that was unfair. But Sue knew the adult me, she had *witnessed* the adult me, and my parents largely hadn't. When Sue believed I could do it, she made me believe, too.

School was school: helpful, overwhelming, boring, necessary. I studied operations, research and development, financials, and marketing. I worked on creating a business plan and learned how to apply for a loan. Every time I grappled with the notion that I was about to drain my entire savings and willingly go back into debt, I felt sick, but there was no getting around it. I needed the money, and I didn't have the sort of family that I could ask to borrow it from. Nor would I have wanted to. My pride wouldn't let me. This was something I had to do on my own.

My new teacher also made it clear that I needed to start looking for a business location immediately. Unfortunately, it wasn't the only location that needed finding. I arrived home after my first class to discover a letter from my landlord slipped underneath my door. My lease was ending on July first, and if I wanted to renew, there would be an increase in rent. The rent was already more than I felt comfortable paying on my own, but I'd been planning to make it work somehow because I didn't think I could handle becoming single, starting a business, and moving into a new place all in the same year. Now I had no choice.

"He only gave you two weeks' notice?" Kat asked. "Is that legal in America?"

"I think so? I don't even want to live here, but it was the one thing in my life that I didn't have to deal with. I was gonna figure it out next summer."

I chose to take it as a sign that it was stupid of me to keep ignoring the rent; I had to move someplace more affordable. This was not the time to indulge. But a glance around my apartment made me want to cry again. My one-bedroom with crappy furniture didn't feel like an *indulgence*. I supposed now I needed to find a studio. A less-than-one-bedroom.

I announced it that way at work the next morning. "I need to find a less-than-one-bedroom."

Macon was confused, but when I told him about the letter, the audacity of the timing infuriated him. "I don't have time for anger," I said. "I have to go to work, go to class, write a business plan, find a business location, and now find an apartment and move everything I own in two weeks. Not that it will take me long to move everything I own," I added bitterly.

He didn't even think about it. "You can stay with me."

My heart stopped. What did he mean by that?

"You can take the spare room. Edmond's room."

I checked to see if any of our coworkers had overheard. They hadn't. But my glancing around made him conscious of them, too. He hadn't been talking loudly, but he lowered his voice even further. "Until you have time to find your own place, of course."

"That might not be for a while."

"That's okay. It'll give you a chance to save up some more money."

"You want me to live with you *rent free?*"

"Why would I charge you? You've done so much work on my house. You've already paid."

I was stupefied. "Macon . . ."

Did he look hopeful?

"I can't live with you," I said carefully. *Because it's confusing. Because it would mean different things to each of us. Because I might never want to leave.*

But he didn't ask why, and I don't know what reason he filled in. His energy faded and darkened. He slid away into subdued professionalism. "So you need to find a studio."

I was still reeling at the idea of being his roommate. Sleeping so close to his bedroom and standing naked in his shower while he wandered around on the other side of the door. I couldn't believe he'd made the offer like it was nothing. That meant it *was* nothing to him. He was only reacting poorly because I'd discarded the idea so quickly.

He suggested the free apartment-hunting website that we often directed patrons to, but I'd already glanced through it and had immediately gotten stressed out. It had clarified why my rent was being raised so significantly. *Everything* in Ridgetop was more expensive than it used to be. For the price I was paying now, I could get a studio, except . . . I was already paying too much. Only a handful of properties would actually save me money.

I spent the next few days viewing these apartments on my lunch breaks but ran into a string of bad luck. At the first stop, I made the mistake of telling the landlord that I wanted a more affordable location because I was quitting my job to open my own business. Suddenly that place became unavailable. I learned my lesson and kept my mouth shut. But the other apartments had already been claimed by the time I showed up, and there was a lot of competition even for the ones at my current price. I was looking at increasingly poor spaces with increasingly higher rents, and everything was falling through.

"You don't by any chance have a room you're renting out?" I began asking patrons, because it seemed like every homeowner *did* have a room they were renting out these days. A number of them answered in the affirmative, but all of their spaces were reserved for the tourists on Airbnb. I could see Macon holding his tongue. If I asked, I knew Edmond's room was still mine, but I couldn't accept that.

I emailed all the employees in the library system, an act that was frowned upon, but I was leaving, and I was desperate. Nobody had anything available, although I did receive a reply from Stephen at the East branch wondering if it was true that I was opening a bookstore and could he apply for a job? He was interested in similar work with fewer volatile banners. We'd only met once, but I liked him, and he had a good reputation. I told him I'd be in touch, which gave me a bounce of energy that deflated the instant I returned to my search. I even considered texting Cory to see if he knew of any available places, but my last shred of dignity wouldn't allow it.

Mika checked in three days before I had to move out, wanting to hear how my classes were going and asking if I needed any help finding the business location. "I'd love your help," I said, "but I can't start looking until next week. I have to be out of my apartment by Saturday, and I still don't have a place to live."

I thought I'd told her, but apparently we'd only been discussing the bookstore. After asking some follow-up questions, she chided me, "I wish you'd told me sooner! I might have something. It's not great, but . . . it sounds like you don't need something great?"

Desperation overrode trepidation. "What sort of not great?"

She and Bex were turning an addition on their house into a single-occupancy rental space. In case something scary happened with the economy again—which felt less like an *if* and more like a *when*—and the dojang couldn't pull through, they'd already have another source of income. "The toilet and shower have been installed, but we haven't hooked up the sink or oven yet. Or installed any cabinets. I'll have to talk to Bex, but you could pay us either in work or a small amount of rent or some combination of those. We could draw up a contract so the parameters would be clear."

"Mika, that sounds *very* great." I was trying not to cry.

"Don't say that until you see it," she said.

I saw it the next morning before work. It was smaller than every other place I'd toured—a micro-studio, my friends called it. The room was rectangular and spanned the back side of their house. Still under construction, it was covered in sawdust and plastic sheeting. Their kitchen was on the other side of the main wall, and I'd be permitted to use it until the studio's kitchen was installed. My queen-size mattress was too big for the space, and they hadn't purchased any furniture yet, but Bex told me they'd buy a new twin bed that weekend. The deal we worked out was that I would help them get the space ready to rent and pay a minimal fee to cover water and electricity, but the space would be mine through the end of the year, and I could break the contract whenever, without penalty, if I found someplace better.

It was a horrible space. It was a generous deal.

I took it.

The studio wasn't big enough to hold everything I owned, so I asked Macon if Edmond's room was still available. His posture straightened until I clarified that I'd like to store some of my belongings there through the end of the year. When I told him about my new place, he looked dubious. "You'll be washing your hands in the shower? Getting your *drinking water* from it?"

"Only until the sink is installed."

"Ingrid."

"It's not as bad as it sounds. And hey! I'll learn some new skills."

Macon didn't speak for several seconds. Then he said stiffly, "The room is still yours—for you or anything you need to store."

"Just my stuff. Thank you."

He offered to help me move. I wanted to say that I could handle it, but I did need help, and a man's stronger muscles would admittedly be useful. It was a late shift, but we had no time to waste, so Macon followed me home after closing so we could take the first two carloads to his house. I'd been collecting cardboard boxes, and my books and vinyl were already packed. I pointed them out, but instead of grabbing them, he scrutinized my entire apartment, ending with my bedroom. My move had finally given one of us permission to enter the other's most personal space. His arms crossed as he glanced between my bed and my dresser. "I guess we could borrow Richard's van again. We'll need it for your couch and bookcases, too."

"Oh, none of that is coming with me. I'll leave it by the dumpsters and post a message about it on the Buy Nothing group."

"I thought your new place wasn't furnished."

"It's not. But there's no room for any of this."

He turned toward me, and I was surprised to see that he was angry.

"It's all bowed in and falling apart anyway, see?" I struggled to yank open a dresser drawer, showing him that the bottom had collapsed. "Particleboard. That's why I can't sell it."

"What about your bed?"

"I don't want that either."

"But it looks fine," he pressed.

"Listen, there's a reason why Cory didn't want any of it either, okay?" I didn't mean to be sharp, but the mention of my ex was enough for Macon to drop it.

We loaded the boxes into our cars and still had a little room left, so we hunted for smaller items to fill the empty pockets. "What about these?" Macon pointed to my bedside lamps. "You'll need one, but probably not both. I could take the other for you."

"I hate those lamps. I'm not keeping them either."

"What's wrong with them?"

I lifted one up, and he laughed when it *ding ding ding*ed.

"Well, you'll still need one," he said. "Don't get rid of them both."

I wouldn't need any kitchen equipment for a while, though, so we packed up some of that and headed to his house. I hadn't been there since I'd started school and was ashamed to see that I'd left his living room in such a chaotic state. He assured me that he didn't care, but then we had to drag several items from Edmond's room into his study to make room for my belongings, and the chaos grew. It was almost midnight before all my boxes were stacked inside his spare room.

"As always, I don't know how to thank you," I said. We were exhausted and needed to crash. We had to work the next day, and then we still had to move the rest of my things.

"As always, I'm paying you back for labor you've already done."

"Well, dinner's on me tomorrow." A few hours earlier, he'd fed me leftover pasta freshened up with a generous handful of leafy herbs. It hadn't tasted like leftovers at all. It had been delicious, adding to my tab of guilt. Yes, I'd been helping him, but I liked being in his house, so the equation felt lopsided. I was getting something out of it.

It didn't occur to me that he might be getting something out of it, too.

I went home at lunch the next day and hastily packed up most of my bedroom. I crammed everything I didn't want Macon to see (undergarments, vibrators, lube) into a backpack, stuffed my laundry basket and hamper with as much clothing as possible, and then dropped it all off at my new place. The basket and hamper returned with me to carry another round later.

Laundry. I'd forgotten about it, but I doubted Mika and Bex would mind if I used their machines. I could probably do laundry at Macon's house, too, on days when I was already over there painting. I tried not to feel depressed about being back to where I'd been in college—a person without my own washer and dryer. It was actually worse than that, though, because the new studio was smaller than my first apartment. Much smaller.

After work, Macon and I threw everything in my bathroom into boxes. It was a strange reversal. I had seen his toiletries, and now he was seeing mine: menstrual cups, dandruff shampoo, eczema cream, pimple patches, tooth-whitening mouthwash. "Do you need this on top?" he asked, rattling my night guard in its plastic case. I was too busy to be anything but grateful. I crammed it into my pocket so it wouldn't get lost.

We emptied out the rest of my bedroom, refilling the basket and hamper and tossing the rest haphazardly into other bags. He forced me to take one lamp and a bedside table.

When we arrived at the studio and I turned on the lights, he looked stunned.

"I know." I headed off the lecture. He hadn't even seen the sawdust and plastic sheeting; Mika and Bex had already cleaned that up. "But it's only temporary. I'm dumping everything in that corner, so just pile it over there as high as it will go. I'll probably have to store some more of this at your place, but I don't have time to go through it all right now."

He just stood there clutching an armload of my belongings. He was only a few inches taller than me, but his body seemed huge in the space. That's when I realized the ceilings were unusually low.

"I know," I said again.

"Ingrid." He said it in that familiar, sad way, as if I were the one breaking him somehow. It didn't feel fair.

The door flew open behind him. Relieved, I launched myself into Mika's and Bex's arms. They were both small, but while Mika was delicate and gentle, Bex was wiry and muscular. Mika was wearing a sheer blouse and gold earrings that dangled just past her bobbed hair. Bex kept their hair closely cropped for ease of maintenance and wore stylish tracksuits almost exclusively. Tonight they were attired head-to-toe in classic Adidas.

"We're so happy this is going to work out," Mika said.

"And we're sorry it's such a dump," Bex said.

I glanced at Macon, worried that he would voice his agreement, but he'd rearranged his features to look less aggravated. "This is my friend, Macon."

Mika's eyebrows shot up.

Shit. I'd forgotten that I'd mentioned him to her at the café. I couldn't tell if Macon had caught her reaction. Everybody shook hands, I made sure they all knew each other's pronouns, and then my new landlords helped us unload the cars. When we finished, the pile of my belongings nearly touched the ceiling.

"Is there any more?" Bex asked, and Macon laughed darkly.

Mika frowned with worry. "Do you need help? I know everything has to be out before tomorrow."

I started to say no, because they were doing enough for me already, but Macon interrupted. "We could use your help carrying the bigger furniture down to the dumpster. Nothing is heavy, but it's unwieldy, and Ingrid's place is on the second floor."

Mika changed into a T-shirt—even the plain white tee looked prettier on her than it would on most people—and then my friends returned with us to my apartment. Keeping my promise of dinner, I ordered an extra-large pizza from a local joint called Pizza Friend, honoring Macon's rules: not a chain, vegetable toppings only, and the box would be his to compost. He seemed pleased but also embarrassed that I remembered his outburst so precisely.

He and Bex began hefting away the unwanted furniture while Mika and I packed up everything that remained. My downstairs neighbors showed up, hearing that I was giving things away for free. They claimed a bookcase in exchange for helping us carry out the mattress and couch. The pizza arrived, we devoured it, and then, eventually, my apartment was empty.

My friends were still chatty, but I had grown quiet. The final item we lugged out was the vacuum cleaner, which I'd just used to sweep the floors one last time. Hopefully I'd at least get the deposit back. I'd have to contact Cory to give him his half. It was our last remaining financial tie.

"Does the vacuum go to your place or mine?" Macon asked.

"You don't have room for it," Bex said to me. "Why don't you let him take it, and you can borrow ours?"

It was disheartening to say goodbye to so many of my possessions, but what was one more? Everybody got in their cars to leave when I remembered that I still needed to post a photo to the Buy Nothing group. I hopped back out and jogged over to the dumpsters. Everything was heaped in a jumble in the darkness. The second lamp dinged as I approached. The sound was mournful, as if it knew this was farewell.

I looked up at my building. The lights in my apartment were off.

Not my building. Not my apartment.

I closed my eyes to smell the pines, but all I inhaled was the stench of garbage. Behind me, a car door opened and shut. Unhurried footsteps approached. Macon wouldn't drive away until I did; he had only left me behind that one memorable night.

"It feels like I've reverted a decade," I said without turning around. A lump rose in my throat. "Like every single thing that I accumulated in my twenties is worthless."

"It's not too late. We can still take it with us."

"No, you saw it. It's all trash."

He came to a stop beside me. "Which is why you aren't reverting. You're graduating."

I only laughed to push down my tears.

"You were right," he said. "You don't need any of this anymore. You have better things coming."

I wasn't sure I believed him, but it had been a long night, and we still weren't done. I took the photo. It was dark, but it would do. Free stuff was free stuff.

It was late when we finished, and I had continued to unravel as we unloaded the last of my belongings into his spare room. I was finally getting ready to leave when he pointed out that I had no bed to sleep in that night.

I sighed. "I know. I'm just gonna sleep in a pile of clothes."

"Why don't you stay? I'll take the couch, and you can take my bed."

"No, it's fine. I'm so exhausted that I won't even notice my clothes aren't a bed."

"You shouldn't be driving when you're this tired. Seriously, just stay here."

"I'm not going to stay here."

"Why not?" His frustration was rising. "Just take my bed."

"I'm not taking your bed."

"Fine, my couch."

My sudden eruption was volcanic. "I'm not sleeping in your house!"

"Oh my God." He put his hands to his temples. "What is happening? Why the fuck not?"

"Because of the thing! You know. The thing."

"What *thing*?"

"That time I tried to kiss you!" I covered my mouth as if I could swallow the words back down whole.

His eyes widened, and he took a step back. "That was . . . that's not . . ."

"See? It's still weird. And your friendship means too much to me. I can't afford to lose it. I can't afford to lose *anything else* right now."

He sat with that for a long moment.

"It's just a bed," he said finally, quietly. "Or a couch."

I took the couch.

Macon was right. It was just a couch, but in my exhaustion, I'd twisted everything up. I didn't know what I had been thinking. I *hadn't* been thinking. But now that the house was quiet and I was alone with my thoughts, I couldn't imagine a single scenario in which him giving me a place to sleep for one night would have led to me . . . making another move on him? Was that what I was afraid of? My overreaction didn't make sense, and now I'd soured things between us again.

We hadn't spoken much after I'd agreed to stay. He'd brought me a blanket and pillow, and I'd brushed my teeth using his toothpaste and my index finger. Tomorrow was Saturday, so we had to go to work. I needed to shower, but I'd have to do that at my new place in the morning because I also needed to change. I knew I should just leave, but that would feel rude.

Although he was down the hallway and behind a closed door, his frustrated presence loomed over me. A purring cat might have provided solace, but he had locked Edmond in the bedroom with him, presumably so Edmond wouldn't bother me.

The couch was lumpy and uncomfortable. Weeks ago, we'd hefted it into the center of the room so that it wouldn't get splattered with paint. Now moonlight cast gloomy shadows of the ladder, buckets, brushes, and tarps. The entire room had been dismantled, yet nothing had been painted. I didn't have time and still had no idea how to pull off the promised bookshelves. And if I couldn't figure those out here, how could I possibly figure out the shelving for my store?

My restless mind cycled through the list of things that I still had to learn and do and figure out. I had to help finish the studio, and then I had to find another apartment. And I only had a month left of paychecks and health insurance, and then I had to figure out those things, too. And the classes would teach me some of the skills I needed to know, but they were another thing I had to keep up with while simultaneously applying for a loan and finding a business location. And Mika would help with that, but I'd always imagined Macon helping, too—and then I was right back to thinking about the humiliation of implying that I was afraid I might make another move on him. How else could he have interpreted my freak-out?

No. Ingrid. No.

The blanket was too hot. I sloughed it off. My minty, toothpasty finger found a hole in the couch's upholstery and couldn't stop touching it. My fiddling hands. The pillow smelled like Macon. I had the strangest sensation of wanting to smash my face into it, kiss it as if I were a child pretending, which filled me with shame and fury. I tossed and turned. Sweated. The crickets and katydids thrummed with summer heat. The scent was overwhelming. I pushed my finger all the way into the couch's hole, and then I did it again and again and again.

July

DATE DUE	BORROWER'S NAME	ROOM NUMBER
JAN 25		
FEB 19		
MAR 30		
APR 17		
MAY 10		
JUN 03		
JUL 22		

CHAPTER TWENTY—SIX

At the first hint of dawn, I folded the blanket, used the toilet, and headed for the door.

"Are you leaving?" Macon's voice was low and scratchy with sleep when he appeared at the threshold between the hallway and living room. He squinted at me because he wasn't wearing his glasses. His hair was a disaster, and he needed to shave.

My heart thumped. It was unfair how attractive a man could look in the morning, even when he was exhausted, even when he was a friend, even when that friendship was strained. I cleared my dry throat. "I need to shower and change. I was gonna text you."

"Breakfast?"

"No. I'm okay."

"Okay," he said after a moment. There was nothing else to say.

My new place was only five minutes away, so close that I felt even stupider for having spent the night. I arrived in a state. It took ten enraging minutes to find my shower toiletries, and then the instant I was naked, I realized all the windows were uncovered. I turned off the overheads and showered briskly in the early morning light. My unit was in the backyard, so it was fairly private, but I still felt exposed. I'd forgotten to look for a towel, so I squeegeed my body with my hands and shook off the rest of the water like a dog. Work didn't begin for another three hours, so I curled up—nudely, wetly, miserably—on my clothes and crashed until my alarm went off. Then I dug through the pile again, found some clothing that would do and about half of my makeup. My hair dryer could have been anywhere, so I twisted my hair into a damp and lifeless bun.

"Morning, neighbor!" Bex called out as I trudged to my car. They were drinking coffee on the front porch. Their chair was tipped back, their feet up on a table. I adjusted course and wandered over. "We didn't realize you came home last night until we heard the shower," they said.

When I explained that I hadn't, they gave me a closer look. Their eyes were naturally dramatic with thick brows and long lashes. After an intense appraisal, they slid their mug across the table to me. I rarely shared beverages postpandemic, but—after only a brief hesitation—I accepted.

"So." Their thick brows waggled. "Macon."

"It's *really* not like that."

My tone was dour enough and their respect for privacy was healthy enough that they grinned but smoothly changed the subject. "We'll have a bed for you by the time you get home."

"Any plans for covering the windows?"

"Shit." The front chair legs thunked back onto the porch. "Sorry about that. No idea, but we'll take care of that today, too."

I thanked them for everything, including the coffee, and made it to the library on time. Sue and Alyssa chattered like noisy songbirds while we prepared to open, but Macon arrived even later than usual and in an extraordinarily grouchy mood. His dark eyes were underscored with even darker circles, and his hair was still smashed and poofed and sticking out in all directions, a warning to anyone who dared speak to him.

Alyssa did not heed the warning. "What were *you* up to last night?"

Before he could destroy her for such a banal ribbing, I stepped in. "It's my fault. He helped me move." I neglected to mention that it had been the second night in a row.

Sue looked surprised. She knew about my apartment woes, but Macon and I had yet to divulge the full extent of our friendship. It shouldn't have felt illicit, but it did. Or perhaps not revealing it was what made it feel illicit. "You should have asked us, too," she said. "We could have lent a hand."

"Yeah," Alyssa said, though if I had asked her, she probably would have claimed to be busy. (I didn't blame her. It sucked helping people move.)

"I'll call you next time," I said grimly.

Work was hectic from the moment the doors opened. A puppeteer arrived for the summer reading program, shortly followed by a tsunami of children. Alyssa managed the event on the lakeside porch, but even inside the branch it was packed and loud. Macon twitched at every cheer from the crowd, ready to incinerate the puppets in the fireplace. A steady line plowed past our desk, and it wasn't until after our later-than-usual lunches that the library finally calmed.

Macon put his head on the desk, muffling his voice. "Fuck. This. Day."

"Were you able to get any sleep last night?" I asked.

"Very little." His head lifted. "You?"

"Nope."

A toddler screeched in the children's area, and our eyes bugged. We waited. The kid shut up, and Macon's head dropped back between his arms on the desk.

I had to say it so we could move past it. "I'm sorry about last night."

He turned his head to the side to look at me again.

"I genuinely don't know what got into me. Are we okay?"

"Yeah. Of course." His words implied that it was obvious, but a measure of tension relaxed from his facial muscles.

We didn't make any weekend plans because it was understood that I needed to get settled. When I returned to my new place that evening, a dozen plastic milk crates were scattered across the backyard, and a brand-new mattress was on the studio floor. It was exuding a gassy chemical smell, and the windows were all the way open. I hadn't slept on a twin bed since leaving my childhood home. Once Cory and I began to visit as a couple, my parents had replaced it with a larger size. I'd forgotten how small they were.

Mika arrived swiftly at my door. "There are sheets, I promise. Nice organic ones. I'm washing them right now. And the bed frame is on order, but it should only take a week."

"Better than my accommodations last night," I joked. Despair gripped me.

"We also ordered bamboo window shades, but until they arrive we can hang up some old towels. Would that be okay? We didn't want to do it until we checked with you. And I thought we could stack up those crates and use them for open shelving for your clothes. They were in our basement, so I had to hose them off, but they should be dry now. I can help you set them up."

"Sure. Yeah, thanks."

Mika could tell that I was down, and she looked worried. "I'm sorry it's this bad."

"It'll be fine soon enough."

"It *will* be."

Bex entered with a stack of folded towels. We set to work nailing them over the windows, and then we dragged all my belongings to the other side of the room to make space for the crates. We bound them together with zip ties and shoved the structure against the side wall.

Bex put their hands on their hips. "What a shithole."

"Who are your landlords?" Mika said. "I'm gonna send Bex to taekwondo their asses."

At least it was funny to them.

They invited me inside for dinner, and we made a quick pasta dish with cherry tomatoes and fresh basil, which was fine but not as good as Macon's. Mika followed me back to my unit afterward. Bex had already done enough, and although I was friends with them both, Mika was my friend-friend. My primary friend. I didn't want to place any additional burden on Bex. They seemed glad to be ordered to stay behind, and I didn't see them for the rest of the night. Mika and I folded, rolled, and arranged as much of my clothing as possible, but there was still a lot left over, so we extracted the cold-weather items and packed them back into my car along with most of my shoes and handbags. I'd have to store them at Macon's.

We said good night, and I crawled between the new sheets in my new bed. Toxic gas still perfumed the air. The crates were positioned behind my head, and everything else lay before me. Summer insects droned in a familiar cacophony. The house beside me was quiet.

I had never relied on this many people for help before. Gratitude churned with shame around the micro-studio, lulling me into a deep, dark sleep, and I didn't wake up until nearly ten. After remembering that I'd have to go into the main house for breakfast, I decided the first item we needed to tackle was installing the studio's kitchen.

But not yet. Not this weekend.

I stayed in bed for another half hour, not wanting to face the day. It was hard to get over how depressing it was to see the sunlight filtered through somebody else's old bath towels. Eventually my bladder forced me to get out of the micro-bed to use the micro-toilet, and then I took another micro-shower. After a regular-size bowl of cereal in the regular-size main house, I was itching to scram. Without texting him first, I drove my final carload of belongings over to Macon's.

I was surprised not to find him in the garden, and he seemed surprised to find me at his front door. He was wearing yet another black T-shirt, pajama bottoms, and socks with sandals. I noticed the footwear immediately, and his toes curled in a cringe. His expression hardened.

"Hey, I'm in no place to judge anybody for anything," I said.

He stared me down for another defensive beat and then, satisfied that I wasn't going to tease him, relaxed into confusion. "Sorry, did I forget something? Do we have plans for today?"

"No. I should have texted." I lifted my armload of coats in explanation. "I just wanted to drop off a few more things. What's left in my car is the last of it, I promise."

His socks and sandals shuffled aside to let me in. "I have to teach my mom how to use her new phone this afternoon, so I've been treating myself to a lazy morning. Edmond and I are doing laundry and reading in bed."

"That last part sounds good, at least."

"You're welcome to join us." Belatedly realizing that the implication was *in bed*, he winced. "That's not—"

"I know, I know. We just went over that, remember?" I glided past him with my coats, glacier-cool, but my insides burned.

We didn't speak much as he helped me unload the rest of my car. It didn't take long. I had no reason to linger but felt defeated and unfulfilled. I sensed that he wasn't ready for me to leave either, but we were without a task.

I was heading toward the door when he thought of something. "Oh! I've narrowed down the green." He led me to a wall where only two paint cards remained, a rich green called Hunting Party and a similar shade with a hint of brown called Forest Floor.

"I prefer this one's name." I pointed at Forest Floor. "But Hunting Party. That's the one."

He smiled. "I agree."

"Maybe I can work on it next weekend."

"There's no rush," he said, but I didn't like the unfinished job hanging over me. I was heading back toward the exit when he started talking again. "Remember that windstorm last week? My next-door neighbor, the one who moved into Shawn's old place, lost this massive branch from his walnut tree. He's been using my compost pile, so he asked if it would be okay to saw it into pieces and put them in there, but I had a better idea."

Suddenly I felt tired. I wanted to stay, but I also didn't want to talk about work of any kind.

"A cat tree. A literal cat tree. I'm thinking in that corner," he said, pointing between the fireplace and front windows. "You know, because it would go with our theme. And Edmond would love it."

We both glanced at Edmond, who was perched in his usual place on the back of the couch. His watchful green eyes were focused on a crow that was hopping around in the mulch outside, and the white tip of his black tail was twitching.

I frowned. "How big is this branch?"

"Big."

"How would we install it?"

"No idea. I'll research it."

Macon seemed to think that we could do anything. I didn't want to discourage him, so I let it go for now, but the project seemed beyond me in terms of time, skill, and energy. My weariness grew, and I made another move to leave.

"Have you had lunch?" he asked, almost desperately. Always trying to feed me.

"I just had breakfast."

It came out more annoyed than I felt, and he looked hurt. Lunch would have been perfect, an idle afternoon would have been perfect, spending any amount of time with him in his magical storybook cottage would have been perfect. But instinct, or maybe self-preservation, shouted at me to flee. He clammed up and didn't stand in my way.

CHAPTER TWENTY-SEVEN

The temperature rose to peak summer and never dropped, not even at night. Days blurred into weeks. Kat announced that I was allowed to get bangs now, but the urge had passed. I worked and went to class. I became a member of the American Booksellers Association and started taking additional classes, studying their materials behind the circulation desk. Macon read them, too, because they were there, and so did Mika. I helped her and Bex screw together the bed frame, hang the window shades, and install the micro-kitchen—mini fridge, tiny sink, narrow counter, upper cabinet, lower cabinet, two-burner stove—and they helped me search for a business location.

Three potential properties were available. One we ruled out immediately. The space was decent, and it had the most affordable rent, but it was situated on a side street downtown that tourists never noticed and that most locals didn't even know existed. It was an alleyway of melancholia, a monument to failed shopkeepers. We all agreed the energy was too ominous.

The other two properties were mixed. There was a beautiful storefront on a fairly prominent street downtown, but the space was on the small side and the rent was at the highest end of my budget. The more reasonably priced location also came with significantly more square footage, but it was located in a sterile strip mall. The neighborhood was popular enough, but the Tick-Tock Bookshop had been downtown, and I'd been imagining my store there, too.

It was easy to make an argument for either property. Mika argued more for downtown and Bex more for the neighborhood, but they both waffled. A decision had to be made, and I did not feel equipped to make it no matter how many times the property managers unlocked their doors for me. I began to lose sleep again, fearing that both locations would soon be claimed by other renters and I'd be forced to lease the shop in the alleyway.

Yet somehow—I don't know how—I still managed to make it back over to Macon's for a grueling day and a half, during which we primed and painted his living room. The change was staggering. The dark green walls felt both naturalistic and lavish. It was like standing beneath the sheltering canopy of a dense forest but also like standing inside the library of a very old, very moneyed estate. However, the bookshelves still needed to be built, and he still needed dining room chairs, as well as all the curtains and rugs. I apologized yet again for leaving the project incomplete and for the fact that I had no idea when I might be able to return. Most likely, it wouldn't be for months. Even more likely, next year.

"I waited twelve years before doing this much," Macon said, gesturing around. We were wearing our matching Colburn County shirts again, now streaked with Hunting Party. "I can wait that much longer."

He offered to make me an early dinner, and I accepted. Finishing the walls had been an unexpected balm and a boost to my energy, and even though I had a stove now, it was challenging to cook in such a confined space. He sent me into the garden with instructions to gather some yellow crookneck squash, which were spilling out of their beds, as well as some flat-leaf parsley, green onions, marjoram, and catnip. He gave me scissors and a basket, and it felt enjoyably like playing pretend. The spell was broken when I had to use my phone to identify the marjoram and catnip, but I still returned to the kitchen feeling pleased with myself.

"I didn't realize humans even ate catnip," I said cheerfully, setting my bounty down on the counter.

Macon plucked out the sprig and tossed it to the floor. Edmond trotted over, gave it a verifying sniff, and then rubbed his cheeks fervidly against the leaves.

"Oh," I said inanely.

But Macon smiled. "Some people do use it to make tea. It won't harm you, at least."

This was one of the many things I appreciated about him. He never made me—or any library patron—feel bad when we didn't know something. Although he had the air of somebody who might be condescending, he was always generous with his knowledge. He wasn't a snob.

After rinsing everything off, he patted the herbs dry with a towel and then set me to work chopping them up. He stood beside me, grating the squash. His arms were tan from the summer sun, and the back of his neck had tanned, too. I'd never contemplated his neck before. It looked so masculine, that line where untidy hair met skin—

My pulse throbbed.

He stopped grating. Without turning his head, he glanced at me.

I dropped the knife and hurried to the sink to wash my hands. Cool water, not hot. On the floor, Edmond rolled blissfully back and forth over the catnip. I excused myself, and by the time I had collected my wits and dared to return from the bathroom, Macon was already frying all the ingredients together into fritters. He was almost unbearably attractive. The relaxed confidence in the way he stood over the sizzling stovetop, the way he held the spatula. The ease of his domesticity.

I nearly bolted again.

Another glance at me, this one more curious than tense. He was making sure I was okay. If we had been a couple, he would have asked me, but because we weren't—and because I had run to the bathroom—he didn't. I was fine with this. Let him think my problems were digestive.

On the countertop was a jar stuffed with frilly dahlias and dill. To be useful, I carried it to the back porch table along with the chairs, which were still in his dining room. Then I set the small table, and soon he appeared with our plates.

When we finally sat, I wondered how I'd ever get up again. Turning sideways, I slumped and allowed my legs to stretch out beside the table. I did it because I was sapped, but I confess it also turned into a test. Or maybe a dare. Could I provoke him into looking at my bare legs again?

When I had arrived the previous morning, I hadn't considered that he had only ever seen me in pants and work-appropriate dresses and skirts. I'd selected my outfit because it would be another blisteringly hot day. But my shorts were quite short, and my legs were quite long, and as I'd let myself into his house, he'd stumbled and tripped over the perfectly flat floor.

He'd been careful to keep his gaze respectfully averted ever since.

He was also wearing shorts that weekend, and it was the first time I'd ever seen *any* part of his legs. There was nothing remarkable about them other than ... everything. It was an entire portion of his body, ankle to above the knee, that I had never seen before.

Maybe it was the heat; maybe that was why I was so turned on. The angel's trumpet flowers were in heavy bloom. They draped over the nearby fence like hundreds of swirling orange skirts, their sweetly intoxicating fragrance mixing with the nectarous honeysuckle that tangled along the fence beside it. A hidden frog croaked for its mate, and a pair of bright yellow goldfinches splashed together in the stone birdbath a few feet away, unconcerned by our presence.

"I'm glad we've become away-from-work friends," I said, because I needed to reestablish our relationship out loud.

He plopped a generous dollop of sour cream on top of his fritters, still not looking at my legs. "So am I."

"How awful would it have been if I'd left and we'd never hung out again?"

Macon made a noise of disgruntlement. "It won't be the same without you."

I knew it was true because I would have hated for him to leave me behind, but I still relished every time that he said it. "I'm sure whoever replaces me will be nice," I said diplomatically.

"No." He stabbed a fritter. "They'll be dull, and I'll hate them."

I laughed, which made him smile. I felt lucky to see his smile so often now.

Something occurred to me, and it seemed unbelievable that I'd never considered it before. I sat up, tucking my legs back underneath the table. "Hey, would you have any interest in working at the bookstore? I could use a cranky and knowledgeable man such as yourself."

The smile faded. It took longer than I expected for him to answer.

"No," he said.

It was a punch to my chest, and I flinched.

His smile returned, but it was gentler. "I've already thought about it. And I appreciate the offer. But I believe that what I do—providing free reading materials and resources to the community—is noble work. The public can be a pain in the ass. But this service is my calling."

I laughed a little, but a deep sadness washed through me. He was right, and it must have been why I had never considered asking him before. Macon was a librarian. His convictions had always been strong. I believed in them, too, but not with the same steadfastness or intensity. Librarians and booksellers traveled on parallel paths, but those paths were not the same. It was why I was leaving, after all.

I took a bite and was surprised to discover that the sour cream was lemony. The additional tang complemented and elevated the fritter. "I understand," I said, swallowing. "Although if you ever change your mind, the offer remains on the table."

"Thank you."

The first firefly of the evening hovered between us and blinked. Macon's eyes tracked it for a few seconds before he continued. "You must be excited, though. You're almost out."

"It feels like I'm making a huge mistake. I've been so busy that none of this has felt real, but . . . it's starting to feel real."

"You'll feel better once you've settled on a property. I still think you want the place downtown," he added. "Your voice sounds more wistful when you describe it."

I liked that he listened to me that closely. "It just feels like so much," I said, and he knew I was talking about money.

"You don't have to tell me, but how much *do* you have?"

Although we talked openly about our finances and each had a general idea of what the other could afford on a day-to-day basis, we'd never flat-out stated the specific contents of our bank accounts. Revealing the exact number would feel like standing naked before him.

I hesitated—and then told him exactly how much I had.

I was grateful that the darkening sky hid the warmth rising in my cheeks. I was proud of the amount I'd been able to save, but the number still made me feel small in the world. And being so forthright meant admitting that I was putting everything I had on the line for this.

Macon looked quietly surprised in a way that felt rewarding. Like maybe he hadn't expected the number to be as substantial as it was, since he knew it hadn't been that long since I'd paid off my student loans. He set down his fork with a solemn nod, an acknowledgment of the trust I had placed in him, and sat with the number. But when he finally spoke, it wasn't about money. "Take me with you the next time you view those properties. I'd like to see them."

The entire garden lit with electric-yellow fireflies.

"Okay," I said, as if it wasn't what I had wanted this whole time. I hadn't asked because I'd already asked so much of him this year, and I was aware of how much he had already given me. I hadn't wanted to impose on him with yet another request.

He joined me the following night after work, even though it was another late shift. As always, I was running out of time and had none to waste. He drove us to the neighborhood location first. Although the strip mall exterior was uninspired, the other stores and the parking lot were all decent, and the visuals could be improved with the sort of over-the-top, eye-catching window displays that Mika was so talented at creating. I was describing a scenario she'd pitched that involved colorful paper lanterns when the property manager arrived.

He was wearing his best mask of enthusiasm, but the mask was cracking, and it was obvious he felt hassled to be meeting with me again. He perked up in earnest when he noticed I'd brought Macon, as if a man might convince me to hurry up and make a decision already. He unlocked the door and began delivering his usual boastful spiel directly to Macon.

Unfortunately for him, Macon could read people quickly and had zero patience for blowhards. He strode inside and didn't acknowledge the man again.

I showed Macon the building, where everything might go. He didn't say much, but he asked insightful questions. Nothing needed to be repaired or brought up to code. Overall, it was in great shape. At one point, though, he looked down and frowned.

"It's brand new," the property manager said right behind us.

But I understood that Macon wasn't judging the state of the carpet, just the fact that there was carpeting at all. Whenever I imagined a perfect bookstore, it had wooden floors that creaked with age. It was historied and higgledy-piggledy, not modern and ready-made. I didn't need to say any of this out loud. I knew him well enough to know that this was what he had been imagining, too.

We drove to the downtown property. There were a few employee parking spots behind the building, but there wasn't a customer lot. This was a negative but not a dealbreaker, because it wasn't usually difficult to find street parking. And unlike the other location, this one had curb appeal. The facade had two huge windows on either side of the door, elaborate scrollwork, and decorative molding. It looked beguiling . . . but also shabby and beaten up.

The interior needed a lot of work, too. The second property manager was already there when we arrived, a woman who politely waited out of the way while I walked Macon around. Everything was coated in a thick layer of dirt and grime, a contractor would have to fix the lighting and the restroom, and the whole place smelled potently of its former life as a store that sold fragrances, soaps, and lotions. The other property was spacious, and this one was cramped. But it was also easy for me to imagine where everything would go, to imagine moving between the shelves and displays, to imagine arriving to work there every day. I could almost hear the steady heartbeat of the grandfather clock inside the Tick-Tock Bookshop.

Macon leaned his weight forward, and the hardwood creaked beneath his shoe. He looked at me and smiled.

"It needs a ton of work," I said. "And everything would be crowded."

"But there's something charming about a crowded bookstore, isn't there?"

"There is," I agreed.

"And it has good bones."

"It does."

"And it would be nicer to deal with her than the other property manager."

"It would be." I sighed. "But the rent."

"But the rent," he agreed.

We were standing near the front windows. I turned to ask the woman a question when my eyes caught on the view outside. The other shops and restaurants and businesses were shining with warmth and life. Crowds of people were strolling around and laughing. A busker down the street was playing a cello. I stared at the scene for a minute or two, a lump of longing in my throat. I had never seen the location at night before. I tried to remember the view from the other property, but I could only picture its asphalt parking lot.

"You have enough," Macon whispered. He was still beside me.

"Barely," I whispered back.

I was close, but I was still hesitant. Afraid to make such a monumental decision.

"You light up in here," he said. "You dim in that other space."

I signed the woman's paperwork and wrote her a check.

CHAPTER TWENTY-EIGHT

During my final class, I presented my business plan and applied for a loan through the school's lending division. It felt like the wrong order to apply for the loan *after* making the first rental payment, so I tried not to think about it too much, which meant it was all I thought about: my hard-earned savings falling, falling, falling through a new hole in my pocket.

My coworkers threw a party on my last day of work. Sue brought in my favorite lemon pound cake that she usually only baked for my birthday, Alyssa brought in a platter of fancy cheeses, Elijah brought in crackers and nuts, and Macon brought in sliced vegetables and an excessive number of dips. They gifted me a postcard of the stained-glass Mary Brisson that we sold to raise money for the Friends of the Library, but they'd put it in a handsome frame so I could hang it up in my new office. They were supportive and excited for me, and I cried several times.

I hugged everybody goodbye except for Macon. I knew I would see him again soon, but it was also too painful.

We both knew that we would never have a better coworker than each other.

August

DATE DUE	BORROWER'S NAME	ROOM NUMBER
JAN 25		
FEB 19		
MAR 30		
APR 17		
MAY 10		
JUN 03		
JUL 22		
AUG 04		

CHAPTER TWENTY-NINE

Amira Najafi was born in the earliest hours of August. Baby and mom were both healthy and well, apart from Brittany's fury that she had been pregnant nearly two weeks longer than expected. Even Reza's dedication to being on time couldn't make Amira arrive any faster.

I understood a little of what Amira was going through. She was transitioning from one phase of life into the next, and that required a lot of work. She was going as fast as she could.

All of my waking hours were now spent inside my empty store. Finally, I had something substantial that belonged to me, and I was doing everything I could to open its doors quickly. My stupidly ambitious goal was October first, but my reasoning was sound and practical. I needed the tourist dollars that would arrive with the changing leaves. Autumn was Ridgetop's prime tourist season, and downtown would be packed with potential customers that I couldn't afford to miss—nor could I afford to miss the holiday sales that would immediately follow. Those few months represented an enormous percentage of my projected yearly sales, and the season that came after would be the slowest part of the year. I couldn't risk opening the store any later.

If I didn't meet a reasonable-but-still-considerable sales quota by the end of the year, the store might go under as quickly as it had appeared.

No pressure.

I wouldn't hear about the loan until the end of the month, so I continued to drain my savings and stretch each dollar as far as possible. The loan officer at Ridgetop Means Bizness assured me that my chances were good, but I wouldn't feel good until I actually had their money. Plan B was a traditional bank, although my chances there were a lot less likely. Plan C was my family. I prayed I would never need Plan B and prayed I would never, never need Plan C.

Those early days and weeks were frantic. I trashed and recycled all the junk left behind by the previous renters and scrubbed every surface, ceilings to floors. The dust was thick, the dead flies abundant. To save money, I didn't run the air conditioning, and I sweated and cursed through a raging headache from the scent of the old fragrances, which were baked into everything. The fumes in the heat were horrific. I kept the doors propped open to circulate the air, and sometimes people wandered in off the street to see what I was up to. Everybody gagged when they smelled the strong cocktail of perfumes and cleaning products.

"Jesus Christ," said a woman whose shirt was moving. "How can you stand that?"

"What's underneath there?" I asked, unable to suppress my curiosity.

Her eyes narrowed protectively. "My pet rats."

"Ah, that's Shanelle," the owner of the toy store next door to me said later. Her storefront had dozens of whirligigs spinning in the wind outside, which I hoped would also attract children to my children's section. "She's churlish but harmless. Have you met Clyde yet?"

"Which one's Clyde?"

"The guy with the flapping dentures who tells jokes and riddles."

Clyde had popped in earlier that week to ask, "What smells better than it tastes?" I'd expected some crack about my store, but the answer had been an inoffensive groaner. "A nose!"

"Oh, he's a sweetheart," I said.

The toy store owner gave me a tiny pleased smile, and I sensed that I had passed a test. "It's a great neighborhood," she said. "Your bookstore will fit right in."

On the other side of me, on the good corner lot, was a tenderly named coffee shop. Kindred was, unfortunately, the same coffee shop that Gareth and I had gone to shortly before the first time we made out. But despite my memories coloring it with this uneasy tinge, its owners were also friendly—especially once they learned my store would not have a café.

"We thought we might have to throw a rock through one of your windows," the wife said.

"Which would have been a shame since you just cleaned them," the husband said.

Mika couldn't quit her job until September, but during her off-hours, she scraped and sanded and repaired the exterior. Bex joined in when they could, too. Meanwhile, I kept at the interior. Thankfully, the main layout and back room were already useable, but the restroom needed to be redone, and getting the lighting right was vital. I met with contractors, plumbers, and electricians, trying to find people who could start work immediately, and scoured the town for discounted fixtures. But even the cheap ones were expensive, especially the shelving. And the most affordable shelves were metal, but I didn't want metal. Metal felt so clinical.

In the middle of all of this, Macon suddenly appeared.

I confess that I'd been hoping to see him sometimes in the evenings after his shifts—that maybe he would drop by and lend a hand—even though, unlike Mika (and by extension Bex), he had no stake in the business. But he was busy with his own life, helping at his mom's house and working in his garden. The grueling process of preserving the harvest had begun.

So my heart gave a startled leap of joy when his car pulled into a spot right in front one Monday morning. He almost looked disappointed to see me. I climbed off my ladder (his ladder, I was borrowing it) to greet him with a huge smile. "What are you doing here?"

"You weren't supposed to be here yet," he said. "It was supposed to be a surprise."

"I've been starting early. While the temperature is merely miserable, not scorching." For the last two days, I'd taken over the work outside and had been painting the wooden part of the exterior. It traversed the length of the store on top, framed the windows, and then extended a little beneath them. There were lots of fiddly decorative bits, and the whole thing required several glossy coats. Though the job itself wasn't fun, it was exciting because it was the first time I was getting to make my mark on the space. "What was supposed to be a surprise?" I asked.

"Oh my God." He was staring up at my work. "Is that Hunting Party?"

"I loved it so much that I wanted to throw my own party. I hope you don't mind. It's such a perfect bookish color."

His expression was astonished. He was still absorbing it, entranced. "Of course I don't mind. You helped pick it. It's your color, too."

I laughed. "It is, isn't it?"

"It looks beautiful. It looks so great."

I'd almost texted him a photo, but then I'd gotten curious to see how long it would take for him to recognize the color in person. (An instant—that was how long it had taken him.) My smile grew. "What was supposed to be a surprise?" I asked again.

He shook his head, as if coming out of a daze, before glancing at me.

"What?" I asked, because I wasn't sure what the glance meant. Instead of replying, he opened one of his car's back doors and hefted a tall planter out of the seat. It was an attractive piece of cochineal red pottery. "Macon!"

He carried it to the entryway and set it down with an *oof*.

"Where did you find this?"

"Hold on," he said, then went to his car and returned with a second one. He set it on the other side. "I bought them a few years ago for my mom's house. She never uses them, and I'm tired of filling them and watering them myself, so they're yours now."

"I can't take your mom's planters—"

"If you hate them, they can be temporary. But you need something out here. Everybody has flowers downtown."

"I don't hate them. I love them. They're gorgeous. I don't know what to say."

He strode away again, back to his car.

"I don't know where I'd put a third one," I joked.

He began hoisting bags of soil and plants from the trunk. "Consider them a housewarming gift. A store-warming gift."

"The store already has plenty of heat, but thank you. This is so thoughtful."

"I also brought these." He held up two iron brackets with long arms. "I wouldn't have installed them without your permission, though. They're for those." He pointed to the front passenger seat, where two hanging baskets with pretty coconut liners were stacked.

"*Macon.*"

"The liners are new, but the baskets are also from my mom's house. And all the plants are extras from my place. I promise it's not a big deal."

I couldn't stop beaming as I helped him unload everything. Yet I still felt a twinge of guilt. "Are you sure your mom doesn't need these?"

"She won't even notice they're gone."

There wasn't enough humor to mask the underlying darkness of that statement. "How's her health been lately?" I asked. So much of the focus this year had been on his aunt.

"Physical health? Fine. Mental health . . ."

I nodded with understanding.

As he slammed his trunk shut, his concern shifted to me. "I won't be in your way, will I? I was trying to do all this before you got here."

"You aren't in my way."

He *was*, a little, but I wanted him there. I was so glad that he was in my way. I wished I could give him a hug—for his mom, for his aunt, for the plants—but it still felt like a thing we didn't do. I remembered the strength of his arms around me. The tightness of his grip.

"Oh my God." He had stepped inside the store now. "It's like an oven in here. What's that smell? I swear it didn't stink that bad before."

"I'm airing it out. I think the paint will help—and all the books."

"Yeah," he agreed. "It'll fade. Is it okay if I look around?"

"No. You came bearing gifts and the door is open, but I'm gonna have to ask you to leave."

He gave me an exaggerated scowl, and I lit up with delight. He smiled and then poked around, appreciating my hard work, listening to my stories.

"You still haven't told me what you're naming it," he said.

"You'll have to wait like everybody else." I felt protective and superstitious about the name, like how Brittany and Reza wouldn't tell anyone Amira's name until she arrived.

"Mika knows."

"Mika works here," I said. I'd needed her help with the signage and hiring the right person to design it, more costs I'd forgotten about. "Nobody will ever be able to spell it," Mika had warned me. "Or pronounce it. Or know what it means." She was correct, but I didn't care. The name was perfect. Some days it was the only thing I felt confident about.

"*I'm* here to work," he said.

"I offered you a job, and you turned it down. Speaking of, how's the library?"

"Boring. Uneventful. It's annoying how many people miss you."

I brightened even more. "Yeah?"

"Everybody keeps asking where you are. I'm beginning to feel insulted."

"I hope you're telling them about the store. I need that free advertising."

"I can't tell anybody if I don't know what it's called."

"Nice try."

"Of course I'm telling them," he said.

"How's Jenny doing?" A library substitute whom we both liked had been hired into my position.

"She's fine." His nose wrinkled. "I hear a lot about the batting order of her daughter's softball team."

I laughed. I didn't want him enjoying her company more than mine.

"Oh, did you hear they're talking about eliminating fines again?" he said. "I called every member of the board of commissioners to plead our case." The idea had been floated before, but the county had a difficult time seeing the benefits, even though it was clear that fines disproportionately affected the low-income families who needed the library's services the most. It felt odd to be on the outside of these conversations now. As I listened to him go on, it seemed like so much longer than two weeks since I'd last sat beside him.

"Look at that," he said, interrupting himself. "How did I miss that?"

His eyes had caught on the mosaicked entryway. A lot of buildings downtown still had them, remnants of their first occupants. I pulled a bag of soil aside so that he could read the name: ROMAN'S in hexagonal tile. It was the delicatessen that had occupied the space nearly a hundred years earlier.

"It's great, isn't it?" I said.

"I'm so glad you chose this place. This is the one."

I was smiling at him again. I'd never stopped.

He grew alarmed. "What? You're looking at me like there's something on my face." He brushed off his cheeks and chin, just in case.

"I'm looking at you like I'm happy to see you. I've missed you."

"Oh," he said. It was hard to tell underneath his summer tan, but I thought his skin reddened as he busied himself with his plants, the mounds of bushy herbs and trailing vines and cheerful yellow and orange flowers.

I climbed back up the ladder. "I've missed you, too, Ingrid."

I'd expected him to laugh and parrot it back to me, but he didn't. His gaze remained affixed to the greenery. I cringed for having taken the teasing too far. Was this his way of politely shutting me down again? Or was he too self-conscious to flirt back? Either way, he worked underneath me and beside me for the rest of the morning.

CHAPTER THIRTY

My search for the perfect bookshelves, or even okay bookshelves, remained fruitless. It looked like I'd have to purchase them new, and they'd probably be veneered, which reminded me of all the flimsy furniture I'd recently discarded. Mika assured me the quality would be better than that, but she was bummed, too. We both craved the softness and hardness and life of real wood.

"I keep imagining the shelves from the old store," I said one morning in her and Bex's kitchen. "Those rounded edges, all those knots and scratches."

"Do you remember that unusual display that spiraled?" she asked. "They don't even sell things like that. Someone must have made it custom for Len."

"What ever happened to them?" Bex asked. "Did he sell them when he closed the store?"

Mika and I paused with our cereal spoons halfway to our mouths. We glanced at each other and then shook our heads. We didn't know.

"I have no memories of it," I said, "but I'm sure he did. They had to have been valuable."

Bex shrugged. "Might be worth calling Carla to ask."

"No, I wouldn't want to bother her with that."

But Mika was sitting up straighter. "Why not? What's the harm in asking?"

I didn't have an answer—it just felt uncomfortable to contact our old boss's widow.

"I'm calling," she said. And she didn't wait. She still had Len's home number. Carla picked up, and Mika walked out of our hearing range. I looked at Bex in desperation, as if they could still stop her. They shrugged again and poured another bowl of shredded wheat.

Only a few minutes later, Mika returned with a massive grin.

I'd been to Leonard and Carla's house once before, when they threw a holiday party for the Tick-Tock staff. None of us particularly wanted to do it, but we felt like we should, and then we all enjoyed ourselves, yet we never did it again. Socialization can be a lot for book people. I remembered their house being plain but trim on the outside and cluttered and well loved on the inside.

When Mika and I pulled up, the lawn was scraggly and weedy, and the bushes were so overgrown that they blocked the windows. The old station wagon in the driveway looked undriven. Our jubilant mood turned somber and trepidatious.

The doorbell was broken, so we knocked. To our surprise—it seemed like a house where its occupant would be moving slowly—the door opened straight away. Carla looked older, yet she was still clearly Len's spry other half. She ushered us in and talked over our greeting. "I can't believe your timing! It's serendipitous. You can see the state of it," she said, meaning her house. "It's gotten to be too much for me to take care of alone. I'm finally ready to downsize, but it's so overwhelming. I've been meaning to list all those bookshelves online and dreading it."

"I still can't believe he didn't sell them with the store," I said.

"You know Len," Carla said with a dark laugh. "That man kept everything."

This was true. His office and back room and registers had been crammed with items that he no longer needed. "But maybe I *will* someday," he'd always said whenever one of us had begged to empty out the entire drawer stuffed with silver paperclips. Or the cubbyhole jammed with old water bills. Or the shelf bowing from the weight of dot matrix printer paper.

Mika gasped and softly touched my arm. "Do you hear that?"

Carla led us over to the grandfather clock's place of honor in her sitting room, pleased to see how excited it made us. The clock was about head height with a decorated face, and the wood was stained a dark green reminiscent of Hunting Party. Its rhythmic heartbeat was deep and stately, and suddenly I could smell and feel the bookstore that had surrounded it for so many years. My farmor and farfar had also owned a grandfather clock, but the pitch of theirs had been high and conspicuous. The sound of its tick had jumped out of its surroundings instead of melding into them. But this clock enveloped its listener in steady reassurances.

We stood before it for some time, sharing stories and memories.

"But you girls aren't here for this," Carla said. Even though, in a way, we were. She guided us toward the garage. When she opened the door, Mika and I startled. The station wagon was parked in the driveway because there was no room for it inside. The space reminded me of that first stressful weekend in the micro-studio when everything was piled to the ceiling.

"You're welcome to anything in here," Carla said.

"This is all of it," I said. "It really is still here."

"I told you it was."

"We'll take everything. How much would you like for it?"

"I *also* told you it's already yours, as long as I don't have to help haul it away."

I'd been stunned when Mika had shared this news, and now seeing the fixtures in person, I felt stunned all over again. "Carla. I can't."

She shook her head as if it were nothing, when really it was everything. "I just need it gone. And Len would have been thrilled for you to have it. He would have been so glad to know another bookstore was coming to town—and that the two of you were opening it."

Those were the words I needed to hear in order to accept her gift. Because I did believe it would have tickled Len—a lifelong curmudgeon, an elder Macon—to know that his two bubbliest hires were following in his path. He'd complained about everything, he'd been mean as piss to the people he didn't like, and he'd stunk of cigarettes from his frequent smoke breaks. But he'd always had a sweet spot for us because we'd always had a sweet spot for him.

I made arrangements for pickup next month and insisted that Carla call me when she was ready to move so I could help. The least I could do was bestow my free labor on her.

As Mika and I drove away, I imagined being the one to buy Carla's house. The boxy structure was drab and needed a ton of repairs, but I was positive I could turn it into something brighter and more interesting. But even Carla's modest neighborhood was too expensive for me, especially now.

"What's wrong?" Mika asked. "I thought you'd be over the moon."

I *was*, so I forced my thoughts to return to the miracle that had just occurred. I tried not to think about how many years it might take for me to be able to afford a house. Or even rent one. Or how if the bookstore failed and I lost everything, the clock would start all over again.

CHAPTER THIRTY-ONE

And then a second miracle occurred: the loan came through early. It had been at the forefront of my mind all month, knotting my shoulders and sabotaging my sleep, despite being assured by the lender that it would almost certainly happen. But then it *did* happen, ahead of schedule, and the release of pressure was like an open fire hydrant on a summer's day.

The day had already been better than the two before it, when I had painted the ceilings. Ceilings were exhausting, neck-straining work. But the electrician had done his job quickly—a third miracle—so the ceilings had been ready for me. And now they were ready for the new light fixtures. And now I had the money to buy them.

I had also met Amira that morning, which had given me perspective. Yes, I was tired, but not as tired as Brittany and Reza. It seemed significantly less strenuous to build a bookstore than to raise a newborn. Amira was beautiful and hungry and sleepy and good, but I was still grateful that she was theirs and not mine. I had stopped by to drop off a load of clean and folded clothes. This had been my baby shower gift: washing their dirty laundry via porch pickups and drop-offs so they wouldn't have to interact with me. Both sets of grandparents had been in town for the baby's first week, so I'd started after they had left, but this was the first morning that Brittany had the energy to crack open the door to say hello. It was also the first time I'd ever seen her without makeup. She still looked gorgeous, although perhaps more like a gorgeous disaster.

"I hear our washer and dryer running at odd hours, but I still don't understand how you find the time," Bex said.

Bex was helping me paint the walls, a much more gratifying job than the ceilings. It was also a smaller job because we weren't touching the areas that were exposed brick. Mika had helped me select the perfect pale, warm color of yellowing pages—a hue so natural in a bookstore that it wouldn't even be noticed. An extension of the books themselves.

"Easy," I said. "I stopped doing my own laundry." I was elated and riding high about the loan. I had *all* the energy.

"Speed, maybe. Adderall or Ritalin."

"Do you see what I'm wearing?"

"Impossible to miss, darling. Very cute bra."

I laughed. I was down to my last tank top—plain white and now forever splattered with paint—and a special-occasion push-up bra with a red floral pattern. The bra was extremely visible through the tank top, but I was beyond caring. I did not have time to care.

My phone chimed. The volume was on because I was waiting to hear from Mika, who didn't know about the loan yet. She had an online shopping cart full of computers and other equipment ready to go, and I was eager for her to hit the purchase button. The text wasn't from her, but I grew even more excited. "Macon says not to eat. He's bringing over dinner."

"For you or for all of us?"

"Probably just me. Sorry."

"No worries." Bex set down their brush. "I'll wash up and meet Mika. We'll grab something and join you." The store she worked at was a short walk away, and there were plenty of restaurants in between.

I was singing to myself when Bex returned from the restroom. They liked hip-hop and dance, and since they were doing me a favor, we were listening to music instead of my usual audiobooks. We'd started with the good stuff and had switched to the trashier stuff after the loan came through. I was thoroughly enjoying it. "You know," they said, pausing near the entrance, "for somebody who isn't your boyfriend, Macon sure acts a lot like your boyfriend."

My roller paused.

"He brought you flowers," they said.

"He brought plants for the store."

"He's come to 'check on them' twice."

"That's only because he doesn't trust me to water them."

One of Bex's thick eyebrows rose.

"You guys are helping me, too," I pointed out.

"Because my wife is quitting a good career to work here. We are highly motivated to help you succeed. What's his motivation?"

"He's my friend."

"Are you sure?"

My throat felt swollen, and I swallowed.

Bex shook their head with a quiet laugh and left.

No, I wasn't sure. I thought I had been sure, but then I had been wrong, and now I was somewhere in between. I did sense that he was attracted to me. He definitely enjoyed my company. But my own desire was so strong that I feared I might be misinterpreting him again.

But if Bex could see it, too, did that mean it was real?

It wouldn't take long for him to arrive. I raced to the restroom, toweled off the sweat, and rinsed my face with cool water. Redid my messy bun. Added lipstick. Thank goodness my legs and armpits were recently shaved. What else, what else? Too late to do anything about the outfit, though I realized with a jolt that I *wanted* him to see me like this—wearing less than he'd ever seen before. My reflection was pink and flushed but radiant and electrified. Hopefully my own version of a gorgeous disaster.

I hurried back to my roller. It was dusk, and I turned the music up loud, some synth-y European club song, ridiculous but thumping. He would arrive any second now. I resumed painting, my hips swaying to the beat. I wanted him to see me having fun. I wanted him to see me feeling good, feeling cute, feeling sexy. I wanted him to *see me*.

"Ingrid," he shouted, and I jumped and nearly dropped the roller.

I burst into laughter. "Macon!"

He was standing frozen in the doorway clutching a large Pyrex container, almost as if he was afraid to come any closer.

I set down the roller. The beat changed, picked up, and I danced toward him with my arms raised and an enormous smile. "The loan came through!"

It took a moment for him to process what I'd said because he was watching me so intently. My long bare legs. The floral-patterned bra. His blatant, uncharacteristic gaping filled me with a rush of power. He blinked—and then again. "That's great," he said, a little choked.

I laughed and danced all the way up to him. "I'm celebrating."

He seemed stunned but let out a flustered laugh as I took the container from him and set it on the floor. I kept dancing even though he hadn't moved an inch. Without ever having been told, I knew Macon didn't like to dance. Cory liked to dance. Cory actually *loved* to dance, and he was good at it, too. About as good as I was, at least. But I didn't need Macon to dance with me. I could dance with him.

The music throbbed. Still laughing to myself, I bounced and gyrated around him: arms, legs, belly, pelvis, chest. He stood, ground to the same spot, embarrassed but enraptured. Like he wished it would stop but also very much hoped it would continue.

I wanted to touch him. I didn't dare.

A pen from work was still tucked behind his ear. Still dancing, I slowly, teasingly pulled it out. Then I popped it into my mouth and playfully bit the end.

His eyes were wide and locked on mine.

No. Ingrid. No.

His expression looked so familiar that it knocked the wind out of me. My body froze as Mika rushed me from behind, shouting, "You got the loan!"

She and Bex had come in through the back door. Their appearance jumped me back to life. Mika and I ran into each other's arms and shrieked, but part of my shriek was also fear. I didn't know if Macon was about to tell me no again—I didn't *think* he was—but if he did, I couldn't bear the rejection. Yet it felt equally unbearable to remain in this fraught limbo.

I needed him to make a move.

I needed him to say yes.

The song changed. Bex turned the new one up even louder, and then the three of us began dancing and laughing together. I waved for Macon to join us, an invitation I knew he wouldn't accept, and he shook his head vehemently.

I loped back over to him, catching my breath. I held out the pen.

He didn't take it.

"Whoops." I wiped it off on my shirt. "Sorry. I got carried away?"

He was staring at the pen or my tank top or maybe my bra. I think I had broken him. Attempting one last flirtatious gesture, I slipped the pen back behind his ear. His hand automatically went to it. I waited, hoping, for him to do something. Anything.

He looked away from me, breaking the tension. "I can't stay."

My disappointment was crushing.

"I just came to drop that off." He gestured to the Pyrex. "I made dinner for my mom, and it's been a while since I fed you, so . . ."

"Okay." I couldn't keep the frustration out of my voice. "Well. Thanks."

His gaze whipped back to me. I was surprised that he looked frustrated, too. Perhaps even angry. "I still have to deliver hers."

"Oh," I said. Feeling a little shittier.

We stared at each other, the bass still vibrating. My friends still dancing. He glanced over at them. Suddenly I saw the decade between us, the differences in our responsibilities, and felt young and judged in a way that I didn't like. His mouth opened to say something, but then he changed his mind and bit it back. He was struggling, and I did not feel like helping him. When he finally spoke, his voice was too low, and I couldn't hear it above the booming music.

I held a hand to my ear.

"The color," he said, speaking louder and pointing to the walls. I think he tried to smile, but the lines of his face were so agitated that it looked like a grimace. "It's good. It's like . . . the slightly aged pages of a novel."

It killed me that he knew this. That he saw this. That we interpreted the world in such a similar way. He made me want to scream. I wanted more than paint colors and friendship flowers and pity meals. I wanted *him*.

"I like it, too," I said, snatching up the dinner and stalking away.

"I overwhelmed him," I told Kat a few hours later, still feeling ornery but also writhing with humiliation and regret, "with the stupid dancing."

"Yeah," she said with brash confidence, "but he was into it."

"Then why didn't he make a move?"

"Because you weren't alone, and he doesn't strike me as the type of guy who'd take a risk when other people are watching."

She wasn't wrong, but my frustration still raged like an inferno.

"I'm sorry he's the only thing I call you about anymore," I said. Our FaceTimes had become rare since I'd become so busy with school and then the store.

"Hey, remember the first year of Howie's life when I disappeared on you?"

I cracked a glum smile.

"Was it a big deal?" she pressed.

"Of course not. You were adjusting to a life-changing event."

"Exactly. You're in a new season of life, and a lot is happening right now. I know it doesn't mean that you're gone or that you don't care about me. And I also know that when things calm down, you'll be back. And I'll still be here—just like you were for me."

"How do you know he was into it?" I asked, unable to help myself.

Kat grinned. "Because he watched you dance for the whole song."

CHAPTER THIRTY-TWO

Something was burning. Smoke drifted into my nostrils seconds before the black clouds started billowing from the hood of my car. I swore and pulled over. The tow truck took ninety minutes to arrive, and as I climbed into its cab, red-faced and sweat-soaked—it had been an entire month of feeling like a chicken roasting on a rotisserie—I tried not to get angry at the driver. It wasn't his fault the miserable heat had yet to break. Nor was it his fault that I hadn't had anything to read while I waited.

He drove us—my car and me—to the mechanic's garage, where Harvey shook his head with smug disappointment. "I told you."

"I know," I snarled, and stomped off toward Macon's while he fixed it.

It was a small blessing that I knew Macon would actually be at home on a Wednesday. He was taking his annual two weeks of vacation time to harvest and preserve his garden. I expected to find him elbows-deep in veg, so I was startled when his car drove past me.

The street was empty, so he stopped and backed up. He rolled down a window. "Were you coming to see me?" He looked startled, too, as he took in my bedraggled appearance. "Are you okay?"

Since he hadn't taken the bait when I'd looked flushed and sexy at my store a few days earlier, it was hard to care that he was seeing me flushed and unsexy now. He'd been seeing me like this for months, anyway. I slid into the passenger seat. "My engine overheated again."

"Fuck."

"Yeah. And I have a load of tile in the car that I need to take to my contractor. Would you be able to drive me back to the mechanic and help me get it to my store?"

Another car appeared behind us, so Macon began to drive. "Uh, actually, this is a bad time. Can it wait an hour?"

It couldn't—my contractor had started on the restroom and needed to see what tile I'd picked out, and he was texting me demands for updates—but it also could. Because as peevish as I currently felt toward Macon, I was still asking for a favor, and he had never turned down one of my requests before. He seemed to be anxious and irritated for a reason that had nothing to do with me. "What's going on? Are you okay?"

He glanced at me, hesitant.

"What?" I asked again.

His mouth tightened in a way that told me he was thinking. Whatever it was, he didn't want to share it. As the ponderous silence dragged on, I turned my head toward the window—to give him privacy but also to hide my exasperation. I felt him look at me again.

His grip squeaked as it tightened on the steering wheel. "My mom just called."

All of my attention turned back to him.

"Apparently, she hasn't been paying her property taxes, and—for whatever fucking reason—the tax office in the courthouse closes at noon on Wednesdays. I could either drop you off back at the mechanic and then swing by when I'm done—"

He took a deep breath.

I waited for the *or*.

"—or you could come with me."

It was understandable that he might feel embarrassed about his mom, but accompanying him to the tax office didn't seem like a big deal. Despite my confusion, I softened my tone. "Yeah. Of course I'll come. Thanks for helping me."

He nodded but didn't relax. Instead he grumbled, "I was in the middle of canning tomato sauce when she called. Now the flavor's going to be off."

"I guess . . . I'm glad it's her ruining your morning and not me?"

This caught him off guard, and he almost laughed. "Oh, you're ruining my morning, too. Because now I'm gonna get home even later. My sauce is fucked."

Even with his dark tone, I knew he was teasing me. But I winced anyway.

"So what happened with your car?" he asked.

I told him and felt vindicated that the part he hated the most was the idea of being stranded without a paper book. I could have borrowed an ebook from the library, but I hated reading on my phone, so it had felt like a sign that I should reply to some emails instead.

Suddenly he pulled into a driveway. We were only a few streets over from his house, and the one before us reminded me a lot of Carla's, modest and plain. The yard was also nondescript, but unlike Carla's, the grass was mown and bushes were pruned. And that's when I understood.

"*Oh*. Is this your mom's place? Is this where you grew up?"

"Yeah. Sorry, we have to stop here first."

He turned off the car but made no move to exit.

"Would you like me to wait here?" I asked.

He shook his head with resolve, and then he looked at me. The intensity of his stare swallowed me whole. "No, I want you to come in. You should come in."

My throat dried. "Okay."

"You should know . . ."

I waited for him to finish, but his gaze broke away again.

"I know," I said gently. Meaning: *I've met her before. I know she's unwell. I promise I will not judge her or you.*

"It'll be good for her to see a different face," he said as we climbed out.

It made me self-conscious about my appearance. My hair was in two disheveled braids, so as we headed to the front door, I hurriedly undid them, smoothed everything out, and rebraided them. Macon unlocked the door using a key from his own ring but hollered before entering. "Mom? I've brought someone. We're coming in."

The house was stuffy, not much cooler than outside. Teetering stacks of shipping boxes and crumpled packaging were everywhere. Hardly any floor was visible underneath it. Macon glanced at me, trying to gauge my reaction. I flashed him an encouraging smile. His mother appeared on the other side of the cardboard and made her way toward us through the chaos, which took some effort.

"Do you remember my friend Ingrid from the library? The one who's been helping with my house?"

I hadn't considered that he might have talked about me with her, but it did make sense that she'd seen all the new work. I liked knowing that I'd made it into their conversations.

"Of course I remember." She had a big smile, and she was dressed neatly, which I'll admit I hadn't been expecting.

"Hi, Ms. Nowakowski. It's nice to see you again. Sorry to barge in on you like this."

"Please, call me Lynn." Her voice was friendly though somewhat frail. Since the last time I'd seen her, it was as if she'd transitioned from a young senior citizen to an elderly one. Macon had told me that she'd been older when she had him, but she also seemed much older than my parents. "And I don't mind, as long as you excuse the mess. It doesn't normally look like this."

Wondering what on earth she'd been ordering, I nodded and kept smiling.

Macon glanced at me again, visibly uncomfortable.

"Look at you," she said, taking me in. She had his same coloring, but her features were nothing like his, which made me wonder about his dad. Macon knew his father, but only barely. He'd dated Macon's mother briefly and hadn't been interested in raising their child. Because of that, Macon was equally, hostilely uninterested in him. "You're as pretty as I remember."

I glowed, immeasurably happy to receive a compliment from his mother.

"It's nice that you've been helping him," she continued. "He's been showing me photos. It looks so much better than it used to. It needed a woman's touch—that's what I've been telling him ever since Dani moved out."

Macon looked like a pained teenager silently pleading for his mom to shut up. Meanwhile, I tried to conceal my surprise that she hadn't seen our work in person. I knew her agoraphobia had been worsening as she aged, narrowing the areas she was willing to visit. It was why she had stopped coming to the library and running her own errands; most locations were now outside of her radius. But I had assumed Macon's house was still a safe space. It had never occurred to me that the reason why he always delivered his meals to her was that she was no longer able to come to him.

"It's been a fun project," I said. "I've been enjoying it."

"And now you're opening a bookstore?"

Again, I was surprised and pleased that she knew. I answered her questions for another minute, and then she invited me in farther to sit and have a glass of iced tea.

"Mom, we have to go." Macon had started rooting around on the console table beside us, which was covered with junk mail. "Where are the letters?"

"They're in the basket," she said with matching impatience.

"What basket?"

"The one underneath the table."

He removed a teetering stack of empty shipping boxes from on top of a decorative basket and tossed them onto another pile across the foyer. They landed with a bang that made his mother wince. When he looked inside the basket, he seemed stunned. "What is this?"

The basket was stuffed with unopened envelopes.

"That's where I put the important mail, for safekeeping."

"Mom. You can't ignore these. You have to open them, or at least tell me so I can go through them. I thought everything important was on your coffee table."

"Well, I keep it there *now* because the basket is full. That's how I found the new letter."

"I need it. Where did you put it?" He was already heading toward what I assumed was the living room, but he glanced back at me. "Would you mind looking through that for anything from the tax department?"

"Of course." I began flipping through the mail—financial institutions wanting her to sign up for new credit cards and charities wanting her to donate money, but also letters from insurance companies and her bank and a variety of bills. Some of it was stamped overdue.

Macon returned quickly with the necessary letter in hand.

"How about we borrow this and I sort through it on the way there, since we're in a hurry?" I said. I wanted him to examine its contents, but I also didn't want to embarrass Lynn.

"That's a good idea. Mom, I'll bring this back later, okay?"

"Be *careful*," she said. "That courthouse floor is slippery. And the roads downtown are so crowded and dangerous. All those one-way streets."

He hugged her and kissed her cheek before holding the door open for me.

"It was nice seeing you again, Lynn," I said, carrying the basket out.

"You come back anytime," she said to me. "Be careful!" she shouted at Macon again.

"I will," he said.

We didn't speak again until her house was out of view. He had just shown me something intimate and painful and real. I felt certain that nobody else had been granted access to this part of his life since Dani. Even though I wasn't entirely sure what I had witnessed, I understood that it was a window into his difficulties and responsibilities. He had made himself vulnerable to me for perhaps the first time ever, and I held the weight of that trust as if it were sacred.

"There are a few more things in here that you should probably look at," I said quietly about the basket on my lap. I sifted through it again.

Macon released a heavy sigh. "I'm sure there are."

"So . . . I'm guessing she always has that many boxes lying around?"

"I break them down and recycle them whenever I'm there. Since she hardly leaves the house, she has everything delivered. I've told her a hundred times to let me know what she needs so I can pick it up, but she already feels bad about how much I do for her, so she doesn't like to ask. And stuff like that"—he gestured to the basket—"stresses her out, so she pretends it doesn't exist. I asked her to start putting it on the coffee table so I can look through it when I'm there, but I didn't know she had all that, too. Apparently, she's been getting these notices about her property taxes for months. I don't know what compelled her to finally open one this morning, but thank God she did, because the county is one day away from putting a lien on her house."

"I'm sorry. I didn't know it had gotten that bad. I mean, I guess I did. But I didn't *know*."

"One day away," he said again.

"Is she . . ." There was no delicate way to ask, but I felt like he'd given me permission. "Is she a hoarder?"

"Not in the way you're thinking of. But if you're wondering if the rest of her house is that crowded, the answer is yes. Just not with such obvious trash. It's all stuff that makes her feel safe. Prepared for any emergency."

"And she doesn't come to your house anymore?"

"She hasn't since Dani moved out. All that empty open space freaked her out. She's weird about empty spaces."

"Is that why you never filled it? To keep your mom away?"

"What?" He glanced at me sharply. "No."

"Sorry, I didn't mean . . . I don't know what I meant." The idea had slipped out before I'd thought it through. Macon was obviously trying his best to take care of Lynn. My insensitive questions reflected more about my relationship to my own parents.

"You know, that's the third person you've tried to blame for the state of my house," he said. "Dani, Bonnie, my mom. But I've been telling you the truth. It wasn't any of them. It was me."

I felt so ashamed. "I'm sorry."

We rode in silence for a minute. He stretched his neck to the side and groaned. "Maybe you're not entirely wrong." His energy shifted from aggravation to nervousness, which made *me* nervous. "It's possible I haven't been in a rush to fill that space because . . . she'll probably have to move in with me. Eventually. I'm not sure when, but sometime in the next few years."

"Oh."

He glanced at me again, and I tried to keep my expression neutral. I wasn't sure how to react. I wasn't sure why this news had caught me so off guard.

"It's a lot of work, having to take care of both houses," he said. "And things like this are going to keep happening. And worse. She needs care, but I don't want to send her to a home, and I doubt I could afford it anyway, and I'm the only family she has now that Bonnie . . ."

Macon trailed off. He had visited his aunt a few weeks earlier when she'd left rehab, though I'd only found out about it after the fact. He said she was doing okay, but he'd sounded more wary than hopeful. A neighbor had fed Edmond while he was away. He hadn't wanted to bother me because I was busy with the store. I wished he would have bothered me.

"Well," I said, "Lynn is lucky to have a son like you."

His voice thickened. "It sucks. You're young, so your parents aren't there yet. But it sucks."

You're young. It jumped out at me—one of my fears about why he might not want to be with me. I didn't like that it was there on the tip of his tongue.

"She looks good, though," I ventured.

"My mom has a lifetime of practice pretending that nothing is wrong. Just don't try to take her on a walk. Or to the doctor. Or to the pharmacy."

"Will you even be able to get her into your house? Won't she want to stay where she is?"

"Oh, she'll fight me. But I'll win. It's one thing to have my mother move in with me, but I am *not* moving back in with my mother."

"Plus," I said, "your garden."

A beat, then a small smile. "Plus, my garden."

"I'm sorry," I said again.

"How are your parents? You haven't mentioned them in a while."

"They're fine. Doing their thing. Excited about the wedding."

"I thought maybe they'd come up here and help you with the store."

I laughed once. "That's not their style."

"What do you mean?"

It was always difficult to explain my relationship to my parents to other people. "They're good parents." It was how I always started because it was important. "They're supportive. They love me and believe in me. They're also just . . . not the sort of parents who will ever physically be *there* for me. It's not like you and your mom. I rarely see them. We don't talk often. When I stopped answering their texts during everything that happened"—I waved in the general direction of the first half of the year—"they accepted it and didn't ask me what was going on. They're living their own lives, just like Riley and I have always been expected to live ours. We've always been counted on to take care of ourselves. I can't imagine asking them for help."

He thought about it for a moment. "That sounds like a lot of pressure."

I squirmed, having just witnessed the pressure that he was under with Lynn. "It's really not. It's nothing like the sort you're under."

"It's just a different kind, that's all. And it explains why you hate asking for help."

"What?" I actually laughed again, but it was incredulous. "I've been doing nothing *but* asking people for help. Remember this morning? When I asked for your help? It's why I'm sitting in your car right now?"

"Yeah, but it pains you to do it. Even though you're always helping everyone else out. You're good at giving but not at receiving."

It stung. Not like he'd said something unkind, but like he'd said something true.

We fell into another silence. By the time we reached the courthouse, I had found five more letters about unpaid property taxes. I stuffed the bundle into my tote bag, and we hastened into the clean, echoing building. Macon strode ahead, confident in his destination. His hair was frizzy from the humidity, which made my chest ache. As we rode the elevator to the third floor, I smoothed down my braids again. The frizz was so much cuter on him than on me. But when the elevator dinged, I looked up to find him watching me in the murky reflection of the steel doors. They split open, fracturing his gaze, and he quickly looked away, hurrying out and down the hall.

I followed slowly behind him with a pounding heart. What *was* this strange relationship we had? This friendship loaded with stolen glances? I knew how I felt about him, but I was still confused about how he felt toward me. He had never made a move. Not one. But perhaps now that he'd let me in with his mom, he was on the verge of letting me in elsewhere.

He was already inside the tax office when I caught up with him. I handed him the letters and took a seat, figuring he'd want privacy. Thankfully, there was only one person ahead of him at the window. I checked my phone and texted the contractor that I'd be there soon.

"Ingrid." Macon's voice was low and quiet.

I looked up, expecting him to say something more, but his eyes were unexpectedly gigantic and alive. They darted toward the clerk's window.

I glanced over and held back a gasp.

Our eyes locked again in delight.

I scrambled to my feet and got in line with him.

"Be good," he whispered.

"I'm always good," I whispered back.

When the person in front of us left, we stepped oh-so-casually up to the window of one Mr. Ken Fondness. A printed sign, worn and curling with age, was taped to the wall beside him: PLEASE REFRAIN FROM MAKING SMALL TALK WITH THE CLERK. My smile widened into a delirious grin. Ken Fondness was futzing with something on his computer.

"*Hi*," I said.

Ken Fondness frowned.

Macon cleared his throat, a noise meant for me, and handed over the letters. He explained that he needed to pay his mother's taxes, and Ken Fondness grew irritated.

"I don't need this," he said, gesturing to the mail as if it offended him to even see it. "But since you're tardy, there's a form you'll need to fill out before you can pay."

"Okay," Macon said.

"I don't have it here. I'll have to retrieve it," Ken Fondness said as if we were a major inconvenience in his day that ended at noon.

"That's fine," Macon said. "I can wait."

Ken Fondness shot him a hassled look before stalking away. Afraid he was still within earshot, Macon and I communicated silently. I pointed with excitement at the library copy of an old boat book sitting beside his computer. Macon raised both fists in the air with glee.

Ken Fondness returned with the form, and we chilled. Macon filled it out while Ken Fondness typed something up.

"It's nice to see you away from the library," I said. I couldn't stop myself.

Ken Fondness looked up from his computer screen. He didn't point at his sign to get me to shut up, but he glanced at it irritably.

I beamed back at him.

Macon finished the transaction, and we scooted out the door with ten minutes to spare. "I love him," I gushed in the elevator. "I love grouchy old men."

"I'm aware, and I'm grateful for it."

The temptation dangled right there, but I was too hyped to allow myself to read anything into it. I would pocket that and save the indulgence for later. "Do you think he recognized us?"

"Of course he recognized us. And I think seeing us together outside of the library has now tarnished his opinion of me." Macon's tone was droll but his smile was teasing, because Ken Fondness had still never forgiven me for my pirate blunder.

I laughed as we exited back on the main floor.

As we passed a huddle of lawyers, Macon lowered his voice. "He's been doing the same job for thirty-six years and no one can remember him taking a day off."

"He eats an egg salad sandwich and a banana every single day for lunch."

"Excuse me," a man said, interrupting our riffing. He was middle-aged, but it was a rough middle age. His face, limbs, and hair were long and rangy in a reckless way, and he was wearing a T-shirt with an ugly cartoon kid on it. "Are you in a hurry?"

"Yes," Macon said.

Even though I was the one in a hurry, I was curious, and I was in a giddy mood. "That depends."

Macon glared at me.

"We're getting married, and we need a witness." He gestured to an exhausted-looking woman in a nearby sitting area. Three young children were squirming all over her, and two of them were sobbing.

"Oh," I said. "Well, I guess I—"

"How long would it take?" Macon asked the man while still scowling at me.

"It'll be fast," the man said. "A couple of minutes. I've done it before."

"Sure," I said, no longer at ease.

"Great." The man clapped his hands and led the way. Reluctantly, I followed. "Come on, troops, let's go!" he said.

The tired woman and her upset children gathered their belongings. Over my shoulder, I threw a pleading look to Macon, who was staring at me in disbelief. But then he just shook his head and trudged along behind us.

Inside the courtroom, a pissed-off judge kept telling the woman to quiet her kids. Macon and I stood in the back of the unremarkable room, the third child joined in the crying, vows were spoken, and then it was over. I signed a piece of paper, and Macon and I left.

"Felicitations," I said in horror.

"He knew he was getting married today, yet he chose—*he chose*—to wear a Cornholio shirt." Macon glanced at me and then clocked the generational difference again. "*Beavis and Butt-Head?* You didn't miss much."

"I mean, I've heard of it."

"I thought it was funny when I was twelve."

"Do you think that woman's children are okay?" I asked.

"No," he said.

We were both still shuddering as he drove me to the mechanic. "What does marriage even mean when people can just...go and do that?" he said. "Why bother at all?"

Cory and I had once believed that we might get married at the courthouse this autumn. (It was almost this autumn.) I imagined standing beside him in the same bare-bones room before the same irate judge and felt ill. "Fuck," I said, remembering something else. "I still have to buy my maid-of-honor dress. Riley picked out one that's expensive."

"Maybe your new friend will lend you his T-shirt," Macon said bitterly.

When we arrived at the mechanic, Harvey said, "Your engine block cracked because you didn't get a new radiator or hoses last spring."

"Can't I get them now?" I asked.

Harvey scoffed. "You're beyond that fix now."

"So..."

"So you need a new engine," he said, "which will cost more than that car is worth."

"So..."

Harvey frowned at me like I was an idiot, which I suppose, in that moment, I was. "So I'm saying you need a new *car*."

Macon and I transferred the contents of my Volkswagen into his Volvo, all the bits and bobs from my glove compartment and floorboard and trunk, and then we drove to my store to deliver the tile. Tears streamed down my face. I loathed myself for crying in front of him again, and I loathed myself for using his car as a moving van again.

"This fucking year," I said.

"This fucking year," he agreed in a tone that was calm and steady and depressed.

"I can't afford a car right now. Not even another shitty one. I can barely afford that dress for the wedding." He parked and made a move to get out, but I stopped him. "I need a minute. I don't want the contractor to see me like this. I have to look responsible."

"You *are* responsible."

"My car would disagree."

"Well, I've always hated your car, and I'm glad you finally killed it before it killed you."

I rummaged around in my bag until I found a tissue. When I blew my nose, it honked like a goose. What was one more humiliation in front of him?

"Maybe . . . don't get a car," he said.

"What? Macon. I need a car."

"But what if you don't? You live a ten-minute walk from here, and there's a grocery store within walking distance, too. You could get away with not having one for at least a few months."

"What about when I have to go to the salvage store across town?" I gestured to the boxes of decorative tile in his back seat. "I can't ask you to help me every time."

"Why not?"

Because you're not my boyfriend. I didn't say it, but I let it sit between us all the same. The silence grew uneasy. "Because you have a job," I finally said.

"No, you're right," he said, skirting past the awkwardness. Another dark silence descended. A minute later, he sat back up. "Okay." He was trying so hard to fix this problem for me. "If you don't have a car, you can cancel your insurance. Set that money aside and then use it to hire a car whenever you need to go somewhere farther away."

The weight of it all was so demoralizing.

"It would only be temporary," he said.

"Like the studio. Like my savings."

"Hey." He waited until he had my attention. Until I actually looked at him. "You're doing a good thing here. Your bookstore is going to be great."

"*Pfft.*" I turned away toward the nameless storefront. A goldendoodle was drinking water from the bowl I'd set out for dog passersby. The trailing flowers in the hanging baskets ruffled in the breeze. In the windows were Mika's two large hand-painted signs in a sweeping calligraphy: BOOKSTORE COMING SOON! WE CAN'T WAIT TO MEET YOU! My heart lifted a teensy bit.

"Oh my God," Macon said suddenly. "I haven't even told you about cheeseburger leg yet."

My frown was already softening. "What?"

"Months ago, back when we weren't—"

He was going to say *talking*, but I waved him past it.

"Anyway. I had this dream where I rolled up the bottom of my pants, and the skin on my calves was hanging off in these meaty, ground beef–looking, patty-sized shapes. It was a condition called cheeseburger leg." He grinned at my bewilderment. "You were there, and you were appalled that I hadn't gone to the doctor, but it had only been a week."

I put my head in my hands. "Stop trying to cheer me up."

"I thought it might go away on its own."

I turned my head so it was still resting in my hands but facing him.

He lifted one of his pant legs as if to show me. "Those patties were *really* painful."

"Okay," I said.

"Okay what?"

I shoved his arm. "I'll be okay. You can stop now."

Every time I touched him, his fingers found the place where mine had just been. He was still laughing as his hand went unconsciously straight to the spot. "I just hope the condition isn't hereditary," he said. "I'd never be able to get my mom to the doctor."

Finally, I burst into laughter.

His smile widened—and then he shoved my arm back. The brief touch was light but thrilling. My palm went straight to the spot, covering it as tightly as a promise. I would give him the time and space that he needed. He was letting me in, and the wait would be worth it.

September

DATE DUE	BORROWER'S NAME	ROOM NUMBER
JAN 25		
FEB 19		
MAR 30		
APR 17		
MAY 10		
JUN 03		
JUL 22		
AUG 04		
SEP 28		

CHAPTER THIRTY-THREE

The inside of my head was a to-do list that never shrank. For each item crossed off, a dozen new ones appeared, mounting and intensifying the pressure. Everything was riding on opening the store when the temperature dropped, but in the meantime, Ridgetop had just had the hottest August on record, and September wasn't faring any better. Stubbornly, I continued to work with open doors and a borrowed fan, sweating out every gallon of water I drank. I sweated so much that I hardly had to use Kindred's restroom. My own was still under loud and hectic construction.

The moments when time slowed down—the moments I was with Macon—stood alone like islands. He was still on vacation but occupied with his garden. One evening, though, he drove me to a bicycle shop. Via a lengthy text argument, he'd talked me into testing out an electric cargo bike to replace my car, at least temporarily. The insurance money I'd be saving, plus the little I got for selling my old car for parts, would cover the cost. I was more eager to hang out with him than to ride the bike, but after only a few minutes of zipping around, I was sold. We took turns, and he looked as youthful and enthused as I'd ever seen him.

"I'll let you borrow my car if you let me borrow this bike," he said seriously, and I laughed.

"Head trauma is on the rise because fewer people wear helmets on e-bikes, so promise me you'll always wear one," he said seriously, and I swooned.

I recognized now that some of his cautiousness—things like texting to see if I'd arrived home safely and driving a make of car known for its high safety ratings—was a result of being raised by a fearful mother. Still, I liked that he worried about *me*. I liked that he wanted to keep *me* safe. I bought the bike and a cute mint helmet and pedaled happily back to work.

The next island was the day we moved the shelves and other fixtures from Carla's garage into the store. It was all hands on deck—Macon; Mika; Bex; Bex's business partner, Craig, and his truck; two altruistic black belts from their dojang who also did CrossFit and liked to show off their strength; and Richard and his van. I couldn't believe how many people showed up to help.

As we finished loading the last item into the van, Richard, gaunt yet full of vigor, lingered as he said goodbye to Carla. I nudged Macon. "You think?"

"I *do* think," he said, touching the spot on his arm. Sweat was rolling down his forehead, and his glasses were crooked and smudged.

I pointed to the glasses. He took them off and handed them over. I breathed on the lenses and carefully wiped them with my shirt. I'd been cleaning them for years, although I couldn't remember the last time I'd done it. I'd cleaned Cory's glasses, too, whenever I found them lying around our apartment. "Thank you, cleaning fairy," he'd call out when he put them back on.

"Isn't it nice to be able to see the world again?" I said, handing them back to Macon.

"Don't see what's so nice about the world," Macon grumbled. This was *our* usual exchange. But his eyes sparkled cheekily as he got into his car.

Suddenly I noticed Carla was standing behind me. I thanked her again for everything, but she ignored it. "He reminds me of Len," she said.

"Richard?"

"No. Your beau."

"Oh, he's not . . ."

Her expression twinkled. "You're welcome. And yes," she said before I could remind her, "I'll call you when I'm ready to move." I had already opened Macon's passenger door to get in when she added, "And bring your beau again. I like him."

"She likes you," I said to Macon, both of us ignoring the other half of what she'd said. The CrossFit black belts had also mistaken us for a couple, as had the bike salesman.

"Looks like Richard has some competition," he said.

I laughed, secretly pleased that our chemistry was apparent to outside observers. Secretly pleased to be returning to the store in his car, not anybody else's.

But it was a frustratingly long time before I saw him again. My work was nonstop, and with the bartering spirit still going strong, Macon made a deal with his neighbor: yard work in exchange for helping to build his own bookshelves. Then his mom discovered mildew in her bathroom walls, which turned into its own saga. Just as the door to something new had been cracked open, we stopped being able to see each other as often, and never without anybody else around.

Mika finally joined me full-time, and I tried to turn on the air conditioning as a welcome present. It did not turn on. Figuring this was something the landlord would pay for, I was shocked to examine the lease and discover the HVAC system was my responsibility.

I wrote the repairperson a harrowing check.

Stephen from the East branch was officially hired, and then my third employee walked in after seeing the signs in our windows. I recognized her immediately by her colorful leg tattoos—big floral blooms and beloved kidlit characters. She was the server from the diner who had witnessed my breakup with Cory. Jo had worked in a children's bookstore in Georgia as a teenager and in college. She was still young, but she was sharp and enthusiastic and knowledgeable, and I hired her on the spot as my children's specialist.

"We need one more person," Mika said. "Somebody willing to do events and social media."

Stephen was a bit of a Macon (and Len) and had already claimed the back room job of opening shipments and fulfilling online orders, but it was Macon himself who sent me my final employee: Amelia Louisa Hatmaker, the library patron who had gifted us the hot-air balloon voucher. *Her husband just left her for a younger woman,* he texted. *Her résumé sucks because she hasn't worked in twenty-five years, but I think she'd work hard to prove herself.*

I liked Amelia Louisa, and she had the extroverted personality for community outreach that the rest of us lacked. After my own breakup experience, I was concerned about her ability to handle everything amid the turmoil, but Amelia Louisa turned out to be a godsend. (A Maconsend.) Efficient and organized, she also threw herself into setting up the computers and point-of-sale system.

Stephen, Jo, and I ordered books while Mika filled our gifts section with sustainable goods, recycled notebooks, fountain pens, greeting cards made by local artists, and Ridgetop-appropriate stained-glass suncatchers shaped like classic novels. With each new task, our decision fatigue grew, but whenever one of us had a meltdown over quantities or editions or translations, Amelia Louisa reined us back in with the skill that came from being the mother of two rambunctious teenage boys. We didn't have a history together or a rhythm like I'd had with my library coworkers, but I could already imagine baking everyone's birthday cakes.

Cory's birthday arrived, and he began a new decade without me. It made me sad but not mournful. My thirtieth was fast approaching, too. I texted my well wishes, he responded straightaway, and then we exchanged several friendly messages. He'd heard about my store and was astonished and proud of me. *You know,* he said, *that never would have happened if we were still together.* He was right, but the thought had never occurred to me before.

"I thought about inviting him to the wedding," Riley confessed over the phone.

"You always did get along," I said.

"Speaking of, have you bought your dress yet?"

Fuck. Fuck, fuck, fuck.

"I'll take your silence as a no."

"Oh God. I'm sorry. I just paid for this huge repair that I hadn't budgeted for." My mind raced to find the money. It was fortunate that I'd been saving on apartment rent throughout this ordeal because that banked money had been rescuing me from these surprise expenses. Unfortunately, my sister hadn't picked out a regular dress. It was designer and outrageously expensive. It cost the same amount as a theoretical month of rent, which, this month, I had given to the HVAC unit. "I literally can't afford it. But I'm sure I can find one that looks similar. It'll be okay if I don't match the other bridesmaids *exactly*, right? Since I'm the maid of honor?"

"Iggy. Stop freaking out. It's okay."

"I promise I'll get your approval on whatever I find before I buy it."

"Iggy! Stop it. I'm buying you the dress."

I felt ill. "What?"

But she sounded happy. "Thank God, something I can finally do to help you. Yes. I'm paying for your dress. It's a gift. And we're both going to be happy about it."

"I can't let you do that. That dress is four figures."

"Yeah, and I'm the asshole who picked it out. I'm throwing a wedding that might get media coverage, so it's made me paranoid about everything looking perfect—"

"Wait. You think your wedding might get media coverage?"

"*People* covers high-profile WNBA weddings all the time."

"Jesus."

"I know."

"Doesn't that freak you out?"

"Yes. Hence, the dress. Which I'm paying for."

"I still don't think I can let you do that."

"I'm not giving you the option."

We sat in silence.

"You're stewing, aren't you?" she said.

"I'm trying to figure out how to pay for this."

Riley's voice deflated with a sigh. "Listen, I know Mom and Dad wouldn't pay for this dress for you. And I know you'd never ask them to. I wouldn't either. But just because we don't have that kind of relationship with them doesn't mean we can't have it with each other. Being around Jess's family has made me realize there are other ways to *be* family. We can talk more. We can visit each other more. And you can let me help you with this."

It stunned me.

My sister had told me over the summer that she wanted to help with my store, but since the WNBA season was short, she couldn't afford to miss any time with Jess before she started playing in the Turkish league during the offseason. I'd laughed and told her it was fine. But Riley had been hurt that I had already assumed she wouldn't be there. Even though we were closer to each other than we were to our parents, it had never occurred to me that being there for each other was still a choice. That we could do more to support each other, and that maybe that was also what she'd been trying to get me to do all year: support her.

"I'm sorry." I wilted. "I should have been helping you this whole time, too."

"I mean. We've both been a little busy."

We released pitiful laughs at the understatement.

"Don't tell Mom," Riley said, "but she might have been right that planning a wedding this big in one year was a mistake."

I suspected it was less work than opening a new business, but as the big sister, I let this slide. Which reminded me that I'd let other things slide. "God, I haven't even asked yet. How's Jess coping?" Her team, the Atlanta Dream, had lost its first two playoff games and were already out.

"Jess is tough. She's disappointed but glad they at least *made* the playoffs this year. The team is headed in the right direction."

"I'm glad she's okay."

"So, does this mean you'll let me buy the dress?"

I remembered what Macon had said about me having a hard time accepting help and how true that had felt. I swallowed my pride. "Yes. Thank you."

"Good. Because I already bought it while we were talking. It'll arrive next week. I seriously do not have any fucking time to waste."

"You and me both," I said.

"You and me both," she said.

The malodorous fragrances had finally faded, and the stock—crisp new arrivals—was delivered in overwhelming quantities. The scent was a homecoming, even as our thirsty hands dried out from touching all the paper and cardboard. We were behind schedule, and one Monday, Sue and Alyssa and Elijah showed up to help. I savored this generous reunion and familiar camaraderie. Elijah wielded a box cutter in the back room while Sue and Alyssa assisted me on the floor.

"Too bad Macon couldn't join us," Sue said, as we organized the history sections.

"He's helping his mom today," I said, "but he's already done so much around here."

"Yeah," Alyssa said slyly, "those sunflowers by the registers sure are beautiful."

My skin warmed at the implication. "I assume you recognize them because he also brought in some for the library." Macon often brought in bouquets for the front desk. Mine had been left in the mosaicked entryway a few mornings prior.

"We didn't get any sunflowers," Alyssa said.

"No, we did not," Sue said, adopting the same sly tone.

My heartbeat skipped and picked up.

"Ever since you left," Sue said, "he's been miserable."

"Sounds like regular Macon," I said, still thinking about the flowers.

"No," Alyssa said. "He's *moping*. He's full-time unhappy now."

I paused, a stack of ancient history in hand. He'd complained about work to me but had given no indication that his grievances were anything out of the ordinary.

"You know," Sue said, shifting books beside me slowly and methodically, "he used to want to work at the reference desk." The reference desk was at Rowe Memorial. It was the main library downtown, only two blocks away from my store. "I thought it was strange how he stopped talking about it when you showed up."

Reference librarian was the job I'd always privately believed he'd be great at, even though he'd never mentioned it to me. He'd always seemed content in his current position.

Sue went on, "He didn't even apply for Val's job when she retired two years ago. I tried to convince him to do it, but he shut me down."

I swallowed. "Guess he changed his mind. Guess he's happy doing what he's doing."

"Silly me," Sue deadpanned. "And here I was thinking he wasn't switching jobs because he's in love with you."

Two workers shouted and began hammering in the restroom. I jumped and then cowered, wincing at each blow. Sue and Alyssa exchanged a grin.

"We're friends," I said. This was true. "Our relationship has always been platonic." This was less true. I had many friends, but I only wanted to sleep with one of them.

"Well, since you're such good friends"—Sue thumped a row of books against the end of a shelf for emphasis—"maybe you can encourage him to apply for the reference job that'll be opening up later this year. Ted is moving to Portland."

"Oregon or Maine?" I asked, because I needed the subject to change. Sue had said *love*. She thought Macon was in love with me. The word cracked and splintered my heart open, and the painful shards rattled around inside my chest for days. Making me wish it were true. Making me wonder if it was. Causing me misery and ecstasy and no end of suffering.

And then another heartbreak happened.

We did not meet my goal.

Although the equinox had passed, the weather was still warm, and the trees were only hinting at what was to come. I'd been scrutinizing their leaves all month, praying for them to take their time—to give *me* more time—and they had miraculously obeyed. (Not miraculously. Climate change.) But

October was now a whisper away, and the tourists who'd booked their reservations early were already swelling the streets, yet our shelves were still half empty.

I was devastated. It felt like the store had failed before it had even begun.

If we missed peak tourism, our holiday sales might not be enough to keep the store alive. We'd be opening only to close forever in January. I couldn't endure another January that reset my entire life. It was unimaginable to be so close to losing everything again.

"We'll be able to open in a week," Mika said, comforting me in my office.

I gestured to the two pictures I'd hung: the framed Mary Brisson postcard and a photo of Len frowning, cigarette dangling from his lips, feet kicked up on his crowded desk. "Look how disappointed in me they are."

"*You* are disappointed in you because you gave yourself an unattainable goal. We're doing great. Don't give up on us now."

"I'm not giving up."

"I know you aren't." Her smile turned teasing. "So stop acting like it. Besides, I have news that will cheer you up."

The outside signs were ready for delivery. Mika and I had decided it was crucial to shell out some real money for them, and I was nervous to see if our gamble had paid off. She had hired two local artists: a metalsmith to sculpt our name in distinguished gold capital letters that would span the green length of the storefront, and a woodcarver to create a swinging sign that would hang above the sidewalk. The swinging sign was reminiscent of an old woodcut illustration, a carved stack of books with a big stylized B to match the gold B above it.

Mika was still concerned about the name I'd chosen. Getting signs with the right aesthetics was a way to compromise.

The signage went up on the last day of September. The store glimmered like a jewel box. It looked timeless and cultured. Worthy of notice, worthy of existence. All four of my employees—I had *employees* now—stood with me, admiring the spectacle in the twilight.

"I know I already asked what the name means, but I've forgotten," Amelia Louisa confessed.

I felt his presence before I saw him. The energy and excitement swirling around inside me shifted to greet him as he approached us from behind.

"Bildungsroman," Macon said to Amelia Louisa, his eyes locked on the golden letters. "It's a novel that spans a protagonist's formative years, often from youth into adulthood." His gaze cut away to find mine, brimming with admiration. "It's perfect."

"It even ties in with the history of the building, the old deli." I pointed at the mosaicked entryway. "Roman's."

"I love it," he said sincerely. Still looking at me.

Love. I beamed up at my bookstore. "I do, too."

October

DATE DUE	BORROWER'S NAME	ROOM NUMBER
JAN 25		
FEB 19		
MAR 30		
APR 17		
MAY 10		
JUN 03		
JUL 22		
AUG 04		
SEP 28		
OCT 07		

CHAPTER THIRTY-FOUR

The personalized Bildungsroman items arrived, everything thoughtfully designed: the free bookmarks to tuck into purchases, which were gorgeously illustrated but easily compostable; ethically made shirts and hats and totes; and custom mugs crafted by a local potter. Seeing the store name in print was a thrill, and I was proud of the product line we'd come up with.

Amelia Louisa gave us the rest of our point-of-sale training while her teenaged sons stamped the Bildungsroman logo onto countless brown paper bags and followed Jo and her tattoos and dyed-black hair around like lovesick puppies. They helped her create my dream centerpiece for the children's section: a fake fireplace inspired by the one at the library. She'd found a shabby but handsome antique mantel, and they painted it to complement the walls. Inside the mantel, they painted impressionistic flames. Fairy lights illuminated a stack of real logs, and they placed a cozy round rug in front of it with adorable child-size wooden chairs.

Banned Books Week had already passed in September, but Mika and I gave it an extension by crowding one of our front windows with challenged titles. In the other, we placed seasonal reads arranged on a scale from cozy autumnal to blood-chilling horror.

And finally, our shelves filled in with the expected sections but also the sections we'd been looking forward to the most: local authors, regional reads, and staff picks, plus temporary displays like Books Down Under (a table honoring Kat's favorite Australian fiction), The Book Was Better (novels that had recently been adapted for film or television), and Book Xanax (gentle stories where nothing too stressful happens).

"Ingrid!" Mika called out the evening before we opened. "We need a tie-breaker."

I emerged from the back room, tangled in more fairy lights. I'd picked up a box stuffed with them from a garage sale, and I wanted to hang them everywhere during this first holiday season. My coworkers were huddled near a display of books that we'd deemed fantastic despite their intimidating size.

"Jo and I want to call it 'I Like Big Books and I Cannot Lie,'" Amelia Louisa said.

"While Mika and I prefer 'I Promise They're Worth It,'" Stephen said.

"Not to be one of those people," I said, "but those are both great."

"The first one," Macon said from a row over, "because all the other displays also include the word *book*." He'd stopped by with another carload of plants and was tucking them into the store's nooks and crannies. They were cuttings from the same plants that filled the library's nooks and crannies.

"Damn." Stephen ran a hand through his graying floppy hair. He was a floppy guy in general, from his posture to his cardigans. "That's a good point."

"Just make sure they all have shelf talkers," I said, before moving toward Macon. "People will need more convincing to buy those."

"Give me a stack, and I'll fill some out while I'm at the library," Macon said.

I leaned against the bookshelf beside him. Not sexily but exhaustedly, arms still tangled in unlit lights. "Are you *sure* you don't want a job here?"

His eyes remained focused on his work. "I don't want you to be my boss."

My heartstrings zinged to attention. His tone was as carefully modulated as ever, but he'd left plenty of room for interpretation. I debated on a flirtatious response but then remembered my failed dance. "They're all so cute," I said, switching to the plants. Something safe. He'd been caring for the cuttings all summer long in his greenhouse, another thoughtful vegetative gift I hadn't known was coming. "I'm afraid I'm going to kill them."

"You won't," he said. "I'll teach you."

He'd also donated a dozen pumpkins for our window displays. He'd grown them for their flavor, but they were still beautiful. "Next year, I'll plant some decorative varieties," he'd said, concerned that I was disappointed somehow. *Next year!* was all I heard. He was planning for a future that assumed my store would still be open—and that I'd still be in his life.

He stopped futzing with the pilea and gestured to the lights. "Need some help?"

I held out my arms.

Slowly and patiently, he began to unravel them. I closed my eyes while he worked around me. He smelled like potting soil and aged library pages and leather bindings and the bars of soap from his house that I had learned were eucalyptus mint.

"Ingrid," he said quietly.

I startled awake—and then a second time to see him so close to me.

"Did you fall asleep?"

"I'm tired," I said.

"I gathered that. I was afraid you might fall over."

"Speaking of jobs," I said.

"Were we?"

"Sue mentioned that a reference position is opening up. Are you gonna apply?"

He frowned. "Did she ask you to ask me?"

"Yeah, but you should do it. You're qualified, and it'd be a good match for your strengths and interests. The work would be more engaging, too."

He handed me the cord, neatly wrapped. He'd untangled the entire strand without ever touching me. I wanted him to touch me again.

"Plus," I said bravely, "Rowe is so close. We could have lunch together."

"Ah. The real reason emerges. You just want me to cook for you."

I understood he was teasing me. But was it flirtatious? His serious tone still made it impossible to tell. "Obviously," I said, going for it this time.

He didn't volley back. "Apparently, a few people are interested in the job. People who are better with people. I have a difficult time imagining them hiring me over somebody like . . . Candice from West."

I pretended to vomit, and he gave me half a smile. We both found Candice exhausting. She was the sort of person who volunteered for everything and then tried to invent *new* tasks to do. But I was also surprised to hear him talk down on himself. "You're better with people than you think," I said. "And you're great with the unhoused community and the mentally ill. That matters at Rowe." Libraries were a safe and warm space for vulnerable people, and our downtown location received the highest volume of them by far. Macon was calm and patient with a lot of difficult people that other librarians couldn't handle. "*You don't give yourself enough credit.* You said that to me once, but you don't give yourself enough credit either."

His expression grew puzzled. "When did I say that?"

"At the 911 call center." It was the day we'd admitted that we would have missed each other if we'd been sent to separate locations. It had felt like a confession, some sliver of unspoken truth cracking through.

"God," he said. "Remember that time we worked at the 911 call center?"

"Seriously. What the fuck. But also, we were sent there because they trusted we could do the job."

"Yeah, okay. I see what you're getting at."

"I'd hire you. I *tried* to hire you," I said, which made him almost laugh. "I mean, you definitely won't get the job if you don't even apply."

"You're starting to sound inspirational, which you know I can't tolerate."

"My bookstore opens tomorrow. I'm allowed to feel inspirational."

"So it does." His voice softened with affection. "So you are."

CHAPTER THIRTY-FIVE

Our doors opened to the sweet brown scent of autumn. The temperature had finally dropped, and a crisp wind chilled the air. We bustled around like eager squirrels gathering nuts, still setting up shop and wondering how many people would notice that our closed sign had flipped to open. We'd decided to wait a day before setting out the A-frame sidewalk sign with its handwritten entreaty for customers to come in. We needed to make sure everything was running smoothly.

Our first customer was a tourist from Chattanooga, and her first purchase was a popular romantasy. She held up the novel and agreeably posed for a photo with me for social media. And then—as easy and impossible as that—we were in business.

Clyde the joke man passed her on the way out. "I've got a special one for you this morning," he called out, dentures flapping.

"Hit me," I said.

"Why did the librarian become a bookseller?"

I was touched before he even got to the punchline.

"Because she wanted to start a new chapter in life!"

"*Clyde*," I said, almost tearing up.

"I would like to buy something," he said. "Something cheap."

It made me laugh. I sold him a greeting card for his granddaughter's birthday—it turned out we shared the same date—and he had a skip in his grandfatherly step as he exited.

Macon arrived a few minutes later, popping in before work. The cheerful bell on the door surprised him, and he looked up. "A final gift from Len," I said, hurrying to meet him. He was carrying a heavy-looking slow cooker. "Mika found it in one of the drawers."

"It's from the old shop?"

I nodded, beaming, and slipped the ladle out from underneath his arm. "We've already had two customers!"

"Oh my God. That's great."

I finally realized the importance of what he was holding. "Is this what I think it is?"

"Don't tell my coworkers. I haven't had a chance to make it for them yet." The slow cooker was filled with pumpkin spice latte made with real pumpkin, not a flavored syrup. He usually brought it to the library on the first day of autumn. He set down the appliance behind the registers, and I lifted its lid to smell the heavenly brew. *Coffee, pumpkin, cinnamon, ginger, nutmeg, cloves.*

"Your timing is perfect. I'm actually a little cold. Didn't think I'd ever be cold again."

He took in what I was wearing, a short-sleeved blouse that he'd seen an infinite number of times before, and it dawned on him. "Your winter clothes are in Edmond's room."

I laughed. "I realized that this morning, too."

"Well, stop by whenever."

"It feels like an eternity since I was at your house."

"I agree," he said with an unexpected catch in his voice.

And there it was, that hum of electricity, that gravitational pull between us, and I *know* he felt it too because his body leaned in closer. His mouth parted as if he were going to ask me something. Or suggest something. But then my entire staff swooped in, descending upon the slow cooker, and his mouth and body closed up again. Our connection was severed.

He headed for the door, clearing his throat. "I just wanted to say congratulations. To all of you. And good luck." The bell rang again as he exited.

Amelia Louisa inhaled a deep whiff of latte and sighed. "If I didn't know any better, I'd ask for your permission to date him myself."

I turned toward her sharply.

They all laughed at me.

"Like I said," she said, grinning, "I know better."

Every recent interaction with Macon had been laced with this tension of being observed. We hadn't been alone in so long. I wondered what might happen the next time we were.

Frustratingly, I didn't have the opportunity to stop by his house for another week. The store was busier—more *noticed*—than I'd expected, which was exciting for business but ruinous for my spare time. Our restroom remained under noisy construction. It was a mystery how we had managed to put together an entire store while my contractor had failed to finish a single room. I fantasized about skipping a year into the future: listening to the hushed shuffles of browsing customers, feeling settled into the pace of the business, and living . . . wherever I'd be living. Knowing that I still had to move made me anxious, and I had to keep forcing myself back to the present. The present, which was loud with power tools. Where I was worried about sales and the possibility of failure and losing that dream of the future. And all of my money, too.

But the present was also rich with hope. Our first local author showed up and signed stock and promised to send in her author friends. Amelia Louisa arranged our first event and, at the request of several customers, organized our first book club. Many of our earliest walk-ins gave us helpful advice. Others, who had never worked in retail, gave us awful advice. And several times a day, somebody strode through our door and exclaimed, "A bookstore! I didn't think there were any of these left in the world. Aren't you scared about—" and then they would name the Bad Place. These people never bought anything because they weren't book people, so their words didn't faze us. Everybody else was happy to have a bookstore in town again.

"How are you?" Macon asked when I finally appeared on his doorstep.

"Frazzled," I said, but my smile was enormous.

"I've been wanting to stop by, but I also haven't wanted to bother you. I know you need to get into the new rhythm."

"Please bother me," I said, unpacking the slow cooker from my backpack and handing it over. "It's clean, but you'll probably want to wash it again anyway."

He lifted the lid to inspect the situation, and his brows rose to discover that the pot was packed with tightly rolled tank tops.

"Space is precious on a cargo bike," I explained.

He nodded in appreciation. "Smart."

"You should know Stephen is still talking about those lattes, and he's not a talkative guy— Edmond!"

Edmond Dantès trotted into the room, and I dropped to the hardwood to greet him. He started purring as soon as I touched him, a soft sound like crackling static.

"Have you missed me? I've missed you." I glanced up to say something to Macon but then caught sight of his bookshelves, which had been built but were not yet painted. I gasped. "You didn't tell me you and Phil had started."

"We're working on the cat tree now. I've been sanding and oiling the wood."

"And the chairs!" I made a beeline for his dining room. "I love them."

"Do you mean it?" he asked nervously. He'd found a full set at the Habitat for Humanity store and had texted me a photo. They had a cute shape, and I'd liked them immediately.

"Yes. Screw my mismatched plan. These look great. They're perfect."

"Would you still recommend painting them?"

"God, yes." They were a trashed-looking shade of putty. "Red."

He looked doubtful, which made me smile again. "Like the accent color in your kitchen," I said.

"I don't have an accent color in my kitchen."

"But you *will* once I finally get around to picking out the rug and curtains."

It made him laugh. I loved making him laugh.

"What about the couch?" He motioned toward the living room again. "It's been looking a little worse since the rest of the upgrade."

"Destroy it. Burn it. Toss the ashes into the river and piss on them."

I was on a roll, but he was taken aback. "Didn't realize you had such strong feelings about it," he said. "Noted."

"That couch is a physical manifestation of depression."

"What would you replace it with?"

"I'll text you some links. Help me with the rest of my stuff?"

We unloaded the rack and pannier bags from my bike and carried everything inside. I'd only been able to cart over my summeriest clothing. I'd have to drop off another load later, but as I dug through my belongings in Edmond's room, I grew worried. "Am I missing some boxes?"

"Shit." Macon flinched. "Yeah, I moved a few into my bedroom to make it easier to reach the litter box. They've been there for so long they've become invisible."

"Oh no." I was mortified. "I'm sorry."

"I promise it's fine. Like I said, I forgot about them."

"Well, *I* promise I'll get them out of here as soon as I have a new apartment."

I followed him into the only room that I'd never been inside of before. I'd seen more of it since that first night cat-sitting, as I passed nearby whenever I used the bathroom, but my inconvenient interest in it had prevented me from examining it up close. Macon's bedroom was small but cozy. The walls were the same beaten-up white that his other rooms had been, the same color that his study and Edmond's room still were. There was the large dresser and mirror that I remembered, as well as the matching side tables and lamps and a queen-size bed. The furniture was nondescript but sturdy, and the bed was draped in a surprisingly nice quilt.

"Who made that?" I asked.

"Bonnie. She gave it to me as a housewarming gift, even though the house itself was already practically a gift."

"That was sweet of her. How's she doing, anyway?"

He thought about his response. "She answers when I call. She sounds okay. That's more than I get from her when times are bad."

I nodded, unsure what else to say.

He gestured to the quilt. "That was one of the only things I had left when Dani moved out. She even took the mattress," he added.

This statement jumped out as if it were written in bold ink. It sounded like he wanted me to know that his mattress was new. (At least I hoped it was new. I hoped he hadn't found it wherever he'd found the couch.) Was he remembering how he'd carried the mattress that I had shared with Cory to the dumpster? Was he thinking about how this was the first time that I'd ever stepped foot inside his bedroom?

As I searched through my boxes, his energy seemed to pulsate. "Have you started looking for a new place?" he asked.

"I'll look in January when the store slows down. Or goes out of business, ha. I can't deal with anything else right now."

"Oh," he said quietly.

And it struck me: Did he think a relationship counted as *anything else?*

With a pounding heart, I tested him. "Hey. I know you've never met them, but Brittany and Reza are hosting a birthday dinner for me next weekend. Mika and Bex will be there. And I know you hate parties, and I do, too, but this one will be small and simple. Like that one here at your house all those years ago? It's okay if you don't want to come, though," I added, providing an escape. "You don't know everybody, so it might be uncomfortable—"

"No," he said. "I mean, yes."

"Really?"

"You *are* inviting me, right? You didn't actually say that."

"Yes."

He swallowed. "I'd love to come."

My whole body tingled in response. It wasn't a date. But it wasn't not a date.

While I didn't normally do anything special on my birthday, it had been a *year*, and thirty was a loaded number. I'd been hoping Macon would host the celebratory dinner, which would have been a tricky ask, but then Brittany and Reza had surprised me by showing up at the store, Amira in tow, and offering first. And now, just like that, Macon was in. *I'd love to come.* My mind played this on repeat for the next week, hearing the swallow beforehand.

On the twenty-second of October, Mika, Bex, and I arrived early to Brittany and Reza's house, bearing wine and my favorite foods. (I'd instructed Brittany and Reza not to cook; they didn't need any additional burden right now.) Macon surprised me by arriving on time, although it dawned on me that I'd only ever seen him arrive late to work. He'd been punctual whenever I'd asked him to be somewhere. In addition to my requested dishes, he was also carrying two bouquets of garden flowers, a big one for me and a smaller one for the hosts.

"Where's mine?" Bex joked, and Macon looked so insecure that I wanted to hug him.

I hugged the flowers instead. Flowers! He'd brought me flowers again.

"How thoughtful," Brittany said. "Thank you." She still had a lingering distrust of him because of the incident in January. We'd both been so busy that I hadn't been able to fill her in on how much he'd been helping me. But Macon didn't know that her opinion of him was low, and I was relieved that she had decided to behave.

I officially introduced everyone who didn't know each other, and then we unwrapped the containers and heated what needed to be heated. Evidence of an infant was everywhere—bottles drying, piles of burp cloths, a carrier, a bouncy chair, blankets on the floor—but the house had been vacuumed, and it smelled warmly of beeswax. Two honeyed tapers were lit on the table like they'd been at Ramadan. And once again, Brittany's appearance was polished and on point.

"You didn't have to do all this," I said, feeling guilty.

"We're just grateful that you were okay with us hosting," Reza said. They weren't ready for babysitters or spending an entire evening away from home.

"Where *is* the baby?" Mika asked. "I'd love to meet her."

"She's asleep," Brittany said.

All conversation froze.

"She's in the back with a white-noise machine," Reza said, reassuring us. "She'll be awake soon enough, though."

"I love her and want to spend every second of every minute of every day with her," Brittany said. "And I'm fucking exhausted and need her to sleep more than two goddamn hours in a row." Her polish had already worn thin, and it made me love her even more. She placed Macon's flowers between the tapers before turning on us. "And don't even *think* about giving me advice because we've tried it all, and I don't want to hear it."

After a brief and awkward pause, Bex gave her a dashing smile. "I'm confident that none of us have any advice to give you."

Brittany exhaled. "Thank God."

"Our moms have been a lot," Reza explained.

We gathered at the table. Brittany sat at the end nearest to the hallway and Amira, and Reza sat across from her. Mika and Bex sat beside each other, and I sat beside Macon. Despite sitting beside each other for years, there had always been distance between us at the circulation desk, and we always sat across from each other at his house. As everybody tucked in and laughed and shared stories, I tried to remember the last time we had sat this close together. It must have been at one of the all-day all-staff meetings at the main library. We always sat beside each other in the sea of folding chairs, but that was in fluorescent lighting with a hundred coworkers, and this was in candlelight with two couples and us.

His profile was achingly familiar. The line of his nose and chin, the slope of his shoulders. But his hands looked larger and more alive as they moved beside me. Our elbows bumped, and our forearms brushed. Each time, we murmured an apology, reining our limbs back in. Though our arms were clothed, my skin shivered. Macon felt solid. Not abstract, like in my murky thoughts before slumber, but like muscle and sinew and bone. He was wearing a nice button-down that I'd never seen before, and I was wearing a dress that he'd never seen before, and I felt pretty and happy, surrounded by my friends in the flickering glow.

As the meal progressed, Macon even opened up and began sharing stories, too. Everybody was enjoying themselves. I couldn't have asked for a better birthday.

"We forgot to toast!" Mika said.

Our wine glasses were almost empty, but everyone turned to look at me.

Mika lifted hers. "Ingrid, you've had a horrible and sensational year." Everyone laughed. "But I'm proud of everything you've accomplished, and I'm so grateful to be back inside a bookstore. Thank you."

Bex raised their glass. "And *I'm* thrilled to have no financial stake in it."

Everyone laughed again, and Brittany added, "To Ingrid and her bookstore."

"To Ingrid and her bookstore," everyone chorused.

My skin was flushed with joy and prosecco as everyone clinked glasses. Macon's and mine clinked together last. He held my gaze as he spoke. "Happy birthday, Ingrid."

I was beaming. "Happy birthday, Macon."

Everyone froze in surprise—then burst into fresh laughter. When I realized my mistake, my flush transformed into a full-bodied blush. Macon's eyes lit up with delight, but he was the only one who wasn't laughing.

"I've had a very busy year, and I'm very tired," I said.

"Happy birthday, Mika." Bex clinked their wife's glass, which started a new round of everybody wishing everybody else a happy birthday. Amira cried from the nursery. Brittany and Reza both vaulted to their feet, but she waved for him to sit back down and left.

"So, when is your birthday, Macon?" Mika asked.

"November twenty-third," I answered.

Everybody stared at me again. "I can name all of your birthdays, too," I said defensively. And then, to remove the pressure from myself, I said, "He's also having a big one this year."

Their collective gaze shifted, and I immediately regretted thrusting him into the spotlight.

"Forty," he said. It made him the oldest at the table by six years. There was a subtle undercurrent as they processed that he was a full decade older than me. When we were younger, a difference like that would have meant something, but it had long stopped mattering to me.

Mika smoothed away the tension with a warm smile. "Happy early birthday."

"Hey," I said to Macon, diving straight back into awkwardness. I blamed the wine. "This is the first time since we've known each other that we've both been in our thirties."

Macon's expression tightened. "For a whole month and a day."

The tension ratcheted up another notch, and I realized I still hadn't taken my attention away from him. I shifted toward the others and brightened my expression. "Well, this isn't where I expected my life would be at this age, but . . . I like where it's headed."

"I'll cheers again to that," Bex said with a third raise of their glass.

But it turned out that Macon wasn't done. "Where did you think you'd be?"

The directness of his question in front of people he hardly knew surprised me. Perhaps the wine had loosened him, too. "Definitely not in an under-construction micro-studio," I said.

Everyone but Macon laughed again.

"In my own house," I said, because he was waiting for an honest answer. I couldn't look at him, though. "With somebody I love. But the bookstore has been a wonderful surprise."

"Do you ever want kids?" Reza asked.

"Reza!" Brittany admonished from the baby's room. I laughed and called back that it was okay. But now everyone at the table was interested in my response. The intensity of Macon's gaze told me *he* was interested in my response.

"No," I said.

"Even if you find the right guy?" Reza asked.

Something smacked against the hallway wall. Mika leaned back in her chair to see what it was. "Brittany threw a stuffed bunny."

Reza looked sheepish. "That means I shouldn't have asked, and you don't have to answer."

"I don't mind," I said. Although I did, a little, but only because of Macon's presence. Yet I also wanted him to hear my response. "Cory wants children. I don't. It's one of the reasons why we broke up."

"Oh," Bex said, "I'm sorry."

"It's okay. There were many reasons. And we're both happy with our choices."

"We're considering adoption," Mika said quietly.

Bex shied but took Mika's hand. They gazed at each other with so much love that it hurt my heart. "You'd be great parents," I said.

Macon's preference was the only one left unstated, and once again, it felt paramount to steer the conversation away from the topic. I started to ask Reza a question about Amira when Macon spoke up unexpectedly. "I've never been interested in having children either."

His eyes were on Reza, but he was talking to me. He wanted *me* to know. I sat very still.

"My relationship with my college girlfriend ended because of that," he said.

"Oh," I said. I hadn't given much consideration to his girlfriends before Dani, although I knew there'd been two previous serious relationships: one in high school and one in college. Around the time he and Dani had broken up, in one of his darker moods, he'd referred to himself as a serial monogamist.

Another delicate silence descended, thankfully broken by Brittany's loud reappearance. She was still zipping up the top of her jumpsuit. "Who wants cake?"

Somehow, Reza had managed to find enough time to bake an elaborate dessert: three layers of airy lemon cake with tart raspberry jam between each and a gorgeous ring of whole raspberries on top. "It's more summery than autumnal," he said, "but lemon seemed cheerful. Like you."

He hadn't witnessed a shred of my cheerfulness that year, so it felt good to hear that he still thought of me that way. I couldn't help but glance at Macon. He nodded in agreement.

"Lemon cake is my favorite," I said to Reza.

Brittany slapped a hand against the side of her head. "We forgot candles."

"This is perfect," I said. "Just as it is."

"Blow out the tapers," Bex said, and the others agreed. And who was I to turn down a wish? They placed the candlesticks before me, and I closed my eyes. Surrounded by love, I felt my fears about the future dissolve. I wished for my friends to all have a good year.

We devoured the cake, the conversation moved along to safer topics, and everybody helped clean up. When Brittany and Reza began sagging against each other, I steered the party toward the door.

And then Macon surprised me again.

He hugged me goodbye.

It was the first time he'd purposefully touched me since the shove in his car, the first time he'd hugged me since I was crying in his house. The contact was so charged I nearly whimpered. Breathing in his familiar and comforting scent, I clung to his back tightly and for longer than I normally would have. His heartbeat quickened against my chest.

"Happy birthday," he said, voice so low and close that it resonated through me.

He started to pull away, then changed his mind and kissed my cheek. It was the way that any friend would kiss another friend's cheek, except my knees weakened. And then he stepped away from me so quickly that his stubble scratched my skin.

I was frozen and speechless.

"It was nice to meet you," he said with a wave to Brittany and Reza.

"Oh, Ingrid, I forgot," Reza said, wide awake again. "Brit wanted to show you Amira's room. Thanks for coming, Macon!" He slammed the door closed behind him.

My four friends stared at me.

"Why isn't that happening?" Bex asked.

"I can't believe you two aren't fucking," Brittany said. Her eyes widened. "Are you fucking?"

"No!" My voice lowered in case he could still hear us. "And I don't know why it's not happening. I would very much like for it to happen."

Brittany, Reza, and Bex all hooted.

I turned to Mika for guidance, but she shook her head. "It doesn't make sense to me either. It's been clear since the day I met him that he's into you."

"Yeah," Brittany said, "I used to hate him for turning you down, but I like the guy I met tonight. You should try again."

Bex wheeled on me. "What does she mean, 'turning you down'?"

"You don't know?" Reza looked excited.

"You just told me you had a crush!" Now even Mika was getting worked up. "You didn't tell me you'd tried to hook up with him."

"I tried to kiss him, and he *emphatically* said no."

"When was this?" she asked.

"January," Reza said. "We drove her around afterward trying to hook her up with somebody else."

"That didn't work either," Brittany said.

"Happy birthday, Ingrid," I said. "Let's talk about the most humiliating night of your life."

"Well, whatever was holding him back," Brittany said, "it's gone now."

"He literally just kissed you," Reza said.

"Ten months later and on the cheek," I said.

Everyone jumped to argue about whether that counted as a move, and then Mika said simply, "He's shy."

We all stopped.

"That's it." Bex's hands dropped to their hips. "I think that's actually it."

"But we've been friends for *years*," I said.

"Yeah, but isn't that what makes it scary for you, too?" Mika said. "That you're afraid you'll ruin what you already have?"

"I did try. More than once. Sort of."

"No," Brittany said. "He's a shy librarian, and you're a badass businesswoman, and that means you're going to have to make the first move—again."

CHAPTER THIRTY-SIX

I texted Kat later that night while I was brushing my teeth in my micro-sink. *Everybody here is trying to convince me that I should make another move on Macon.*

She responded immediately. *Everybody there is correct.*

!!! Why didn't you say something???

You were busy opening a bookstore. But yeah, that guy is obviously in love with you.

A rush swept through me, so powerful I thought I might collapse. I typed, deleted, typed again, and hit send. *I think I'm in love with him.*

I KNOW, Kat said.

My legs buckled. I slid to the floor, clutching my toothbrush and phone against my chest. I pressed my forehead against the sink cabinet. Terror and pain coursed through me as the full depth of my own truth was revealed. I didn't just like him. I didn't just want to sleep with him. I didn't just want him to be my boyfriend.

I loved him, and I had been in love with him for a long time.

Much longer than this year.

I tried to think back, but dizziness clouded my mind. I had pushed down and buried and denied my love for him—my complete and total adoration—for so long that I couldn't pinpoint when or where or how it had begun. It had never been there, yet it had always been there.

No. Ingrid. No.

I dropped the toothbrush and phone. My hands, all ten wriggling fingers, clawed at my chest. I wanted to rip out my own heart to stop the agony. I was in love with Macon, and now that I knew it, I could never go back to being just his friend. I had no choice but to try again. And if he rejected me—I didn't think he would, but oh God, what if he did?—I would have to finally accept it. But then our friendship would also have to end, because I couldn't fathom being able to survive in his presence anymore.

The time had come to either move forward together or separate forever.

CHAPTER THIRTY-SEVEN

Early the next morning, the leaves reached their explosive peak. The mountains were a riot of reds and oranges and yellows, a fiery blaze against the chilled air.

It was a Monday. He would be home.

I love him, I thought as I climbed onto my bike.

My heart was in my throat.

"I love you," I practiced to the trees.

"I'm in love with you," I practiced to his mailbox.

"Please tell me you love me back," I practiced to his front door.

"Ingrid," he said, opening it in shock. He was crying. "How did you get here so quickly?"

Our embrace wasn't happy. I held him as his tears turned into sobs. I led him back inside, and we sat at his dining room table because his couch was already gone.

It was Bonnie, I learned.

She was gone, too.

CHAPTER THIRTY-EIGHT

Macon left town. I wanted to go with him—I didn't want him to be alone—but he asked me to watch Edmond, and I also didn't know how I could leave the store yet.

Bonnie had overdosed three days earlier, but she had only been discovered that morning by a neighbor. Secretly, shamefully, selfishly, I was relieved that she hadn't died on my birthday. That those two dates would never be tied together for him. He used his sick leave to take care of her body and complete the other necessary arrangements regarding her estate. Will, her stepson, was still in Myanmar and was unable to fly back for two more months. They decided to wait and hold her memorial in the new year. At least I would be able to attend that.

I stayed over at Macon's house. After a quick discussion, we realized it made more sense than me pedaling back and forth between the bookstore and my studio and his house. And then, because his couch was gone, suddenly I was in his bed.

There are clean sheets in the bathroom closet, he texted that first night.

I remember, I said because I had emptied out his entire bathroom to paint it.

What I didn't say was that I had no plans to change the bedsheets. My body trembled as I turned down the quilt and slid between the sheets and blankets for the first time. His aroma was overwhelming. Desire stirred within me, then ripened. He was grieving, my carnal reaction was ill-timed, and it was wrong to be doing this in a friend's bed, but I touched myself anyway, tumbling and writhing. Had he thought of me here, too? I imagined him wanting me as desperately as I wanted him, and I came, shuddering hard into my own hand.

I slept deeply, embraced in his warm scent, and awoke with my hand still in place.

During the daytime, at least, I kept my wits about me. I dropped off the meals for his mom that he'd forgotten to leave with her, and I checked in with him frequently but not annoyingly, mostly over text but twice over the phone. I loved hearing his voice, even when it was broken. I wanted him to return home. I wanted to tell him what I *needed* to tell him.

I lavished my attention on Edmond in his place. I treated him to the special cat grass that was growing in the greenhouse, brushed his furry little tuxedo, and indulged his mischievous curiosity by leaving my suitcase open so that his white mittens could inspect and pull out each item inside. It wasn't long before he was sleeping beside me in bed at night.

Thinking of getting a cat for the bookstore, I texted along with a sweet picture of him, limbs stretched and tufty belly sprawled out against my legs.

Allergies, Macon replied, bursting my bubble. But then a heart appeared beside my photo.

He was right, of course. Too many people were allergic. *Maybe when I get a new apartment*, I said, thinking about how comforting it would be to come home to a soft companion.

It took a few minutes for him to respond. *I can definitely imagine a cat in your future.*

Was that as carefully worded as I hoped?

By the time he returned, eight nights after he'd left, I had worked myself into another state. I threw open the door, welcoming him home with this ridiculous notion that it was natural for me to be there. But my appearance caught him off guard.

"I thought you'd already be gone," he said.

He was a few days unshaven, and the lines of his face were heavy with grief. How easy it had been to forget that while I'd been living in a fantasy—in his house and his bed with his cat—he'd been alone in Bonnie's empty house, mourning a devastating loss.

It wasn't the time.

It wasn't the moment.

"Just wanted to make sure you made it home safely. I'll be off now," I said, rushing to grab my suitcase. At least I was already packed. At least I had already washed and changed the sheets. I paused at the door to give him a hug. His body was loose with exhaustion. "I'm so sorry," I said for the hundredth time that week as I started to pull away.

But then his grip tightened around me.

"I should have gone back sooner." He was choked up. "I left her in that house all alone, and I'll never have a chance to undo that."

"Oh, Macon," I said with sorrow.

It took a full minute for him to break away from me.

"There's broccoli cheddar soup in the fridge," I said.

His voice lifted, faintly. "You made it?"

"It's nothing fancy. But at least you won't have to cook tonight." This was underselling it. I had tried very hard to make a worthy soup, but I didn't want him to know that. I only wanted to nourish him like he had done for me.

CHAPTER THIRTY-NINE

The next day was Halloween, and all of us booksellers (except for Stephen) dressed up. I wore the same Kiki costume—red bow and blue dress—that I had worn every year to the library. After work, I soared on my bike like a broomstick through the crunchy leaves and boisterous trick-or-treaters in Macon's neighborhood, thinking I'd help him hand out candy. Wondering if he'd had time for a jack-o'-lantern. Wondering if he'd carved them friendly or scary.

His lights were off.

I flew home.

November

DATE DUE	BORROWER'S NAME	ROOM NUMBER
JAN 25		
FEB 19		
MAR 30		
APR 17		
MAY 10		
JUN 03		
JUL 22		
AUG 04		
SEP 28		
OCT 07		
NOV 12		

CHAPTER FORTY

Two weeks after my birthday, my events coordinator convinced me to throw another party. It was the grand opening of Bildungsroman, a month late, although Amelia Louisa assured me this wasn't uncommon. "We'll say it's for the community, but really we need to bring in an enthusiastic crowd to make sure we meet our sales quota," she said.

"I'm going to pretend the party is for the new restroom," Jo said, because we were all grateful it was finally done. "You should include a picture of the toilet on the invitation."

So, despite wanting to be there for Macon, despite needing to know if my feelings were reciprocated, I put in even more hours at the store. Amelia Louisa helped me hire a restaurant on our street to cater the party and to build goodwill. We contacted the downtown business association (we were a new member), the local newspaper (barely a pamphlet), and some local news websites (reach unknown but probably equally dire), and she booked an interview for me on our public radio station.

Friends and family were invited. My sister was still unavailable, but my parents actually wanted to attend. It had been so many years since I'd had an accomplishment worth celebrating that I hadn't even considered the possibility. I discouraged them because I didn't have a room for them to stay in.

"You're busy with the wedding," I said, which was true. "Come visit me in the new year." I was proud of my store but still ashamed of the studio. I didn't want them to see how broke I was or how much I'd put on the line. Even more so, I didn't want the distraction from whatever was happening—or not happening—with Macon.

I'm sorry, I texted him, *but I have to invite you to another party.*

Has it already been a year since your birthday? he texted back.

Grand opening. I know things are rough right now, so obviously I don't expect you to come, but I wanted to let you know.

Oh, that. It's already on my calendar.

It is??

You emailed the flyer to every library.

I felt embarrassed. Right. Of course.

He started typing again without waiting for my response. *Unless you don't want me there? Your invitations always sound like pardons.*

I would love for you to be there, I said quickly.

And then I worried that the word was too much, even in this context. His reply didn't arrive for several minutes. *Okay.*

The next few days were a storm of stress and anxiety, but then Saturday night arrived, and the store transformed into the very essence of love. Brittany and Reza and Amira. Carla and Richard, who didn't show up together but who immediately found each other in the crowd. Jamal from Ridgetop Means Bizness. Clyde the joke man. Librarians from all the branches, not just mine. I recognized library patrons and authors and illustrators, and then strangers appeared. We had hoped for a big gathering but had mentally prepared for a small one, but people stayed—and more people kept coming. The bookstore had never been so alive.

I was on my tiptoes, searching the room to see if Macon had materialized, when somebody else walked through the door. I gasped. He saw me, too.

"Cory!"

He grinned, weaved his way through the crush, and kissed my cheek. It was exactly what Macon had done on my birthday, yet nothing like it. My knees didn't weaken. There was no quick jerk away, no scratch of stubble.

It was what a kiss from a friend was supposed to feel like. I threw my arms around him, and he laughed.

"Iggy! The store is incredible."

"Thanks for coming. I didn't know if it was weird to invite you."

"Are you kidding? I would have been pissed if you hadn't." He gazed around in genuine wonder. "I mean, look at all this! You did it."

I beamed. "I did."

"Gosh, Ig," he said, taking me in again. "You look beautiful."

I was wearing a red sleeveless dress with a twirly full skirt and a dramatic square neckline that had a delicate scalloped edge. It was my maid-of-honor dress, though it didn't look like one. My sister had good taste, and she'd chosen well. I never would have been so bold as to wear it before the wedding, but Riley had asked me to. It was her way of being there.

"Thank you," I said. I felt beautiful *and* loved in it.

We didn't have long to catch up because there were other people I needed to talk to and shake hands with, but it felt good to see him. It felt good to know he still cared about me. And it felt good to have no regrets about separating.

A short time later, he found me again, a supportive stack of purchases in hand. He had to go, but first he wrapped me in a proud hug with his available arm. I felt happy in his embrace. Cory knew me in a way that nobody else ever would, but there were also so many aspects of myself that stretched beyond him now. That he would never know. And these parts of me were reserved for somebody else.

Elijah and his mom snagged my attention next, and I got to brag to her about how Elijah had whipped my science fiction and fantasy section into shape. And then Mr. Garland serenaded me with a few flattering and embarrassing bars about a vivacious shopkeeper. And then I spotted Shanelle, so I brought her a hunk of cheese from the caterer's table to split between her rats.

And then—

There he was. Tucked against the regional books. I don't know how long he'd been standing there, but he was angled away from the crowd, examining the display.

My entire body illuminated. I was certain my skin began to glow.

"Excuse me," I said, and floated away.

People called my name, and I said hello but didn't stop.

He glanced over at me—a glance that told me he was assessing the situation and had been assessing it for some time—and startled because I was actually headed toward him. My smile was radiant. His eyes didn't leave mine. My skirt swished against me and didn't stop until it was touching his legs.

"Hi," I said.

Macon looked pained but also lit up from within, exactly how I felt.

"Ingrid," he said, as if he couldn't say any more.

He was still wearing his work clothes, a rumpled button-down and corduroy jacket that I'd seen innumerable times. His hair was unkempt. Every single aspect of him was familiar, yet now that I understood that this was love—now that I was ready to tell him—he seemed surrounded by a strange aura.

"Did you get something to eat?" I asked. "A farm-to-table place did the catering. I think you'll approve."

"Not yet. I will." He smiled, but it slipped away. "Uh, I saw Cory on my way in."

My glow dimmed. I took a step back, muscles tightening.

He shook his head as if to say I'd misunderstood. "I think it's great that he came. I'm glad you're still friends."

"Oh." My limbs loosened. "Me too. It was nice to see him."

"You look . . . the store looks . . . it's all very pretty."

He winced, but my heart nearly burst out of my chest. It was the first time that he had ever acknowledged me as attractive. In all our years together, he had carefully avoided the subject. Even on workdays when I had dressed up a bit and it would have been normal for a friend or coworker to say, "You look nice today," the words had never crossed his lips.

My friends were right: Macon was shy. I had always known this, but he was so confident in his work and in our conversations that he was good at masking it. It was easy to forget. But it was obvious—so obvious—now.

Macon was shy, and Macon liked me.

I was *beaming*.

He looked rigid and uncomfortable, as if his shoes were pinching his feet. Then he took a deep breath. "You arrived at my house only two minutes after I texted you about Bonnie."

There it was. I'd been wondering how long it would take for him to realize it was impossible for me to have arrived that quickly. I nodded, heart thundering.

"Why did you come to my house that morning?"

"Ingrid!" Jo shouted over the crowd. "The registers are down!"

"Shit." I bit my lip. "I'll be right back, okay?"

As I jostled my way through the sea of readers, I glanced back over my shoulder. He was still watching me. I gave him another smile, trying my best to convey to him: *I've got this. I've got you. I understand everything now. You've done enough, and I'll take it from here.*

But when the crisis had been averted and my staff were ringing up the sales again, I returned only to find that he wasn't there. Frantically I circled the store. He wasn't anywhere. Guests drew me into conversations, and while the mingling and handselling were great for business, they were terrible for my emotional state. When the crowd finally thinned hours later, I kept expecting him to reappear, as if he'd been hiding behind a chair and waiting for everyone else to leave. But he was gone.

The store didn't fully clear out until after ten. In what should have been a moment of triumph, disappointment crushed me. Mika and I sent the others home while we cleaned up. Bex stayed to help us and sweep the floors.

"Are you okay?" Mika asked, sensing my distress.

"Of course," I said. But I was miserable because Macon had called it a night without me. I'd have to text him in the morning and see if he wanted to meet up. I'd been waiting all year long for him—I'd been waiting years for him—but to wait one more sunrise felt agonizing.

Bex danced in their emerald green tracksuit and spun the broom. "Success!"

The night *had* been successful, and it upset me that I had been distracted for all of it. I forced myself to reframe the last few hours. A crowded store was what I had been working so hard to achieve. The community had been generous, and sales had been strong. Amelia Louisa had been right; the additional boost was almost enough to compensate for the store opening a week late. As long as we had a healthy holiday season, we had a good chance at surviving. But we still had to have a healthy holiday season.

The three of us finished up. I hadn't ridden my bike because I was protecting my dress, and their car was parked down the street because our small employee lot had been full. We grabbed our coats, switched off the main lights, and stepped outside. The fairy lights twinkled in the front windows. I draped my arms around my friends, finally experiencing the expected rush of gratitude, and we stared up at the shining gold letters above. The early November air was crisp and cold. The moon was a waning gibbous, bright enough to light our path.

A figure stepped out of the shadows behind us.

We startled—and then my friends laughed with relief. But my breath caught.

"Sorry." Macon was wearing his thick duffel coat. His Paddington coat. I hadn't seen it in months, and he hadn't been wearing it during the party. "I didn't mean to scare you."

Bex grinned. "Are you here to walk us home?"

"I didn't see your bike," he said to me, "so I thought you might want company."

Mika gave me a squeeze, and then she and Bex slid away and strolled ahead.

"I'm sorry I left." Macon's expression twisted with agitation. "I wasn't dressed warmly enough for a walk. And I thought you might need a coat, too."

With a surge of pleasure, I realized he was holding one of my coats that I'd left behind in Edmond's room. It had been lying on top of the boxes.

"But . . . I forgot you wouldn't be alone. And it's autumn. So of course you already have a coat." He cringed with embarrassment.

I was so happy and giddy that I was speechless.

We ambled toward my neighborhood, fallen leaves crunching underfoot. As Mika and Bex drew farther ahead, they reached out and took each other's hands. The act was simple but devastating. That physical bond, that companionship, represented everything I wanted.

Macon was still holding my coat, but his empty arm swung beside me.

I extended a brave pinky, searching. It brushed against his hand, and he flinched. But then his arm stopping moving. His hand stilled completely. I tried again. My finger slipped between two of his, and his fingers pressed back. A thrill shivered through me. The rest of my hand moved in, and then his large hand took over and swallowed my small one entirely. His grip was strong and firm. Elation spread through me so swiftly I almost fainted.

Ahead of us, my friends gave me savvy nods, then got into their car and drove off.

Macon and I didn't speak.

We didn't look at each other.

We didn't want to break the spell.

Without letting go, our hands explored. Pressure there. Feathering here. A rub there. We were learning each other's lines and contours. Although we had known each other for years, we were discovering the shape of something new.

When we entered my neighborhood, the trees grew large enough to disperse the moonlight. They towered and locked branches together overhead. Their few remaining, clinging leaves quivered in the wind. Our breathing grew shallow. The energy between us darkened and throbbed. For several minutes, we continued to walk in heavy, questioning, expectant silence. When our feet finally sank into the gravel driveway, he hesitated.

I tugged him forward and led him behind the house.

The night deepened around us. The streetlights grew out of reach.

At my door, our bodies turned toward each other. Our heads moved in close and then backed away. We stared at each other for a few seconds, but our gazes were too intense, so our eyes closed. Perhaps this made the transition easier, made us less self-conscious about how well we knew each other in every way except for this one.

Our mouths parted. His breath was warm against mine.

He pulled me into his arms, still holding my extra coat. My hips pressed forward and discovered he was hard. Another thrill shot through me. I rocked against him, slowly.

He sucked his breath in.

My chin tilted up.

Ready.

Our mouths met with aggression. With greed and want and desire and frustration and five long years of repressed yearning. I cried out, and the noise unleashed something inside him because he kissed me harder. I gasped. Our eyes flew open at the same time, but then he looked down, watching my chest rise and fall. I fumbled to get my keys out of my tote.

We kissed again, panting, and our teeth clashed. The door opened, and we fell inside. My bag and the extra coat fell to the floor, then our actual coats and his corduroy jacket. Our bodies arched and dug against each other, enjoying the feel of less in the way. The room was so dark it was almost black. His arms were strong, and I reveled in the reality of his chest, the hard muscle and bone of it, a structure that was holding us both up. We kissed with so much force, it was as if we feared the other person might still mistake our intention for something else. His lips traveled down to my throat, down to my collarbone, and then I grabbed him by the hair and pushed him into my breasts. They were straining against the low neckline of my dress. His mouth lowered the neckline farther until he found what I wanted and sucked. I shuddered. My arms clasped behind his head to hold him in place. He tried to grope my ass, but the full rustling skirt of my dress made it difficult. I reached up to unzip it, and he moved to help.

"Careful," I whispered. It was the first word either of us had spoken.

He froze.

"It's for my sister's wedding."

He relaxed and chuckled silently against me. Silence wasn't necessary, but we were both aware of the thin wall that separated us from my friends' kitchen. Now that we had paused, we heard movements issuing from inside their house. Afraid that our pause might turn into a full stop, I guided his hand to my zipper.

"Wait," he whispered, which was not a word I wanted to hear. "Do you have something?"

I told him I was on the pill and felt him exhale. Neither of us had expected to be in this position tonight. He unzipped me carefully, as requested. I removed my shoes and then he helped me step out of the dress. I unhooked my strapless bra and let it fall as I steered him backward toward the bed. Urgency returned. He wrestled off his shirt as we toppled onto the blankets. Our bare chests crushed against each other for the first time. Our hearts were beating wildly. He kicked away his shoes and took off his glasses. We kissed again, and as his tongue parted my lips, his hand slipped between my legs. Through the thin cotton of my underwear, it was obvious I was ready for him. I wriggled it down, fumbling with the waistband of his pants, and he quickly stripped away the rest of his clothing. He entered me, and it was a frenzy. Thrusting, bucking, bouncing, riding. Our hunger was desperate and ravenous. I came first, and he came only seconds later, as if he'd been barely holding on, waiting for my release.

We fell back onto my bed, sweating and gasping and in shock.

A minute passed. Another. As our breathing regulated, our bodies began to feel more and more crowded. Finally, I squirmed to the side to give us both some room and then realized there wasn't any. I laughed once. He stirred against me in question.

"Twin bed," I whispered.

He laughed quietly. "It's *so* small."

"I guess we should have done this at your place?"

"Next time," he said, and I closed my eyes to thank the universe.

A different pressure moved to the forefront. "Be right back." I slipped out of bed, but then an uneasy thought occurred to me. "My bathroom doesn't have a fan. Or even a door yet."

"That's okay." Amusement undercut the seriousness in his voice. "I'm an adult."

It was the best and most Macon reassurance. I was smiling as I padded down the short corridor to the far corner. The laminate floor and cold porcelain chilled my bare skin. I relieved myself and returned, and then he got up to do the same. His hands tapped against the walls and kitchen countertop as he felt his way to the back. The sheets and blankets were askew, heaped and bunched and falling off. I straightened them out, slid beneath them, and listened. The mundanity of the sounds was unexpectedly comforting: the urination, the flush, the hand washing. Another human being moving through my space.

He navigated his way back to me with more assuredness, but when he leaned over to get into the bed, his entire frame stiffened. "Do you, uh, want me to stay? Should I go home?"

I turned onto my side, facing him, and then scooted my spine against the wall. I patted the empty space between us. He climbed in. His skin was still radiating a blissful warmth, and my vision had adjusted enough to the darkness that I could see him better now. His features were miraculously familiar, but they also contained a new openness. It was as if there was more of him than there had ever been before. He was studying my naked body with wonder and disbelief.

I couldn't resist a coy smile. "So you *do* like me."

"Ingrid," he said, his expression collapsing. "I have always liked you."

My gaze turned downward. "So what changed?"

"Between now and . . . January?"

"Yeah."

"Nothing."

I looked up sharply.

"Ingrid." His voice cracked as he spoke my name again. "I love you. I've been in love with you for years. It's possible that I've been in love with you since the day we met."

A wave of happiness crested inside me—and then crashed onto the familiar rocks of sorrow and confusion. "But you rejected me. You told me no."

"Because you tried to kiss me at work. With no warning. While you still had a *boyfriend* whom you planned to *marry*."

"There was warning," I said meekly.

"I assure you, there was not."

"The marriage wasn't definite."

"It was on the table."

The ugly heat of shame spread through me again. "You're right. I'm sorry."

"It's okay. You were going through something."

"I'm still sorry."

"I know." He gave me a sad smile before groaning. "If only you knew how many nights I've lain awake, wondering if I'd fucked up and lost my chance with you forever. But I wanted you to want *me*, not just any warm body. I didn't want to be a fling. And then after you and Cory broke up, you said you didn't want to date anybody for a long time. You were grieving the end of your relationship. I didn't want to step in at the wrong moment. I couldn't handle being a mistake that you might regret later."

"So . . . you were waiting?"

He nodded. His expression was fearful and hopeful.

"Macon," I said. "I was at your front door two minutes after that text because I was already on my way there to tell you that I love you. I've been in love with you for years. And it's possible that I've been in love with you since the day we met."

His eyes closed. Tears reflected the dim moonlight.

"When Cory and I made our stupid, absurd plan, you were the first and only person I thought of. I did want you specifically. Desperately. But you're right, I didn't think about what would happen to you after that month was over. I didn't understand the position I was putting you in. And I didn't understand that this intense *thing* between us was love."

"What did you think it was?"

"Lust."

He laughed, wiping his cheeks. "It was that, too."

"When did you know?"

"I *didn't* know that you loved me. But I suspected. I hoped."

"When did you fall in love with me?"

"Immediately," he said. "And gradually."

The warmth of recognition poured through my body.

"When you arrived at work," he said, "you were . . . so much prettier than your predecessor." We laughed again. My predecessor was a retired woman with four grandchildren. "And you radiated sunshine. Actual sunshine, not like those awful people who force their optimism onto you. It felt good to stand in your atmosphere."

I beamed, but he grew serious.

"You were also young."

"Too young?" I asked.

"Maybe. Yes. Probably."

"But not anymore?"

"No." But then he sounded worried when he asked, "Am I too old?"

I leaned in to kiss him. "No."

"I mean," he said, a minute later, "it's not like I've been *pining* for you this whole time. I had Dani, and you had Cory. I was happy to be your friend."

I kissed him again.

"There was a little pining," he said into my mouth, and I smiled against him.

"A lot of pining," he said heavily after another minute.

"Hey." I pulled away from him. "Can I ask you something?"

His brow rose with amusement because we were already past asking for permission.

"Why did you and Danielle break up?"

"Ah." He grew serious again. "You mean, was it because of you?"

I must have looked hopeful because he gave me an apologetic smile, as if he was letting me down gently. "No. Our differences became clear during lockdown. We couldn't stand each other by the end. We parted on decent terms, but we'll never be friends. We don't speak."

"Oh."

My disappointment made him smile again, even though it was unfair of me to feel that way. "*However*," he said, "the pandemic—working together at that call center—did make me feel closer to you. And I think that's when I began to hope." His fingers threaded through mine and took hold. "So perhaps you did play a role."

"Do you still talk with your other exes?"

"Occasionally. They're both married with children, living lives I've never wanted."

"I don't have any other exes."

He hesitated. "You don't count any of those guys from earlier this year?"

"Oh my God. *No.*" I laughed, but I could see that his mind had already arrived at the follow-up question. "You're wondering how many of them I slept with, aren't you?"

"It's none of my business." But then he grimaced. "Also yes. And no."

"Two. The two you can guess," I added.

"So we're even."

He was telling me that he'd only ever slept with his three girlfriends, which was what I'd suspected. It also meant he hadn't been with anybody since Dani, which was also what I'd suspected. A powerful yearning rose within me again. I closed the gap between our bodies.

Our first time had been quick. The release of our suppressed feelings had resulted in an atomic detonation. Slowing down the explosion would have defied the laws of nature.

Our second time was religious. Contemplative and meditative and languorous, we moved together in awe that this had finally happened, that it *was* happening, that it would *continue* to happen. Our bodies listened and responded, ecstatic with each new revelation. Worshipful of the deep communion. And the universe opened up before us, bathing us in a brilliant and shimmering light.

CHAPTER FORTY-ONE

We slept for a few hours, but we both woke early, each conscious of the other's every shift. The narrow mattress enhanced the experience, but we would have been aware and awake even if we had been sleeping on a king. We studied each other as dawn broke through the bamboo shades. The growing light gradually revealed more of our bodies, our freckles and blemishes and scars.

"You're so beautiful," Macon said, touching the mole on my cheek with reverence. "I've never seen anybody so beautiful."

My skin tingled. I ran my fingers through his disheveled hair, stroked the stubble on his face, traced the lines of his ear and nose and lips. He stayed very still.

"I love you," I whispered.

"I love you," he whispered back.

"We're allowed to say it now."

"Out loud, even."

We kissed, long and slow, but my eager energy built and built and built until I had to pull away for it to gush out. "It's just that I like you *so* much."

He gave me the amused look I'd seen so often—the look he gave only to me—but he also appeared to be melting with happiness.

"Honestly, if you knew how much I like you," I said, "it would probably freak you out."

"Oh God, Ingrid. I'm obsessed with you."

I leapt into another kiss, and he kissed me back intensely before moaning and burying his nose in my hair. "Fuck, you smell incredible," he said.

I laughed.

"I'm serious. You leave this fruity, citrusy smell in your wake, and it's been driving me insane for years. I would drink an entire bottle of your shampoo, whatever it is."

I nuzzled my face against his chest, giddier than I had ever been in my life. "It's my conditioner. Mango citrus."

He inhaled again and released a growl. "My bathroom has smelled like this ever since you left. Whenever the shower steams, I smell you. Your scent is still embedded in my towels."

Another erection pressed against me, asking a question.

I shoved him onto his back and climbed on top.

"What time do you have to be at work?" he asked afterward. It was a Sunday, so he had the day off.

"I'm not going in today."

He propped himself up on his elbows, surprised.

"Mika has been trying to convince me to take a day off ever since we opened. I'm finally going to do it."

"Oh my God. I have you for the entire day?"

"What should we do?"

His arms wrapped around me, pulling me back into him. "First we're going to bundle up and walk to my house." We couldn't stop kissing each other. "Then I'm going to make you pancakes." We could have devoured each other. "And then we're going to fall into my bed and stay there for the rest of the day."

"Can I bring a book?"

"Absolutely. Although I doubt you'll have time to read it."

"Maybe in the morning."

"Yes," he agreed, "maybe tomorrow morning."

"I suppose that means I should pack an overnight bag."

"Yes," he said. "Or you can borrow my things."

"Or mine. They're still at your house."

"I've been taking good care of them."

I smiled as I detached from him and climbed out of bed to stretch my cramped limbs. He stared up at the full length of my body, drinking it in. I handed him his glasses and then dressed with slow intention, a strip show in reverse. My prettiest underthings. I leaned in to kiss him, and his fingers dipped beneath the lace straps of my bra, toying with them, letting them gently snap, taking pleasure in the anticipation of what would come again later. I shrugged on a loose V-neck sweater, and his gaze turned longingly to my legs. I zipped up my pants and buttoned them closed.

He shook his head, almost laughing, as if he still couldn't believe any of this was real. I understood how he felt.

We spent the next twenty-four hours together, reveling in our newfound access to each other's bodies. Although he had been too shy to make the first move, he remained confident in every single move that followed. The sex was exhilarating, our need to possess each other insatiable, but even more, I basked in the sacredness of the everyday—wrapping my arms around him while he flipped the pancakes, leaning against him while we brushed our teeth, draping my legs across his while we read. His hugs were strong and unlimited. I glowed whenever he tucked my hair behind my ears, pressed a hand against the small of my back, rested his head on my shoulder to marvel at our reflections together in the bathroom mirror.

We already knew each other's secret awkwardnesses. We already trusted each other. I wore my night guard. He wore his socks and sandals. And when Edmond made biscuits on me in bed that night, Macon clutched his chest, and his eyes puddled into ridiculous cartoon hearts.

IT HAPPENED, I texted Kat on my way to work the following day.

My phone lit up immediately with a FaceTime request.

"*Tell me* he was worth the wait," she said.

I cackled in triumphant jubilation.

I stayed at Macon's house every night except for when he worked the late shift at the library. It seemed right to set some sort of boundary, however arbitrary, but the hours without him were intolerable. "You're like a teenager with her first boyfriend," Mika teased me. And then Bex always chimed in: "Ding-ding-ding-ding-ding-ding-ding."

It was the sound of my lamp, and the first time Bex did this, I just about died.

But Macon and I *felt* like teenagers, aroused and obsessed. We fucked in the dirt of his humid greenhouse, on the cold tile floor in his kitchen, in the shower when we were supposed to be getting ready for work. We couldn't keep our hands and mouths and bodies off each other.

"You know," I said on one of those early nights, lying exhausted in his lamplight and feeling daring, "my first orgasm in this bed was not with you." His eyes brightened with disbelief, and I turned gleeful. "Don't get me wrong. You *were* in my thoughts."

"Holy shit. When I was out of town?"

"I never changed your sheets. I wanted to be surrounded by you."

"And here I was, disappointed that you *did* change them before you left."

"Of course I did! My guilty scent would have been all over them."

"Oh my God." A hand went to his forehead. "Yeah, that might have actually killed me." He gaped at me through his fingers, laughing. "I can't believe you did that."

"You would have done it in my bed."

"Well . . . I definitely did it smelling your scent on my towels."

I gasped and shrieked with delighted laughter. "What else?"

He was smiling straight at me. He was always *looking* at me now, and I was always looking at him. We didn't have to hide our interest anymore. "What else what?"

"What else haven't you been able to tell me? Like, have you been sniffing the clothes in my boxes, too?"

His expression fell with seriousness. "Ingrid, no. I promise I've never gone through any of your boxes. That would have been such a violation."

That was actually a much better answer. "Really?"

He held up a hand like an oath. "Apart from that one time when I was shifting them around, and one fell open, and one of your sweaters was right there on top. I might have smelled the sweater. It might have smelled unbelievably good."

My feet wiggled against his with excitement. I wasn't into feet, but I liked that it was another part of him that I'd never seen before and now had full-time access to. I liked all of his new parts. "What else?"

He trapped my feet between his to stop them from wiggling. But he was smiling again. "Your turn."

"Your glasses." I sighed. "So sexy."

He wasn't wearing them, and his eyebrows rose.

"Feel free to leave them on sometimes. You know."

The eyebrows rose even higher, but then he turned contemplative. "I suppose they are one of the only things Cory and I have in common, appearance-wise."

"I like a nerdy frame," I confirmed.

"So why did you wear contacts? Before the Lasik?"

Sometimes it still struck me as odd how long we'd known each other—and how well he knew me. That he remembered I'd had the surgery five years earlier. "My vision was *terrible*. The lenses of my glasses were so thick that they made my eyes look even bigger and buggier."

He frowned. "You don't have buggy eyes."

"I do a little bit. It was more obvious when I was younger."

"Your eyes are striking and unique. They're one of my favorite things about you."

I wiggled my feet happily again. "The pen." I reached out and tapped behind his ear, then made a rumbling noise of pleasure. "That too."

"So you're saying you like my accessories."

I laughed. "Yeah. You come with good accessories."

"Okay, since you brought it up ... that night at your store? When you were dancing? I have thought a lot about that moment when you slid my pen into your mouth."

I shrank and finally did look away. "Oh my God, I don't know what I was thinking. I guess I wasn't. I was just horny."

"Yeah." He laughed. "Me too. You also scared me shitless. I didn't know if that was the sort of thing you did with friends or what."

My gaze shot back to him. "The sort of thing I did with *friends?*"

"I don't know! You *did* run off and dance with them the second they arrived. You were in a wild mood. I had no idea what was happening."

"A terrible seduction, apparently."

"The seduction was effective, I assure you."

I grinned and scooted farther into him. I couldn't get close enough. I wanted to crawl inside his body and set up camp.

"On a related note"—he shook his head—"that bra with the red floral pattern. That one underneath your tank top."

"Thought about that, too, huh?"

"Fucking hell. Please wear it again soon."

"You know, you've always been very good at keeping your eyes up here." I pointed at my face. "You've always been respectful. I appreciate that."

"Thank God I don't have to be such a gentleman anymore."

I poked him.

"I try not to be a creep," he said. "But I looked a lot when you weren't looking. I'll leave it at that."

"I looked when you weren't looking, too."

"At my accessories?"

"The back of your neck."

He wasn't sure how to take that. "My neck?"

"Mm, and your arms and shoulders. And ass."

He burst into surprised laughter. I nestled against his chest, and he softly touched my clavicle. "I've saved every photo you've ever texted me." His voice rumbled against my ear. "Even the ones you're not in. Which unfortunately is most of them."

I turned my head to look up at him, and he nodded down at me. "I've spent hours staring at that photo of you and Edmond," he said.

"What photo?"

"That selfie. The one with the bacon book."

I felt pleased but also slightly embarrassed. "If I'd known you were keeping it, I would have sent a better one."

"No. It's perfect. It looks just like you."

"That's because it's a photo," I explained.

He poked me back. "You looked natural. And you were in my house with my cat. It's a good picture."

"This isn't fair. I don't have any of you."

He shuddered. "I hate having my picture taken."

"I know, but I have *none*. After all these years! I want a photo. I want lots and lots of photos of you. I want photos of you and me together, multiple albums on my phone."

"You're the photogenic one."

"Shut up. You're very handsome, and I want to be able to look at your face whenever I want."

His skin warmed underneath me. "Okay."

"Good. Yay."

"Speaking of phones . . . I used to hope those emoji hearts meant something, but you always put them in our work texts, too."

"Yeah, I send hearts to everyone," I said. "Sorry."

"Damn. I wasted a lot of time wondering about that."

"*Now* they'll mean something. I'll switch from red to pink. Only the most special people in my life get the pink ones."

"Glad to hear I've been upgraded, at least." His arm readjusted around me, and he stroked my hair. "You know, I used to worry that I wasn't your type because your ex is so much more playful and extroverted than I am. Like, I bet he sends emojis."

"He does. But everybody should be using fewer of them, so you're still the cool one here. And it was exhausting dating an extrovert."

"I just don't want to end up like my mom, terrified to leave the house. Even though I've never had those phobias," he amended quickly. "I don't want you to worry."

I shook my head against his chest. I knew he hadn't, and I had never worried about that, but it made me sad to think about him worrying about it.

"That's why I push myself to go out," he said.

"Like to my parties?"

"I went to those because they were yours. I wanted to be there. Though yeah, in general, I don't see what's so wrong about not wanting to do stuff."

"That might be the sexiest thing you've ever said."

"You must be tired of doing stuff."

"I'm *so* tired of doing stuff."

He kissed the top of my head. "That reminds me of another thing."

I perked up. "Oh?"

"Do you remember that training session where they taught us how to use the new system?" He was referring to a boring event that had lasted all day and had ended, inexplicably, in an extended social gathering. "Well, I was having a miserable time off in a corner somewhere, and you found me and said, 'I'm gonna leave and grab a burger. Want to come?' And it was like being rescued. You *rescued* me. I don't know why I didn't realize I could just . . . leave on my own. But then we had those great veggie burgers, and we were laughing so hard, and you looked so bewitching in the restaurant's light. And I remember thinking, *uh-oh*."

I burrowed into him deeper. I'd forgotten about that night.

"I told Dani later that you'd saved me—leaving out the *uh-oh*—but apparently, I didn't leave enough of it out because she got pissed off at me. Dani really hated you."

"She did?" I felt strangely hurt, even though I hadn't liked her either. Even though I'd already suspected she didn't like me.

"She didn't care for the way I looked at you. Or talked about you. Or the fact that you were this cute, sparkly woman who sat beside me all day long."

"Sometimes I used to worry I wasn't your type because she was so serious."

"It was exhausting dating somebody so serious," he said, and I laughed. "See? I don't even remember what her real laugh sounded like. By the time she moved out, it had been so long since I'd heard anything other than her sarcastic one."

"I'm sorry."

"I'm not. It only made me more sure of what I did want."

"Sounds like you're talking about me again."

"I'm definitely talking about you again. You're my favorite subject. People should write books about you so I can buy them from your store and read them."

"*The Care and Keeping of Ingrid*," I said.

He laughed. "*A People's History of Ingrid*."

"*How to Win Ingrid and Influence Her*."

"*The Joy of Ingrid*."

"That's the one," I said. My heart was so full it was spilling over. "That's the one they'd write first."

CHAPTER FORTY—TWO

We'd only been together for three weeks when he asked me to move in with him. It was the night before Thanksgiving and his fortieth birthday. I was excited because it would be a rare day off. He was stressed because we were cooking for Lynn; he'd convinced her to come to his house. From me, he'd requested no presents and no fuss, but I had purchased a small gift and planned to make a little fuss. Only things I knew he could handle and would enjoy.

We had already fallen into a steadfast, comforting rhythm. I loved tucking in beside him in bed at the end of the day, knowing we had the whole quiet night ahead of us. We had quickly learned how to sleep beside each other, understood when the other person needed space and when they didn't, and had discovered that we both took pleasure in snuggling close in the early morning, when it was still dark and cold outside but our bodies had stored up a full night's worth of warmth, our limbs tangling against and on top of and underneath each other.

That night, I was wearing one of his T-shirts and nothing else, and we were reading, bathed in the same content afterglow as the characters in old movies who made love and then smoked cigarettes. We liked reading the good passages out loud to each other. It was gratifying to be able to share our books with a partner again. Macon set down his hardcover in his lap, and I thought he was about to preface another selection. His reading voice was first-rate, deep and steady. But when I looked over, I was surprised to find that he looked nervous.

"I've changed my mind," he said. "I do want a birthday present."

I lowered my novel and raised my brows. "Oh?"

"Move in with me."

"Oh," I breathed.

"You'll have to leave the studio soon, and apartments are expensive. This would ease your financial burden." The offer felt familiar. Despite framing it as a gift, he was speaking in his unsentimental librarian voice, and he wasn't looking at me. I wanted sentimentality and ardor.

"You're practically living here anyway," he went on. "You're already sharing the responsibilities and the housework."

I stared him down until I forced his eyes to meet mine. His shyness had returned. "You know," I said, "this is the second time you've asked me to move in with you."

He swallowed. "Say yes this time."

"Why did you ask me the first time?"

"I wanted to help you out."

"Was that all?"

He gave me a smile tinged with remembered heartbreak. "No. I was hoping you'd fall madly in love with your new roommate."

"And why are you asking me now?"

His hands trembled as he removed my book from my hands so he could take them into his. "Because I want you here. All the time. Just like this."

I squeezed his hands back. "Now *that's* a good reason."

We hadn't told his coworkers we were dating yet. The next morning, when Alyssa sent a Grim Reaper birthday GIF to Macon in their work group text, he sent them back a selfie where I was smushed up against him, kissing his cheek.

Got what I wanted this year, he wrote.

Alyssa, Sue, and Elijah all lost their shit, which was tremendously satisfying.

I spent the day assisting Macon in the kitchen. We were using his family's recipes, not mine, which was fine by me. I preferred his cooking, plus he had strong menu opinions because of his birthday occasionally landing on Thanksgiving. ("The timing makes it difficult for me to dislike a holiday that I objectively disapprove of," he once told me.)

Before he left to pick up his mom, I called my parents. I usually FaceTimed them, but I already knew that would be too much for Macon.

"We're both here, shucking corn," I told them.

"Hello." Macon managed to project confidence into the speaker despite his trepidation. "Happy Thanksgiving."

"Ah, the new old boyfriend," my dad said.

Macon swiveled toward me in alarm.

I muted the phone. "Not your age. I don't think. *Old* as in we've known each other a long time." Unmuted it.

"I'm not sure if you remember," Macon said, "but we met once, the last time you were in town."

"I remember," my mom said. "And Ingrid has spoken so much about you over the years."

He studied me, pleased, as he plucked off the corn silk.

I gave him a bashful smile and shrugged. "So I have good news," I said to my parents. "You'll have somewhere to stay when you come visit me this January. I have a new place with an extra room."

Macon's eyes widened as if to say, *This is* not *how you're telling them, right?*

I shrugged again as my parents cheered and congratulated me.

"It's Macon's house," I said. "I'm moving in."

The ear of corn fell from his hands. He looked like he was dying. I walked my phone back to the bedroom as my concerned parents stuttered and asked a lot of questions, the main one being: *After only three weeks?*

"Three weeks plus sort of a whole summer plus five years," I said.

Macon was hovering in the doorway when I hung up half an hour later. "At least they called me your boyfriend."

"You are my boyfriend." We had never actually said the word before.

"I know. I'm just glad they know, too. I like people knowing."

"They definitely know now."

"I cannot believe you told them like that."

"It *is* okay for them to stay here in January, right?"

"Of course."

"Okay. Thanks. I realized belatedly that I didn't ask."

"You don't have to ask me. They're your parents."

It was a good response, yet I felt an odd pang that he didn't add, "And it's your house." But I doubted anything was meant by the exclusion, so I didn't allow my thoughts to linger there. "Speaking of parents," I said.

"Yep." He grabbed his wallet and keys from the top of the dresser. "I'm gonna bring her in through the kitchen door, okay? The living room might freak her out."

I was taken aback but kept it to myself. I knew his mom was afraid of empty spaces, but the living room wasn't exactly *empty*. He'd painted the bookshelves the previous weekend, but they were curing, so they still didn't have any books on them. And he still didn't have a couch. But Edmond's blankets and toys were in there, and the cat tree had been installed. Macon and his neighbor had done an impressive job. The tree was tremendous, spanning floor to ceiling in one corner of the room, smooth limbs and branches. A perfect foresty addition.

I set the table, peeled and boiled the potatoes, and put the homemade rolls into the oven. His errand shouldn't have taken more than ten minutes. My anxiety grew. It was important to him that she come. He wanted her to see all the work we'd done and wanted to remind her that his house was safe. I also suspected that he wanted my first longer interaction with her to be on his territory. I think that felt safer for *him*.

Forty minutes later, they arrived. I watched him lead her through the garden. Although her voice was frail, she had never looked it in the handful of times that we'd met. She did now as she kept stopping and squeezing her eyes closed. She clung to him tightly. Patiently, he guided her to the back door, and I opened it to greet them.

"Mom, you remember my girlfriend, Ingrid."

Of course she remembered me. I could tell he just wanted to call me his girlfriend to complete the saying-words-out-loud circle. My stomach warmed with pleasure.

"Happy Thanksgiving, Lynn," I said.

She was dressed in a nice blouse and jewelry, which made me grateful that I had put on something nicer, too. (Macon was wearing his normal clothes, but I'd instinctively not trusted this to be the dress code.) She was pale and agitated and didn't speak. Macon shot me a frustrated, apologetic look, and I touched a reassuring hand to his back. He led her inside and straight to the table. "Why don't you rest for a few minutes?" he said to her. "We'll be eating soon."

He joined me in the kitchen. *I'm sorry*, he mouthed.

I brightened my expression. *It's okay!*

I brought her a glass of water and then gave her some space to recover. It didn't escape my notice that he'd sat her in a corner where she couldn't see the living room. He was mashing the potatoes, perhaps too aggressively, when I returned. "I'll finish that up and carve the turkey," I said. He'd gotten a small bird because she was coming. "Why don't you go grill the corn?"

I love you, he mouthed.

"I love you, too," I said, cheerfully and aloud.

One side of his mouth lifted in a smile, and he shook his head, but in an affectionate way, as if he was remembering how much he liked me.

I preened.

His head was still shaking as he went back outside. I resisted checking on him and Lynn, figuring they both needed time to regroup, and finished what needed to be done. When I carried the gravy boat to the table (Macon owned a gravy boat! Cory and I had definitely not owned a gravy boat), Lynn's color and breathing had both returned to normal.

"You're clearly a better guest than I am, Ingrid," she said.

"Nonsense." I gave her a friendly smile, only belatedly snagging on the word *guest*. He'd told her this morning that I was moving in. He said she'd been happy for us. But I couldn't dwell on this because I needed to make sure she was comfortable. "We're really glad you're here."

"I'm glad you're here, too. It was so obvious my son liked you."

I laughed. "I wish he'd told *me* sooner."

The back door opened, and we heard him reenter. "Oh, he's the same boy he's always been," Lynn said. "Waiting for the girl to ask him out first."

"*Mom.*" He dropped the plate of corn loudly onto the counter, where it rattled. "That conversation stops now, whatever it is."

Lynn and I grinned at each other, and I returned to the kitchen. Macon gave me an extremely grouchy look, which made me smile even bigger.

"The walls look good," Lynn called out. "Pretty table, too. And I like the red chairs."

"Ingrid helped with all of it," he reminded her.

"Obviously," Lynn said, and I laughed.

"You need curtains, though," she added.

I nodded at Macon like *See?* as we loaded our three plates with roasted turkey, rosemary stuffing, grilled corn, mashed potatoes, butterhorn rolls, and cranberry sauce with candied ginger and orange zest.

"Oh!" Lynn said.

He stilled. "Everything okay in there?"

"I forgot you have a cat now."

"He won't hurt you."

"No, I know. I'm fine. Bonnie used to have a calico, do you remember? Used to run around here. She took it with her when she married Jim."

"Snickers," he said.

"That's right."

A shadow fell across Macon's face. I placed my hand atop his and let it rest. He and Lynn had been arguing recently about Bonnie's memorial service. His mom, unsurprisingly, wanted to hold it in Ridgetop. But Bonnie's life had been in Durham.

When we entered the dining room, Edmond was sitting upright in one of the empty chairs. Macon tossed a piece of turkey to him.

"Did you remember to turn off the grill?" Lynn asked.

Macon sighed. "Yes, I turned off the grill."

"Look at that." She buoyed again at the plate set before her. "You're such a good cook. Isn't my son the most talented chef?"

"He is," I said.

"Ingrid helped, too, Mom."

I smiled and made a gesture to Lynn that said, *Only a little*. "I'm better at decorating— Oh!" I sprang back out of my seat. "Your present."

Macon started to protest, but I bounded off and fetched the bag from where I'd hidden it in Edmond's room. "Happy birthday slash Thanksgiving."

"I told you—"

"Hush and open her gift," Lynn said.

He did. It was a pair of candlesticks made by the same ceramicist who made the mugs for Bildungsroman and two spiraled beeswax tapers dipped by a local chandler.

"I like them," Macon said, sounding surprised.

His mom and I laughed, and I lifted his chin and kissed him.

"Thank you," he said.

"Special occasions require candles," I said, dimming the lights and producing a matchbook from my pocket.

"Careful with those," Lynn said.

"Mom," Macon said. But after blowing out the match, I ran it under the tap to show her that I was safe and trustworthy.

The meal was delicious, the tapers honeyed the air, and Lynn turned out to be a lively conversationalist. She was sharp and curious and well read, and I was relieved we didn't run out of things to talk about. It was easy for me to imagine all the meals and matches and candles that we might burn through together at this table. I hadn't forgotten about her probably needing to move in with Macon someday. There was room for us both here, and I hoped he saw it, too.

Everything was going well until dessert. Macon and I were in the kitchen. I was plating the pumpkin pie, and he was whipping the cream when his mother announced that she needed to use the bathroom. I was surprised when he tensed.

"Macon," she said again, anxiously.

"I heard you. That's fine."

I set down the pie server (Macon owned a pie server!) and went to her. She was wavering on the threshold to the living room with large and frightened eyes.

"Lynn? May I escort you to the bathroom?"

She didn't answer, so I placed a gentle hand on her arm. I tried to guide her forward, but her limbs were stiff. When I tried again, she shrieked.

Macon hurried toward us. "It's okay. It's the same house it always was."

"I can't," she said. "I can't."

"The bathroom is just over there."

"I can't! I want to go home."

"You can do it," he said. "I'll walk you there."

"Take me home! I want to go home!"

Tears were rolling down her cheeks, and I backed against the wall as she flew into hysterics. "Mom, it's okay," he said.

"Take me home," she screamed.

"I'm taking you home." He glanced at me frantically, and I bolted for his keys and wallet. She shrieked again, perhaps because I had crossed into the empty space. The bare branches of the towering cat tree threw sinister shadows across the walls. "Wait," he called after me. "I still have them in my pockets." And then, "I didn't put them down, Mom. Just like I promised, okay? My keys are right here." As he led her out of the house, he coached her breathing. "Do what I do. We're going to make our exhalations longer than our inhalations."

I flashed back to sobbing on the library's restroom floor, Macon crouched beside me. How many times in his life had he spoken those exact words? When had it started? Still in shock, I scraped our plates and loaded them into the dishwasher. I pictured him as a child, how scary it must have been—and then how humiliating once he grew older. I thought about his aunt again, better understanding the support and freedom she must have provided for him.

When he finally returned, I was sitting at the table with two slices of pie.

"Happy birthday," I said quietly.

"One night." He slumped into the chair beside me. "I was hoping we could get through one night."

"You got her here. We had a wonderful dinner. That's a good start."

"I knew the living room would freak her out."

"You said that, and I didn't believe you," I admitted. "But we'll get a couch. And we'll fill the shelves. We'll fill the whole room up and invite her back."

"I miss Bonnie."

My heart broke. "I know."

"I wish you could have met her."

Edmond sprang onto my lap, and the candlelight flickered.

"It's not like she would have been *my* Bonnie anyway. That Bonnie was already gone." Darkness weighted his shoulders. "My mom is all I have left now."

I lifted one of Edmond's paws and waved it at him. "Not all."

He took us in. A smile almost cracked through.

"I'm sorry I made it worse," I said, speaking in a voice and lifting both front paws to gesticulate like a hand puppet. "But I'll learn how to help. I'll read up on it, and you can teach me."

Macon didn't laugh. "That's not necessary. And you have nothing to apologize for."

I think he was trying to absolve me from any responsibility, but it deflated me. If we were to all live here together someday, I needed to be able help her. To help him. It suddenly felt as if I was trying to push my way into his life, as opposed to both of us moving forward together. Yet this was also exactly where I *wanted* to be—with him, in this house.

Edmond had also wanted to belong to Macon and get inside this house. As he yanked his paws out of my grasp, I tried to hold on to him—

engulfed my whole body around him—but he squirmed off my lap and tore across the room.

It was only confusing because all of this was new, I assured myself. Once I settled in, everything else would feel settled, too.

December

DATE DUE	BORROWER'S NAME	ROOM NUMBER
JAN 25		
FEB 19		
MAR 30		
APR 17		
MAY 10		
JUN 03		
JUL 22		
AUG 04		
SEP 28		
OCT 07		
NOV 12		
DEC 06		

CHAPTER FORTY-THREE

It took longer than anticipated to find the time to move the rest of my belongings over to Macon's house. After Thanksgiving came the dreaded Black Friday, and then my little store prepared for the following Small Business Saturday. Amelia Louisa had pulled off the miracle of arranging a signing with Susie Corners, a celebrated but reclusive children's picture book author and illustrator who lived on a farm outside of town. She'd only ever done one event at the Tick-Tock, and it had been before my time. Susie was odd and prickly, but she arrived in her trademark overalls, and her readers (and Jo) were euphoric. For the first time ever, Bildungsroman was slammed from opening to closing, and we had lines at the registers all day.

And then—extraordinarily—we stayed busy.

November slipped into December, and Mika went all out with the holiday decor. Inspired by the piles of shipping boxes in our back room, she trimmed the cardboard into enormous three-dimensional trees and menorahs and wreaths and dreidels and moons and stars. She crafted stockings and a plate of cookies for our fireplace, and Santa's leg to dangle above the flames. She snipped toilet paper rolls into rings and strung them into countless garlands. And everything was twisted and sparkling with white fairy lights. It was a breathtaking sight. Many new customers walked in the door just to admire her creations.

Macon applied for the reference job and was immediately called in for an interview. I was proud of him and not the least bit surprised that they viewed him as a strong candidate. He reported that it had gone well but declined to speculate on his chances. He seemed unusually stressed out about the whole thing, probably because it had been years since he'd tried for something new. I assured him that no matter what happened, the higher-ups knew he was interested now; he would have more opportunities. But I could tell he wanted this one.

We finally made it to the micro-studio early one Sunday morning. It only took two carloads to empty it out, and we dumped everything in Edmond's room on top of the rest of my belongings. The chaotic heap looked so distressingly familiar that I had to remind myself this wasn't another temporary move. We'd sort everything out when we had more time.

First, I needed to keep a promise to my friends.

Macon and I donned our matching Colburn County shirts, chucked out the milk crates, installed the bathroom door, and painted the walls a smoky green that Mika and Bex had picked out. After that, we scrubbed the entire studio from top to bottom and helped them carry in a new dresser. None of us could believe the transformation. The studio had gone from a depressing, bare-bones hovel to a soothing, meditative space perfect for a solo traveler.

"You might want to replace the lamp," I said, handing over the key.

Mika and Bex laughed, but it felt symbolic to leave behind this final piece of my life with Cory as I entered into my new one with Macon.

And then Macon was issued a last-minute invitation to my sister's wedding. I don't know why this caught us both off guard, other than I'd had numerous conversations about the wedding that year, and he'd never been involved in any of the plans before.

"You've been invited," I said, hanging up with Riley and entering the bedroom.

I'd been searching for a missing sweater that I wanted to wear to work the following day. He was already in bed, but he'd overheard enough to understand. He set down his library book with clear apprehension. His expression was strained, maybe even freaked out. "To the giant wedding? The one with the possible media coverage and your entire extended family?"

I understood his dread and reluctance, and my impulse was to help him. My skin flushed as I willingly—hurriedly—provided the excuse. "It's okay. I'll decline on your behalf. I'll tell them you don't have any more vacation time this year."

If anything, his misery increased. "Won't it make me look bad not to be there?"

"Everyone will understand. It's Christmas. It's so last second."

But he looked like he needed to be convinced. Like he *wanted* to be convinced. I sat beside him on the edge of the bed, cupped his unhappy face in my hands, and kissed his lips.

"It's okay," I murmured.

"Are you sure?"

My fingers traced over and smoothed his worry lines. "Of course."

"Rescuing me again." He kissed me back with more intensity. "God, I love you."

I laughed and let him tug me into the bed. As he traveled down lower to thank me with even greater enthusiasm, the book fell to the floor. I saw stars. God, I loved him, too.

But later, when the book was back in his hands and his attention had returned to the hidden social network of trees, I lay on my side of the bed with my lamp off and wondered if it really *was* just the size and scope of the event, the potential media presence, the prospect of meeting my entire family at once—all of which would be genuinely overwhelming—or if an additional factor was involved. Did the wedding itself freak him out? Did marriage?

I recalled the beginning of the year when Alyssa had learned of Riley's engagement and had asked Macon about proposing to his ex. His flattened response. *There were no circumstances under which I would have proposed.* It was easy to interpret this as there being no circumstances under which he would have proposed to Danielle, but a second interpretation was possible, too. And when I'd asked about his high school and college girlfriends, he'd said, *They're both married with children, living lives I've never wanted.* I knew he didn't want children. But what about marriage? Maybe having a father who wanted nothing to do with his mother had made him resent the entire concept. Maybe because he didn't grow up around it—when Bonnie got married, she'd left town—it was possible that he couldn't see any value in it. And then there'd been his reaction after witnessing the awful courthouse wedding. *Why bother at all?*

Were these individualized cases or were they blanket statements on the subject? It was strange, after all these years, that I had no idea what he thought about marriage.

As I squirmed beside him, another wretched—and severely belated—thought occurred to me: I had no way of driving to Orlando for the wedding.

"Fuck," I whispered.

Macon stiffened, and I heard him set down his book. "What is it?"

I rolled over and told him.

"You can borrow my car." He smiled, relaxing with the easy solution. Grateful to be of service again. "I'll use your bike."

"I canceled my insurance, remember?"

The smile faded. Anything related to driving fell into the category of things that he didn't like taking chances with. He thought for a moment. "What about Cory?"

It was jarring to hear that name come out of Macon's mouth in Macon's bed.

"What about him? He's not going to the wedding."

"But is he going home for Christmas? Do you think he'd give you a ride?"

It was a smart idea. And a generous one, an act of trust and love. I scooted against him—kissing up his arm, his shoulder, his face, shoving my arms around his back, crawling onto his lap, climbing up him, wanting to touch and hold every part of him, unable to get enough.

It turned out that Cory *was* going to Florida, and he was happy to give me a ride back to Ridgetop, but he wasn't leaving early enough for me to participate in all the necessary wedding preparations. Macon was trying to convince me to let him pay for an expensive, one-way plane ticket to Orlando when my sister stepped in and saved the day. "We'll drive you there," Riley said. Her apartment in Atlanta was two and a half hours away. She and Jess offered to drive north to pick me up, and then we'd all make the long haul down to Orlando together.

"Surely you don't have time for that," I said. Jess would only have just arrived from Turkey. She'd been granted a very limited window of leave.

"We want to see your store," Riley said, and then her tone darkened. "And I want to meet this new guy you've already shacked up with."

"I told you, he's not exactly *new*."

Riley harrumphed. "Then why isn't he coming to my wedding?"

When I'd told her I'd moved in with him, she'd been happier for me than my parents had but still with significant reservations. In her shoes, I would have felt suspicious and protective, too. I decided not to tell Macon because I didn't want to give him any more reasons to be anxious about their visit. He already felt guilty for avoiding their wedding. Riley and Jess would arrive on a Sunday, stay with us through Monday, and then I'd leave with them early on Tuesday morning. Macon and I borrowed an air mattress from Alyssa and set it up in his study. Then we frowned at the inflated object with concern.

"Where have your previous guests stayed?" I asked.

"Same place you did that first time—on the couch."

"What about Bonnie?" Remembering his couch, I was offended for Bonnie's sake.

"She stayed with my mom. You're the only one I ever offered the bed to."

I swooned.

On Sunday, I hurried home from work to help him. Because Macon's love language was food, he'd been preparing dinner for hours: butternut squash ravioli with a sage béchamel sauce, a Bibb lettuce and endive salad, smashed garlicky fingerling potatoes, and a sticky toffee pudding for dessert. We were still cooking when our guests arrived. Jess slung their bags on the floor and threw her arms around me. "Whaaaaaat this place is like a storybook!" She shouted over my shoulder toward Macon, who was lingering in the kitchen, "It smells amazing in here!"

I always forgot how loud Jess was, but I loved her warm energy. Her body was strong, and her presence was huge. Her hair was loose tonight but on game days, she wore it in a high, tight bun that meant serious business. Her expression was stoic and legendarily intimidating, confident in her status as an elite on the court. But off court, she was an energetic goofball.

Riley looked like what she was: a younger, tougher, nurse version of me. Her blond hair was bluntly but stylishly cropped, and since she'd started dating Jess, her body had grown more athletic, which suited her. We hugged and held on tightly. Eighteen months had passed since we'd last seen each other, when Cory and I had driven down to Atlanta for a game. It had been too long, and a lot had changed.

Macon stepped into the room, looking nervous, though less than I'd anticipated. His professional work face was on, which was masking most of it. But now that I recognized his shyness, it was easier for me to spot it. Jess introduced herself enthusiastically and shook his hand. He glanced down in surprise, and I hid a smile. The roughness of her hands had startled me the first time, too. I'd been worried that she might overwhelm him, but since her friendliness was authentic, he responded to it in kind, easing another notch. My sister was the challenge.

"It's good to finally meet you," he said. "I've been hearing stories about you for years."

Riley was polite but reserved as she thanked him for hosting them.

I showed Riley and Jess around the house, pointing out everything we'd done and still planned to do, so Macon could finish up in the kitchen without anybody underfoot and have a moment to collect himself again. They were impressed, which was gratifying, and Jess sighed with wistful envy. "We won't be able to settle down like this for years," she said, shooting an apologetic look toward my sister. She was referring to playing overseas in the offseason, plus the potential of being traded to another team in another city.

But Riley just said, "We have the rest of our lives," and I could tell it was a common reassurance. As she reached for her fiancée's hand, Riley's engagement ring sparkled.

Settle down, Jess had said. I did feel settled, or at least I figured I *would* once I had time to settle. But I still didn't think of this house as ours, because it wasn't. It belonged to Macon. That unsettled feeling cracked through my exterior again and slithered inside. I grabbed hold of its tail and flung it back out.

He called out that dinner was ready, and we helped him carry the dishes to the table and pour the sparkling wine. Our small feast looked and smelled as festive as the season. We raised our glasses, toasted the brides-to-be, and dug in.

"Dear lord," Jess said. "Is this ravioli handmade?"

"Macon makes everything from scratch," I gushed. "And the vegetables and herbs are all from his garden."

"Not to bring up your ex, Iggy," my sister said, beginning to relax into her usual self, "but this is way better than eating with you and Cory."

"*Riley*," Jess and I said together.

But Macon laughed, not minding that particular comparison.

"There was a lot of frozen pizza," Riley said.

"Who do you think has been feeding your sister vegetables all these years?" Macon said, and they clinked glasses.

"Nothing wrong with a frozen pizza," Jess said.

"Thank you," I said. And then, "Actually, I don't know why we're defending DiGiorno all of a sudden."

Everyone laughed, and I maneuvered the conversation to their wedding because it was what they always wanted to talk about. The dinner was enjoyable. After her austere greeting, I was relieved that Riley seemed to be putting her hesitations aside to give Macon a fair chance. I hadn't known what to expect because I'd never introduced my family to anybody but Cory.

That night in bed, Macon said, "Your sister calls you Iggy."

I knew where this was going. The ghost materialized back into our bedroom.

"I thought Cory was the only one who did that," he said.

"He learned it from her."

Half a minute later, he said, "Am I supposed to be calling you Iggy?"

I lowered my novel and looked at him in surprise.

"Is that what . . . your loved ones call you?"

It was sweet how unsure he sounded, and I considered my reply. "It was, once. But I've been Ingrid for even longer, and you are my *most* loved one."

His eyebrows rose a little. After all, it had only been weeks. "Most?"

It had also been years. "Most."

He sat with that for several seconds and then confessed, "You're my most, too."

The air mattress was a disaster, and Riley and Jess emerged from Macon's study in a foul mood. They'd been bumping into each other all night and had woken up to find the mattress completely deflated. We apologized, unfairly blaming Alyssa.

"We'll figure out something better for tonight," I promised, as Macon shoved conciliatory piles of blueberry waffles and fluffy scrambled eggs at them.

"You'd better," Jess said, giving us a flash of her intimidating game face, "or you'll be the one driving our sore asses all the way to Orlando."

"I just realized you don't have any decorations," Riley said, glancing around with irritation.

Understanding how much they loved Christmas, I felt bad that I hadn't been able to deck our halls before their arrival. "We talked about it, but with the store and the move and the unfinished living room and me going away for the holiday, the effort didn't seem worth it."

"You *always* decorated your place," she said.

It sounded like she was suggesting this wasn't my home. "Yeah, and I have no idea where my decorations are." I tried not to get defensive. "Somewhere between the litter box and all of my books."

"Don't you usually have a tree?" Jess asked Macon.

"Uh, not in the last few years. But I'm looking forward to getting one next year," he added, with a fretful but sincere glance at me.

It was easy to imagine hanging ornaments and listening to Christmas records together, and my heart panged with longing. The exhaustion of the year was settling into my bones. Working this hard had paradoxically given me *more* energy—all of that forward momentum—but now that I was being forced to take nine days off for the wedding, I wondered how I would get through it. And how would the store survive without me? Until now, I'd only taken off the day after Macon and I became a couple and Thanksgiving. It nauseated me to think about being absent during such a crucial sales week. Macon was even volunteering there next weekend, and Bex was taking a few volunteer shifts, too. We were close to the required sales number, but not out of the danger zone yet. It felt like I was abandoning the store when it needed me the most. Like somehow me not being there might cause fewer customers to come in. It made no sense but plagued me all the same. I'd already made Mika promise to text me daily updates.

Thankfully, the scrumptious breakfast lifted Riley's and Jess's moods, and after taking turns in the bathroom, we bundled up and I walked them to Bildungsroman. The branches were bare, and the air was frosty. Macon had planted ornamental cabbages and flowering kale in our outside containers, and the storefront twinkled with its festive window decor. They posed excitedly for a ton of pictures. Jess posted the best to social media, where she had over a million followers, many of them in our region. I wasn't sure how sizable the crossover was between basketball and books, but it was our highest-profile mention so far, and I was grateful for it.

Riley was awed by what I had accomplished inside. Since her opinion ranked second only to Macon's, I basked in her approval. And my coworkers were thrilled to meet Jess and admire her Olympic rings tattoo and hear her stories, which made Riley feel even prouder.

Afterward, she and Jess explored the rest of downtown and grabbed lunch at a cidery while I returned home to pack. Macon and Edmond kept me company.

"A week is so long," I said, feeling needy and clingy.

"At least the wedding will keep you busy," he said. "Hopefully the time will pass quickly." It was a valiant attempt at optimism, especially considering the source, but Macon was lying supine on the bed, equally morose. I wondered if I should have tried to convince him to come with me, but it still seemed cruel to force him into a situation that I knew would make him miserable.

I held up my red dress for him before packing it away in my suitcase.

Macon groaned at the ceiling. "Nobody there will appreciate that dress the way I do."

His anguish lifted my spirits a smidge. "I should hope not."

He suddenly sat up. "I forgot to thank your sister."

"For what?" I was taken aback.

"That dress."

It made me laugh, but his mood slipped back into melancholy, and his body slumped back into repose. "I'll never forget you walking toward me through that crowd. This crimson beacon."

I lay down beside him on the bed. Edmond hopped off. We snuggled into each other, locking fingers, and stayed there quietly for several minutes.

"I'll be back soon," I whispered.

"You just got here, and you're already leaving."

It wasn't an accusation. It was the same unbearable sadness that was pressing down upon me. "I haven't even unpacked, and I'm already packing."

He poked me in a way that said *yes* and also *that was a good one*.

We were tired. We fell asleep together, jolting awake to Jess's voice. "Aw," she said, grinning at us from the doorway.

I bolted upright with a racing heart, in the disoriented panic that sometimes occurs after an unplanned nap. "I have to pack!"

Macon swept me back down onto the bed and into his arms. "You aren't leaving yet. I'll help you finish tonight." He sealed the promise with a kiss to my forehead. It felt so comforting to be coddled that I almost forgot about Jess. Then I realized my sister was standing behind her, scrutinizing us.

I was surprised that Macon's shyness hadn't kicked in; I didn't know all of his limits yet. It gladdened me that he was comfortable showing affection in front of other people. I leaned into his hug and didn't want him to ever let go.

After dinner, a chickpea potpie with fresh thyme and a golden lattice crust, we filled two thermoses with peppermint hot chocolate to share (because we didn't own four), tuned in to the Christmas radio station, and drove to Thistle Lake. On one of the streets behind the lake was a stretch of garish and spectacularly overdecorated houses. The road was slow and crowded, and Riley and Jess rolled down the windows and demanded that Macon turn up the volume. We cruised the lighted thoroughfare three times, my sister and her fiancée singing at the top of their lungs and delighting in the lawn crammed with hundreds of kitsch vintage blow molds, the Ferris wheel stuffed with teddy bears wearing Santa hats, and the McMansion frosted in an elaborate gingerbread overlay with rainbow sugary icicles. I joined in for some of the songs, and Macon laughed the whole time, embarrassed but happy.

"Man," Jess said as we were heading back. "I miss shit like this when I'm in Istanbul."

"American tackiness?" Macon said.

"*Yes*. I love it."

"You're going to Disney World after the season ends for your honeymoon, right?" he asked.

Jess laughed. "I hear the judgment in your voice."

"I swear that was my normal voice."

"Have *you* ever been to Disney World?" Riley asked him.

Macon smiled because he knew this was a test. My family didn't travel much outside of Florida when I was a kid, but we'd spent a fair amount of time at the theme parks near our house. I wasn't fanatical like Riley and Jess, but I did have a fondness for them, and Macon knew it. "Once," he said. "My aunt took me when I was seven, maybe eight."

"I'm imagining a tiny, grouchy you in Mickey ears, and it's adorable," I said.

"I had a good time," he insisted.

"We've gotta get you back there," Jess said. "Next time you visit, we'll all go."

It had never occurred to me to ask Macon if he would ever go to a theme park with my family. It was almost impossible to imagine him riding a flying elephant. "*Would* you consider going?" I asked.

His head cocked as he pondered the question for several seconds. "I would be amenable to joining you."

Amenable! He actually said that. As Riley and Jess cracked up, my heart swelled, and I wanted to eat him up, I loved him so much.

He frowned. "No ears."

"I would never," I promised.

Macon and I gave our bed to Riley and Jess because we'd forgotten to figure out the air mattress situation, and I believed my sister might murder me if she wasn't properly rested before our road trip. Also, I felt guilty for giving an air mattress to a professional athlete whose livelihood depended on taking care of her body. As we slowly sank to the study floor in the pitch dark, we agreed that we should turn Edmond's room into a guest bedroom before my parents' visit.

"We'll have to buy a bed," I said miserably. "Mattresses are so expensive."

"I'll take care of it."

"No, I'll figure it out. I'll find a way to pay for half."

"Ingrid."

"I will, I'll figure it out."

"Would you please let me do this for you? For us?"

The air mattress reached a new deflation point, and our bodies rolled into each other. As we struggled away, he accidentally grazed my face and felt my tears. "Oh my God." He sounded worried. "It's okay if you don't want me to. You can pay for half. We haven't talked about finances yet—"

"It's not that," I said.

"It's not?"

"It's not *only* that."

"What's the matter?"

I sniffled. "I hate crying in front of you now."

"*Why?*"

"Because I've done it so much this year. And because of your mom. You don't need any more—"

"Please leave her out of this. I promise it's not the same thing. I want you to be able to cry in front of me. What's going on?"

"It's just . . . I'm going to miss you so much. I don't want to go."

Although we were already pressed against each other, he gathered me even closer. He buried his face in my hair, inhaled, and sighed. "Mango citrus." And then he swore, readjusting his back against the floor. "I'll miss you, too, but I'll be right here when you return."

"Not *right* here, I hope."

He laughed and kissed the side of my neck. "Even when you're sad, you're funny."

"I'm very sad."

He kissed my throat. My lips.

"Very sad," I said again. Less sadly.

I kissed him back and felt him smile against me. Our hands roamed. Our mouths. We crawled off the rustling air mattress. The hardwood was cold underneath us, so our shirts and socks stayed on. In the darkness, his hands found my hips, guiding us both. He pushed into me and stifled a groan. I bit his lip to further silence him. He pushed in deeper, and I bit my own. I rocked slowly, taking my time. We gripped on to each other, searching for more comfortable positions, pushing and rocking, promising ourselves there was no reason to hurry.

I grew tearful again in the morning, and our kiss goodbye was wet. I couldn't make sense of why I was so upset over one week apart. I tried to stay upbeat in the car for Riley and Jess, pretending I was only worried about leaving the store. I didn't want to put a damper on their celebration. Also, I was highly aware that immediately after they married, Jess would fly back out of the country while I would be returning to Macon. Sulking would have been unkind.

We'd not been on the road for long when Riley swiveled around in the passenger seat to interrogate me. "So, when are you gonna get another car?"

"I don't know that I am," I said, surprising myself. "Maybe we'll get a second e-bike and share his car." We hadn't discussed it, but Macon loved my bike, and it made sense, financially and environmentally. His house was within easy distance of my store. "He could put me on his car insurance, right?"

Jess glanced at me in the rearview mirror. "You and Cory were never on each other's insurance?"

"No, we had our own cars. We didn't need to be."

"We're on each other's insurance," Riley said pointing between her and Jess.

"Yeah, but you're getting married," I said.

Riley shrugged. "We did it a couple of years ago."

It felt as if I'd fallen into a trap, but I didn't quite understand what it was. Riley clarified it with her next question. "Do you think you'll marry Macon?"

I gaped at her boldness, then shook my head with a sputtering laugh.

"Is that a no?" Riley asked.

I turned my gaze away from her. "No."

"So is that a yes?"

"We've been together for six weeks. We haven't exactly talked about it."

"But you moved in together."

"Yeah, because we've known each other for years." How many times did I have to repeat it?

"Does Macon want to get married someday?"

"Like I said"—my voice tightened—"we haven't discussed it."

"But do you know how he feels about marriage in general? Does he *ever* want to get married?"

There were no circumstances under which I would have proposed.

They're both married with children, living lives I've never wanted.

Why bother at all?

The back seat was hot. "I don't know."

"Do *you* ever want to get married?"

Boiling. "I don't know."

"Maybe we should talk about something else," Jess said, finally interrupting.

"No, this is important." Riley removed her sunglasses to prove her point. "You moved in with a guy without talking about the future. He's had a number of long-term girlfriends, none of whom he married. And if neither of you ever wants to get married, that's fine! But if one of you does and the other doesn't . . . Iggy. It's not your house."

"I know!" I snapped.

My sister's voice cracked and softened. "It's just that I don't want another eleven years to pass before you figure this out, because *you'd* be the one who would have to leave. You'd be the one starting over with nothing."

I was stunned. I felt ambushed. I didn't know what to say.

"Listen, I like the guy," she said, still gently. "He's kind and respectful, he's helped you so much with the bookstore and everything else this year, he let you paint his house *your* favorite colors, and he goggles at you like . . ."

"You're the only person in any room," Jess said.

"Exactly," Riley said. "Your friendship reminds me of what you had with Cory, but your interests seem a lot more compatible. Macon seems like a guy who'd rather stay at home."

"*I'd* rather stay at home."

"I know. That's what I mean." When I didn't say anything else, her shoulders drooped, and she put her sunglasses back on. "I'm sure you know what you're doing. I'm sure everything is fine. Just . . . think about having a conversation with him about this before you unpack all those boxes."

CHAPTER FORTY-FOUR

The unsettled feeling slithered back into me—winding around the ache of missing Macon, winding around my fears about the bookstore and my bank accounts—as the car twisted down the mountains and away from Ridgetop. I had thought I was finally standing on bedrock, but what if this was just a layer of strata—as sparkly as mica but also as thin and brittle? What if my life crumbled again? What if I fell through?

No. I loved him, and he loved me. Bedrock.

But what if he never wanted to get married? Would I be okay with that?

What if he *did* want to marry me? Would I be okay with *that*?

Oh God.

I did.

I wanted to marry him.

* * *

It wasn't a question like it had been with Cory. It was an answer.

I wanted to marry Macon and live in his stone cottage forever and help take care of his mother and watch his garden bloom and see my bookstore thrive and bring him to Disney World with my family and then delight in his exasperated reactions to the corporate monoculture. I wanted to grow old with him and raise a series of dignified cats. I wanted to kiss him when our hair thinned and our skin sagged and our knees stopped working and we both forgot the word for "blue." I wanted to die beside him in bed someday, many decades from now, holding hands in our sleep. I wanted to be buried beside him and have our names carved on a joint tombstone so that everyone who ever stumbled across it for the rest of eternity would know that we belonged to each other.

CHAPTER FORTY-FIVE

Being in the middle of wedding preparations didn't help my anxiety. Nor did it help that the tasks didn't keep me as busy as I'd anticipated. Riley and our mom already had the entire operation organized and running smoothly. I shouldn't have been in Florida yet. I should have been with Macon and at my store. I called Mika so often for sales numbers that she ordered me to stop because I was stressing everybody out. And I couldn't ask Macon what he thought about marriage because it was a conversation we needed to have in person. I knew he loved me. I knew he wanted to be with me. But I had no idea what he thought about the concept of *forever*.

There were hopeful signs. After three days apart, I convinced him to FaceTime me for the first time ever. His expression broke when he saw me, and he touched his screen.

"See?" I said. "Technology isn't all bad."

"I hate it with the fiery intolerance of a thousand book banners, but my love for you burns stronger."

I laughed and touched my screen, too.

He requested selfies, and I sent them—but only if he sent some in return. The Macon album on my phone swelled. I stared at his face whenever I was alone.

My extended relatives flew into town, and then Jess's large family arrived, followed by a sea of strapping young women on holiday leave and a reporter and photographer from *People* magazine. More than two hundred guests showed up, proving that my mother's concerns about nobody coming to a Christmas wedding were unfounded. I was the shortest bridesmaid by several inches. The candlelit venue dripped with poinsettias and red berries and pine boughs, and the brides wore white dresses with white Air Jordans. I cried when they held hands and walked themselves down the aisle, I cried when they read their vows, and I cried when they kissed.

The reception was wild. A party full of athletes was very different than a party full of book people. They were not afraid to dance with me, and we danced all night.

The next day was Christmas Eve. When I woke up, I texted Macon a photo of me still wearing my red dress because I'd crashed in it, and he FaceTimed me immediately.

"If you need help with the zipper, I can be there in nine hours."

"The wedding was very them and very fun," I said. "And I am very tired."

His face fell with regret. "I'm sorry."

"What for?"

"I made the wrong decision. I should have been there."

"You had to make the decision quickly. We'd only just gotten together," I said, but my heart squeezed because I wished he'd been there, too.

He still looked upset.

"If it makes you feel better, you would have hated the reception," I said.

"I like your sister. I like Jess."

His serious earnestness made me smile. "They like you, too. And you'll have plenty of time to hang out with them in the future."

Riley and Jess spent their last two days together visiting family, but they were never apart. I thought about how if it had been Macon and me, we would have told everybody else to fuck off, party's over. But they glowed with happiness. They spent Christmas Eve with us and Christmas Day at the hotel where Jess's family was staying. This left me alone with my parents.

"I like that we don't have to share you with Cory's family this year," my mom said, looping an arm around me.

"Ha," I said.

"Maybe you'll bring Macon home next December?"

And it occurred to me that I *did* want to be home next December—in Ridgetop.

Cory's oldest brother had stopped coming to their family Christmases after his wife had given birth to their first child, and Cory and I had fallen into the belief that this was the way of things. That the holidays were meant to be shared with your family until you created your own. It wasn't a bad benchmark, necessarily, but it did exclude the people who didn't want children but still desired traditions of their own, away from their parents and siblings. Suddenly it was clear to me that I had been feeling this way for years, that I had been shackled to a tradition I had outgrown. This wasn't where I wanted to be.

It explained why I had felt such dread before coming here. It wasn't just about leaving Macon and my store behind. It was about leaving *my family* and *my home* during the holidays.

I tried to show my parents what I was missing. Macon was at his mother's house, so we FaceTimed with them. Everyone was self-conscious and overly mannered, but the call was also nice. I hoped to be on the other side of the screen the next year.

And then it was finally time to go home. It was surreal seeing Cory's car pull up in front my parents' house like it had done so many times before. He got out to say hello, and although it was awkward, it was less so than I'd imagined. Instead of the usual hugs, he waved to my mom and shook my dad's hand. He inquired about the wedding and showed the proper enthusiasm for their anecdotes and the photos my mom shared with him on her phone.

Then he regaled them with a story of his middle brother roughhousing him into a palm tree and accidentally bloodying his face against its trunk seconds before their annual family photo. He took off his glasses to flaunt the damage and then shared the picture, to my parents' polite disbelief. In it, Cory's face looked like a crime scene, and everybody was cracking up, his mother most of all. I appreciated Cory's family but felt relieved that I would never have to live with any of them. I wondered if quiet Macon and his quiet mother (no need to disclose the agoraphobia yet) had risen another rung in my parents' minds.

"I'm glad you two are still friends," my mom said to Cory and me, and the awkwardness returned. We said goodbye, and he carried my suitcase to his car. He didn't have to do that anymore, but I doubted he did it because my parents were there. It was just who he was. The smell inside his car was uncanny, familiar yet from a past that already felt very distant. My parents were still watching, so we were stiff with each other until we were out of sight.

Cory exhaled. "Oh my God. That was weird, right?"

The sound of his laughter loosened me. "*So* weird."

"I didn't know if they'd want to talk to me."

"Of course they did. They've always liked you."

"Your dad had more of a vibe than your mom. I don't think he was excited to see me."

"I think he was just confused and didn't know how to act. Thanks for driving me. I know it's weird"—there was that word again—"but I appreciate it."

"Glad for the company. What happened to your car? Did the engine finally die?"

"Yeah. I've been carless since summer, but it's not normally a problem since I live close to the store."

"What about everything else? Groceries and going out? Are you ridesharing?"

"Oh no. My—" I broke off. *My boyfriend has a car* contained a crucial piece of information that I hadn't told him yet. This wouldn't have mattered if the boyfriend were anybody other than Macon.

He didn't miss the implication, though. His grin spread into his voice. "Your *what?*"

"My boyfriend has a car."

Cory hollered and honked the horn with glee.

I shoved his hands away from it. "Okay, okay."

"What's his name, how did you meet?" He glanced over and saw my reluctance. "Oh my God. This is going to be good, isn't it? Please tell me it's embarrassing."

"It's not, it's just . . ." I swallowed. "It's Macon."

The mirth slid from his face. As he processed the information, his expression turned incredulous before it transformed again into righteousness. "I knew it. I fucking knew it!"

"Okay." I gritted my teeth. "Calm down."

"Oh man. Macon."

"You never did like him."

Cory laughed with outrage, but he also seemed to find the situation hilarious. "Yeah, because he clearly had a thing for you. And you clearly liked him back!"

"He was my friend! We were only ever friends."

"Yeah, no." He shook his head, accusingly but jokingly. "It was the way you talked about him. I could see it. I knew."

"Well, *I* didn't know."

He laughed again as he yelled, "How could you not know?"

I shrugged helplessly. It was true that I hadn't been aware. But I also sort of had, and it didn't feel kind to admit that part to him.

"Fuck," he said. "Macon Nowakowski."

I grinned, ready to break his brain again. "We live together."

"*What?* Since when?"

"A few weeks ago."

"When did you get together? Did you hook up last winter when we . . . ?" His face screwed up. "Never mind. It's still weird! I'm not sure I want to know."

"No," I said. "It only happened last month."

"AND YOU ALREADY MOVED IN TOGETHER?"

It made us laugh so hard we both cried.

"I'm not sure how to process any of this," he said.

"It's okay. It's still new to me, too."

A thought occurred to him. "Wait. Does he know I'm driving you home?"

"Of course he does."

"And he's not, like, worried about it?"

I rolled my eyes. "No. He's an adult."

"I know he is. Damn it." We cracked up again before he added slyly, "My girlfriend knows I'm driving you home, too."

"Oh my God. You have been *waiting* to drop that."

He pounded on his steering wheel. "I have!"

"Is it the woman from earlier this year?"

"It is. She's an adult, too," he bragged.

I didn't tell him that I already knew she was older than us. I didn't want him to know I'd looked her up. But there was relief and joy for both of us in getting to talk to somebody who understood, who didn't need anything explained. We'd both been stuck, we'd both had a hellish year, and now we were both thriving on the other side. He told me how he and Holland had met on his very first night out and how they'd kept running into each other all year long. He had never believed in fate. Now he did. I was less certain about fate, but I felt grateful that time and proximity had been on Macon's and my side.

"Do you think you'll marry her?" I asked. It wasn't interrogatory, like my sister's line of questioning had been, and he didn't take it that way. It was more like a continuation of our last conversation in the diner.

"I do."

"*Cory*," I said happily.

"I mean, not yet." He laughed. "I've fucked up in a lot of ways this year. She needs to know I'm steady. But yeah. Marriage, kids. I see the whole thing with her."

"That's great," I said, meaning it.

"What about you?"

There was a swing in my mood.

Cory quieted. "Sorry, Ig. You don't have to answer that."

I explained that I did want to marry Macon, but I feared it might not be what he wanted. That this was a conversation we needed to have soon, and I was dreading it. That I didn't know what I would do if he told me that he never wanted to marry, but that the possibility was real.

Cory's voice hardened. "Don't you dare put that shit off. You have to have that conversation *now*."

"I know, I know—"

"I'm serious. You need to talk to him about this. You can't let this sit between you unspoken. Don't do what we did."

He sounded like my sister. They were right, and it was a horrendous feeling. Imagining losing Macon felt so much worse than actually losing Cory had been.

"Listen," he said, trying to slow my visible spiral, "I don't know what he'll say. I don't know his history. But I do know he's always been into you. And I bet he would have pushed his boring-ass girlfriend out of the way to shove a ring onto your finger years ago if I hadn't been in the picture."

It hung in the air between us for a moment, and then I whispered dramatically, "She *was* boring, wasn't she?"

"And self-righteous. I wouldn't have wanted to marry her either."

"You also didn't want to marry me," I pointed out.

"Yet I almost did just because you're so great."

I laughed.

We didn't stop talking for the entire nine-hour drive, catching up and sharing stories. It turned out that Holland had also obtained an unexpected cat this year, and Cory had also grown attached to it. We shared photos, and I felt smug that Edmond was much cuter in addition to being better behaved. But it felt strange and magical that even though our paths had diverged, they were still running parallel to one another.

The sky began darkening as we neared Ridgetop, and the mountain air was tinged with . . . something else.

SNOW, Macon texted.

I was shocked by the all caps. *It's snowing?!*

Not yet, but it's supposed to start later tonight.

Sounds like it's waiting for me.

It's not the only one, he said, which made my whole body tingle.

"It's going to snow," I said to Cory, and then he got excited, too.

Another text arrived, this one from Mika. *Are you back yet?*

Home in a half hour!

Come to the store, she said. *I have a Christmas present for you.*

Is it SNOW?

You heard! (No. It's something better.)

"I think it's the sales numbers," I told Cory, sitting forward in my seat. "I think we hit our goal."

"Why wouldn't she just text that?"

"I don't know. Maybe she made a cake to celebrate?"

"Do you want me to drop you off at the bookstore or at Macon's?"

I checked the time. "The store. It's a late shift, so he's still at work anyway." I texted the change of plans to Macon and asked him to pick me up at Bildungsroman. By the time we arrived, my stomach was writhing—about the sales, but also about Macon. It felt incredible that I was about to see him again. And so daunting that I would have to confront him about our future.

Cory pulled up to the curb to let me out. I retrieved my suitcase from his trunk, and then he turned on his hazards to pop out and hug me goodbye.

"Oh my God," he said, catching sight of something over my shoulder. "It *is* him."

I turned around. Macon was on the opposite side of the street, waiting to cross. He was wearing his rumpled duffel coat, his hair was disheveled, and his work pen was still tucked behind his ear. He looked exactly like he always had—except now he was mine.

My heart soared.

"I mean, you told me it was him," Cory said. "But yep. There he is."

Macon was checking his phone and hadn't noticed us.

"Ugh," Cory said.

I smiled.

"Well, good luck," Cory said. "I hope everything works out for you two."

"You sure about that?"

He gave me a cheeky grin. "Hey, I can dislike the guy and still want you to be happy." As Macon began to cross, Cory waved with his whole arm and shouted, "I got it from here, buddy."

Macon startled to see us.

"Yeah, she says she's still in love with me, so I'm taking her home."

I punched Cory in the abdomen, laughing. "You dick."

"Hi, Cory," Macon said.

He strolled toward us, calm and unthreatened. I raced toward him and launched myself into his arms. He wrapped them around me tightly and kissed me passionately.

"Hi," I said, gazing up at him.

"Hi," he said, gazing down at me. He didn't let go. I don't think he wanted to, but I also sensed that part of it was for show.

Cory laughed. "Bye, Iggy."

"Bye, Cory. Thanks for the ride."

He got into his car, turned off his hazards, and sped away with a rude series of honks and a middle finger out the window.

Macon was still holding me. He looked delighted.

"He supports my choice," I said, "but he also doesn't like you very much."

"As somebody who was in that exact position for many years, I know how he feels."

I beamed and kissed him again. "I missed you."

"I missed *you*."

"What are you doing here? Shouldn't you still be at work?"

"Library closed early," he said. "Snow."

I laughed. "Oh my God! You got the email early?"

He laughed, too. "We did."

I burrowed deeper into him, breathing in his familiar scent. "Don't ever let me go."

"Okay."

He held me.

"Actually, it's cold," I said. "Let's go inside. But you still can't let go."

"I promise I will never let go of you." As our bodies broke apart, he took my hand. With his other hand, he grabbed my suitcase. I shifted so I could hold on to him with both of mine.

"I have news," he said in a tone that announced it was good. "I got the job."

"What? Macon! That's amazing."

"I found out last week, but I wanted to tell you in person. I start in January. We'll be working near each other again. And I can come for lunch, like you said."

"We can walk to work together!"

"Or maybe I'll get a bike, too. But at least I can drive you on rainy days now."

"Or snowy ones," I said.

"Or snowy ones."

We were standing on the Roman's mosaic. "I'm so proud of you, and I want to hear *everything* about it. But first, I need to get warm and see what Mika wants."

"You do," he agreed.

I gave him a look that said, *You know what this is about?*

He smiled and let go of my suitcase, not my hand, to open the door. The bell rang above our heads. We entered the bookstore, and my coworkers cheered. "There she is!" Mika ran up to us and hugged me. She laughed when Macon and I did not drop hands.

"The store looks great," I said. I was overjoyed to be back.

Everybody was staring at me with an eager, expectant look.

"What?" I said, and then—for the briefest moment—I thought Macon was about to propose. Even though he was not aware of the discussion I'd been having inside my head for the past week. Even though proposing in public was not his style.

But then I heard it: a rhythmic heartbeat, deep and stately.

My eyes brimmed. "Is that what I think it is?"

Mika took my free hand, and together she and Macon led me to the corner where the grandfather clock had been placed.

"But . . . this is too much. Doesn't Carla want it?"

"She called me last week. She said our store looked great, but the sound was all wrong." Mika was smiling and still holding on to me, too. "She *also* mentioned that the clock would be too loud for her new condo. Macon picked it up and brought it here a few days ago."

I pressed his hand—it was another good surprise that he'd been keeping from me—as I said, "She found a condo!"

"She did," Mika said. "Looks like you'll be helping her move next month."

I laughed with a groan. "It's gonna be a long time before I have another day off, isn't it?"

"You just had *nine* of them," she said. "It's my turn."

"You didn't tell her to look closer," Stephen said, as everyone else gathered around.

"Oh!" Mika said. "Look closer."

I was already looking, and I gasped. An index card was nestled into a groove on the clock. A large number was written on it. "Please tell me that's what I think it is."

"It's what you think it is."

I choked up again. "We did it."

"We did."

"Like, barely," I said, laughing and pulling the card out.

She laughed and teared up, too. "Barely counts. We're still in business."

Macon squeezed my hand and let go, allowing Mika and me to fully embrace. And then Stephen and Jo and Amelia Louisa joined in. We cheered and shrieked and celebrated, and then, after showering them with my profuse thanks, I shooed them out the door. It wasn't quite closing time, but the store was empty. Ridgetop was ready for snow.

I carried the index card to my office, centered it on my desk, and snapped a photo for Kat.

AHHHHHHHHHHHHH, she texted back, along with an ecstatic selfie.

I hugged my phone in lieu of the real person.

"You'll have to frame that card and hang it up in here beside Len and Mary," Macon said. "They'd be proud of you. *I'm* proud of you. You worked so hard for this."

"I'm proud of *you*. Look at us with our new jobs."

"Look at us," he said, eyes locking with mine.

My body surged with the renewal of longing from our time apart, and we kissed again until it almost turned into something more. But we both wanted to get home before the snow. He helped me close the registers, lock up the money, and turn off the lights. The grandfather clock ticked its steady reassurance through the darkness.

It's time, it was telling me. *It's time.*

Macon grabbed my suitcase again and wheeled it to the front door. My hands were shaking. He opened the door for me, and the bell rang. "I'm parked a street over," he said, as I ducked and passed underneath his arm. He laughed at my strange maneuver. "What was that?"

But as I locked the door behind us, his laughter trailed off. And when I turned around, I saw that he was remembering the same night that I was.

"There's something I need to talk to you about," I said.

He held my gaze carefully, nervously. "Okay."

"The thing is," I said. And then the rest of my words froze.

"The thing is . . ."

"I want to get married someday," I said.

His eyes widened.

Terror pulsed through me. Now that I finally had exactly what I wanted, I was teetering on the precipice of losing everything. But I couldn't let the view of someone standing before me block my entire future. Not even when it was the right someone. The best someone. I had made an irrational, catastrophic decision at the beginning of the year rather than address my real feelings and face my fears head on. I couldn't do that again. I had to know where Macon stood. I had no choice but to barrel forward.

"And we've never talked about marriage, so I don't know how you feel about it. If it's a thing you ever want to do with *anybody*. But I'm scared to unpack my boxes if it means I might have to repack them in eleven years. And I'm not trying to pressure you or get engaged right now, but I want to have a discussion. I just need to know if it's even on the table—"

"I want to marry you," he said.

My heart stopped. "You do?"

"Desperately."

"Oh," I whispered.

"I didn't know how you felt about it either. And I was afraid I would scare you away if I said something too soon, but I would have married you yesterday. I would have married you a month ago. A year ago. Five years ago."

"But you've had all those long-term relationships. And you've never even been engaged."

"Because I didn't want to spend the rest of my life with them."

"But you want to spend it with me?"

"*Yes*," he said.

The word snagged inside me, rewriting the code, traveling upward and repeating into infinity.

Yes. Ingrid. Yes.

Something cold and wet hit my cheeks. We looked up at the same time. Tiny snowflakes were tumbling and swirling down from the sky. Our eyes met in wonder. But just as I was about to rewrite the second wrong of that night—just as I was about to kiss him and be kissed back—he stopped me with a concern of his own.

"Before this goes any further," he said, and my eyebrows rose at the implication. He smiled, though unease quickly replaced it. "My mom. I don't know if you remember, but—"

"She can take Edmond's room. We'll make it work."

It looked like he wanted to believe me but was afraid to. "She's ill. It won't be easy."

"I know. I want to help. I want to live with you forever, and I understand that that probably means living with her, too."

"It's a big commitment."

"So is marriage," I said, taking his hands again.

"What about children?"

I was thrown. "I thought . . . we'd sort of talked about that already?"

"Because I've never imagined myself with kids, but if you've changed your mind, I would reconsider it. But I need to know now. I need to know if that's something we should discuss. I'm not getting any younger."

My heart swelled, but I was even more grateful that our opinions remained the same. "I haven't changed my mind."

He seemed relieved. "What about the wedding? Big or small or—"

"Small. I don't want two hundred people watching us. But not at the courthouse either. I don't want a *Beavis and Butt-Head* wedding."

He finally laughed. Tears shimmered in his eyes.

"Maybe a ceremony in the garden with just our closest family and friends," I said.

"Yes. Good. But what about beaches?"

Now I laughed, completely thrown. "What?"

"If I'm vacationing, I prefer cold beaches. Rocky, gray, unsuitable for swimming. But most people don't like that, so if you prefer something tropical, I'd be fine with taking turns."

"I already knew that about you." I smiled. "And I also prefer a moody beach."

He tucked a windblown strand of my hair behind my ear and confessed, "I already knew that about you, too."

"But I would like to visit Kat someday, even though the beach in her town is sunny. I've never been outside of the country."

"Neither have I. And I would love to visit Australia with you someday."

"So . . . is that it? Do we know everything about each other now?"

"I think so," he said. Yet I still didn't see it coming. I still gasped as he got down on one knee in the mosaicked entryway. "I don't have a ring."

"Yes." My answer bubbled out before he'd even asked.

The way he laughed and beamed up at me made me feel like I was the only sun he needed. "Ingrid Dahl. Will you marry me?"

"Yes," I said again, nodding and bobbing my head. I helped him stand and pulled him into a sweeping kiss. Our noses were cold, but our mouths were warm. We kissed for so long that the snowflakes fattened and collected on the ground. They dusted our hair and powdered our coats. We kissed until our lips were sore, our bodies were shivering, and our fingers were frozen. We kissed like we had forever.

CHAPTER FORTY-SIX

Macon drove me home. The porch and living room lights were on when we arrived, and the little stone cottage was twinkling merrily in the snow. Edmond's silhouette was in the front window.

"Did you stop by on your way to the store just to turn on the lights?" I asked with delight.

"I did."

I fake gasped. "The electricity!"

"I wanted you to come home to a warm house. *Our* house."

The words settled over me. I tried them out, and they felt good. "Our house." My throat tightened as tears welled in my eyes. "I love this house."

He turned off the car and smiled at me. "I know you do."

"I mean, I might be marrying you just for this house."

He laughed. "Good. Then my evil plan worked."

"What evil plan?"

"To create the perfect house to entrap you. All your favorite colors, your favorite things."

My gasp was real this time. "Riley said that's what you were doing!"

"Yeah. I thought I was being pretty obvious."

Although a thrill ran through me, hurt and worry followed. "But I thought you liked everything. I never would have pushed something on you that I thought you wouldn't like."

He reached for my left hand, and one of his fingers encircled my ring finger. Locking us together. "I know. And I *do* love everything, especially because it reminds me of you. Of us. I think the whole thing is very us."

Holding hands with him was still the most extraordinary pleasure. "It is, isn't it?"

"Come on," he said, encouraging me to get out. "Come see your Christmas present."

"Oh no! You agreed to no presents. I don't have anything for you."

"It's for both of us. You can actually see it from here."

I swiveled around to look, but everything appeared to be the same. "Is it in the garden?"

"Nope."

"Is that a different cat?"

He urged me out again. "Come on."

I hurried to the door and searched for my house key as he hefted my suitcase out of the trunk. I was still combing through the bottom of my tote when he reached me. His keys were still out, so he unlocked the door and held it open for me.

"Oh my God," I said. "The books!"

The long wall of shelving had finished curing while I was away, and he'd transferred all the books from his study into the living room. The space was now cozy and alive. Just like I'd envisioned, the colors of the spines popped against the oversaturation of rich green. It made the books look like old and beloved art. It positioned them as the most important objects in the house, the first things people would see upon entering. They were the books of a librarian and a bookseller. And then I realized they *were*. He had unpacked my books, too, and mixed them in alphabetically with his.

"I realize we didn't discuss organization." He sounded nervous now. "We could switch the placement of fiction and nonfiction. Or if you'd rather keep our collections separate, we could always put my books on that side of the doorway and yours on the other—"

"It's *perfect*. I love that our books are sitting side by side and getting to know each other, rubbing off on each other. All of their knowledge and stories mixing together."

The way he smiled told me it was how he imagined it, too. "Phil thought it was a mistake to build this many shelves, but there had to be enough space for both of us."

Something occurred to me. "But you built them before we started dating."

"Like I said. Phil thought it was a mistake."

My smile grew to match his.

"Oh!" he said. "But that's not your present. Turn around."

I had been so captivated by the books that I had failed to notice all the new furniture—the long green velvet sofa and matching love seat and adjustable reading lamps. They weren't knockoffs of the items I had texted him so many months ago: *Something like this but obviously not THI$*. They were the actual items. My tote bag slid out of my hand and dropped to the floor.

"Edmond was sitting on the back of the couch in the window," Macon said, relishing my reaction. "You just forgot we didn't have a couch."

I turned slowly to face him. "I don't mean to be . . . I don't know how to say this . . . but clearly we forgot to discuss one other subject."

"I'm not a secret millionaire, if that's what you're wondering."

It broke the tension, and I laughed.

"But obviously I haven't spent any money on this house in . . . well, ever. So I have some savings."

"You didn't have to do this. I would have married you without the furniture." I was joking but also not. "Your trousseau already includes a whole house."

"I did try to find similar used versions, but everything you picked out was so special. And I fell in love with the idea of us reading together in this room. So I waited until"—he pretended to gag and choke—"the Black Friday sales, and then Phil let me store it all in his garage. We'll still need to get curtains and throw pillows and a rug, but I didn't want to buy any of those soft things without you."

"I don't know what to say. Nobody's ever given me anything like this before."

"Merry Christmas," Macon said, guiding me toward the sofa and pulling me down onto it with him. The velvet cushions were squashy and comfortable and so much nicer than anything either of us had ever owned before. It was my first furniture made out of real wood. I would never have to worry about it collapsing underneath me. The structure was solid and sturdy.

"What do you think?" he asked.

I beamed. "I think it'll last a lifetime."

Edmond stood up on the back of the couch and leaned forward to bop my forehead in greeting. I'd missed him, too, and nuzzled deeper into his fur.

"My new job comes with a raise," Macon said, "so I'll have more money to support us. You know, during any hard times at the bookstore. Or if things happen with my mom. Or if your parents need help. I want to be there for your family, too."

I cocked my head at him. "Is *that* why you were so nervous about getting this job?"

"I mean, I want the job. I've wanted it since I started working for the library system. I just couldn't bear to leave my favorite coworker."

I was smiling at him again. I couldn't stop.

"But yeah," he said, "I want to be able to help you. And I know I can't solve every financial problem, I'm still a county employee"—we both snorted—"but occasionally I can buy us a new couch. Or a bed for our guests. And we can save up for that trip to Australia."

"And Disney World."

"I was hoping you'd forgotten about that one."

I laughed. "At least we can stay with my parents. We won't have to pay for a hotel." I nudged my body against his. "You know . . . soon my family will be your family, too."

His brows lifted. I don't think he'd made that full leap in his mind before.

"And we have an Olympian now," I bragged.

It made him laugh, but then he sprang back to his feet. "Oh! You have to see the rest."

"The *rest?*"

His smile widened as I followed him into the study. He'd moved the television in there, but with his books gone, the room was nearly half empty. "I thought we could put a desk in here for you, too. Or you could do whatever else you'd like to do with this space." He led me to Edmond's room. "The guest bed will go in here, but the rest of the room can be used for storage. But if my mom has to move in with us someday, maybe we could build another storage shed outside?" In our bedroom, he had already cleared out space for me in the closet and dresser weeks ago, but he showed me that he'd made even more room. "I would have unpacked your other boxes, but it didn't seem right to go through your stuff without you."

"It's actually happening," I said in wonderment.

"What is?"

"I'm not going to be living out of boxes anymore."

It was as if he was proposing all over again. His voice became husky. "It's yours. Everything. And we can paint the walls of these rooms any colors you want."

I shuddered. "I don't want to paint anything else for at least a year."

"Thank God, because neither do I. But I would have, for you."

It was an extremely romantic thing to say, and I kissed him. He responded fervently, guiding me backward toward the bed.

"Bedrooms are great," I said, pulling away, "but let's try out the new couch."

He feigned weakening in the knees and allowed me to lead him back to the living room. I had been so distracted by the books and furniture earlier that I had failed to notice he had also added a number of beautiful potted plants. The house looked like it belonged to both of us. It looked like *ours.* And then I noticed that the largest plant, a four-foot conifer, was strung with unlit lights, a garland of cranberries and popcorn, and ornaments made out of dried orange slices.

As I gasped, he followed my gaze and then swore. "That was supposed to be plugged in," he said, breaking away from me and scrambling to the floor to fix it. "I forgot."

"Macon! You got us a Christmas tree."

"A Norfolk pine," he corrected. "It'll get bigger. I thought it could live in here year-round to go with our forest theme. Unless Edmond starts nibbling on it, and then we'll have to move it outside. It's mildly toxic to cats. But so far, he just likes napping underneath the boughs."

The lights turned on, blanketing us in a warm sparkling glow. My heart melted. "You got us a Christmas tree," I said again.

"I stole the lights from your store. A strand from a display in the back," he said, quick to explain. He stood back up. "Mika said it was okay."

I touched an orange slice gently. "You made these?"

He nodded. Suddenly he looked shy and embarrassed.

It was painful how much I loved him. I pulled his face into mine and kissed him again, loving how sweet he was and how sweet he tasted. He responded with more intensity, and I yanked him down onto the couch with me. Edmond was still sitting on the back of it.

"Scram," Macon growled, shooing him off.

My head lifted to watch Edmond leap from the couch onto his cat tree, and I became aware of one final surprise: the air was fragrant with onions and garlic and cayenne.

"Holy shit," I said in disbelief. "You made dinner, too."

"Of course I did. There's a spicy peanut and sweet potato stew in the slow cooker."

"*How* has nobody tried to marry you before?"

"Because I despise everyone except you and scowl at them and make them scuttle away like little crabs."

"Oh, hush. You do not."

"Sometimes I do."

"Only the people who deserve it."

He laughed.

"This is unfair," I said, thumping his chest. Almost actually angry.

"What is?"

"It's so unbalanced. I'm getting everything, and you're just getting me."

"First of all"—he flipped me onto my back and pinned me—"I'm getting a fucking *bookstore*. Have you ever considered that maybe I'm marrying you for that?"

It honestly did make me feel better.

"Second of all"—his face softened as he took me in—"you *are* everything. You're literal sunshine. You light up my life and bring color into my world, and all I've wanted since the day we met is to bask in the warmth of your glow."

I beamed up at him, radiant with happiness.

"See?" he whispered. "Sunshine."

I tugged on his shirt and pulled him down into me.

"Warmth," he said, pressing against me.

Illuminated by the tree and reading lamps, Macon looked happy, too, surrounded by our green forest, life and stories growing all around him. And perhaps I was his light, but he had guided me out of the darkness and into this new life. Light simply had no purpose without life.

Here, with him, I had found a purpose.

Here, with him, I was filled with life.

ACKNOWLEDGMENTS

I've been working with books since I was a teenager, so my first heartfelt thanks are for my coworkers during the years when I was a bookseller and a librarian. Thank you to Kevin Tobin, who gave me my start in the industry, and thank you to all the other booksellers who saved my life as a teenager and showed me that I had a future to look forward to. Thank you to the librarians who then picked up the reins in my twenties and taught me how to be an adult. I fiercely love and admire all of you.

Thank you to the booksellers at Malaprop's, my hometown indie bookstore, for their vital presence in our community. And thank you to the other marvelous booksellers and librarians around the world that I have been so fortunate to cross paths with in my career as an author. I'm especially grateful for your hard work on the front lines of the current book-banning crisis in America. Thank you for continuing to fight for our right to read the books that make other people uncomfortable.

I'm actually still a librarian—a volunteer now for over a decade. And I'm thankful for my fellow librarians and the patrons at that special library, too. I'm so grateful to still be putting books into the hands of people who need them.

As for *this* book, my agent, Kate Testerman, has always been my champion.

Thank you, Kate, for being by my side since day one. Thank you also to Maria Napolitano for your help internationally and to my outstanding film agent, Dana Spector.

Thank you to my editor, Sara Goodman, for your keen guidance and gemlike wisdom, and thank you for honoring the time and space that I needed to figure out how to write this. What a gift! I don't take it lightly.

Thank you to Olga Grlic for creating a cover that I recognize myself—and Ingrid and Macon—in, and thanks to the entire team at Saturday Books and Macmillan for your incredible support and collective friendliness: Jennifer Enderlin, Merilee Croft, Cassie Gutman, Brant Janeway, Kim Ludlum, Michelle McMillian, Erica Martirano, Althea Mignone, Zoë Miller, Alexis Neuville, Sarah Pazen, Eileen Rothschild, and Erica Young. Thank you to Manning Krull for the beautiful case stamp. And thank you also to all of my publishing teams overseas.

Kiersten White gave me feedback for every single version of this novel and is my constant texting companion. I am forever grateful for her friendship. Alison Cherry gave my sentences a tremendous workout, which gave me a peace of mind. Jade Timms is a brilliant reader and hilarious one-woman podcaster, Myra Simmons graciously listened to me read this entire book out loud, Jeff Zentner swooped in with excellent suggestions during a crisis, and Laini Taylor left behind such kind comments in my margins that I bear-hugged my laptop. David Arnold, Nina LaCour, and David Levithan were also delightful sources of encouragement throughout this process. Thank you, all.

Thank you to my mom and dad for a lifetime of unconditional love, as well to my wonderful mom and dad who live next door to me.

Thank you to my sister. Always my sister.

Thank you to Lauren Biehl and Melisa Pressley for answering my research questions, and thank you to every friend who has ever shared their dating horror stories with me, some of which I have pilfered for this novel. Thank you to the luminous minds in my afternoon meditation group. And I've played the photo game with a number of coworkers over the years, but Lynn Hunter was the first. Thank you, Lynn, for helping me get through those long and tedious shifts.

My biggest thank-you of all is reserved for my husband, Jarrod Perkins, who supports me daily in an infinite number of thoughtful ways. Who is the cheerful sunshine to my gloomy rain cloud. Who helped me paint our house my favorite colors. How lucky we are to have found each other so young, and for it to still be so right.

Finally, this novel was completed in the chaotic aftermath of Hurricane Helene. Ridgetop was inspired by my hometown of Asheville, North Carolina, which suffered a great many losses in the storm. It's still difficult to process and discuss what happened here, but miracles also arose out of the tragedy: kindness, empathy, and generosity. Neighbors helped neighbors, party lines be damned. It gave me a glimpse back into our collective humanity. It reminded me of who we really are and who we can choose to be. Thank you, Asheville. The world is a better place with you still in it.

About the Author

STEPHANIE PERKINS is the *New York Times, USA Today,* and international bestselling author and anthology editor of multiple books, including *Anna and the French Kiss, Lola and the Boy Next Door, Isla and the Happily Ever After,* and *My True Love Gave to Me,* as well as *There's Someone Inside Your House,* which was adapted into a major motion picture for Netflix. She has always worked with books—first as a bookseller, then as a librarian, and now as a novelist. She lives in the mountains of North Carolina with her husband. Every room of their house is painted a different color of the rainbow.